ACRIMONIOUS

REMINGTON FAMILY LAW SERIES
BOOK 1

MARIE FORCE

Acrimonious
Remington Family Law Series, Book 1
By: Marie Force

Published by HTJB, Inc.
Copyright 2026. HTJB, Inc.
Cover design by Hang Le
Print Layout: E-book Formatting Fairies
ISBN: 978-1966871187

HTJB, Inc.
PO Box 370
Portsmouth, RI 02871 USA
author@marieforce.com

MARIE FORCE is a registered trademark with the United States Patent & Trademark Office.

Thank you for respecting the hard work of this author. To obtain permission to excerpt portions of the text, please contact the author at *marie@marieforce.com*.

All characters in this book are fiction and figments of the author's imagination.

CHAPTER ONE

An arduous schedule for the day ran through Julian Remington's mind as he took care of some personal business first thing in the morning.

In. Out. Back in. Deeper this time. A hard push that drew a satisfied moan from his eager partner.

McDavid custody hearing first thing after eighteen months of wrangling.

Partner meeting midmorning if he made it back from court in time.

New client meeting over lunch.

Court at four with Jenna Simsbury, who should get full custody of her three children as of today—again—after months of back-and-forth.

A three-hour gig with his band at eight would round off a sixteen-hour day.

Any number of other things might arise to make an already chaotic day even more interesting.

As a partner at Remington Family Law, Julian never knew what to expect from one day to the next, and he liked it that way. He could be hit with anything, from an emergency custody hearing to a call from one of Hollywood's A-list stars looking for help with a divorce that'd drag on for years, to one of the firm's longtime clients seeking visitation with a grandchild.

Sharp fingernails dug into his back as he picked up the pace, ready for the big finish so he could get on with what promised to be another long, complicated day as one of LA's top family law attorneys.

He doubled down on the deep strokes, going for broke. *Come on, let's get this done.*

She went off with a shout, which gave him permission to take his own pleasure. "Oh, *oh*, Julian... Oh *God, I love you.*"

He stopped short. She what? No, no, *nope*. He abruptly withdrew from her.

She pushed silky dark hair off her stunning face. "What? Julian..."

He'd already dealt with the condom, pulled his pants on and was buttoning his shirt.

"Where're you going?"

"To work."

"But we were..."

"We're done."

Her big blue eyes got even bigger. "Th-this time or for good?"

"Remember when we started this, and I said it was just for fun? When I told you not to get attached?"

Her eyes filled with tears that he so did *not* want to deal with. "I... I didn't mean it."

"Yes," he said with a sigh, "you did, or you wouldn't have said it."

"I take it back."

Julian reached for her hand and kissed the back of it. "You need to find yourself a nice guy who's available for the things you want. That guy isn't me."

Her lip quivered as more tears filled her eyes. "But it could be. We're good together."

"We're good together in bed."

"Isn't that the best place to start?"

"It's not going to happen, sweetheart. I've said that from the beginning when I told you I don't do relationships."

"Yes, but I thought—"

He placed a finger lightly on the full lips that had brought him real pleasure, but not true love. Never that. "You thought wrong."

She was crying openly now.

"I don't want to hurt you, but I was honest from the start about what this was—and what it wasn't."

"You care about me, too. I can tell! Why won't you let yourself have feelings?"

He didn't have time to deal with a question that'd take all day to answer. "Because I don't want to. I've got court in an hour. I've got to go."

Julian had just enough time to run home to shower and change. His driver, Ernie, would pick him up at home and get him to the Stanley Mosk Courthouse downtown for a trial he'd been working toward for a year. He couldn't wait to present the case and to watch his client's ex-husband's face when he presented irrefutable proof of his douchebaggery. While that wasn't an official legal term, it should be. Bryan McDavid was the poster child for the concept.

Stacey got out of bed and followed him to the door, grabbing his arm. "You can't just dismiss me like hired help when you're finished with me." The angry edge to her voice was new and unattractive.

When he turned to face her, he saw she was naked as the day she was born, with her considerable assets on full display. Those assets didn't change anything for him. "That's not what I'm doing."

The tears had dried up, and her pretty eyes seethed with outrage. "I said something I didn't mean. Don't be so dramatic."

"Take care of yourself, Stacey. I hope you find what you're looking for."

"*Julian!*"

She was still screaming his name from her doorway when the elevator doors quietly came together to get him out of there.

Julian leaned against the back wall, closed his eyes and sighed over yet another near miss. Why did they never believe him when he told them—in the bluntest possible words—that he'd never fall in love with them, he'd never marry them or be anything more to them than a hard cock once in a while? Why did they always want more?

What else could he have done or said to prevent this latest in a long list of scenes that occurred whenever he had to remind a woman that he was exactly who he'd said he was from the beginning?

Most people spent their lives waiting and hoping to hear those three little words. For Julian, his brothers and sisters, they were the worst three words in the English language to hear from a romantic partner. Love, as they'd experienced it, was a battlefield, a place where people tore apart those supposedly dearest to them on their way out the door.

No, thank you.

The Remington siblings wanted nothing to do with that four-letter word. The other one, the less socially acceptable four-letter word? They were all for that one, but when l-o-v-e entered the room, they were out the door so fast the heads of their now-former partners were left spinning as they hit the road and never looked back.

Maybe Julian should've clued Stacey in on what he'd been thinking when they were having sex. He should've told her he was reviewing his schedule for the day and making a mental list of things he needed to do ahead of each appointment.

Then she'd know what a heartless bastard he really was and would realize she could do better.

After Julian made a quick stop at home to shower, shave and change into one of the bespoke suits he was known for, Ernie picked him up for court, the one place in the world where everything made sense to him. That's where he helped his clients get out of the very thing Stacey wanted with him. It's where he negotiated the future for innocent children who'd become pawns in their parents' wars, the way he and his siblings had once been.

Ernie handed Julian a tall Americano with oat milk. At nearly seventy, Ernie was a proud Vietnam veteran who still wore a missing-in-action bracelet on his tattooed forearm. He'd been a nineteen-year-old Marine when he was sent to the jungles of Vietnam to fight a war that'd never made sense to him or most of the guys he served with. He'd tell you they'd served their country and would do it again, despite the decades of PTSD most of them had lived with, not to mention the less-than-welcoming reception they received when they'd first returned home.

These days, Ernie hung his hat out at the beach in Venice in a "shack by the sea"—as he put it—with his girlfriend and loved his job as Julian's driver.

"Thanks," Julian said for the coffee Ernie bought for both of them any time he picked Julian up at home.

"How was your night?" Ernie asked.

"Better than my morning."

Ernie glanced at him in the mirror. "How've you already had a shitty morning?"

"Had to give Stacey the bad news that I meant it when I said I don't do relationships."

"Ah, and I take it that went over well?"

"As it usually does."

"Like a fart in church?"

Ernie always made him laugh, even when he didn't want to. "Something like that."

Another thing he loved about Ernie was that he knew

when Julian needed quiet to prepare for the day. Today, he was more interested in brooding than preparing, thanks to the scene with Stacey, which had upset him the way it always did when things went sideways with a woman.

Julian often suspected that eight of the nine Remington siblings had gone to law school just so they'd never again find themselves as helpless as they'd been as children. For ten long years, they'd been the knotted rope in a tug-of-war between their parents that seemed like it would never end. Their lawyer parents had been focused on winning at all costs, regardless of the consequences for their children.

When it finally ended, no one was a winner, least of all their kids. Julian and each of his siblings carried the trauma of that interminable, ugly, public nightmare with them as they helped others disentangle themselves from commitments they'd once expected to last forever. The fallout had been made worse, if that was possible, by the reality TV show their parents agreed to do featuring the spectacle of their divorce, claiming it'd be good for business.

While it had, in fact, been great for business, it'd been mortifying for their children, especially Julian and the siblings who'd been old enough to understand what was happening while they did what they could to protect the younger ones from the worst of it.

If there was one thing he and his siblings had learned the hard way, and had seen time and again in their practices, it was that nothing lasted forever, and it was far easier to be alone than to get involved in something you couldn't walk away from when it no longer worked for you.

He couldn't imagine what it would be like to be *married* to Stacey, or any of the others who'd come before her, once he decided he didn't want to be there anymore. No way would he ever let that happen. Being able to leave—any time he wanted, with his head held high and his conscience clear—was key to his survival in the screwed-up world in which he lived and worked. Every day, he witnessed what people who were once madly in love did to try to destroy each other—and the children they swore they loved more than life itself. He'd found that most didn't love their kids nearly as much as they hated their ex.

Julian wanted nothing to do with that for himself, and neither did his siblings. While they enjoyed bickering with one another as if it were a blood sport, that was the one thing they all agreed on.

After seeing his one serious ex-girlfriend, Aimee Godfrey, recently at her parents' fiftieth anniversary celebration, Julian had been deeply unsettled to realize the feelings he'd once had for her were still there. They'd resurfaced from the deepest, darkest corners of his soul to remind him of how helpless love could make you, especially when it didn't work out.

Aimee was long married to a guy named Trent Morgan, who worked in finance and was some sort of whiz kid when it came to investing, or so he'd heard. They had three beautiful kids—a son and two daughters—and a happy life that seemed to suit her.

She'd gotten lucky.

Julian made a lucrative living off the fact that most people were *un*happy and not afraid to go all out to get free of the person they'd supposedly loved with all their heart once upon a time.

Being alone was better than taking a gamble that more than half the time ended in expensive failure. The Remington siblings had seen what that kind of failure looked like up close and personal, and they were all set, thank you very much.

Stacey would be okay. She'd find a nice guy who wanted a white picket fence in the burbs and a posse of kids.

That man was not, and would never be, Julian Remington.

. . .

AN HOUR LATER, Julian was in Los Angeles County Superior Court, listening to Bryan McDavid and his attorney extol Bryan's many virtues as an involved, caring, safety-conscious parent who should share in joint custody with his soon-to-be ex-wife and Julian's client, Rachel McDavid. Because he had all the evidence he needed to bury Bryan, Julian let him and his windbag attorney, Thomas Driscoll, have the floor for the first thirty minutes of the hearing.

Rachel wanted sole custody due to Bryan's angry outbursts that regularly frightened her and her children, among other concerns that Julian would bring to light when it was his turn to present their side of the argument. Bryan had been unwilling to engage in mediation and had demanded a trial when the matter could've been quietly settled out of court for much less than the trial would cost them, both financially and personally. Nothing about this proceeding would be quiet, if Julian had his way.

Driscoll went on and on about the character references he'd obtained for Bryan, who was by all accounts an upstanding member of the community, a dedicated father to his two young sons and a well-respected auditor, expected to make partner at his CPA firm within the year.

"Mr. Remington and his client would have you believe that Mr. McDavid is one step above a deadbeat, when there's ample evidence to the contrary. He should have shared custody of his sons and a reasonable visitation schedule. Thank you, Your Honor."

Judge Michael Fallows glanced at Julian to give him the floor.

He'd been looking forward to this moment as he stood to hand one set of copies to Driscoll and another set to the judge. "Your Honor, some new information has come to light in the last twenty-four hours."

"Objection," Driscoll said. "We've heard nothing about any new information."

"We only found out about it yesterday," Julian said. "And it's highly relevant to the matter before the Court."

"I'll allow it," the judge said.

Turning to face Bryan McDavid, he said, "Do you recognize these posts?"

On each page was a post made to an X profile called Ramblr26, accusing Rachel of being a neglectful mother and cheating wife.

"'If you encounter Rachel McDavid,'" Julian read from his copy as he watched Bryan begin to shift in his seat the way people did when they knew what was coming, "'you should be aware that she presents herself to be one thing, when she's someone else entirely. She opens her legs to anyone who asks and doesn't give a shit where her kids are when she's doing it.'"

Fallows stared at Bryan, his expression stern.

Excellent.

"Th- that's not me." Bryan directed a hard, hateful stare at Rachel, who kept her gaze focused straight ahead, the way Julian had told her to. "I have no idea who that is. Could be anyone with the way she gets around." He had close-cropped blond hair, cold blue eyes, a goatee and a chip on his shoulder so big, it took up all the extra space in the courtroom.

"Is this your address?" Julian asked as he dropped another sheet of paper on the table in front of Bryan.

Bryan leaned in for a closer look. "You know it is. It's all over the divorce paperwork."

Julian approached the bench to deliver additional documents. "Your Honor, we've tied the IP address for Ramblr26's account to Mr. McDavid's home."

With a glance toward Bryan and his attorney, the judge reached for the documents while Julian stepped back to watch the show. The only thing that would've made this better was popcorn.

While the judge reviewed the documents and the vicious, foul things Ramblr26 had written about the mother of his children, Driscoll leaned in to confer with Bryan in frantic-sounding whispers.

Julian and Rachel had learned about the posts from a mom at the boys' school. Rachel had never met the woman, but she'd called to tell her what was being said about her online. When she'd relayed the information to Julian, she'd been full of outrage and disbelief that the man she'd once loved, to whom she'd given two beautiful sons, would say such vile things about her publicly when none of it was true. She'd never once cheated on him, but he sure as hell couldn't say the same.

Julian had proof of that, too, thanks to his investigator brother Carson, who'd put together a full report on Bryan's extracurricular activities over the past four years. He'd planned to hold that back in case he needed it, but he didn't care for the way Bryan was glaring at Rachel, clearly trying to intimidate her into backing down.

Not on his watch.

"Your Honor, I'd also like to enter into evidence this investigative report that was recently completed detailing Mr. McDavid's extramarital affairs over the past four years. We believe you'll find it helpful in determining a fair settlement as well as custody of the McDavids' young sons. In our opinion, the boys would be detrimentally affected by spending time with a man who speaks so disparagingly about their mother online and conducts extramarital affairs so frequently, we wonder how he'd find the time to care for his kids."

Bryan surged to his feet so quickly, his chair went crashing into the half wall behind him. "*You fucking bitch! You had me followed?*"

"Mr. Driscoll, please remind your client that that language and behavior are not acceptable to this Court, and unless he'd like me to end this right now without any further input from your side, he'll sit down and be quiet."

Driscoll moved quickly to retrieve the chair and plopped Bryan's ass back in it before he made things worse.

After returning to his seat at the table, Julian reached for Rachel's cold and trembling hand. He'd told her ahead of time what he planned to do and warned her to be ready for Bryan to get ugly. But how could anyone prepare to have the person they'd once loved enough to marry and have children with talk to them that way?

Bryan was breathing hard and nearly foaming at the mouth with rage.

Good, Julian thought as he stared him down, *let the judge see how he behaves when he's angry. Maybe he'll grant our request for full custody with a domestic violence restraining order that'll keep him the hell away from her and their kids.*

After about ten tense minutes, the judge put down the documents and looked at Bryan. "This new information, in addition to what I've already read in the file, leaves me with no choice in this matter. The horrible, hateful things you've said online about Mrs. McDavid, even if every word were true, are so revolting that I agree with Mr. Remington that joint custody is not in your sons' best interest. Sole custody is hereby awarded to Mrs. McDavid, and I'm approving the request for a domestic violence restraining order that'll prevent you from coming within one thousand feet of your wife and sons."

Bryan let out a cry of anguish. *"I never laid a hand on them!"* He glanced frantically at his attorney. "How is this domestic violence?"

"Abuse doesn't have to be physical in nature to count as domestic violence, Mr. McDavid," the judge added. "Your behavior has disturbed the peace of your soon-to-be ex-wife and your sons, which is a qualifying factor."

"But I never hit her! She's lying if she says I did!"

Driscoll told him to be quiet.

"I hereby grant Mrs. McDavid sole custody of the minor

children as well as child support in the amount of three thousand dollars per month, due on the first day of each month, and spousal support in the amount of one thousand dollars, due concurrently. The child support, in the amount of fifteen hundred dollars per child, will continue until the children reach the age of eighteen. The spousal support will end only if Mrs. McDavid remarries. The decree will be final sixty days from today, with the initial payment for child support due on the first of next month. Spousal support will begin thirty days after the divorce is final. If you violate the restraining order, you'll be arrested and charged. Am I clear on that?"

Bryan was now softly sobbing as tears ran down his face. "You're really going to take my kids from me after everything she's done to me?"

"She hasn't done anything to you, Mr. McDavid," Julian said, "other than be a faithful, loving wife and mother. You're the one who filed for divorce, refused to engage in mediation and then took to social media to air out your made-up grievances against the mother of your children. If you're looking for someone to blame, you might want to consult a mirror."

"Fuck you, you slick piece of shit."

"This matter is concluded," the judge said. "Mr. McDavid, if you know what's good for you, you'll stay away from your wife and children."

Bryan glared at Rachel. "This isn't over. Count on that, bitch."

"Mr. Driscoll, please inform your client that he can be arrested for threatening Mrs. McDavid, and let him know that this is, in fact, over. You can petition the Court in twenty-four months to possibly modify the restraining order and revisit visitation with your children. I suggest you use that time wisely and invest in anger management classes if you hope to convince the Court to allow you to see your sons."

"*Twenty-four months?*" Bryan asked on a scream. "I can't see them for *two years?*"

"Based on the things you posted about the mother of your children, I wouldn't let you care for my dog," Julian said. "You're lucky it's only two years."

"Thank you for your input, Mr. Remington," the judge said sarcastically. "This matter is adjourned." The judge got up to leave the room.

"I don't get to say anything? You're just taking my kids away *for two fucking years*, and there's *nothing I can do about it*?"

Driscoll took hold of Bryan's arm to lead him from the courtroom. Julian could hear him screaming in the hallway outside the room.

Julian turned to Rachel. "What can I do for you?"

She shook her head and reached for another tissue from the box on the table. "I don't know what to say. I got what I wanted, but at what price? I'll have to keep one eye over my shoulder and worry every second my kids aren't with me."

"As much as I hate to say this, it might be a good idea to relocate somewhere new. We can help you legally change your name and the kids' names."

She nodded, but exhaustion clung to her like a wet blanket after years of dealing with Bryan and his rage while trying to keep herself and her young sons safe.

Julian offered her a hand to help her up. "Let's go back to my office and figure out your next steps."

"Thank you for everything you've done to help me," she said, looking devastated despite her "victory."

"Of course. That's my job."

"You do it very well."

"We try."

As he escorted her from the courtroom, Julian was on full alert for trouble. He had a bad feeling that they hadn't seen the last of Bryan McDavid.

CHAPTER TWO

Julian returned with Rachel to his office on Wilshire Boulevard, in the same building his grandfather had purchased to house his fledgling law practice in 1966. Today, Remington Family Law occupied all six floors and employed more than two hundred people working as family law and estate attorneys, paralegals, accountants, investigators and other support staff. As Julian stepped off the elevator on the fourth floor with Rachel, he encountered chaos within the normally orderly area that housed the partners' offices. What the hell?

"*I demand to see him right now!*"

"Ma'am, this is a place of business, and your tone—and volume—is not appropriate." The calm, reasoned voice of their intrepid receptionist and office manager, Hector Cordeiro, the heartbeat of the entire practice, had little effect on the screamer.

Julian walked around the corner and stopped short at the sight of Stacey yelling at Hector to "*Get Julian Remington before things get ugly.*"

Too late. Already there.

"What're you doing here?" Julian asked from behind her.

When she whirled around, he was shocked by her ravaged appearance. "I need to talk to you! This... This *man* told me I had to leave."

Julian wondered how she'd managed to get past security in the lobby and would be looking into that after he got rid of her.

He glanced at Hector and then at Rachel.

"Mrs. McDavid," Hector said, "let me get you some refreshments while you wait for Mr. Remington."

"Thank you," Rachel said as she gave Julian a questioning look.

He rolled his eyes and was pleased by her hint of a smile. If the scene with Stacey brought some much-needed levity to Rachel, he supposed that was one positive in an otherwise outrageous situation. As he gently took hold of Stacey's arm to steer her toward his office, he felt his colleagues watching him, including two of his brothers, knowing he'd be dealing with the fallout of this shit show for days to come.

If Stacey had truly known what mattered most to him, the last thing on earth she would've done was make a scene here, of all places.

Julian avoided the gaze of his faithful assistant, Matilda "Mattie" Jones, as he went into his office and closed the door, releasing Stacey the second she cleared the threshold.

She whirled around confront him. "I don't know who you think you are, dismissing me like I'm a piece of garbage on the street when you're done with me."

"That's not what happened, and you know it." He went around the desk to check the messages and mail Mattie had left for him. "But if you choose to rewrite the story to fit your narrative, there's nothing I can say that'll satisfy you."

"Don't come at me with your lawyer bullshit."

He glanced up at her. "If you want lawyer bullshit, I'll tell you all about the Domestic Violence Protection Act that allows me to request a domestic violence restraining order against anyone who comes to my place of business and disturbs my peace. I could have you served by the end of the day if you want me to act like a lawyer."

"You wouldn't dare," she said, her bravado seeming to waver somewhat.

"Try me. I've already gotten one restraining order slapped on a client's husband today for the very same reason. The court doesn't screw around when it comes to DV." He came back around the desk and sat on the edge, crossing his arms and keeping his pose casual even as he seethed with anger. "Here's how this is going to go... You'll walk out that door, go straight to the elevator and press the down button. You'll leave this building and never come back. You'll never call me or text me, even on someone else's phone, or show up at my door again. If you do, I'll be in court so fast, you won't know what hit you. Is there any part of that you don't understand?"

Her chin wobbled, and her eyes filled with tears. "What I don't understand is why you have to be such a heartless asshole."

"I'm exactly who and what I told you I was at the beginning, when I was very clear about what *wasn't* going to happen between us. Do you remember when I said I don't do relationships or commitment or happily ever after? Do you recall when I said, very bluntly, that you weren't going to be the one to change my mind about these things and to please spare us both the agony by not trying to? Any of this ringing a bell?"

She looked down at the floor.

"I'm not sure what else I could've done to avoid having you come to my office to make a dramatic scene that does nothing but piss me off."

Looking up at him as tears ran down her face, she said, "I just wanted to talk to you."

"Now you have."

"So that's it? We fuck like rabbits for a month, and then it's over?"

"That's it."

"Something's wrong with you."

He held her gaze without blinking until she looked away. "Let me give you a little piece of advice, Stacey. When people tell you who they really are, *believe* them. It'll save you a lot of heartache in the long run."

She swiped angrily at her tears. "I don't know how you sleep at night, treating people this way."

"I sleep great because I never lie to anyone, which is more than a lot of people can say. Just because you don't like my truth doesn't make it any less valid. Now, I have work to do. Can you find your way to the elevator?"

She stared him down for a long moment that ended when she finally looked away. "You're a dick. I hope you get what you deserve in this life."

He wanted to wish her the same, but remained silent, giving her the last word while hoping he wouldn't see her again.

Stacey stormed out of the office, slamming the door as she went. Through the glass wall, he could see her heading for the elevator, chin raised in defiance of anyone who might get in her way.

Good.

He exhaled a deep breath as he took a seat behind his desk, turning to look outside while taking a minute to calm the hell down. While that wasn't the first time he'd been confronted by an angry ex who'd expected to be the one to break through his defenses when it came to commitment and forever, it was the first time—and hopefully the last—it'd happened at his office, where he technically worked for his father. No doubt Corbin was being fully briefed on the ugly scene and would interrogate Julian about it at the partner meeting.

Turning back to his desk, he picked up the extension and dialed 9 for Security.

"Security, Danvers. What can I do for you, Mr. Remington?"

"I'd like to know how Stacey Wilson was allowed up to the fourth floor, where she made a huge scene, demanding to see me."

"Oh no. I'm so sorry. I'll look into what happened. We had two new people start this week, and it's possible one of them let her through."

"She would've told them she was a close friend of mine, which she was until I ended things with her. Please remind them that everyone who's sent up must be cleared by us first."

"I'll take care of that right away, sir. Won't happen again."

"Thank you."

Julian put down the phone and ran a hand through his hair as he tried to find the inner calm that propelled him through chaotic days in the family law trenches. Despite the surgical way in which he'd dealt with it, the encounter with Stacey had left him unsettled, even though everything he'd ever said to her was the truth.

Remaining unencumbered required honesty, and he was always, *always* honest in his dealings with women. He didn't want a girlfriend or a partner or, God forbid, a wife. He wanted fun and sex and occasional companionship, but even that'd become more trouble than it was worth in recent years. Stacey wasn't the first to go out in a blaze of glory when he decided to end a commitment-free arrangement.

He was better off alone than fighting these kinds of battles with people who refused to believe him when he told them what wasn't going to happen—ever.

A knock on his door had him sitting up straighter, preparing to answer questions from his family and colleagues about what'd happened with Stacey, which was the last thing he felt like doing.

His twenty-nine-year-old brother, Jackson, who worked as Julian's associate, came in and closed the door behind him. Like most of the Remington men, Jackson had wavy dark hair and brown eyes. He sported a soul patch under his bottom lip that drove their father almost as crazy as their brother Carson's longish hair did.

"Everything all right in here?"

"It is now."

Jackson leaned against the closed door. "You need anything?"

"Better security, but I've already spoken to Danvers about that."

"I was wondering how she made it up here."

"Apparently, a couple of new people are still learning the ropes."

"Let's hope they learn quickly. Dad is looking for you at the partner meeting."

"I'll be right there."

"I'll let him know. Rachel McDavid's sister came to pick her up, and they're getting the boys from school. She said she'd let you know where she ends up."

"Thank you for handling that for me."

"No problem. You sure you're okay?"

"All good."

"I'm working on getting a digital copy of the restraining order for Rachel," Jackson said. "Will keep you posted."

"Thanks."

After his brother left, Julian gave himself another minute to get his shit together. He'd been off his game since he'd seen Aimee at her parents' party during the holidays. She held the distinction of being the only woman Julian had ever loved, but it'd been over between them for almost twenty years. He hadn't given her a thought in ages until he'd run into her—literally—at the party. Two weeks later, he was still trying to understand how his feelings for her could've resurfaced so swiftly that they'd taken his breath away and left him spiraling ever since. He would've thought he'd become immune to such things. Finding out otherwise had been a huge shock to his system.

Aimee's oldest kid was nearly an adult. That's how long they'd been out of each other's lives. He shouldn't have felt a single thing for her except nostalgia when they'd come face-to-face for the first time in years.

But the reminder of what'd once been a wild, uncontrollable love had left a bitter taste in his mouth, as if he'd been chewing on burnt popcorn, or something equally revolting. It had ended badly, which had been entirely his fault.

After his parents' hellacious divorce was finally settled with them sharing joint custody of their minor children, he'd vowed to never get into a situation like the one his parents had dragged him and his siblings through. As they came of age, each of them had joined him in disdaining relationships that might lead to marriage. They figured if they avoided commitment and everything that went with it, they could also avoid that kind of nonsense for themselves.

They'd gone so far as to take an alcohol-fueled vow one evening to never give in to the temptation and had agreed to a full-family intervention if they strayed off course. Each of them took that vow seriously and had remained true to it for years.

At twenty-one, however, he'd been so in love with Aimee that he couldn't imagine a day without her, let alone the rest of his life.

Back then, Carson had zeroed right in on Julian's dilemma the way he always did. "How in the world can you be thinking about forever with anyone at age twenty-one? Especially since you know all too well what 'forever' looks like." Their parents' divorce had been ongoing at the time, souring most of them on relationships. Julian had been the exception, having gone all in with Aimee from the second they first met.

His brother had been right, though. Julian had been far too young to make serious commitments to anyone, especially since he hadn't even finished college yet and had three years of law school to get through before he'd be worthy of someone like Aimee. Even though she'd grown up as the daughter of Max Godfrey and Stella Flynn, who were Hollywood royalty, she was a go-getter. She'd started her dance studio by then, as she was five years older and light-years ahead of him in more ways than one. During the three years they were together, he'd felt so lucky that a woman of such stunning beauty, intelligence and accomplishment had loved him.

Ending their relationship had been excruciatingly painful and messy, especially since their parents were longtime friends. But when he'd tried to explain that it was too much too soon, she'd told him to grow the hell up and act like a man rather than a little boy pretending to be a man.

That'd hurt. A lot.

Mostly because she'd been right, as usual. He hated that he'd broken her heart when she'd taken such a big chance on him to begin with. When everyone in her life had told her she was crazy to date a much younger guy, she'd told them to mind their own business. She'd truly loved him, and he'd thanked her for that by walking away when shit got real. He'd instantly regretted it, but she'd refused to ever speak to him again.

Aimee had moved on quickly with Trent, so quickly, in fact, that Julian had wondered if she'd loved him as much as she'd said she did. Aimee and Trent had married within eighteen months of her breakup with Julian, and their son was born a year after that. Her life had gone on as if he'd never happened, but judging by the stricken look on her gorgeous face at the anniversary party, she hadn't forgotten him either.

His desk phone buzzed with a call from his assistant, Mattie. "Yes, ma'am?"

"Partner meeting starting in your dad's office."

"I'm on my way."

"Are you okay, honey?"

"I'm fine. Sorry about the scene."

"You didn't make the scene, bebe."

As a grown man and a partner in a law firm, it should've annoyed him to be called childlike nicknames by his assistant. But since he'd known Mattie all his life, it didn't bother him in the least, especially since she never called him any of her many nicknames for him in front of anyone else. He'd inherited the formidable Matilda Jones from his grandfather when he retired shortly after Julian attained junior partnership.

"Tell my dad I'll be there in five."

"Will do. Reminder that you have lunch with Cresley Dane at the Ivy at two. Not that I think you'd forget lunch with a supermodel or anything."

Julian chuckled. "Yep, it's on the radar."

"I'm sure it is."

They were both laughing when she ended the call.

He loved working with her and dreaded the day when sixty-year-old Mattie would announce her retirement. Not that he expected that to happen for a while, since Mattie, who'd never married, would tell you that her job was her life and the Remingtons were her family. She spent every Thanksgiving and Christmas with them and visited Julian's grandfather at his senior care facility every Wednesday evening without fail.

They all loved her, and Julian's brothers envied him for having her on his team, where he hoped she'd stay forever.

After the amusing conversation with Mattie, he felt better and ready to shed the lingering disquiet from the encounter with Stacey. It went against everything he believed in to allow a woman to cause drama in his life, let alone at his workplace. The second that happened, he was gone. A few, like Stacey, felt they could change his mind. Little did they know that his life philosophy came from the kind of experience that should've broken him and his siblings.

Instead, it'd made them stronger and resolved to avoid the kind of nightmare they'd endured as kids. They'd had no control over anything then. Now they were in charge and setting their own rules. Anyone who didn't like those rules wasn't welcome in their lives.

He gathered his notes for the partner meeting and left his office, winking at Mattie as he went past her command post. People said she resembled Phylicia Rashad, a comparison she encouraged. True to form, she was stylishly turned out in a dark purple suit that was probably Chanel or Dior, sky-high heels and nails that matched her suit. That her nails always matched her suits was a source of constant amazement to him.

She was an icon in every possible way, as well as the most loyal friend and assistant anyone could ever hope to have.

As he walked down the long corridor toward his father's office, he sensed people watching him through the glass walls of their offices. They'd love to know the details of what'd led to the public showdown with Stacey. But they wouldn't hear any more about it from him.

Julian almost groaned out loud when he saw Nova Morales, one of the younger paralegals, coming toward him. That she had a massive crush on him was one of the worst-kept secrets in the place.

"How're you doing, Julian?"

He kept moving as he went by her. "Just fine, Nova. Hope you're having a great day."

"You, too!"

Nova was exactly what he should've wanted in a woman. She was young, ambitious, ruthlessly intelligent and sexy as all hell, with extravagant curves, gorgeous dark hair and eyes and lips made for sin. In another life in which they didn't work together, she wasn't more than a decade younger than him, and he hadn't vowed to remain single, he might've returned her interest. In this lifetime, he kept walking as she probably turned to watch him go with her heart in her eyes. That's how

Mattie described the way Nova gazed at him when she thought no one was looking.

He had no time for such foolishness.

Julian greeted his dad's assistant, a serious young man named Luka Woodruff.

"Go on in," Luka said without looking up from what he was doing. He wore his light brown hair combed straight back and sported a Rolex that'd been a Christmas gift from Corbin the year before.

In Corbin Remington's office, the senior partner held court at the head of the huge conference table, where the partners had gathered, including Julian's brothers Carson and Griffin. They had several other partners who specialized in forensic accounting, estate planning, real estate and taxation, all of whom had worked for the firm almost as long as Corbin had.

Julian's brother Ethan was a senior associate, specializing in real estate and community property. Having their own people managing some of the more intricate aspects of high-income divorces set Remington apart from many other family law firms.

"Nice of you to join us," Corbin said with a grin for Julian. As always, every silver hair on his head had been combed into submission and held in place by artfully applied pomade. Regular golf outings kept him tanned and trim, and his custom-tailored suits made him look like the California Super Lawyer he was, even as he glanced at the chunky watch on his wrist.

His father valued punctuality as much as he did loyalty, and while his tone was teasing, his message was anything but.

"Sorry I'm late," Julian said as he took a seat next to Carson.

"We're just getting started." Corbin zeroed in on Julian. "Everything all right, son?"

"Yep. We finally settled the McDavid case this morning,

with Rachel getting sole custody, thanks to Carson's excellent work."

"That guy made it easy," Carson said in the gruff, no-nonsense tone that was his hallmark. He prided himself on being the only Remington sibling not to waste three years of his life in law school.

Julian wondered if his father had asked Carson when he was getting a haircut yet, as he did at the start of every partner meeting. Carson ignored him every time and went on living life on his own terms, regardless of their father's opinion. Even though Carson wasn't an attorney, he was still a partner in the business.

"Good job on finishing McDavid," Corbin said. "How'd the father take the sole custody news?"

"Not well at all," Julian said. "We were granted a DVRO, but I'm not sure that'll keep him away from the wife and kids. She may be looking at relocating."

"And the situation with your friend..."

The question was laced with subtext that included the not-so-subtle message to keep his romantic nonsense out of Corbin's office. "Handled. Won't happen again."

"See that it doesn't."

It was on the tip of Julian's tongue to tell him to shut up with the boss crap, especially in front of the others. If there was one thing he and his brothers hated about working with their father, it was his propensity to talk to them like he had when they were teenagers—in front of the people they worked with.

But since he often went days without crossing paths—or swords—with his father and boss, Julian bit his tongue and reminded himself that the pros far outweighed the cons.

Most of the time, anyway.

Lauren Teller, who was in her late fifties but looked a decade younger and oversaw their forensic accounting practice, shook her head in dismay. "Why does the woman always have to relocate to stay away from a man who's legally prohibited from going anywhere near her?"

"That's a good question without a reasonable answer," Julian said. "It shouldn't be that way, but sometimes they feel safer disappearing into a new life where the ex-husband can't find them."

"It's madness," Lauren said.

Julian had represented Lauren's sister two years earlier when Holly had fled an abusive marriage. She'd ended up moving from LA to Michigan to get away from her ex, taking Lauren's young niece and nephew with her.

"Agreed," Julian said. "But we can only do what we can for them and hope the RO keeps them safe."

After a knock on the door, Griffin's assistant, Mei Chen, came in to hand him an envelope. "Just signed for this. They said it was urgent." The pretty young Chinese woman was freaking brilliant, according to Griffin, who often said he couldn't function without her.

"Thanks," Griffin said.

She nodded and left the room.

"Moving on," Corbin said, "what else is happening?"

"I'm meeting with Cresley Dane at two," Julian said. "She's dealing with some flak from her son's father."

"I could take that for you if you're too busy," Carson said with a grin.

Julian laughed. "Thanks, but I've got it covered."

"Lucky bastard," Carson muttered.

"Someone's gotta do it," Julian said to his brother.

"Son of a bitch." Griffin stared down at a sheet of paper. His normally tanned complexion had gone stark white. He was the one true blond among the brothers, having gotten their mother's fair coloring, as had their sister Jordan.

"What's wrong?" Corbin asked.

"I... uh..." Griffin gathered his stuff and got up. "I've got to go."

"Wait, son..."

Griffin didn't stick around to hear what his father had to say.

Corbin looked at Julian. "Go see what's wrong, will you?"

"I'll try."

Julian gathered his stuff, left the conference room and went to Griffin's office.

Mei nodded to acknowledge him as he approached Griffin's closed door and knocked.

Julian didn't wait for his brother to reply before he entered the office. "What's up?"

The stricken look on Griffin's face was so out of character as to be concerning. "Remember McKenna, who I dated last year for a couple of months?"

"Vaguely."

"She was the extra in that Marvel movie."

"Oh right. What about her?"

Griffin had a wild look in his eyes as he held up the piece of paper that'd been delivered during the meeting. "She's claiming I'm the father of her daughter, which is impossible. There's no way that kid is mine."

"So you never slept with her?"

"I did, but I never take any chances in that regard, as you well know. She's not my kid."

None of them took chances in that regard. "Take a paternity test and shut it down."

"Yeah, I will, but fuck, man." Griffin ran a trembling hand through his hair. "I haven't heard from her in more than a year, and then she drops this bomb on me?"

"Did you know she was pregnant?"

He shook his head. "She never said a word about it to me."

"Damn. You want me to handle it for you?"

Griffin's entire demeanor brightened. "Would you?"

"Of course." Julian took the notification from him, noting the name of the attorney as he scanned the letter. He thought it was interesting that the issue of support wasn't mentioned, which was usually the first thing requested in situations like this.

"The last thing in the world I want is a kid," Griffin said. "You know that, Jules. Get me out of this, will you?"

"I'm on it. I'll let you know when and where for the paternity test. In the meantime, try not to panic. You were careful."

"I'm always careful, for the same reason you are."

"Is she the type to try to trick someone into paying for her kid?"

"Not at all, which is the terrifying part. She was really cool. I liked her."

"So what happened?"

Griffin shrugged. "The usual. She wanted more than I had to give, and eventually she moved on. It was nothing dramatic. More like a fizzle than an eruption."

"Consider yourself lucky," Julian said.

"I take it you ended things with Stacey earlier."

"How'd you guess?"

Griffin grunted out a laugh. "Just a hunch."

"I'm thinking about becoming a monk."

"That'll be the day."

"Honestly, though, I'm seriously considering a vow of celibacy. No one ever believes me when I tell them I'm not looking for anything serious. They all think they're going to be the one to change my mind."

"Little do they know that nothing will ever change our minds."

"Exactly. I mean, google our family if you want to know why we're like this."

"For real."

"Was Dad busting Carson's balls about his hair before I got there?"

"First item on the agenda, per usual."

"Why doesn't he give up on that?"

"For the same reason he wouldn't give up on the custody battle with Mom. Neither of them has ever met a fight they didn't think they could win."

"Which makes them excellent attorneys and—"

"Horrible parents."

"Couldn't have said it better myself," Julian said with a smile. It'd taken them a long time to mostly forgive their parents for what they'd put them through, and each of them had struggled with whether to join firms headed by their parents after law school. In the end, the Remington name and reputation had been too much to pass up, but none of them would ever forget the past. "I'll touch base with McKenna's attorney and keep you posted."

"Thanks, Jules."

"Anything for you."

As he left Griffin's office, he thought about the many times the nine of them had said those words to one another over the years. That was their mantra as they navigated life and work as an unbeatable team. Despite many differences of opinion and the usual sibling crap that came up from time to time, there was nothing they wouldn't do for one another—and they'd proven that countless times over the years.

While Griffin could easily deal with the McKenna matter himself, it'd be better for Griff to have an impartial third party keeping emotion out of the equation.

Before he left for his lunch with Cresley Dane, Julian reached out to McKenna's attorney to set up a call in response to the certified letter.

Julian was prepared to do whatever it took to get his brother free of this situation as quickly as he possibly could.

CHAPTER THREE

The Ivy on North Robertson Boulevard was doing brisk business when Ernie dropped Julian at the curb. He spotted Cresley at one of the patio tables, under an umbrella. She was working in the area and had asked to meet him there.

"My client is already here," he told the maître d'.

"Have a nice lunch, Mr. Remington."

He was a regular there, so they all knew him, and everyone in the place certainly recognized Cresley, a stunning blonde Southern California beauty who'd become an internationally known supermodel at twenty. Ten years later, her career was hotter than ever.

"Hope I didn't keep you waiting for long," Julian said when he sat across from her and extended a hand. "Julian Remington. Nice to meet you."

"I just got here myself." She gave his hand a squeeze. "Nice to meet you, too. Thanks for making the time."

"Of course."

Before he could say anything else, a waiter appeared to tell them about the eggplant pizza special and a goat cheese appetizer.

"What can I get you to drink?"

"I'll do sparkling water with lemon, please," Cresley said.

"Same for me."

"Be right back with your drinks."

"What looks good to you?" Julian asked as they looked at menus.

"That eggplant pizza has my name all over it."

"You want to split it?"

"That'd be great. With a salad?"

"You got it."

They put aside their menus.

"So what can I do for you?"

"As I mentioned when I called, I have a seven-year-old son named Ty." She smiled as she pulled up a photo on her phone of a blond child as gorgeous as his mother. "The undisputed love of my life."

"He's adorable."

"He's perfect in every possible way, and I want to keep him that way by not letting his deadbeat father anywhere near him."

"From what I've read, you've been a single mom from the start and won a custody battle with your ex-boyfriend when your son was a baby. You have sole custody, correct?"

"That's right, but he's recently slithered out from under his rock and is making noise about having a relationship with Ty. That's the last thing in the world I want for my son."

The waiter brought their drinks and asked if they were ready to order.

"We'll do the eggplant pizza special and the main course salad to share," Cresley said.

"Coming right up."

Julian had pulled a small yellow notebook and a pen from the pocket inside his suit coat. "Tell me about the ex," he said after the waiter left.

Her deep sigh set the tone. "His name is Marlon Beckett, and he's also a model, although his career hasn't really taken off the way he expected it to, and honestly? I think his newfound interest in Ty is more about money than anything else."

"Does he have another job besides modeling?"

"Not that I know of. When we were briefly together, his philosophy was to spend all his free time keeping himself in shape and ready for any jobs that came along. Which meant he didn't have the second job to pay the bills everyone else has at the beginning."

"What's his relationship been with Ty since he was born?"

"Nearly nonexistent. Every year or two, he sends him something cool, usually the current 'it' thing. The most recent gift was a drone. Of course, Ty was thrilled with it, and I was furious because I had to figure out how to fly a drone when I had a million other things going on. That's how he rolls. He pops in with some grand gesture that thrills Ty, and then we don't hear from him again for ages."

"Does he pay child support?"

Cresley snorted with laughter. "Rarely. And when he does, it's just enough to keep himself from getting arrested."

The waiter returned with their pizza and salad. "Can I get you anything else?"

"I'm good," Cresley said.

"Me, too. Thanks."

"Enjoy."

They helped themselves to salad and slices of pizza.

While Julian dug into his food, Cresley picked at hers.

"What's happened recently to put you on alert?" Julian asked between bites.

"It was something he said in a text." She picked up her phone, found the text and handed it to him.

I want to see more of Ty, Marlon had written. *Before you say no, ask yourself if there are things you wouldn't want made public, things that might embarrass you—and Ty—or if it would be easier to just let me see him once in a while or maybe even share custody.*

The text had Julian putting down his fork and wiping his mouth with the linen napkin. "What's he got on you?"

Her lovely blue eyes filled with tears. "I'm a... um... a member at Club Quantum."

The club, owned by the actors, director and producer behind Quantum Productions, including Aimee's superstar brother, Flynn Godfrey, was for practitioners of the BDSM lifestyle. Julian had spent some memorable evenings there himself, but not recently.

"How does Marlon know that?"

"He must've followed me and saw me go into the building. I'm not really sure how he found out what goes on there, but he knows."

"When were you last there?"

"About three weeks ago."

"How often do you stop by?"

"A few times a year. It's a stress reliever, and it gives me an outlet without all the hassle that comes with relationships."

"You don't have to justify it to me," he said with a grin. "I used to love hanging out there. I go way back with Flynn's family."

All the way back to when I used to be in love with his older sister...

"It's hard to explain to people who don't get it," she said.

"Believe me, I know. They think it's something sick or twisted, when it's one of the healthier ways to express yourself sexually."

"Exactly! There's no crap like there always is in vanilla relationships."

"I love that about it. In fact, the crap has been piling up lately. I might need to go back to the lifestyle and take a break from the madness."

"I totally get that, and it helps that you understand."

"I really do."

"Marlon certainly knows there's nothing wrong with being a practitioner of the lifestyle, but he's also fully aware that it'd be embarrassing for me to be outed. I've just signed a big new deal with D&G, which includes an airtight morality clause, so this is the last freaking thing I need right now. Not to mention it breaks my heart that he's probably more interested in money than he is in his amazing, beautiful, bright, funny son."

She used her napkin to dab at tears that seemed to infuriate her. "I need him to go the hell away, even if it means paying him off."

"I don't recommend that, unless it includes an ironclad NDA and a signed agreement indicating it's a one-time payment in exchange for him keeping his mouth shut about you and his son, and never again asking you for anything."

"To be honest, I might consider that to be rid of him."

"Do you have a number for him?"

She used her phone to find it.

Julian wrote it down as she recited it.

"I only have it because everything I read when Ty was first born said it was in his best interest to keep his father in his life, even if the contact was limited. He's never heard me say a bad word about Marlon. I figured over time he'd get the picture without me having to draw it for him."

"He will. They always do."

"He's already putting the pieces together."

"Kids don't miss much."

She smiled. "He misses *nothing*."

"I'll see what I can do to make this go away for you."

"Thank you. My friend Marlene said you're the best."

"Marlene Powers?"

"Yes. We're best friends."

"She's awesome. How's she doing?"

"She's started dating again, and that's been amusing. She's so out of practice that she has no idea what to say to anyone."

Julian laughed at the funny face she made. "It's tough out there."

"Don't I know it! I've basically given up on finding someone."

"That's usually when it happens."

"What's your story?" she asked with a coy look that might've turned to interest if he'd encouraged it, which he never would. Not with a client. "Marlene said you're an international man of mystery."

He laughed. "Hardly. I'm stubbornly single and planning to stay that way." Not even a supermodel of her caliber could tempt him to change his life rules.

"Is that because of the drama and mess you see in your work?"

"Partially." She didn't need to hear about the ten-year custody battle, although it wouldn't take her long to find out about that if she went looking. "People don't realize what a nightmare it can be until they've decided to end their marriage, divide their assets and fight over what's best for their kids."

"I had a front-row seat to Marlene's divorce." She shuddered. "If that didn't cure me from ever wanting to be married, nothing will."

"That was a tough one for sure."

"Do you wonder why people bother to get married?"

"Every single day. I feel like it should be a requirement that they have to read the California divorce laws before they can get a marriage license."

"That'd be something."

"I wish I had a dollar for every client who's told me that if they'd known what would be involved in getting divorced, they never would've gotten married."

"I bet you're popular at cocktail parties."

Julian laughed—hard. "I'm a good time had by all."

"Marlene told me about your parents. I'm sorry you guys went through that."

Ah, so she *did* know their history. He shrugged as if it didn't matter, as if it hadn't dictated most of the big decisions he'd made for himself as an adult. "Ancient history now."

"She said you and your siblings all work for one parent or the other. What's that like after all the animosity?"

"It's... interesting. For a time, I thought about going in a different direction, but the firm my grandfather started is legendary, and I would've been a fool to start from scratch somewhere else. So I sucked it up and went to work for my old man. It's not without its challenges, but for the most part, he leaves us alone to run our practices as we see fit. He nags us about stupid shit, such as the length of my brother Carson's hair or my brother Jackson's soul patch. Don't get him started on Griffin's tattoos or Roman's pierced ears."

"He's old school," she said, smiling.

"As old as it gets, but he's a freaking rock star, so we put up with his nitpicking."

"I see him on TV all the time."

"He's their first call when there's a huge celebrity split and always has a great take on what's ahead for the couple."

"I've learned a lot from him about community property and other such things."

"He's a family law master class, and so is my mother, which is another reason why we all sucked it up and went to work for the family businesses. As much as we still resent them for what they put us through, we respect them both as the brilliant lawyers they are."

"Do they speak to each other these days?"

"Just to say hello, most recently at my youngest sibling Roman's college graduation a few years ago."

"I can see why you'd want to avoid all that for yourself."

"Yeah, it's actually not that hard to stay above the romantic fray when you've come from what we did."

"I really appreciate your time today. I feel better knowing you'll be looking out for me and Ty."

"I'll do everything I can to help you. Did my assistant send over the retainer paperwork?"

"She did, and I sent it back an hour before our lunch."

Julian reached for the check that the waiter had left on the table. "Great, thanks. I'll keep you posted on any developments."

"Let me get this," she said.

"No way. It's on me. Clients don't pay. Well... for lunch, that is."

He was glad to leave her laughing after a tough conversation about protecting the person she loved best—not to mention her own reputation.

It burned his ass the way people tried to make a consensual sexual relationship into something deviant just because the concept was unfamiliar to them. He'd always believed that if more people participated in the BDSM lifestyle and all the incredible communication that went with it, there might be fewer divorces.

He texted Ernie for a ride back to "home base," as they referred to the office. His faithful driver came around the corner five minutes later in one of the black Mercedes sedans the firm provided to transport them around the famously congested city during the workday.

Julian slid into the back seat.

"Tell me everything about the lunch with the supermodel," Ernie said as he headed toward Beverly Boulevard. He was obsessed with all things celebrity. "Don't leave anything out."

Julian chuckled at Ernie's shamelessness. "Just another day at the office, my friend."

"Sure it was. Spill the deets, man. I'm living vicariously."

"The deets are that she's a really nice person, concerned

about her kid, the way most mothers are, and in need of a little legal help."

"What's the issue?"

"You know I can't tell you that."

"I keep all your secrets, Counselor. Going on ten years now."

"I'd trust you with my life, Ernie, but some things are too personal to share even with you."

"Sounds juicy."

"Nah, just another client with problems she needs me to solve."

"You're absolutely no fun today."

Julian smiled as he looked up from a review of his notes from the meeting with Cresley. He'd make a call to Marlon when he got back to the office to get the ball rolling toward making him go away. "It's been a day and a half, and it's not over yet."

"Heard about Stacey the smokeshow storming the office."

"Yeah, that was fun."

"I assume that didn't do much to advance her cause."

"Nothing at all. I believe she's now clear on where we stand, which is over and done with."

"You need to find yourself a nice girl to settle down with. Have a couple of kids and a white picket fence. A dog would be good, too."

"Sometimes I feel like you don't know me at all, Ernie."

The older man's guffaw made Julian smile. The time in the car with Ernie was always a highlight of days that were often full of lowlights.

CHAPTER FOUR

Isla Santana wasn't sure when exactly she'd decided that she needed a backup plan, but now that her husband, Gabriel, had returned after being gone for weeks and was in one of his rages, she was glad she'd prepared for this moment. She ushered her children, one-year-old Mila and three-year-old Theo, ahead of her into the crawl space and then replaced the panel she'd cut months ago in the wall inside the main bedroom closet, while praying the seams wouldn't show from the outside.

She'd checked to make sure the light didn't shine through in a dark room to give away their hiding place. It didn't, so she turned on her phone's flashlight so the kids wouldn't add being afraid of the dark to the list of traumas they'd take away from the many other incidents that preceded this one.

Isla found the battery-powered light she'd stashed there months ago, hoping she'd never need that or the days' worth of provisions, diapers, wipes, toys and games she'd carted into the space while the kids were next door with their devoted neighbor and friend, Mrs. Ventura. On the way into the crawl space, she'd also grabbed her laptop and chargers for the computer and phone, which she plugged into the power strip attached to an extension cord that she'd pushed through a hole in the wall months ago and then patched with spackle.

Isla had tried to think of everything they might need for a day or two, if necessary. She couldn't think beyond having prepared for a couple of days. What would happen after that…

The sound of screaming, glass shattering and thumps could be heard through the wall, each one causing her—and the children—to startle in response.

She thought about calling 911 but was too afraid the call might be overheard through the thin wall, so she was counting on Mrs. V or one of their other neighbors to make the call.

As she held the kids close to her, she whispered to them how important it was to be as quiet as possible. They'd had "quiet contests" night after night, until it had become a game they enjoyed, while she hoped they'd never need the skill.

Now that the incident she'd prayed would never come to pass was upon them, the kids clung to her, scared speechless by their father's rage and aware, even at their young ages, that if he found them, it wouldn't be good.

Tears slid down her cheeks, wetting the soft, downy hair of her babies as they burrowed into her, their anchor in the storm.

Gabriel… *Her* Gabriel… Her sweet, adorable, loving, sexy husband had left her a little at a time over the ten years they'd been together, an excruciating undoing that'd intensified the day he'd gone missing for six hours while she was pregnant with Theo. He'd returned a totally different person.

She still didn't know where he'd been or what'd happened, but the spiral since then had been profound and terrifying. Despite pleas from her and other people who cared about him, he'd refused to seek medical care for an issue that was obvious to everyone but him. He'd said he was fine and that they should all mind their own business and had been especially vicious toward Isla when she'd begged him to tell her what was wrong so they could try to fix it.

She would've left him a long time ago if she'd had the resources.

He'd eventually lost the job he'd loved at a design firm, but even that hadn't gotten his attention. Mrs. V had urged her to leave. If only it were that simple...

Isla hadn't worked since Theo was born and couldn't support herself and two young kids on her own. They'd been living on a wish and a prayer for a while, but since Gabe lost his job, things had been tighter than ever, especially since it'd taken a couple of months for unemployment benefits to kick in. Thank God his company laid him off rather than firing him, or they would've been completely screwed.

Glass smashed close to where she and the kids trembled in fear. Isla liked to think he wouldn't harm them, but she wasn't sure of that anymore. She no longer knew the man she'd once loved with all her heart. She didn't love him anymore and hadn't for quite some time. How could she love a man who wouldn't do whatever it took to care for himself and his family?

No, the love was long gone, despite a brief moment of reconciliation two years ago that'd led to Mila. The respite hadn't lasted for even a week, and when she'd discovered she was pregnant, she'd experienced total despair, wondering how she'd ever care for *two* kids in this hellacious situation. But the minute the nurse laid Mila in her arms, she'd understood the meaning of things happening for a reason.

She hated that her babies knew the terror of being hunted by the man who should've been their protector, that they understood at such young ages how vitally important it was for them to stay quiet.

More smashing as he screamed for Isla. It went on long enough that the kids eventually fell asleep, while she remained on full alert.

She was delirious from the energy it took to stay in such a heightened state of awareness while he continued to scream and yell and smash things that used to mean so much to her. Now all she cared about was getting herself and her children out of this nightmare alive. After this incident, there were no choices left. They had to leave, even if it was with only the clothes on their backs.

She had to get her children away from him and never look back.

A loud banging noise followed by a commotion had her sitting up straighter. Her extremities were numb from holding the same position for so long with two children asleep in her arms.

She couldn't tell what was happening on the other side of the wall, but she heard muffled voices, a struggle, more screaming and then... silence.

Her phone lit up with a text from Mrs. V. Isla realized she'd missed several frantic messages from her over the past two hours. *Where are you? The police arrested Gabriel.*

Isla rearranged the children so she could type. *Hiding with the kids in the crawl space behind my bedroom closet.*

A few minutes later, she heard a voice. "Isla, this is Officer Samuelson with the LAPD. We have your husband in custody. It's safe to come out."

She put the kids on pads on the floor that she'd gotten to serve as beds, if necessary, and pushed open the panel.

A young, handsome police officer with brown skin and caring brown eyes was there to greet her. "I'm Officer Samuelson. Are you all right?"

"Y-yes, I think so."

"And your children? Are they with you?"

She nodded. "They're asleep."

"Let's get you guys out of there and settle you somewhere safe."

"What'll happen to Gabriel?"

"He's being taken to Central Booking on domestic violence charges."

"He's not well. Something is wrong."

"He'll be fully evaluated. Are you able to get your children?"

"Yes." She crawled back into the hiding place that had possibly saved their lives and handed Mila and then Theo to the officer. Thankfully, they never stirred as they were relocated.

Isla collected the bags of essential items as well as her phone, computer and chargers and left the space behind while saying a silent prayer of thanks for the protection it had provided them.

As she blinked at the sudden onslaught of bright lighting, she was unprepared to face the absolute wreckage of their home. Everything that could be smashed was in pieces on the floor. Gabriel had destroyed every lamp, dish, glass, bowl, vase and even some of the kids' toys, using Theo's baseball bat, which had been abandoned on the living room floor.

"Is there somewhere you and the kids could go for the night?"

"We can't stay here? The bedroom... I can clean it up."

"No, I'm sorry. This is a crime scene. You'll need to relocate."

She thought of Mrs. V, who'd been unable to have children with her late husband and was sad to not have grandchildren like her friends did. Isla had told her about her parents dying when she was in middle school and that Gabriel didn't see his family, so she was sad that her kids didn't have grandparents.

They'd become close friends, filling a void for each other. Before things got really bad with Gabriel, they'd taken the kids to lunch and the park and on walks through the neighborhood. More than once, Mrs. V had pleaded with her to leave, but Isla couldn't make that happen financially, and

Mrs. V lived on a tight budget that prevented her from helping.

Mrs. V had said more than once that she was afraid of losing them to one of Gabriel's rages. Isla didn't blame her for that. She'd had a front-row seat to the disintegration of their marriage, and her fear for Isla and the kids had put distance between them over the last few months.

All these thoughts went through Isla's mind in a matter of seconds as she tried to decide whether she and the kids would still be welcome with Mrs. V. She really hoped so. "I... I could ask my neighbor."

"Would he think to look for you there?"

"Maybe, but I don't have anyone else I can ask." She wasn't about to call her brother to tell him what Gabriel had done when Denny had told her not to marry him in the first place. He knew nothing about how bad things had gotten.

"Do you want me to ask her for you?"

"I'll text her." When Isla picked up her phone, she noticed her hands were shaking as the last few hours caught up with her in a surge of adrenaline and terror. She took a deep breath and typed the message to Mrs. V.

The kids and I need a place to stay tonight. Could we borrow your sofa?

She could see that the message had been delivered and read.

A full minute passed before she saw the dancing bubbles that indicated her neighbor was replying.

Of course.

Relief flooded her system. She had no plan B or money for a hotel. Their small nest egg was long gone, their credit cards maxed out, and the unemployment money had already been depleted for this month.

"We can go next door," Isla told Officer Samuelson.

"I'll help you move the children."

Two other officers cleared a path through the glass disaster to the door. One of them took Theo while Samuelson had Mila. Isla followed them, carrying their belongings and keeping her eyes on the door. She didn't want to see the destruction of the home she'd lovingly created for her family.

She'd have to come back at some point to get the rest of the things that could be salvaged, but for now, she couldn't bear to look at what he'd done to their home.

Mrs. Ventura waited for them in the doorway to her apartment, stepping aside so the officers could carry the children inside. "Take them to the second bedroom on the right," she said. "The bed is ready for them."

"Thank you so much," Isla said to her.

"I hope this'll be the end of the road with him before he kills you or the children."

"You know I would've left a long time ago if I could've afforded it."

"I'm sorry. I'm not judging you. I swear."

"I wouldn't be surprised if you were. I'm judging myself."

Mrs. V put an arm around her and guided her into the apartment.

Officer Samuelson asked for Isla's contact info and promised to let her know when she could return to the apartment. Then he handed her his card. "Please call me if you need anything at all."

"Thank you for your kindness."

After he left, Mrs. Ventura put a pillow, sheet and blanket on the sofa.

"Could I please check on the kids?"

"Of course. You know the way." She'd set up a cute little room for them to nap when they stayed with her on the rare occasions when Isla needed a sitter.

Isla found the kids still sound asleep and cuddled up to each other. She sat on the edge of the mattress and ran her fingers through their soft blond hair as tears slid down her cheeks. "I'm so sorry," she whispered. "You guys deserve so much better than this. Somehow, I'm going to fix it. If it's the last thing I do, I'm going to make this right for you."

She kissed them both, adjusted the covers, put the light on inside the closet and walked out of the room, leaving the door open so she'd hear them if they woke up.

Thank God they'd slept through the worst of it.

"Do you have everything you need?" Mrs. V asked.

Not even close. "Yes, thank you again for putting us up."

"I hope you can get some rest, honey."

Not at all likely. She hugged her friend. "Thank you for everything. I know it wasn't easy for you to call the police."

"I came home about forty minutes ago and couldn't figure out what I was hearing until I heard him screaming for you. And then when you didn't answer my texts, I thought..."

Isla hugged her again. "I'm so sorry. We were hiding, and I didn't see the texts."

"I can't believe you had a hiding place right in the apartment."

"I realized a while ago that I might need it."

"I was hoping he was gone for good this time."

"Me, too. But I'm not going back. I don't know what I'm going to do, but I'll figure something out."

"Maybe you should finally tell your brother just how bad it's gotten."

Isla had resisted that with every fiber of her being. Denny's strenuous objections to her marriage had caused a rift between her and the older brother who'd finished raising her after their parents died in a helicopter accident. When they saw each other, Isla had pretended everything was fine, because she'd been determined to find a way out on her own.

The last thing she'd wanted to do was tell Denny he'd been right about Gabriel, or that she was in big trouble.

"I'll think about that," she said to Mrs. V, knowing she had few options other than to call her brother at this point. He'd checked in regularly, but they weren't close anymore, and that'd been almost as painful a loss as her parents' deaths when she was in eighth grade.

"This is no time for pride, sweetheart. You need help, and he's your family."

"I know."

Mrs. V hugged her. "Get some rest while you can."

"I'll try."

Isla went to the sofa and sat, trying to regulate her breathing and get her heart rate back to normal. Her body hummed with adrenaline, her fight-or-flight response still fully activated, even though Gabriel was in police custody. The thought of him being locked up, even after everything he'd done to deserve it, was devastating.

She took a series of cleansing breaths and then reached for her phone to call Denny. Even if he was tempted to say, "I told you so," he would still help her. Of that, she was certain. She'd hoped to figure out a plan on her own before she had to make this call, but now she was completely out of options.

"Hey," he said, "what's up? I'm on my way to a gig on Sunset." He played lead guitar in a sixties and seventies cover band called Canyon that was so popular, they could've played seven nights a week if it weren't for their pesky day jobs. "What's up?"

"Something happened."

"What? Are you all right? Are the kids?"

"We are now, but Gabriel... He... he smashed up the apartment."

"He did *what*? Where were you and the kids?"

"Hiding."

"Isla, what the hell? Where were you hiding?"

"I made a place behind the closet wall if we ever needed to hide from him."

"You... you *prepared* to hide from him?"

"Just in case."

"Can you hear how *insane* that sounds?"

"Yes, I can, Denny, but what was I supposed to do with two little kids, no money and no way to move out?"

"You should've called me!"

"So you could tell me how you were right and I was wrong from the start with him?"

"Have I said that?"

"No, but I couldn't bear the fact that I didn't listen to you and ended up in this impossible situation with two precious little kids to care for."

"Where are you now?"

"My neighbor took us in because my place is a crime scene thanks to Theo's baseball bat."

"Jesus fucking hell. Where is he?"

"The cops took him."

"Which means he'll probably be out on bail by the morning. I'm going to talk to my friend Julian about this."

"The fancy-pants Hollywood divorce lawyer? I'm sure he'll jump on taking my case, especially since I can't afford to pay him."

"He'll do it if I ask him to. We go way back. Been playing together since high school."

She'd been in elementary school then, so she didn't know many of his friends from that era. She barely remembered living in the same house with him until he moved back home from college after their parents died.

"Ask if he can refer me to someone cheap."

"You don't want cheap for this, Isla. You need someone who gets results, and that's Julian."

"He's probably three hundred bucks an hour, and don't say you'll pay it, because you can't afford it any more than I can." Julian had negotiated Denny's child support and alimony payments *down* to three thousand a month.

"We gotta get you away from that guy. God, I told you not to marry him!"

"You were right! Is that what you want to hear?"

"No, I want to hear you're leaving him for good this time."

"I want to. I just can't seem to figure out how that's going to happen when I haven't worked in three years and can't do four and a half times the rent upfront, or whatever nonsense they want these days."

"I'll see Julian tonight and call you after."

"Thanks."

"I'm sorry about this, Islands in the Stream. You deserve better."

The silly old nickname he'd given her years ago brought tears to her eyes. "I know I do, but damned if I can figure out how to get it."

"Let me see what I can do."

"Don't commit me to paying him anything. I couldn't even if I wanted to."

"I know. Try not to worry. I'm on it."

"What? Me worry? When everything I own is smashed to smithereens and the so-called love of my life is in jail?"

"That jackass is not the love of your life. He's just the sperm donor for my awesome niece and nephew. You haven't met the love of your life yet."

"If you say so."

"I say so, and as the big brother, I'm always right."

Her chin quivered at hearing him tease her for the first time in years. "Whatever you say."

"I'll call you later. Don't go out anywhere that he can get to you if they spring him."

"Nowhere to go."

"I'll call you back."

When the line went dead, she put down the phone and stretched. "Goodbye to you, too, big brother." Was he overbearing? Incredibly. But he was also the only man in her life who'd never once disappointed her. He'd been there for her at every stage of her life, moving her into her first apartment and helping her and Gabriel move even after taking an immediate dislike to a man he'd deemed not worthy of her.

As Denny had been going through a difficult divorce at the time, she'd encouraged him to focus on his own life and butt out of hers. She wished now that she'd listened to him when he said he'd gotten a strange vibe from Gabe and didn't feel comfortable around him.

Isla had chalked up his objections to no one ever being good enough for his baby sister, but it'd been more than that. She'd been a fool not to listen to him when he sounded the alarm about Gabe's unpredictable behavior. Love and the desire to rebuild the family she'd lost when her parents died had blinded her to things that should've stood out like massive red flags. The disappearing acts had begun while they were dating, but she'd figured he was busy, seeing friends, playing basketball and, occasionally, even working.

His spotty employment track record and the fact that there was no contact with his family were other concerns Denny had zeroed in on.

"Not everyone is close to their family," she'd said, "and besides, what does that have to do with me?"

"*Everything*," he'd said. "I want to know why he doesn't talk to them, or vice versa—and you should want to know that, too. People don't go no-contact with their families for no good reason, and from what I know about him, *he's* the reason."

He'd been right about that. She saw that now, for all the good that did her.

After their parents died, leaving Isla and Denny alone in the world to fend for themselves, he'd tried to guide and advise her, but like most people in their teens and early twenties, she hadn't wanted his advice or his guidance. She'd said she was in love with Gabe and intended to marry him, no matter what her brother had to say about it.

"God, I wish I'd listened to you," she whispered. "But

then I wouldn't have my babies, and they're worth all the hell and heartache that Gabe has put me through. But now... Now I have to leave him for good. I can never go back to him."

The thought of starting over on her own with two young children was so overwhelming as to give her chest pains, but she'd do whatever it took to keep herself and her kids safe. That meant leaving Gabriel once and for all and never going back.

CHAPTER FIVE

Julian was tuning his bass when his longtime friend Denny Clarkson approached him, looking troubled. He was a big dude with floppy blond hair and a kind, friendly face that was unusually tense.

"Hey, man, how goes it?" Julian asked.

"I need your help."

"What's up?"

"Remember my sister, Isla?"

"Of course." While Denny often mentioned her and her young kids, Julian hadn't ever met her. "Younger than us, right?"

"Yeah, by seven years. She's in trouble with a hopefully soon-to-be ex-husband who's escalating."

"How so?"

"He busted up their apartment."

"Busted it up with what?"

"A baseball bat. Everything is smashed to pieces."

"Where was she?"

"Hiding with the kids."

Julian raised a dark brow. "In an apartment?"

"She'd made a hiding place behind a closet in case she ever needed it."

Julian was stunned—and amazed—that she'd planned for such a thing. What did that say about what she must've been dealing with before this? "How long has this been going on?"

"I'm not really sure. She's kept me at arm's length since I told her not to marry him, but if she's calling me for help now, it must be bad. We gotta get her away from him before he kills her."

"Has he ever hurt her physically?"

"Not that I know of, but like I said, she cut me out of the day-to-day after I disapproved of the marriage."

"Is she somewhere safe now?"

"She and the kids are with a neighbor for the night. He's locked up. For now, anyway."

"Can you bring her to my office in the morning?"

"She can't afford you."

"We'll worry about that after we ensure the safety of her and her kids."

"She won't be able to pay for anything. I think he's probably wiped them out."

"We have some leeway for pro bono work." Julian didn't have time for pro bono, but he'd do it for Denny. They'd been playing together in one band or another for more than twenty years. "You okay to play tonight?"

"I will be." Denny ran both hands through his hair, trying to pull himself together. "I wish she'd told me it was this bad before it got to this point. Maybe I could've gotten her out of there."

"I've found that not much can be done until the injured party decides he or she has had enough."

"I think maybe she's there. She sent me pictures of the apartment. It's total carnage."

"Could I see the pictures?"

Denny pulled out his phone, found the pictures of the destruction and handed the phone to Julian.

"Holy shit."

"She said there's almost nothing left except clothes and the kids' toys, and even that is covered in broken glass."

"What's his deal?"

"I honestly don't know. She's kept her distance from me for almost as long as they've been married. I probably messed up by telling her straight out not to marry him, but I had the strongest feeling that it was a mistake. Of course, she didn't want to hear it, and it really changed the groove between us. I had no clue about what she's been dealing with, and I feel guilty about that."

"All right. I'll do what I can to get her off the merry-go-round, but I have to caution you... Unless she's fully on board with making a break, there's not much I can do for her. I can ask for a restraining order that's not worth the paper it's printed on if she's not determined to keep him away from her and her kids."

"I'll talk to her again later and get a feel for where she's at, but I think she knows it's over."

"Keep me posted. I'll do everything I can for you and your sister."

Denny gave him a bro hug around the heavy bass guitar. "I owe you one."

"It's no problem."

"Yes, it is, and don't pretend like I'm not taking you away from shit that earns you seven hundred bucks an hour."

Julian grinned. "You're never going to let me forget I told you that, are you?"

"Not in this or any other lifetime."

"What can I say? When you're good, you're good."

Denny rolled his eyes and went to set up his equipment. "Try not to sprain your ego, Counselor."

"Haha, my ego is unsprainable."

"What's lawyer boy spewing about now?" Troy Warren asked as he joined them. The keyboard player wore a black leather vest full of patches and pins collected from every club, bar, festival and event he'd ever played at. The vest put his sleeve tattoos and impressive biceps on full display, which helped to ensure he wouldn't go home alone.

"His ego is as healthy as ever," Denny said.

The band's drummer, Stix Murillo, and his sexy girlfriend, Vixen, one of three lead singers, came rolling in, holding hands as always. The guys liked to tease Vixen about what her mother was thinking when she'd given her daughter that name. She always had a saucy reply such as, "Wouldn't you like to know?"

In fact, Vixen was her stage name, and she hoped to become as famous as other single-name stars such as Pink and Cher. Her real name was Vivian, but Stix had warned them never to call her that, as she was fully committed to building a career in the music business as Vixen.

The band made enough money to keep her mostly afloat while she reached for the stars, but she'd mentioned being disappointed by how long it was taking to break out.

Julian wasn't going to be the one to tell her how many people came to LA seeking fame and fortune only to never get their big break. However, her incredible voice was a big reason the band had become so popular. She had a Stevie Nicks vibe that had people following them from gig to gig, giving them the kind of fan base that often led to bigger things. He had a semiqueasy feeling about the band taking off, knowing he wouldn't be able to take the ride that the others craved. As much as he loved playing live, and this band was the best one he'd ever been part of, it wasn't his big dream, or Denny's.

Since the rest of the band was constantly struggling for money, Julian refused payment for gigs he was happy to do for free because the music gave him a much-needed outlet away from work.

They rocked the classics for three long hours with one thirty-minute break, during which Denny checked in with his sister. Julian reached out to a contact at the LAPD who confirmed that Gabriel Santana would be their overnight guest at the city jail with an arraignment scheduled for nine o'clock in the morning. Due to the severity of the damage done to the apartment, his friend said, the DA was recommending Gabriel be held without bail while he awaited trial. The outcome would depend on the judge, and Denny's sister needed to be prepared for her husband to be released on bail.

Julian told Denny what he'd learned from the LAPD.

"Well, it's a relief that he won't get out tonight. I'll let her know in case the LAPD hasn't gotten around to notifying her yet."

"What's the plan if he gets sprung tomorrow?"

"I don't have one. I'd take them in if I could, but my place barely has room for me. The child support and alimony are killer, as you know."

"I could loan you the money to get a place big enough for all of you."

Denny hesitated before he said, "The family money is invested for her."

"She doesn't know about it?"

He shook his head. "I was afraid the husband would blow through it, so I kept it from her. She has what she needs to move out."

"You need to tell her that."

"She's going to be pissed that I kept it from her."

"Not as pissed as she'd be if he'd squandered it."

"I hope that's the case. Thank you for helping."

"Always. Bring her to the office in the morning. We'll figure out next steps."

"Will do. Appreciate this."

"No worries."

After they finished their gig, Julian helped pack up the

equipment and then headed for the exit, eager to get home after a long-ass day with another on tap for tomorrow. As he drove home, he thought about Denny's sister and hoped he could help her figure out a plan to get free of her violent husband before something happened to her and her kids.

His practice tended to cater to high-income clients due to the firm's reputation and their hourly rates. However, he tried to help those of lesser means whenever he got the chance. In fact, his active pro bono practice was often a source of contention with his father, who preferred that they stay focused on clients with big bucks.

Making use of his skills and experience to help people who were less fortunate was important to Julian, who'd led an extraordinarily privileged life. Despite the nastiness of his parents' divorce, the rest of his childhood had been somewhat gilded thanks to their professional success. He volunteered one Saturday a month at a shelter for women who'd experienced domestic violence and made himself available to friends who needed help, like Denny, even if they couldn't afford to pay him.

His siblings agreed that their pro bono work made them feel better about charging exorbitant rates to clients who could easily afford them.

As he drove up the hill toward his home in Laurel Canyon, Julian thought of his grandfather, Spencer Remington, and how he'd built the family business into a local institution that'd gained national prominence under Corbin's leadership. With every passing year, the firm's annual gross grew exponentially, which gave them the resources to fund things like in-house estate, accounting, real estate and taxation specialists, which set them apart from most smaller family law firms.

When the shit hit the fan in a Hollywood marriage, Remington was usually the first call both parties made, and if they didn't call the original Remington practice, then his mother's firm, Kate Remington Family Law, was right up there on the list of the most desirable representation. His three sisters, Jordan, Kaidan and Gillian, worked for their mother's firm, as did two of their female first cousins.

They joked about the boys versus girls in court, as they frequently were on opposite sides of high-profile cases, but they strove to leave the animosity in court, as they were determined to stay close outside of work.

On the way home, he hung a left on Lookout Mountain Avenue, passing the house his maternal grandmother had once rented, back when she'd made music with the likes of 1960s and 1970s luminaries Joni Mitchell, David Crosby and Stephen Stills, among many others. In fact, Joni had been her neighbor. Freida Lewis had been a legend in her own right as a successful singer/songwriter who'd inspired her grandchildren's appreciation for classic rock, folk and the other sounds that'd come from the incredible era in which Laurel Canyon had been at the center of the LA musical universe.

He was driving his first-generation black 1971 Porsche 911, which was among his most-prized possessions, even if it became more of a money pit with every passing year. Thankfully, the band had someone to manage their equipment, or the bass would've been hanging out the window on his way home.

Driving the old car brought him joy, especially as he downshifted to navigate the twisting turns of Laurel Canyon, his ears popping as they always did when he went higher into the hills. His brothers liked to say he'd bought a house up there so he'd never have to invite them over, as parking was at a premium on the narrow roads. When it had come time to buy his own home, Julian hadn't looked anywhere other than the neighborhood his grandmother had helped to make famous with her illustrious friends back in the day.

He pulled up to his two-story contemporary-style home on Sunset Plaza Drive. The exterior was dark gray brick with wood accents and a light blue smoked-glass garage door. He pressed the button to open the double-sized door and parked next to the matte black Mercedes G-Wagon SUV he used when he needed to go farther than Sunset for a gig. He was under no illusions about the Porsche and believed her days were probably numbered, so he drove her as often as he could.

Inside the house he'd owned for seven years, Julian disarmed the security system and flipped on the lights in the kitchen he'd fully renovated over two years of weekends with light wood cabinets, a tile backsplash in several shades of blue, matching stone countertops and stainless-steel appliances. He went to the fridge, grabbed a beer, turned on the teardrop lights over the island and sat on a barstool to check his email and messages to wrap up one workday before the next one began.

He had a text from Rachel McDavid: *Bryan showed up at the boys' school trying to sign them out, but thankfully, the admin is aware of the situation, knows he's not authorized and refused him. Is this something that needs to be reported to the Court?*

Julian sighed as he typed his response. *Absolutely. I'll take care of that right away. Where are you now?*

Staying with a cousin in Sherman Oaks until I figure out a plan. Bryan doesn't know her, so he wouldn't think to look for us here. The boys are upset because I told them they can't go back to their school, but of course I can't tell them why, because then they'll hate him, and I swore I'd never make them hate him... That's turning out to be harder than expected. Instead, they'll hate me for things I didn't cause. I can't even think about what might've happened if he'd succeeded in getting them from the school. Is he angry enough at me to harm them? I'd like to think not, but I'm not sure anymore.

I'll reach out to the Court and Bryan's attorney as well to remind him that his client is under a restraining order and showing up to his sons' school is a violation of that. The judge may consider contempt charges, which are criminal misdemeanors.

Thank you for all your help. I can't believe it's come to this, but here we are.

If Julian had a dollar for every time a client had expressed that same sentiment, he could retire early. A romantic partner becoming a threat came as a shock to those who'd put their trust in them. The threat could be physical, emotional, financial or all of the above, and it came from the person who was supposed to keep them safe.

Hang in there, he replied to Rachel. *We'll keep pushing until he gets the message.*

She gave his text a thumbs-up.

He sent urgent messages to the Court and to Thomas Driscoll, Bryan's attorney, letting them know of the incident at the McDavid sons' school.

Then he listened to a voicemail from Marlon Beckett. "Returning your call. Happy to talk about a settlement with Cresley whenever you're available."

Funny how Julian hadn't mentioned anything about a settlement when he'd first reached out. He'd call Beckett in the morning to see what he had to say, and then he'd figure out how to make him go away and leave Cresley and their son alone.

He also had a message from Jenna Simsbury thanking him for the "gangsta move" that'd resulted in her husband agreeing to her request for full custody of their three children rather than having his financial misdeeds entered into the public record at trial. This had occurred after months of her husband refusing to consider mediation.

Once again, Carson and his investigative team had come up with exactly what Julian had needed to push the case to a satisfactory conclusion for their client.

Michael Simsbury would have visitation with the children and would pay hefty child and spousal support while also taking full responsibility for the massive debt he'd accrued in both their names. Julian was pleased with the outcome for a client who'd seen her immaculate credit destroyed by her ex-husband. Additional court action was underway that would hopefully restore her credit, but it wouldn't happen overnight. In the meantime, she was struggling to restart her life free of her ex-husband, but with lousy credit and three children to care for as a single mom.

Jenna's case was yet another example of how unfair life, love and marriage could be.

Julian downed the rest of his beer, stood, stretched and headed upstairs to bed, seventeen hours after he woke up in Stacey's bed, only to be reminded why he almost never spent the night with a woman. He'd been exhausted last night and had fallen asleep without intending to.

He'd given her hope by staying. That'd been a tactical error he wouldn't soon repeat.

CHAPTER SIX

Isla woke on Mrs. V's sofa with a deep feeling of dread and despair. It took her a minute to recall the events of the day before that'd led to her hiding out in her neighbor's apartment. A soft sob from the back bedroom had her getting up and going to the kids so they wouldn't wake Mrs. Ventura before dawn.

Mila was sitting up in bed, her hair in a mass of blonde ringlets around her chubby little face. Her lip quivered, and her eyes pooled with tears.

"Mama's here," Isla whispered as she snuggled up to her little girl, praying Theo would sleep for a while longer. She had none of their toys or anything to entertain them at this hour, which added to her already considerable anxiety.

She ran a soothing hand over Mila's back, hoping she'd go back to sleep.

Denny was coming at nine to pick them up for the meeting with his attorney friend. Since she could no longer afford to pay a sitter, she'd have to take the kids with her, which certainly wasn't ideal. But what else was she supposed to do?

Mrs. V played bridge on Tuesdays and looked forward to seeing her friends. Isla would never ask her to miss that, and she had no one else she could ask on short notice.

In the weeks that Gabriel had been gone this time, Isla had come out of the fog of survival mode to realize how increasingly isolated she'd become from the friends who'd sustained her after she and Denny lost their parents.

She'd been supported by a close group of girlfriends who'd been by her side as she finished middle school and entered high school while navigating profound grief and fear about the future. Denny had left college in Colorado and moved home to serve as her guardian. Their parents' life insurance had allowed Isla and Denny to remain in their home. They'd muddled through, somehow, despite frequent clashes over Denny's "parenting," which had largely consisted of him saying *no*.

That had turned Isla into a lying rebel. She'd defied him openly, shutting off her phone so Denny wouldn't be able to track her down and ruin her fun. He'd been furious with her, but that hadn't stopped her from continuing to evade him.

Gabriel had entered the picture during that vulnerable period and had been an incredible source of love and support. The more he'd encouraged her to depend on him, the less she'd seen her friends—and her brother, who'd hated Gabriel from the get-go and had pleaded with her not to marry him.

She could see now that the isolation had been Gabriel's plan all along. The critical remarks he'd made about her brother and each of the women she'd been close to had chipped away at her belief in them. He'd been offended any time she made plans that didn't include him. Eventually, she'd said no to their invitations often enough that they'd stopped asking her to do things.

Her excuses always involved Gabe and work and, later, the kids, but her friends had partners, jobs and kids, too, and they still found time for one another. She saw photos of their frequent outings on Instagram and always felt sad and left out, but what did she expect? If you said no often enough, people stopped asking and moved on without you.

And now here she was, on her own with two little kids and no one other than a kindly neighbor she could call on for support, which was probably exactly what Gabe had hoped to achieve.

She'd started college as a commuter to UCLA but left after two years to play house with Gabriel for a few years before they got married. Since she hadn't finished college, she had fewer employment options now that she'd be seeking a divorce and full custody of her kids. How in the world would she ever support them? Before Theo arrived, she'd worked as a receptionist for an ophthalmology practice in Beverly Hills, but after Gabe landed his dream job with the design firm, he'd encouraged her to give up her job to stay home with Theo to save money on daycare.

Now she could see how quitting her job had further cemented his total control over her and their finances. Tears slid down her cheeks as she picked through the ruins of a once-promising life that'd been derailed by loss and compounded by bad decisions. She'd trusted the wrong person with her love, faith and security, and now she faced the daunting task of unraveling her life from his and starting over. But how she'd do that with two little ones counting on her for everything was beyond her ability to comprehend on that first morning after near disaster.

Isla thought of it as a near disaster because most of the things Gabriel had destroyed could be replaced. The few special items she'd taken from her parents' home were still in boxes in the same closet that'd provided sanctuary to her and her children. Those treasures were safe, as were her babies, which was all that truly mattered. She'd figure out the rest one step at a time.

Somehow.

. . .

AT NINE O'CLOCK, Denny pulled up in the silver Toyota Tundra he drove for his work as the owner of a small construction company. He carried coffees for both of them as he met her at the driver's side of her red Hyundai SUV, which was three months behind on payments and probably about to be repossessed. He helped her load the kids into their car seats while they squealed with delight at the special attention always paid to them by Uncle Denny.

Over time, she and Denny had papered over the earlier cracks in their relationship, but there was still tension between them that usually disappeared when the kids were around. Denny was an amazing, caring, loving uncle to them, and they adored him.

Mrs. Ventura had given her a key and told her to come and go for as long as she needed to. Her kindness had reduced Isla to tears as she'd hugged and thanked the older woman.

"Now, now," she'd said. "No need to get maudlin over it."

There was every need in Isla's mind, as Mrs. V had just given her and the kids a place to stay while she figured out their next move. Although, if Gabriel was released from jail, he'd probably come right back to their building. He was aware that she'd become close with the older woman next door, even if he'd tried to discourage it, calling Mrs. V a nosy old biddy who wanted to know their business.

"Did you sleep at all?" Denny asked as he drove Isla's SUV to Beverly Hills, toward an attorney and a divorce she couldn't afford. Her stomach was in knots. Mrs. V had made pancakes for the kids, but Isla had only sipped at coffee.

"Some."

"After they finish processing the apartment, I'll help you rescue whatever can be saved."

"You don't have time for this."

"I took the day off."

"Denny! You can't afford to do that."

"How do you expect me to think about anything but you and the kids after what he did? I'll make up the day on the weekend. Don't worry about me."

She would worry about him and the mess she was making of both their lives. They'd already had far more mess than their share.

"Do you know anyone who's hiring?"

"Not off the top of my head, but I'll put out some feelers."

"I texted Georgia about working at the bar." She'd worked with Georgia at the ophthalmology practice. She'd left to manage the Whisky A Go Go, an iconic Sunset Boulevard bar and music venue. She'd told Isla to hit her up if she ever needed to make real money. Isla had filed that info away.

Stopped at a red light, Denny looked over at her. "How will you work nights with the kids?"

"Mrs. Ventura said she was fine with watching them. They'll be asleep when I leave. Georgia says I'll make great money there."

"And put up with guys hassling you nonstop?"

"It's fine. It's easy money at a time of day when I have someone to watch the kids."

"What does she do if they wake up wanting Mommy?"

"She'll figure it out. They know her."

"How well do they know her?"

"Well enough. Stop, will you? I have to do *something*."

"I can't bear to think of you working in that meat market with all those jackasses panting around after you like they did when you were younger."

"I'm older and fatter after having two babies in three years. They won't even notice me."

"Sure they won't."

Thankfully, he let the matter drop. After finally escaping a controlling husband, no man, not even her beloved brother, was going to tell her how to live her life. She'd never let that happen again.

Isla scrolled through her phone, looking for a way to expend the nervous energy that made her feel like she'd had five glasses of champagne. As if. She stopped on a post from TMZ that showed supermodel Cresley Dane laughing at an outdoor table with a handsome, dark-haired guy. As a fan of all things Cresley, she read the caption and gasped when she saw his name was Julian Remington. "Isn't this your lawyer friend?" She held her phone so Denny could see the image.

"Yeah, that's him."

"Is he *dating* Cresley Dane?"

"Not that I know of."

"Sure looks like it to me. *That's* the guy you're taking me to see? He looks like a supermodel himself." Guys like him thought the world revolved around them. She was fresh out of patience for that kind of big-dick energy. She'd been married to it for six years and had had enough.

"He's a good guy and a fucking brilliant lawyer. That's what you need right now."

"Fucking brilliant," Theo said from the back seat.

Isla glared at Denny.

"Sorry. I'm out of practice. My kids swear like sailors." They were twelve and fourteen and lived with their mother in Santa Monica. Isla hadn't seen them in more than a year.

"Awesome."

She and Denny coexisted in uneasy silence as they drove by Rodeo Drive, Lexus and Audi dealerships, Saks Fifth Avenue and other fancy boutiques. Denny hung a right to enter the parking garage at a six-story white stone and blue glass building on the corner of Wilshire Boulevard and Rexford Drive, otherwise known as the high-rent district.

"This place smells like money," she said. "Are they printing it here?'

"May as well be," Denny said with a gruff laugh. "The

Remington family is filthy rich, but Julian's cool. He's one of my longest-standing friends in music."

"How come I've never met him?"

"You haven't been to one of my shows since I've been playing with Canyon, the band we're in together now."

"Sorry about that."

"Don't be. As I mentioned, I don't want you hanging out in smoky bars with pervy guys harassing you."

"You recall that I'm thirty-one, and you're not the boss of me, right?"

"What did you say? I can't hear you."

Half the time, she wanted to punch him in the face. The other half, she wanted to cling to him and beg him to make her feel safe the way only he could. Right now, the punch to the face was the prevailing desire.

She and Denny each carried one of the kids into an elevator that deposited them into a fancy marble lobby, where they reported in at a reception desk.

"Dennis Clarkson to see Julian Remington."

"Do you have an appointment?"

"We do."

"I need ID from both of you, please."

They worked around the kids to produce their driver's licenses.

The security guy made a phone call and then gave them visitor badges that they were asked to keep visible.

"Jeez, it's easier to get into the Pentagon," Isla said while they waited for the elevator that would take them to the fourth floor. She wondered what it might be like to work in a place like this. The ophthalmology practice had been in a strip mall.

"Julian said there was an incident earlier this week, and they've tightened things up even more than they were. They have to be careful with security. They've had instances where someone who lost a case against them tried to hunt them down."

"Really?"

"Oh yeah, it's a concern. You help take someone's kids or money from them, they're furious and could be dangerous afterward."

"I wouldn't have thought it was dangerous to be a lawyer."

"Family law is an emotional battlefield. They have to be super careful that scorned spouses and parents who lose custody don't come looking for them. Julian told me once that they have an employee whose sole job is to make sure their addresses and personal info can't be found online."

"Wow. That's crazy." She hadn't realized that family law could be dangerous, but considering the battlefields upon which their wars were fought, it made sense.

When they stepped into the elevator, Denny let Theo press the button for the fourth floor and then pulled him back right as he would've pressed all the other buttons, too.

"Buttons!"

"You can press more on the way back down," Denny told him.

"Now!"

"Later."

Theo squiggled against his uncle's tight hold.

"Remember what Mommy said about behaving in the office building," Isla reminded him.

"Business," Theo said.

"That's right. People are doing *business*, and we have to be quiet."

He put his finger to his lips and said, "Shhhh."

"Very good."

Denny smiled at his nephew. "He's too cute."

"And he knows it."

Mila rested her head on Isla's shoulder, seeming overwhelmed by the odd series of events that'd transpired over the past twelve hours. She'd been unusually quiet and withdrawn since she woke up for the second time with her mother and brother in bed with her. She'd asked for her toys, and Isla had promised to get them for her later.

The thought of confronting her destroyed home was so devastating that she couldn't allow her mind to go there. She was taking this surreal day one step at a time, beginning with the movie-star-handsome lawyer Denny was bringing her to meet.

They were shown to an office where a sharply dressed woman greeted them with a warm smile. "Denny and Isla," she said, "I'm Julian's assistant, Mattie Jones. And who are these doll babies?"

Isla was immediately in love with the kind woman and in awe of her gorgeous black-and-white-checked suit coat that she'd paired with a red scarf, the kind of effortless style that Isla admired in other women, as she'd been born without that gene. "This is Theo and Mila, and they've promised to be very quiet in your office building."

"Aw, that's so sweet of you guys." She offered them candy from the bowl on her desk, ensuring they'd be her best friends forever. "Have a seat. Julian is finishing up with another client and will be right with you. Can I offer coffee or another beverage while you wait?"

"I'd kill for another coffee," Denny said.

"Me, too," Isla said.

"How do you take them?" Mattie asked.

"Both just with cream," Denny said.

"Coming right up."

"Thank you," Denny said.

"She's so nice," Isla said.

"Julian says she's the only reason he gets anything done. She keeps him on schedule and never lets him forget anything important."

Isla liked hearing how much Julian appreciated an obvious

treasure like Mattie. She gave him a few points that took him out of negative numbers in her mind. And yes, she knew it wasn't fair to think she had him all figured out before she even met him, but she sure as hell knew his king-of-the-world type and didn't think much of it.

Mattie returned with two coffees in cups with lids, which Isla appreciated with the kids squirming on their laps. From her suit coat pocket, she produced two juice boxes and a pack of vanilla sandwich cookies. "I figured it had to be snack time, right?"

"Snack," Theo said as he zeroed in on the cookies.

"Thank you so much, Mattie," Isla said.

"My pleasure."

Ten minutes later, the door to Julian's office opened, and Cresley Dane came strolling out in all her stunning glory. *Good God,* Isla thought. It almost hurt to look at her.

She smiled at Isla as she went by. She was already past when Isla started wishing she'd said hello or done something other than gape at the woman with her mouth hanging open like a fish out of water. A cloud of expensive perfume followed Cresley as she headed for the elevators.

"Holy smokes," Denny muttered. "She's even hotter in person."

"Put your tongue back in your mouth."

"I could say the same to you," her brother retorted, making Isla laugh.

How long had it been since she'd laughed at anything other than the silly things the kids did?

"Julian will see you now," Mattie said.

They collected the kids and made their way into a massive office with two glass walls overlooking Neiman Marcus on the other side of Wilshire. The scent of Cresley's expensive perfume lingered in the air.

Julian, who'd shed his suit coat and rolled up the sleeves of a crisp white dress shirt, stood to come around the desk to welcome them with handshakes. He wore a navy-and-purple silk tie, dark navy pants and a silver watch. "Isla, it's so nice to finally meet Denny's favorite little sister."

"Nice to meet you, too." She was almost as dazzled by him as she'd been by Cresley, and he smelled every bit as incredible as she had. He was a lot to process, which was why she didn't tell him she was Denny's *only* sister. Besides, he probably already knew that. "Thank you for seeing us."

"My pleasure. And who are these two cuties?"

Had she really almost forgotten that the kids were with her? "This is Theo and Mila."

Julian reached out to shake hands with Theo, who looked him in the eye the way Isla had taught him and said, "Nice to meet you."

Smiling, Julian said, "You as well, sir. This is your sister?"

"Yeah, but she's shy."

Mila had buried her face in Isla's shoulder to avoid looking at him.

"I was shy when I was little, too. Luckily, I grew out of that, or my job would be torture." He gestured to a gathering of sofas and chairs. "Please have a seat. Make yourselves comfortable."

"Impressive digs, Counselor," Denny said. "I mean, I knew it'd be something, but this…"

"I can't take any of the credit. My grandfather had good taste in office space sixty years ago. The place has aged well."

And he was humble. So much for preconceived notions. He was about six two or three, with wavy dark hair, soft brown eyes and just the right amount of facial hair. His smile was warm and welcoming, his face radiated kindness, and Isla immediately felt safe in his presence. That was an odd realization since she really only ever felt safe with Mrs. V and Denny these days. She'd expected to meet a man whose success had made him pretentious and probably full of himself and had to admit her preconceived notions had been unfair.

Theo couldn't take his eyes off the man who'd treated him like an adult and not a bothersome child, which was what Isla had expected him to do when little kids invaded his workplace.

"Are you all set for drinks?" Julian asked.

"We are, thank you," Isla said. "Mattie took good care of us."

"She's the best."

"So you and Cresley Dane, huh?" Denny said with a smug grin. "Keeping secrets from your buddies?"

Julian smiled. "She's my client, and what was reported on TMZ was a business lunch that's now causing us a number of headaches, but enough about that."

He directed his attention to Isla, and the impact was similar to how it felt to look directly into the sun. "Denny showed me the photos. I'm so sorry for what was done to your home."

"Thank you."

He glanced at the kids. "If they want to get down to explore, there's nothing they can hurt in here."

"Are you sure?"

"Absolutely. It's all boring old books. Let them roam."

"Do you want to look at Mr. Remington's books?" Isla asked Theo, who nodded. He loved books. "Don't touch anything, okay?"

"You can touch the books, Theo. But some of them are really heavy, so be careful."

Theo made muscle arms. "I'm strong."

"Wow," Julian said, "look at those biceps! There's a basket of toys over there, too."

Hearing that, Theo perked up even more. "Let's look at the toys, Mila!"

She squiggled out of Isla's arms to follow her favorite person wherever he chose to lead her.

"They're beautiful kids," Julian said.

"Thank you. I got lucky with them."

"Yesterday was a rough day for you guys."

"Yes." Understanding that he was easing her into the point of this meeting, she glanced down at a gorgeous area rug in shades of blue. "The latest in a series of tough days."

"Denny told me about your hiding place in the apartment. I'm truly impressed with your ingenuity."

She gave him a small smile. "I was hoping I'd never need it."

"Do you want to tell me about what led to you setting it up?"

Isla took a second to organize her thoughts and began with the thing she most wanted him to know—that she wasn't a fool for love. "I... I used to wonder why women didn't just leave when their domestic partners turned out to be dangerous or unstable or unkind or whatever it was. I'll admit to having judged friends who put up with awful crap for so long." She accepted a tissue from the box Julian offered her. "I've learned the hard way that it's not as simple as deciding to leave, especially when you haven't worked outside the home in years and have two kids to think about."

"Nothing about this situation is simple," Julian said in a kind, gentle tone that made her want to curl up to him and let him make it all better.

She shook off that thought almost the second she had it. The only one who could fix this was her, and she needed to remember that.

"After what happened yesterday, I'd advise that we immediately request a restraining order that'll keep your husband away from you and the children while we figure out our next steps. Would you be okay with that?"

"How does that work?"

"Basically, it's a court order that requires him to stay at least a thousand feet from you and the kids."

Isla had been determined to get through this without becoming overly emotional. That was turning out to be easier said than done. She wiped away more tears. "How long would the order be in effect?"

"For as long as it's needed. I'd suggest we start with a year and reassess later."

"A year?" That would officially make her a single mother. She glanced at her kids, who were engrossed in the trucks and blocks they'd found in the basket—for the moment, anyway. "Will he have to help financially?"

"We'll request spousal and child support."

"That doesn't mean we'll get it, though, does it?"

"You should be awarded reasonable support. The question is whether he's able to pay it. What does he do?"

"He... Well, he was working for a design company, but he got laid off a while ago. He's been collecting unemployment that barely covers the basics. I can pick up some hours at a bar where my friend is a manager. My neighbor will watch the kids for me."

"I don't want her doing that," Denny said.

Isla turned on him. "I don't *want* to do it, Denny, but I have to do *something*. The bar is easy money, and my friend from the doctor's office will look out for me. It's the only prayer I have of hanging on to the apartment. I... I don't know where we'd go if we can't stay there."

"Would it be possible for you to move to a smaller place for now?" Julian asked.

"I suppose that's an option. I need less room since most of what I own is wrecked."

"When you're able to, it would help if you could make an inventory of everything he destroyed so we can seek restitution."

"I'll make a list. None of it was worth much."

"It was to you."

The statement went straight to her broken heart. "Yes, it was."

"I ask all my clients the same questions: What's your ultimate goal for the future, and how does your spouse fit into that?"

It'd been so long since Isla had allowed herself to have goals that she took half a minute to think about it before she replied. "I suppose the most important goal is a safe, peaceful, happy childhood for my kids. They deserve that." She pressed the wadded-up tissue to her eyes again. "As far as how Gabriel fits into that... He doesn't. He's clearly got a medical problem of some sort, whether it's addiction, mental health or something else. He's refused to seek help, and I've learned that it's almost impossible to force an adult into treatment if they don't want it. I hoped he'd work out whatever he's been going through, but after yesterday, I can't hope for that anymore."

"That's understandable. Is it your intention to end the marriage and request custody of your children?"

Isla's chin wobbled as she nodded. In that moment, all she could remember was how much she'd once loved Gabriel and planned to spend the rest of her life with him and their children. A long time ago, she'd realized that wasn't to be. She'd begun to bide her time until she could make a break from him. In order for that to happen, however, he'd needed to come back from wherever he'd been for weeks—and when he finally had turned up, he'd taken the bat to their home.

"I hate to talk about business at such a difficult time, but there's paperwork I need you to complete so I can represent you. I'd also like your permission to ask our investigators to look into what he's been up to during the times he goes missing. Would that be all right?"

"I... I can't pay for any of this."

"I understand. We take a number of pro bono cases each year, and yours will be one of mine."

"How can you do that?"

"It's an important part of my practice. It allows me to help people who can't otherwise afford quality representation. Is that a yes on the investigators?"

"Yes, please."

"We'll also need to talk assets and liabilities and other such details. We'll set yesterday as the official date of separation, which is a critical benchmark in a divorce case."

"I'll never be able to thank you enough."

"Me, too," Denny said gruffly.

"Anything for you, pal," Julian said with a smile that encompassed both of them.

CHAPTER SEVEN

Isla had touched Julian deeply with her quiet strength at a time of deep despair over the demise of her marriage. Petite, with light brown shoulder-length hair and lovely brown eyes, she looked nothing like Denny, who was much taller and a true blond. While Julian had never met Denny's parents, they'd already been friends when Denny had been forced to step up for his younger sister long before he was ready for that kind of responsibility.

After Isla signed the retainer agreement and went to collect the kids, Denny said, "I need a minute alone before we go."

Julian reached for the signed retainer. Mattie would see to listing Isla as a client in their internal database so no one else in the firm would agree to represent her husband. "I'll ask Mattie to show Isla and the kids my dad's fish tank."

"Thanks."

To the kids, he said, "Do you guys want to see my dad's super cool fish tank?"

"Yes!" Theo exclaimed.

They abandoned the toys on the floor and ran over to their mom, who held out her arms to them. She scooped them up in a practiced move that impressed Julian, who had almost no experience with little ones except for his siblings. But he hadn't been solely responsible for them when they were younger and couldn't recall ever scooping up two of them in one smooth move the way Isla had.

He opened the office door. "Mattie, Isla and the kids would like to see Dad's fish. Would you mind taking them?"

"You got it. Follow Ms. Mattie, and I'll show you the way."

"Thank you."

"What's going on?" Isla asked Denny when she realized he wasn't going with them.

"Band business. I just need a minute."

"Don't talk about me."

"Please... Don't be so full of yourself."

She gave him the exasperated look that sisters had been giving brothers for all of time and carried the kids out of Julian's office.

"She's not taking any of your shit," Julian said to his friend when they were alone. "I love that."

"Everything I've ever done has been to try to protect her. You believe me, right?"

"I do."

"When our parents died... I had no clue what to do with a young girl who'd lost the most important people in her life while trying to manage my own shock and grief. I came home from Colorado and became her legal guardian, which was more complicated than you might think."

"I can't imagine what that would've been like."

"It was tough. She had to do what I told her to, and I tried to be reasonable, but I had no clue what I was doing, and we fought. A lot. Especially as she got older and wanted more independence. We muddled through, you know? One day at a time, as they say, but it was the hardest thing I've ever done. When she met Gabriel, she was immediately gone over him, but he always made me uncomfortable. There was just something... off. I don't know how to explain it, but I was adamantly opposed to her marrying him, which was the first time we were seriously at odds since our parents died. We didn't speak for months."

"That must've been rough."

"It was the worst, and it happened right around the time I was leaving Revenge Tour, which was also horrible." The breakup of Denny's first real band had been a nightmare that'd cost him three close friends.

"I remember that."

Denny ran his fingers through his mop of hair. "That's why I kept the money hidden from Isla. I had zero faith in her husband."

Julian thought about the divorce he'd brokered five years earlier for Denny and his ex-wife, Kath, in which the money from his parents had been treated as community property, since he and his wife had used some of it to buy a house, among other things. Denny had been the executor of their parents' estate as well as Isla's legal guardian until she turned eighteen. All the money that was left to them would've gone to him to manage for both of them.

"I've never told Isla about the money because at first I didn't trust her not to burn through it during her rebellious stage, and then I didn't trust Gabriel not to go through it like a madman, the way he apparently has with all their other money. I'm afraid she'll hate me for not telling her before now."

"You said she knew you didn't want her to marry Gabriel. Maybe she'll understand why you didn't tell her about the money."

"She won't. She'll never speak to me again."

"You're her family. You and the kids. She won't turn her back on you if you tell her you kept this from her to protect her."

"I don't know what to do. It's been eating me up inside for a long time because I knew they struggled financially, but I had no idea that things were this bad with him. She always told me everything was fine, the kids were great, things were good. I was so afraid of Gabriel looting the whole thing, which is the only reason I never told her about it. I helped her out with college, paid the upfront costs on their apartment. I did what I could to help them without giving away to him that there was more."

"Tell her that."

"I can't."

"Do you want me to talk to her?"

Denny brightened considerably. "Would you?"

"Sure." Julian would do it to help his friend, even if the situation was awkward. Isla had the right to the money her parents had left for her. "Remind me of the details again. It's been a minute since we settled your divorce."

A few minutes later, Isla returned with Mattie and the kids, who were excited about the fish tank and wanted to show it to their uncle.

Denny picked up Mila and took Theo's hand. "Show me."

"Is that okay?" Isla asked Julian. "We're disrupting your whole office."

"It's fine. My dad loves when people enjoy his tank. Did you see him?"

"No, just his assistant, Luka."

"Ah, okay. He must be out of the office, or he would've come out to see the kids. He loves kids, which is probably why he and my mom had nine of them."

"You have *nine kids* in your family?"

"I do," he said with a smile. "I'm the oldest of the Remington banana republic." He gestured toward the chairs. "Have a seat for a second?"

"Oh, um, okay."

She was lovely, with pale skin suffused with a rosy glow

that became more so when she was flustered. Her eyes conveyed warmth and humor as well as anxiety on behalf of herself and her children. If he'd met her under other circumstances, he might've wanted to get to know her better. Under these circumstances, she was off-limits as a client. Not to mention, she was the beloved baby sister of his close friend.

"Denny has something he needs you to know, but he's concerned you'll be angry with him for not telling you before now."

She sat perfectly still, seeming to barely breathe while she waited for whatever new bomb was about to drop on her life.

"I offered to talk to you about it because he wants you to know that he loves you very much, and everything he did was to protect you and your children."

"Please tell me. You're scaring me."

"Your parents left you money. Denny has kept it from you because he was afraid Gabriel would burn through it."

She let out a cry of distress. "*Oh my God*! Is that even legal? Can he do that?"

"As the executor of the estate, it was within his purview to manage it as he saw fit. And I want to add an important point. That you didn't know about it until today keeps it out of Gabriel's reach in the divorce. It'll be treated as your separate property as opposed to community property that you'd be required to divide with him."

"How much is it?"

"They had a million in life insurance between them. Half went toward support for you guys after they died, and the other half was divided between the two of you. Two hundred fifty thousand was invested conservatively for you and is at about six hundred thousand now."

She covered her mouth with her hand, as if trying to contain her shock. After a moment of charged silence, she said, "If they left him the same amount, then why is he living in a shithole apartment and working like a dog to pay his child support?"

"Because he's invested the money for his retirement."

"I can't believe he decided this for me like I'm still a child."

"Let me ask you something... If he'd told you about it six years ago when you turned twenty-five, how would you feel about giving Gabriel half of whatever was left during the divorce proceeding, assuming there was anything left?"

"If it was mine, why would I have to give him half?"

"Because if you had access to the money during the marriage, it most likely would become community property under California law. That means half of it would be owed to him upon divorce, especially if you'd used any part of it for household expenses, rent or a mortgage or anything that benefited both of you."

After giving her a minute to process that information, he added, "Denny protected what was yours from being lost to a man who'd take a baseball bat to your home and possessions while you and your children hid in fear for your lives."

Her eyes went bright with tears.

Julian handed her a tissue. "I'm sorry to be blunt like that, but it's the truth. I'm not just saying this because he's my friend, but Denny protected you and your assets. He did you a huge favor."

"I guess the good news is now I can afford to pay you."

"No charge for Denny's sister. He's been my friend for twenty years."

"That's very kind of you. Everyone has been so kind." Isla covered her face with the tissue. "I'm sorry."

"I'll give you a minute."

He left his office, closing the door.

"Everything all right?" Mattie asked.

"It will be. Not today, but in time."

"Her kids are precious. The little guy is so polite and inquisitive. They loved the fish."

"I figured they would."

"Are you okay? You look strange in the eyes."

He loved the way Mattie said things—and how well she knew him, which was helpful most of the time. "This is a tough one."

"Aren't they all?"

"Some are worse than others. Is Carson in his office?"

"Haven't seen him yet today. Want me to track him down?"

"Nah, I'll text him. Any word from Marlon Beckett?" Julian was eager to get Cresley's situation resolved before Beckett decided to go ahead and release dirt on her to the media. The picture of them having lunch at the Ivy hadn't helped the situation, as Cresley was now concerned about publicity she didn't need with a potential custody battle looming.

"Nothing yet. I've left him multiple messages and tracked down his management and left a message with them, too. He probably looked you up and realized it'd be easier to avoid you than deal with you."

"That's on-brand for him. Thanks for being thorough."

Denny and the kids came down the hallway toward Julian's office.

His friend's gaze met his, full of questions.

Julian gave a subtle nod, indicating that Isla was still in his office.

"Is she okay?" Denny asked.

"She will be. I explained what could've happened to her assets if you'd told her about them sooner. I think she understands why you did it."

"So she doesn't hate my guts?"

"I don't think so, but you'd have to ask her about that."

"Come on, kiddos," Denny said. "Let's go find Mommy."

. . .

ISLA WAS quiet as Denny drove them back to the apartment complex where she planned to spend the rest of the day cleaning up the mess her soon-to-be ex-husband had made of their home. While she was in the meeting with Julian Remington, she'd received a text from Officer Samuelson, letting her know that her apartment had been fully processed, and she was cleared to return. *Please be careful*, he'd added. *There's glass everywhere.*

Even though she was relieved to hear she could return to her home, several other thoughts cycled through her mind on repeat as she processed the eventful morning.

First was that Denny had hidden money from her parents because he was afraid Gabriel would spend it all. Second, his friend Julian might be the most gorgeous, kind, sincere man Isla had ever met, and why in the hell was she thinking about him when she had much bigger concerns?

"What's his story?" she asked Denny, to make conversation, or so she told herself to justify the question.

"Who?"

"Julian Remington."

"Oh. Um. Like, you want to know about..."

"Is he married?"

"God no," Denny said with a snort. "He'd rather have gonorrhea than a wife."

"So he's got commitment issues, then?"

"Nah, nothing like that. His folks, both of them high-powered family lawyers, dragged him and his siblings through an endless custody battle back in the day. It cured them of wanting marriage or permanence. Not to mention, they spend their days unraveling other people's happily ever afters."

"I suppose that'd spoil all things romance for them."

"For real." He glanced over at her when they were stopped at a light. "Are you pissed?"

"I was, for a minute... And then Julian explained what you saved me from, and now... I'm sad."

"Because of what I did?"

"No. I'm sad you felt it was necessary."

"I'm sorry, Islander. I never trusted him. I wish I'd been wrong."

"I should've listened to you."

"If you had, we wouldn't have your babies, and that would've been tragic. They're the best. I like them better than my own kids."

"Haha, that's because one of your kids is a teenager, and the other will be soon."

"Exactly. I hear they're not dicks for the rest of their lives."

"Language!"

"Sorry. I'm so out of practice with watching my mouth."

"Get it together before Theo's talking like a construction worker."

"Yes, ma'am."

After a long silence, Isla said, "I want you to know... I'm pissed with you for holding out on me about the inheritance, but I understand why you did it, even if the reason you did it breaks my heart."

"You've had enough heartbreak to last a lifetime, kid. It's time to turn the ship around and chase joy."

Isla glanced at him. "Where'd you hear that?"

"My therapist."

"You have a therapist?"

"Have for a long time. You ought to get one. Highly recommend."

"What do you talk about?"

"Everything. All the hard stuff no one else wants to hear about."

"I want to hear about that stuff."

"You've got enough of your own."

"That doesn't mean I can't be there for you the way you've been for me. I mean... you gave up your whole life for me."

"Temporarily."

"For five years. That's not nothing."

"I'd do it again in a heartbeat."

"Did I ever say thank you?"

"You don't have to."

"Yes, Denny, I really do. What would've become of me if you hadn't stepped up?"

Their parents had both been only children, and their grandparents had died years before their parents did. She would've ended up in foster care without him.

"It was never a question that I'd take care of you."

"But it meant putting your own dreams on hold for five important years." When their parents died, he'd been playing with a band that had gone on to secure a recording deal, without him. They were still together and opening for some big acts these days.

"Eh, whatever. If I hadn't stepped up for you, I wouldn't have met Kath and had my kids. Things work out the way they're meant to."

"Do you believe that? Really?"

"I want to. I mean... Everything in life is so fu—"

"Denny!"

He grinned at her. "*Freaking* random. I like to believe there's some sort of higher power at work. Otherwise, most of it would never make sense."

"I can't believe Mom and Dad dying was meant to be."

"The thing about believing in meant-to-be is that you have to take the bad with the good. It's all preordained, before we're even born."

"When did you get all deep and philosophical?"

"I've always been that way."

"How did I never know that?"

He shrugged. "We haven't seen as much of each other lately as we used to."

"Because of G." Isla glanced at the kids, who were watching a movie on an iPad.

"I never wanted that. I hope you know…"

"Yeah, I do. I didn't at the time. I thought you'd be an AH to any guy I brought home."

"I wouldn't have been. I liked Aaron. Remember?"

Isla hadn't thought of her high school boyfriend in ages, so long that it seemed he'd been in another lifetime. "Yeah, I do." Aaron had gone to college out of state, while Isla stayed in LA, trying to figure out what she wanted to do with her life, working in bars to pay the rent and chipping away at college one or two classes at a time. She'd met Gabriel through work friends and had fallen madly in love over the course of that first heady week together.

"I might not have married him if things hadn't happened the way they did."

"You can still finish school and do all the things you wanted to do."

"I suppose." School felt daunting to her with two little ones to care for, but less so than it would have before she'd found out about the money. "I guess the good news is I can keep my apartment."

"And not work."

"Oh, I'm still going to work."

"Not at a bar!"

"That's where I can make big bucks."

"You don't need it."

"Yes, I do. The money is a huge relief, but we both know how expensive life is, and with college to think about and all the other life expenses, I need to do this for me—and my kids."

"Mama no work," Theo said.

"It's okay, honey. Don't worry."

"No work."

"See?" Denny said. "He agrees with me."

Isla glared at him.

They picked up lunch for the kids on the way home, and after they'd eaten, Isla put them down for a nap in Mrs. V's guest room. Once she was sure they were asleep, she and Denny took the baby monitor next door to deal with the carnage. Because she'd tried not to look too closely on her way out of there the night before, she wasn't at all prepared for just how bad it was.

"Holy fucking shit," Denny whispered.

Isla was blinded by tears that she swiped away in furious disbelief that this was her life. That the man she'd chosen to love, out of all the men in the world, could've done this to their home. She was determined to hold it together and clean up so she and her kids could get back to some semblance of normal.

"Isla."

She turned to face her brother.

"You can't stay here. The minute he makes bail, he'll be right back here, even with the restraining order."

"Where am I supposed to go?"

"Let's get you out of here. You can't stay here or next door. You'll be like sitting ducks, and who knows how angry he'll be after a night in jail? He's apt to blame you for everything. I... I can't leave you here with the kids. Look at what he did. You're not safe here."

"I have no money to move, Denny. Even with this newfound investment account, I don't currently have the money, and my cards are maxed out."

"We can get you access to the money today. Whatever it takes to make it so he can't find you."

She glanced at him. "I'm not sure what to make of this new information about our finances when we've spent years trying to survive on next to nothing." Another thought occurred to her. "Is this why you live in that shithole apartment? Because you didn't want me to know there's money?"

"I didn't want *Gabriel* to know about it. I never felt right about keeping it from you, but after I had to give a chunk of mine to Kath, I was more determined than ever to protect yours."

"Tell me how you were able to keep it from me."

"You would've come into the money when you were twenty-five. By then, you were all about him. Every instinct I had told me to keep your money away from that guy, so I petitioned the court to postpone the maturation date until you were thirty. It's in an account that you'll have access to today because Julian told us Gabriel can't get at anything that you didn't have until after the date of separation."

Hearing the lengths he'd gone to in order to protect her softened her toward him. "Thank you for always doing what was necessary to protect me, even when I wasn't looking out for myself."

"If I'd had any idea it'd gotten this bad," he said, gesturing to the shattered glass that covered every inch of the place, "I would've made the money available to you. I swear it."

"I didn't want you to know it'd gotten this bad."

"I'm sorry you felt like you had to keep it from me. That's my fault."

"No, it's Gabriel's fault. All of this is his fault."

"Yes, it is. Let's find you a new place to live—today."

Resigned to having to move to keep herself and her kids safe, Isla nodded. "Okay."

They spent the next hour picking through the shattered remains of her home to salvage clothing, toys, bedding, towels and other things she'd need in her new place. When she'd gathered up as much as she could fit into the bins, boxes and suitcases she had on hand, they moved it all to Denny's truck.

"What do I do about this place?"

"Is the lease in your name or his?"

"His."

"Then you leave him to deal with his own mess."

"If I can afford something better, let's look for a house I can rent that has a little yard for the kids."

"I have a friend who's a Realtor. I'll call her."

"Thank you for everything, Denny. Not just today, but always."

"We're a team, you and me."

He used to say that all the time after their parents died, leaving them to face an uncertain future on their own.

"Yes, we are."

"Let's figure out what's next for you and your kids."

CHAPTER EIGHT

Julian was finishing up another long day at the office when his brother Roman came in with more mail. "Look at you. Making two deliveries in the same day. How's the mail room treating you?"

"As you well know, it totally blows. It's so boring, I want to stab myself in the eye with a letter opener."

Julian smiled at his youngest sibling, the one who looked the most like him with a few of his own embellishments, including diamond studs in his ears and sleeve tattoos he was required to keep covered at the office. "Ah, yes, I remember well what it was like to want to use the letter opener for something other than its intended purpose. But the good news is, you're almost done."

"Two more weeks until I go back to school, and what does it say about our mail room that law school is looking good to me?"

Julian laughed. "It's a rite of passage, my friend, and trust me, someday you'll be thankful to Dad for making you start at the bottom." Each of them had found it "easier" to come into the family business having spent some time in the trenches during college and law school vacations, even if it had sucked at the time.

Roman helped himself to some of Julian's good bourbon and reclined on the sofa as he pulled off his tie.

"Make yourself at home."

"Don't mind if I do."

"I'm looking forward to having you here every day." He'd always had a soft spot for his youngest sibling, who'd been born when Julian was thirteen.

"Yeah."

"You're not excited about joining the family business?"

Roman took a long drink of bourbon. "Did you ever want to do something other than this?"

"Like what?"

"I don't know. Anything. We could practice any kind of law. Why family law?"

Sensing an existential crisis brewing with his brother, Julian got up and fixed himself two fingers of bourbon, bringing it with him when he sat across from Roman. They were due for their monthly dinner with their siblings in forty-five minutes, but the restaurant was walkable from the office, so they had time.

"You're not the first Remington to face that burning question."

"I'm usually the last one to do everything."

Julian chuckled at the matter-of-fact statement. "Every one of us has been where you are, questioning the meaning of life and whether the family business is what we wanted."

"It's strange sometimes... How you guys have memories of things that happened to all of us that I barely remember. The drama didn't have the same impact on me that it did on the rest of you."

Julian had experienced a totally different childhood from Roman's in many ways. Roman had told him before that he felt guilty for not carrying the same trauma the others did from the ugly custody battle between their parents.

"Don't get me wrong, I'm grateful not to remember most of it. Hearing what it was like for you guys is always hard. It's just that I don't feel the same pull to the profession that the rest of you do because you want to help other kids avoid what you went through."

"That's not the only reason we chose family law." Julian put his glass on the coffee table and rested his elbows on his knees. "Part of it was the opportunity to join an established, well-known, successful practice and not have to start from scratch the way most people do."

"I get that, but what if I want to do something totally different and make my own mark in another part of the profession?"

"Then that's what you should do."

"Dad would flip out. He loves having everyone working together—and so does Mom."

"You're not living their lives. You're living yours. Work will take up a big chunk of your time. If you don't love what you're doing, it'll be a slog."

"Does this ever feel like a slog to you?"

"Not really. I mean, there're days when it's *a lot*. You leave emotionally drained from battles you're fighting for people you'd never know if their lives hadn't blown up in their faces. I met the sister of a longtime friend today after her husband took a baseball bat to their apartment yesterday."

"Is she okay?"

"She and her kids are fine because she had the foresight to set up a hiding place inside the apartment in case they ever needed it."

"Wow."

"I know. She had it ready for them to spend days there if they had to. I can't stop thinking about how crazy things must've been for her to realize she might need a hiding place at some point."

"And she couldn't have left?"

He shook his head. "The husband burned through all their money, and the credit cards were maxed. She was in a tough spot and still is. Even though we've requested a restraining order, we're worried about what he'll do when he makes bail. Being able to help someone like her feels really good."

"I'll bet it does. That's amazing how she had the hiding place ready."

"It really is." Julian didn't mention how he'd thought about Isla all day after their meeting and found himself wanting to know more about her, which was a somewhat unusual development. She'd truly impressed him in more ways than one.

While he always felt for whatever his clients were going through—and often related to their struggles in a way that most attorneys never could—he rarely found himself wanting to get to know them better or wondering what they were like when their life hadn't just imploded.

"Jules... Did you hear me?"

"What?"

"I asked you where she hid."

"Oh, um, she cut a hole in the wall behind the closet and made a place for her and her kids to be in case he came home in one of his 'rages,' as she calls them."

"Shit, man. I can't imagine having to live like that."

"I can't either, but it's another reason why family law can be so satisfying. We're able to help people like her get out of unsafe situations."

"What do you do when it's the husband who hires you?"

"Men can be victims of all the things, too, but as you build your practice, you can be more particular about who you represent. If you find out your potential client is an abusive asshole, you can just say no."

"Yeah, I guess that's true."

"Unless you're working as a public defender, you always have a choice about who you represent—and who you don't."

"Do they ever try to hide who they are from you to get you to take their case?"

"Sometimes, but I make sure I know exactly who I'm representing before I agree to take them on. If they try to hide their shit, I put Carson on it. If there's shit to be found, he'll find it."

"He's a badass."

"He sure is."

"You could always work with him if you'd rather investigate than litigate."

"I've thought about that. I don't know. We'll see. I gotta pass the freaking bar before I do anything."

"You've got this. I have faith in you."

"I wish I were so confident. Standardized tests are still my worst nightmare."

Roman had dealt with attention deficit disorder since he was a child and had been medicated for it since middle school.

"You're taking the test-prep class this semester, right?"

"Yep and let me tell you how much I'm looking forward to that. Not."

Julian laughed. "'Get it over with and get on with it.' That's what Grandpa said to me when I was right where you are."

"Speaking of him, he called me yesterday to ask if I could take a run out to Ojai to check on the ranch, but I won't get to that before I go back to school since Dad has me working nonstop. Can you get out there?"

"Yeah, I'll take a ride out there as soon as I can. No worries. I'll call him and tell him I'm doing it."

"Maybe he'll want to go with you."

"I doubt it. He doesn't like being in the car that long anymore. He says it aggravates his arthritis."

"I can't believe he's going to be ninety-four."

"Right? And still going strong for the most part." Julian checked his watch. "We need to go."

Roman sat up, finished the last of his drink and handed his glass to Julian. "God forbid the girls give us shit about always being late."

"Ain't no one got time for that."

"Hey, Jules... Thanks for listening just now. I appreciate that you didn't try to stuff the family business down my throat like everyone else would've done."

"It's a long life, man. You gotta be happy."

"Are you? Happy?"

Julian rarely thought about such things. "Yeah. I guess. I mean... It's all good."

That was what his brother expected him to say, but only he knew how out of sorts he'd been since he ran into Aimee Godfrey and was reminded what it'd been like to be truly in love—and how empty and off his game he'd felt ever since.

He kept hoping he'd shake off the lingering disquiet, but that hadn't happened. Instead, it had gotten worse, and for some reason, the unsettled state was only more so after his meeting with Denny's beguiling sister.

What the hell was that about?

JULIAN WALKED WITH ROMAN, Griffin and Ethan toward THE Blvd at the Beverly Wilshire, where they had dinner every other month with their sisters in the Wilshire Dining Room, away from other customers so they could speak freely about matters they wouldn't want overheard. The other months, the brothers trekked into downtown to meet their sisters close to their office.

On the way to dinner, Julian held Griffin back. "Are you set for the paternity test tomorrow?"

"Yeah, I guess."

"It's just a cheek swab. No big deal."

"Sure, no big deal that could set off a nuclear bomb in my life."

"You said the baby isn't yours, and this'll prove it."

Griffin gave him the same wild-eyed look as the day before. "What if she *is* mine? What do I do then?"

"You offer support and go on with your life."

"While knowing I've got a kid out there growing up without me?"

"Let's wait and see what the test says before you go down that road."

"It's all I can think about."

Julian couldn't imagine how stressful it would be to get a letter like that from an ex he'd moved on from a long time ago. He'd do everything he could to support Griffin through this, no matter what the test revealed.

The brothers were not at all surprised to find their three sisters already at the table with glasses of wine and sharing the burrata-and-watermelon appetizer.

The girls stood to greet them with hugs and kisses.

"Good to see you," Julian said to Jordan as he hugged her and then Kaidan.

"Have you lost weight, Jules?" Gillian asked as they embraced. "You're looking gaunt in the face."

"I am not."

"Are too."

"His face is always weird," Carson said when he joined them in time to overhear the comment.

"Shut up. All of you."

Kaidan laughed. "I miss this nonsense when I haven't seen you boys. Said no one ever."

"Right," Griffin said. "You miss us all the time."

"Where's Jackson?" Jordan asked Julian.

"I have no idea."

"Aren't you his boss?"

"Yeah, but I'm not his keeper." Julian sent a text to his brother asking where he was.

On the way. Was waiting for the RO to come through for Isla Santana. Just got it and sent her a copy.

Ah, okay. Thanks.

"He's coming," Julian said as he set up a text to Isla, relieved to know the protective order was now in place.

My associate (and brother) Jackson said he sent a copy of the restraining order to your email. If Gabriel comes home, call 911. Don't hesitate.

Yes, thank you. I appreciate the fast work. I've relocated to a short-term rental off Laurel Canyon Boulevard. He wouldn't be able to find me here.

Julian's heart did a funny stutter at the mention of Laurel Canyon. That put her in his neighborhood. Not that it mattered.

Glad to hear you've relocated. Let me know if you need anything. I'll be back to you with next steps in a day or two.

Thanks again for everything.

He sent her two thumbs-up.

"Earth to Jules," Jordan said.

"Oh, sorry. That was a new client escaping a DV situation. Jackson was waiting for her RO to come through, and I wanted to touch base with her about it. He's on the way now."

"Phones away, y'all," Kaidan said.

The others grumbled, but they put their phones in pockets or purses, as they did whenever they managed to carve out some time to spend together. Otherwise, they'd be tending to work rather than catching up.

"Remingtons!" Their waiter friend Leonardo smiled as he stood at the head of their table. He had dark hair streaked with silver and a warm, welcoming demeanor. "How's life in the divorce trenches?"

"Busy as always," Julian said.

"Who's missing?" Leo asked.

"Jackson," they all said.

"Let's get some drinks going while you wait for him."

Leo took their orders for drinks and more appetizers and promised to be right back.

Jackson arrived a few minutes later, apologizing for being late as he took a seat next to Roman after hugging each of his sisters. "What's up, bitches?"

"Sit down and shut up, Jack," Jordan said, attempting a stern expression that made them all laugh.

"Romy, it's nice to have you with us," Kaidan said. "We miss you when you're up at Stanford."

"I miss you guys, too," Roman said glumly. "I can't wait to get back to LA full time."

"One more semester, and then we're all done with school," Griffin said. "That's hard to believe."

"How many years has at least one of us been in law school?" Ethan asked.

"Too many," Gillian said. "Jules, you're what, thirty-eight? So you would've gone... sixteen years ago? So that's how long one or more of us has been in law school."

"Except for the smartest one who chose not to waste three years of his life in boring old law school," Carson reminded them.

"When are you taking the bar?" Jordan asked him.

"July."

Carson had made a bet with his siblings that he could pass the exam without going to law school. They were holding him to it.

"Roman can help you study," Jackson said with a smile for their youngest sibling.

"We can do flash cards, Carson," Roman said.

"Eh, who needs that shit?" Carson said. "I'm going in cold. I've been studying by osmosis for years."

Julian shook his head as the others laughed. "Good luck with that."

"What's everyone getting?" Kaidan asked.

"Whose turn is it to pay?"

"Jackson," the others said as one.

"Fuck my life," he muttered.

"Your days of freeloading off us are over, baby brother," Ethan said.

Carson coughed. "Says the ultimate freeloader."

Ethan flipped him off.

Just another night out with the Remingtons, Julian thought as he relaxed a bit for the first time since "the encounter" with Aimee.

"I'm getting the seventy-six-dollar Chilean sea bass," Griffin said with a grin for Jackson.

"There's a fifty-dollar limit per sibling," Jackson said. "I'm only an associate!"

"Please," Kaidan said. "We know how much you make."

"My rent is four grand!"

"We told you not to sign that lease," Jordan said.

"You had to have that fancy apartment in Brentwood," Gillian added.

"My place is *fly*," Jackson said with a smug grin.

"For four grand a month, I want a view of the Pacific," Griffin said. "Oh wait, I have that."

"When you're not crashing at my place because you don't feel like driving home to Malibu," Ethan said.

"That's what brothers are for," Griff said.

"I'm going to start charging you rent," Ethan said.

"You can try."

"Speaking of rent, how's it going with Mom, Kay?" Julian asked.

"I'm living the dream with her as my weekday roommate," Kaidan said sarcastically, "and my boss."

The others laughed even as they winced with empathy for Kaidan, who'd offered their mom her spare bedroom after Kate's home was lost to the terrible Palisades Fire last year. Thankfully, Kate decamped to her weekend place in Santa Barbara every Friday afternoon, giving Kaidan a break.

"Since I'm taking a big one for the team by putting up with Mom, I'm not paying for dinner until she moves out," Kaidan said.

"All in favor, say aye," Jordan said.

"Aye."

That was one thing they could easily agree on. While they loved their parents, the siblings carried complicated feelings from their childhood that they were still contending with as adults, especially working as they did for the family firms.

"Hey, Jules, I got a call from Gabriel Santana this afternoon, looking for representation," Gillian said. "I pulled the police report and saw that you'd filed for an R.O."

"Actually, I did that," Jackson said. "All real work in his practice is done by me."

"Pipe down," Julian said to his brother—and associate.

If Gabriel was calling around to lawyers, he must've made bail. "I need to text my client to let her know her husband is out on bail." While he did that, he said to Gillian, "Not that he can afford you, but you might want to look into what he did to their home before you decide to represent him. If she hadn't hidden herself and her kids from him, he might've killed them with the same baseball bat he took to their home."

"Yeah, I took a pass based on the police report," Gillian said. "He asked if one of the other lawyers in our firm might be interested, and I said no."

"I hope he's getting that answer from everyone he calls," Julian said.

"Some scumbag will take him on," Gillian said. "And then you'll make them both sorry they were born."

"Yes, I will."

"Heard about what you guys pulled off with the McDavid case," Jordan said, "how you tied him to the vitriol online. That was well done."

"That was all Carson."

"Not all of it," Carson said, "but the most important part was me."

They laughed at his predictably cocky reply as their appetizers were served.

"Don't act like savages," Julian said as they swooped in like a gaggle of hungry seagulls.

"You're not the boss of us," Jackson said.

"Um, I hate to point out the obvious…"

"Eff off. We're not at work."

"I'm having some issues with my associate," Julian said as the others laughed. "He's a bit insubordinate."

"Please, I cover your ass like nobody's business."

"Don't talk about Julian's ass when we're trying to eat," Roman said to more laughter.

"Hurry up and finish school, Rome," Jordan said. "We need you back in town to stay."

"Can't happen soon enough for me," Roman said.

"How's your friend Gwendolyn?" Jackson asked, earning him a fierce glare from Roman.

"Shut your face."

"What? I'm just asking."

"Who's Gwendolyn?" Carson asked.

"No one," Roman said. If looks could kill, Jackson would be dead as a doornail.

"You're just asking for Carson to launch an investigation by being evasive," Griffin said. "Fess up."

"She's a friend from high school. We reconnected over the holidays. Nothing to see here."

"Uh-huh," Jackson said.

"Fuck all the way off." Roman was hotter than Julian had seen him get over anything in a long time. He'd been a hot head as a kid and had done years of therapy to deal with his anger issues. "I'm never staying with you again."

"Knock it off, Jack," Ethan said. "Leave him alone. I'd much rather talk about whether Jules is seeing Cresley Dane, and if he isn't, how can I get her number?"

"I'm not seeing her, you idiot. I'm representing her, and no, you can't have her number."

"Our entire office was talking about you dating a supermodel today," Jordan said, grinning at Julian.

"Freaking TMZ," he said. "If only they'd bothered to confirm it before they put us on blast."

"What fun would that be?" Ethan asked with a smirk. "For them..."

"Right? Poor Cresley is fending off everyone she knows because she had lunch with a guy."

"Not just *any* guy," Jordan said. "*Only* LA's most eligible attorney."

Julian groaned and rolled his eyes while the other fools cheered for Jordan finding a way to work that nightmare into the conversation. He'd never forgive the local magazine that'd given him that ridiculous "honor" two years ago.

"We're in the biggest fight ever," he told Jordan, giving her the stone face he used in court when he wanted to intimidate someone.

She laughed. "I can't help what other people say about my big brother. I'm just reporting the facts, Counselor."

"Fuck off with the facts."

"Um, that could get you disbarred, bro," Carson said.

"What do you know about getting disbarred?" Julian fired back.

Everyone else laughed.

"This family is a shit show," Gillian said.

"And we wouldn't have it any other way," Ethan said.

"So how long are you stuck with Mom?" Roman asked Kaidan. "Or should I say, how long do you have the pleasure of her company?"

"The contractor said it could be *two years* until her place is rebuilt."

"Stop it," Julian said. *"Two years?"*

Kaidan moaned. "I can't live with her for that long. I just cannot do it. I love her, but... Two years of her asking me where I'm going, who I'm going with and what time I'll be home..."

Julian winced. "Damn. Old habits die hard, huh?"

"*So* hard." After a pause, Kaidan said haltingly, "You guys... I need to tell you something."

The siblings fell silent at her unusually serious tone.

"What's up?" Ethan asked.

"I'm not sure how to say this."

"You're scaring us, Kay," Jordan said. "Whatever it is, just say it. We'll figure it out together like we always do."

Kaidan bit her lip, which put Julian on edge. His feisty, defiant, ass-kicking sister was never hesitant or nervous like she was now. "I think Mom and Dad might be back together."

CHAPTER NINE

Kaidan's words landed like a bomb, rendering her boisterous siblings completely speechless.

"*What?*" Carson said for all of them. "What the actual fuck are you talking about, Kay?"

"Don't yell at me! I'm just saying... There's a vibe."

"What kind of vibe?" Jordan asked tentatively. "And why haven't you said anything before now?"

"I wanted to wait until we were all together," Kaidan said. "Do you guys remember what it was like between them before it all went to shit?"

"Nope," Roman said. "I only know the shit."

"Same," Jackson said.

"Me, too," Gillian said.

The three youngest had vague memories of the bad times and even fewer recollections of the good years.

"When they were together—and happy—Mom was different. She was lighter, giggly and silly."

"You're talking about *my* mother?" Jackson asked. "Giggly and silly?"

"I know what she means," Julian said. "I remember that."

"I do, too," Carson said. "She was like a teenager in love around him."

"Yes!" Kaidan said. "Exactly. Over the last couple of months, I've heard her on the phone at night, behaving just like that, and then, this past weekend, she disappeared."

"What does that mean?" Griffin asked. "How can a grown woman disappear?"

"She turned off her location and went dark for the whole weekend," Kaidan said.

"She did," Jordan said, nodding. "I tried to call her twice about work stuff, and she never returned the calls. When I looked to see where she was, her location was turned off. I can't remember a time that's ever happened. When I asked her about it this week, she said she forgot to check her voicemail."

"That also never happens," Kaidan said.

"I thought it was weird," Jordan said, shifting uneasily in her seat.

The idea of their parents back together, after one of the most contentious divorces in history, was almost impossible to believe.

"That's *so* weird." Gillian crossed her arms in a protective pose that tugged at Julian's heart. "She's always available."

"Why do you assume it's Dad she's talking to?" Carson asked suspiciously.

"Because I've never heard her behave that way with anyone else."

"That doesn't mean she hasn't met someone new," Carson said. "Why in the hell would she ever go back to Dad after what they put each other—and us—through for ten goddamned years?"

Leonardo stopped short as he approached the table. "What's wrong with you guys? You look like you've seen a ghost or something."

"Or something," Roman said for all of them.

"Ready for more drinks?" Leo asked.

"*So* ready," Carson said.

After they'd ordered another round and Leo had walked away, Ethan said, "I can understand wanting it to be true."

"That's not what this is," Kaidan shot back at him. "Them back together is the last freaking thing I'd ever want."

"Same," Griffin said as everyone else nodded in agreement.

"I'm merely saying the preponderance of evidence has me wondering if it's possible," Kaidan said.

They all looked to Carson, who put up his hands to fend them off. "No way am I investigating whether our parents are rekindling an old flame that nearly swallowed us whole. No. Way."

"You could find out faster than the rest of us," Jordan said.

"Get someone else to do your dirty work. If it's true, I want nothing to do with it."

Leo approached the table to take their dinner orders but stopped when he seemed to sense the tension was still strong. "Should I come back?"

"Give us a few minutes, Leo," Julian said. "Thanks."

"You got it, Counselor. No rush."

After Leo walked away, the silence persisted, which was so unusual when they were together that it put Julian's nerves on edge. "You guys, listen... While I appreciate that the evidence might point toward a reconciliation, there's no way they're back together. They're barely civil to each other when they *are* together, which is hardly ever. It's been three years since they saw each other at Rome's graduation."

"They see each other at bar association stuff," Jordan said.

"They do?" Julian asked. "Since when is Dad going to those meetings?"

"He rarely misses one," Gillian said.

"How did we not know that?" Julian asked his brothers.

"Maybe he's checking out for something else because he doesn't want us to know he's going to be somewhere that she is," Ethan said.

Again, the siblings were silent as they pondered the possibility...

"Are we going to eat?" Carson asked. "Cuz I've got other shit to do tonight." He signaled for Leo to come take their orders.

"Everything all right, family?" Leo asked.

"Yeah, all good," Julian said. "Let's order."

After dinner, which Jackson paid for with much bitching and moaning, they parted with hugs and promises to set a date for the next one on the girls' side of town.

"Do you think it's true?" Griffin asked Julian the second they walked away from their sisters to head back to the office.

"No, I don't." Eating dinner had been a chore thanks to the huge knot of anxiety that'd settled in his chest at the mere mention of their parents rekindling a romance that had wrecked their lives for a time. Julian had taken most of his lobster pappardelle to go for lunch tomorrow. Hopefully, the sick feeling would pass when one of his siblings produced proof that Kaidan's theory was nonsense.

They'd agreed to be on alert for clues. Well, everyone but Carson had agreed to that. He'd reiterated his earlier statement that he'd have nothing to do with it either way.

It had to be nonsense.

There was no way...

"Jules," Roman said, "did you hear me?"

"No, sorry. What?"

"What if it's true?"

"It's not, so let's move on."

It couldn't be.

That was the end of it as far as he was concerned.

AFTER SHE'D PUT her kids to bed, Isla poured a glass of the wine she'd gotten at the grocery store, where she'd stocked up on the way to the rental. She figured she'd earned the wine after the two days she'd just had. Since emerging from her closet hideout, she'd been waiting to feel heartbroken that her marriage to Gabriel was finally over. She'd thought she might feel regret or a longing for what used to be.

Rather, her prevailing emotion was relief.

It was over.

Done.

Finished.

Forever.

According to her new lawyer, she had a very strong case for sole custody of her kids, and apparently, her parents had left her money that would make everything easier. Hearing that news had been almost as shocking as Gabriel taking a bat to their home. She'd assumed all their resources had been used to pay for essentials as Denny finished raising her while he commuted to college at UCLA.

In the whirlwind of revelations uncovered as she took steps to end the marriage and move out of their apartment, she'd barely had a second to process any of it. Now that she could reflect, relief was the pervasive emotion.

In truth, the demise of her marriage had been a slow-rolling train wreck or, as she'd seen it described by someone online, death by a thousand paper cuts. That phrase had spoken to her soul. Day by day, week by week, month by month, the paper cuts had added up to a gaping wound that'd scabbed over but never had the chance to properly heal before he did something to reopen it.

And the cycle would begin all over again.

As she'd carved into the drywall in the back of her closet, hoping to find a space where she and the kids could hide if it came to that, she'd been fully aware of the absolute insanity of what she was doing and why she needed it. After having Mila completely on her own, suffering from postpartum depression while caring for two kids and wondering where her husband was for the first month of their daughter's life, the marriage had been over for her. She'd been biding her time ever since, looking for an exit ramp that he'd delivered with a baseball bat.

She'd begun to move on from him mentally and emotionally even before he smashed up their home, forcing her to make the actual move to leave him for good.

Tonight, as she sat in someone else's house, surrounded by things that didn't belong to her, she was more at home than she'd been in the apartment for quite some time. She felt safe, hidden within a city of millions in a place he'd never think to look for her. For once, the massiveness of Los Angeles was coming in handy rather than frustrating her with traffic, crowds and other challenges that came with city living.

She exhaled fully for the first time in years.

Years.

It'd been *years* since things had been "normal" with Gabriel.

Years of her life that she'd never get back had been lost to an unknown adversary, an illness or an addiction or something that'd taken him over and away from her. She wondered if knowing what was wrong would make her feel better. At one time, it would have. Now, it didn't matter anymore. She hoped he'd get the help he needed so he could maybe someday have a relationship with his children, but that'd be up to him. All her begging and pleading for him to get help had fallen on deaf ears, and now...

She was done.

Isla drank her wine and gazed at the framed posters of musicians she didn't recognize on the wall above the sofa in a house on a street named for a president she'd barely heard of. Woodrow Wilson. She had vague memories of learning about him in school, but no solid info on him that she could easily recall.

The Realtor Denny had called had told him the short-term rental that'd checked all her boxes had historical significance to some musician she'd never heard of but whom Denny had gushed about while Isla had made sure the windows were locked.

She couldn't care less about historical significance. The only thing that mattered was that she and her children were safe and secure and had enough money to eat tomorrow.

Hearing that Denny had protected her money from Gabriel had been both shocking and devastating. But thank God for him, as she'd thought a million times since they lost their parents. They'd been union camera operators who met on the set of a film when they were twenty-one and had been together ever since. Denny and Isla had taken some comfort in knowing they'd be together forever in the afterlife.

Twenty-year-old Denny had stepped up for her then and so many times since that she couldn't possibly count them all. If she'd known when she first got together with Gabriel that her brother was hiding money that was legally hers, she would've been outraged. In her righteous indignation, she might've said or done things that could never be unsaid or undone. There was no question that, if it'd come down to a choice back then, she would've ended her relationship with her brother to preserve her bond with Gabriel.

What a fool she'd been, but thankfully, she hadn't lost her brother, too. That would've been truly tragic.

Here, she thought as she looked around at the cozy room full of musical memorabilia from the sixties and seventies, comfy couches, terracotta tile and other Spanish accents, she was more at peace than she would've thought possible on the day she met with a divorce attorney.

Speaking of Julian, her phone chimed with a text from him.

Gabriel is out on bail. He's been served the restraining order and been told to stay at least one thousand feet from you and your children. I have some more paperwork for you to fill out. If you'd like, I could drop it off on my way home. I live up the road from where you are in the Canyon. Or I could messenger them over tomorrow.

Oh hello. *Yes, please, bring me the papers, you sexy devil,* she thought.

Stop it, Isla. You're about to file for divorce after your husband got himself arrested for smashing up your apartment. The last thing in the world you should be doing is crushing on your divorce attorney.

But he'd been so kind, so understanding, *so gorgeous.* And he'd smelled pretty damned good, too.

If she was going to hell for thinking her divorce attorney was sexy, then at least she'd go happy.

Her actual reply was all business. *Sure, that'd be great. You've got the address on Woodrow Wilson Drive?*

Yep, I know that house. It's a landmark. I didn't know it was being rented.

I heard it's got history. To me, it's a safe haven.

See you shortly.

Oh my God, he was coming over soon!

She ran for the shower and was still dripping as she rifled through suitcases on the floor, looking for something to wear. Jeans and a T-shirt were the first things she found, so she grabbed them and went to get dressed and dry her hair.

She didn't want to look like she'd gone to any trouble as she put on lip gloss, mascara and some powder to matte the shine on her forehead that came from the cold sweat she'd broken into as she tried to find everything she needed to look presentable when nothing was unpacked or put away.

"You're getting *way* too excited about a lawyer dropping off paperwork for your *divorce*," she told her reflection as she gave herself a good once-over in the full-length mirror in the bedroom to make sure she didn't have toilet paper stuck to her foot or underwear hanging out of her jeans.

Deciding she looked as presentable as she ever did these days, she straightened her hair and then went to finish her glass of wine while reminding herself he was coming as her lawyer and nothing else.

"You're in no position to be getting excited to see any man, let alone your freaking divorce attorney. How many of his clients fall madly in love with him? Probably most of the women—and maybe some of the guys, too. You'd be the latest in a long line, so knock it off and get real."

CHAPTER TEN

By the time Julian knocked on Isla's door thirty minutes later, her nerves had been calmed by a second glass of wine that'd put her in a mellow mood as she greeted him.

All her pep talks might never have happened, because the minute she opened the door to him, she was reminded why she'd had such a strong reaction to him earlier. He was... *beautiful*.

"Come in," she said, stepping back to admit him.

"I've driven by this house a thousand times and always wanted to see the inside."

"I'd give you the tour, but the history is lost on me. I didn't even remember that Woodrow Wilson was a president."

He laughed, and oh my... What laughter did for his already handsome face... It ought to be a crime to look like him when you spent your days unraveling marriages.

"This house was the home of the legendary Cass Elliot from the Mamas and the Papas back in the sixties."

Isla gave him a blank look that made him wince.

"Come on! 'California Dreamin''? 'All the leaves are brown...'"

He could sing, even if the tune rang zero bells for her.

He groaned dramatically. "You're killing me."

"I'm sorry," she said with a laugh as she led him to the kitchen. "Denny gave up on me recognizing his musical heroes years ago. I'm more of a Swiftie than a classic rock kind of girl."

"Mad respect to Taylor, but you're missing out by not checking out the classics, too."

"Duly noted. I'll look into Cass Elliot."

"Mama Cass. She was incredible. Fun fact, she helped to put together the legendary trio of Crosby, Stills and Nash."

Isla did her best to look impressed but was clearly at a disadvantage in this conversation.

"Look them up, too. You won't regret it."

"I'll do that."

"Sorry to go on about music, but you've moved into a neighborhood that defined the LA music scene in the sixties and seventies. Check out the Laurel Canyon playlist on Spotify. You'll love it. I'll send you a link to that and a couple of others."

She held up the bottle of wine to ask if he wanted some.

"Sure, just a quick one."

Isla poured him a healthy glass, hoping he'd stay for a minute. Or two. "How do you know so much about that era when you're…"

"Thirty-eight," he said with a grin. "My maternal grandmother was a singer and songwriter who was part of the Laurel Canyon scene back in the day. I got my education and my love of music from her. She made sure all her grandchildren understood the musical history of our home city."

"Did she know any famous people?"

"She knew *all* the people. Joni Mitchell, Cass Elliot, Crosby, Stills, Nash, Young, Zappa, Morrison. Her stories were the thing of legend. Sex, drugs, rock 'n' roll, and all of it right here in the Canyon. She lived up here her entire adult life and is the reason I bought up here."

"That's very cool."

"You have no idea, but you will if you check out Laurel Canyon's musical history. The LA music scene was basically founded right in this neighborhood."

"I'll definitely check it out."

"Anyway, I didn't mean to go on about it," he said with a sexy grin. "But you're staying in *Mama Cass's* house."

"Have a look around."

His eyes glittered with unrestrained delight that sent a surge of something that might've been desire straight down her backbone. Holy shit.

"Do you mind?" he asked.

"Not at all."

He took his wine with him as he wandered into the living room for a closer look at the framed images of legends that now made more sense to her after what he'd said.

"This is amazing," he said of the painting depicting Cass Elliot. "That's the rest of her band, the Mamas and the Papas. And look, you've got Frank Zappa, Neil Young and Joni Mitchell, too. I have that same poster of Joni's *Blue* album at my place."

"There's another one of hers in the bedroom. *Ladies* something."

"*Ladies of the Canyon*, another classic."

"Do you have a degree in music or something?"

"Nah, just a grandmother who brought me up right. She taught me to play the guitar when I was five, and I've been playing ever since. She exposed me to all the best music."

Isla curled up on the sofa with her drink, thrilled when he sat in one of the overstuffed easy chairs. "Is she still with us?"

"Nah, she died about ten years ago. I miss her every day. We were buddies."

"That's so sweet." *This is a man a girl could fall madly, deeply in love with,* Isla thought, that was if she wasn't about to file for divorce with him as her attorney. "What was her name?"

"Freida Lewis. Look her up. She's got songwriting credits on a few songs that hit the charts at various times. She was friends with Joni and Cass and the other ladies of the canyon and had affairs with a few of the guys, too. She never would tell me which ones."

"Gee, I wonder why not?"

He laughed. "I told her she'd become a prude in her old age, but she said her lips were zipped about who she slept with back in the day. But, she added with a twinkle in her eye, I'd be impressed with her taste in men."

"I think I would've enjoyed hanging out with her."

"Oh, you would have. My friends were crazy about her. She used to have us up for weekends when we were in high school and let us drink beer and smoke pot and swim in the pool at all hours. My mother would've flipped out if she'd known that."

"She wasn't like her mother?"

"God no. My grandmother was a hippie flower child, and my mom was all about conformity. When she announced her plans to go to law school, my grandmother almost sprained her eyes from rolling them."

"Whereas most parents would've been thrilled if their kids took that path."

"Freida wasn't most parents. She was all about bucking the system, and my mother is all about working within it."

"Which one are you more like?"

"I've got some of both in me. I mean... I work within the system as an attorney, but I'm always looking for creative ways to manage it on behalf of my clients."

"Manage it how?"

"Well, there're a lot of nuances to be found within the law, if you're looking for them. I've had clients who would've ended up paying an ex a lot more in spousal support if we hadn't negotiated other things the ex was interested in as part of the settlement."

"That's an interesting approach."

"Well, any divorce lawyer worth their retainer is looking for ways to save their clients money in the long run. That's why our firm is focused on mediation and trying to stay out of court. The longer these things drag on, the more it costs everyone involved—except the lawyers."

"Wouldn't it be in your best interest to let it drag on?"

"Financially, yes, but ethically? Not so much. Our firm is well established thanks to my grandfather and my father, and we don't need to engage in the games some attorneys like to play to eke every dime they can get out of their clients. In fact, we call out that practice when we encounter it in opposing counsel. I've filed my share of ethics complaints against attorneys who are in it to squeeze as much money out of their clients as they can with little regard for what'll be left for the client to live on after they litigate the hell out of their divorce —and inevitably end up where they would've been without the protracted battle."

He offered a sheepish grin. "And that's probably way more than you ever wanted to know about being a divorce attorney."

"Actually, you just told me the most important thing about yourself. That you put ethics ahead of financial reward. Could I ask you something else that's probably way out of line?"

"Sure. Go for it."

"How many of your clients have fallen in love with you on their way to divorce court?"

"Oh, um, well…" His face flushed adorably, and her crush exploded into full-blown desire.

In the thirty seconds of charged awareness that passed between them, Isla realized how long it'd been since she'd felt real desire.

Years.

"I'm sorry. I didn't mean to embarrass you."

"I think you enjoyed embarrassing me."

She laughed. "Maybe a little. You've got to admit it's a reasonable question."

"Is it, though?"

He held her gaze, seeming as perplexed as she was by whatever seemed to be happening between them, and then he shook his head as if trying to clear his mind of salacious thoughts.

Isla wanted to tell him not to try so hard to move on from this perfect moment, one unlike anything she'd experienced before. *Stop it*, she thought. *Just stop. You're in no place to be looking for magic with someone else when you're still married and nowhere near being free to pursue something new.*

But, oh, how she wished she were free to lean in and kiss this beautiful, sweet man who was looking at her the same way she was probably looking at him.

"I, uh, wanted to talk to you about the paperwork I brought."

That suddenly, reality returned to remind her he was a lawyer delivering documents that would lead to the dissolution of her marriage. And that was all he'd ever be to her—a means to a long-overdue end.

JULIAN DROVE AWAY from Isla's house feeling an urgent need to put some distance between himself and his friend's sister before he did something that could never be undone. He'd wanted to kiss her so badly, he'd nearly forgotten all the many, *many* reasons why he could never do that. First and foremost, he was her attorney and was ethically bound to serve only her legal needs, but even more importantly, Denny trusted him to see his sister through a difficult time in her life. He needed to stay focused on the job at hand and not on how adorable she'd been while needling him about his clients falling in love with him.

And yes, it'd happened a time or two, usually toward the end of a long grind when he'd picked up on a vibe from a client that she might be interested in continuing their relationship once her divorce was finalized. It'd happened twice before the divorces were even final, with a not-so-subtle suggestion that they meet for a drink. The subtext had been clear... They were hoping for much more than a drink.

He'd never once crossed that line with a client, and he wasn't about to start now. But that he'd been truly tempted... His mind whirled with disbelief as he drove the short distance from her place to his. And holy shit, she lived close to him in that rental. In a city the size of Los Angeles, Denny had settled her right down the road from him.

As he drove the G-Wagon into his garage, he was still wondering what the hell had happened just now. He'd planned a quick stop to drop off the documents and had ended up drinking wine with her and going on about musical history that she had no connection to. But from the second he'd stepped into that storied home, he'd been captivated by her. Their conversation had flowed effortlessly, and her interest in hearing his stories about legendary musicians who'd lived in their neighborhood had seemed genuine, even though she'd never heard of them.

He'd send her a couple of playlists to listen to so she could get a sense of where she was now living and what had taken place there once upon a time.

"That's a great way to take a step back and pretend like nothing weird happened just now," he muttered as he walked into his house, dropping his work bag inside the door and kicking off his shoes.

He'd already been reeling from the bomb Kaidan had dropped at dinner, which was probably why the encounter with Isla had taken on an odd vibe. His emotions were all over the place after hearing his notoriously contentious parents might be back together.

For fuck's sake.

That just couldn't be true. Their children had barely survived their first rodeo with those two, who'd torn each other—and the nine of them—apart over a decade of battle that'd led them both to be the kind of family lawyers who tried their best to never let that happen to their clients.

Ironic, right?

They'd done everything wrong in their own divorce, which had cost them both millions of dollars and untold agony for everyone involved, but they worked hard to keep that from happening to strangers who were clients.

Julian cracked open a beer and sat on a stool at the island, thrust back in time to an era he tried to never think about lest he be derailed by emotions he'd spent years in therapy putting behind him. As the eldest of the nine siblings, he'd been on the front lines, often absorbing painful hits in an attempt to protect his precious brothers and sisters. He'd done whatever he could to keep them sealed off from the worst of it, often at his own expense.

He regretted nothing, but if his parents were back together…

The very thought of it filled him with unreasonable rage that he'd kept hidden from the others at dinner. He'd been so shocked by Kaidan's comments that he'd ceased to function for a few minutes as she spelled out the somewhat irrefutable evidence that something was up.

He honestly didn't want to know, but he also didn't want to be blindsided if it was true.

He checked his phone for the first time in two hours to find a flurry of texts from his concerned siblings, each of them looking to him for guidance on how to handle this latest chapter in their family's sordid history.

If only he had the answers they were looking for.

He responded to each of them with the same thing. *Let's not worry about something that may or may not be true. Reminder that we're not children anymore and don't have to be dragged into anything that goes down between them.*

That was probably why he'd reacted the way he had to Isla. He'd gone there in a state of shock and had been comforted by her kind, sweet demeanor.

That's all it was.

It'd been a lot lately, between running into Aimee, the culmination of several intense cases, the scene with Stacey and now hearing his parents might be reconciling. No wonder his reaction to a simple conversation with a woman was way out of character.

Women didn't get to him. He didn't allow that to happen. Ever. And his close friend's younger sister? As lovely as she was, she wouldn't be the exception to his rules.

He'd send her the playlists he'd promised her, and that would be that.

CHAPTER ELEVEN

In the morning, Julian was driving to the office when he took a call from Cresley Dane, who wanted to know whether he'd heard back from her son's father.

"Nothing yet."

"That son of a bitch."

"This happens a lot when they realize the other party has retained counsel and is getting serious about dealing with them. They tend to go to ground."

"What can we do to smoke him out? I'm terrified he'll release something to try to damage me."

"If he does that, we'll make him very sorry."

"The scandal alone would cost me lucrative contracts, Julian. We can't let him smear me. It'd be the worst-possible time."

"Let me talk to my brother Carson, our lead investigator, and see what he suggests. I'll get back to you in an hour or two?"

"Thank you so much."

"I know it's hard but try not to worry too much. The fact that he knows you've got an attorney on the case makes him less likely to do something stupid that could end up costing him a lot of money as well as any prayer of seeing his son."

"I wish he cared about seeing his son, but he doesn't. He's after money. It's no coincidence that he resurfaced right after my new deal was announced. He wants his piece of the pie."

"Well, that's not going to happen. I'll talk to Carson, and one of us will get right back to you, okay?"

"Thanks, Julian. I feel better after talking to you."

"No problem at all."

"On another note, I've heard from every friend I've ever had asking me who my sexy new man is."

"Great," he said with a groan. "The Ivy might've been a mistake."

"It wouldn't have mattered where we were. They would've found me. This is the part of my job that I hate the most. I can't even have lunch with a man, who is my *attorney*, without it being all over TMZ that I'm in a new relationship. Ty even heard about it at school!"

"Ugh, that sucks. Freaking paparazzi."

"They're the worst."

"We're on the job. Try not to worry."

"Thank you again."

He ended the call with Cresley and called Carson.

"What's good?" Carson said when he took the call.

"The usual insanity. I might need you on Cresley Dane's case after all."

"Sign me up, brother. Does she need me to get right over there to provide comfort and counsel?"

"Easy, killer," Julian said with a chuckle. "I need you to find her deadbeat baby daddy, who's suddenly resurfaced looking for money right after she signed a big new deal. And he allegedly has some dirt on her that'd prove embarrassing if it got out. For some reason I can't quite fathom, he's not returning my calls."

"And you're such a nice guy."

"Right?"

"Send me what you know about him, and I'll get on it. If you wanted to mention to Cresley that I'm handling it *personally*, that'd be fine with me. In fact, you should feel free to send over her number so I can reassure her myself."

"You're a clown."

"She's a *supermodel*, my dude. What's wrong with you that you're *not* interested?"

"Other than her being my client?"

"Yeah, other than that."

Why did Isla's pretty face pick that exact moment to pop into his mind, reminding him all over again of how connected he'd felt to her the night before?

Julian shook off those thoughts as quickly as they'd appeared. "Gotta go. I'll get you the info on the baby daddy as soon as I get to the office."

"I shall be waiting with bated breath."

"Gross. You ought to do something about your bait breath if you're setting your sights on a supermodel."

Carson was laughing when the line went dead and his Sirius XM picked up with his favorite channel, Classic Vinyl.

"Idiot," Julian said even as he smiled about Carson's foolishness. He had no trouble whatsoever attracting female companionship. In fact, if he set his sights on Cresley, she'd probably be interested, supermodel or not. She was only human, and the ladies *loved* Carson.

He turned up the volume to sing along to the Badfinger song "Day After Day" as he drove past the Beverly Hills Hotel in the neighborhood where they'd been raised on Lomitas Drive. Corbin now lived alone in the big house.

Anyway, about Carson and women... It wasn't that they didn't dig Julian, too, but for Carson, it'd always been seemingly effortless in a way it'd never been for Julian. When they were younger, he'd been the awkward one, while Carson was Mr. Smooth from about sixth grade on. Sometimes Julian felt like he'd never truly outgrown his awkward stage, especially since his goal was to stay single forever.

Most women didn't want to hear on the first date that there was no chance of any kind of future. Once in a while, he met one like Stacey, who said they wanted the same things he did, until they went and fell in love and ruined a good thing.

He was relieved to have not heard any more from her since their office standoff the other day, but he had an uneasy feeling he hadn't seen the last of her.

When he pulled into his parking space at the office, he texted the info about Marlon Beckett to Carson.

Got it, Carson replied. *On it.*

Using his ID card for access, Julian took the elevator from the parking garage to the fourth floor and greeted Hector at the reception desk.

Hector waved him over.

"What's up?" Julian asked him.

"So it's none of my business, but..." Hector looked around to make sure no one would overhear him. "That woman Stacey... She's going off on you online."

"How do you know?"

"I, uh, looked her up to see if she had anything to say. People like that never go away quietly." He handed Julian a slip of paper. "Her socials."

"Thank you, Hector. I appreciate this." And he meant that, but it was mortifying to have one of their employees cluing him in about an ex trashing him online.

"The stuff she's saying about you... It's obvious she doesn't know you at all."

"I'll take care of it."

"I figured that's what you'd say."

Julian forced a smile for Hector, who looked upset. "This is when all those years in school pay off."

Hector laughed and then reached for his ringing desk phone.

One of the central facts of Julian's life was that no matter how early he left his house in the morning, he never, *ever* got to work before Mattie. She was always waiting for him with a smile, dressed to the nines with coordinating nails, ready to help him conquer the day. Today, she wore a red suit with a black silk blouse and a black-and-red scarf.

He handed her the skinny latte he picked up for her along with his tall Americano every day on the way in.

"Thank you, my love," she said as she followed him into his office, closing the door for their daily coffee and planning ritual.

Before Hector had told him about Stacey's latest salvo, he'd been wondering about how he might go about finding out what was going on with his parents without Carson's involvement, as that would usually be his first move.

Julian had debated whether to ask Mattie about whether she'd picked up on anything about his parents being back together, but if anyone would know, it was her. Somehow, she knew everything that went on with everyone. Carson often said he wanted to steal her for his team because she already knew everything they were trying to find out.

"What's wrong?" she asked when he was seated at his desk and she was in one of his visitor chairs.

"I want to ask you something…"

"You can ask me anything. You know that. Why does my Julian look so distressed?"

"Have you heard any rumblings about…"

She raised a brow.

"My parents being back together?"

Her expression conveyed pure shock that answered his question. *"What?"* she asked in a whisper. "Back together? Good Lord, no. I haven't heard anything of the sort."

Julian exhaled a deep sigh of relief. If Mattie didn't know about it, it probably wasn't true.

"Where in the world did you come up with such a thing?"

"You know how my mom is staying with Kaidan during the week since the fire?"

Mattie nodded.

"Kaidan says there's a vibe."

"Tell me more."

He detailed the evidence Kaidan had presented to them the night before, from the giggling to the disappearing act over the previous weekend.

"Huh," Mattie said, looking contemplative. "I've not picked up on anything on that, but..."

"What?"

"If it's true, and that's a huge *if*, they'd be very careful to keep it on the down-low because, you know..."

"The nine children who work for them would be furious?"

Mattie winced. "Something like that." She shook her head. "Didn't see that one coming."

"You and me both. If it's true... I just can't."

"They have to know it'd be the biggest scandal since the first one they caused, at least within their close circles. Well, actually, it'd be a huge story to everyone, since your dad has made himself into a TV star."

"The very possibility of it makes me ill." Julian had a thought and felt his eyes go wide. "The Godfreys' anniversary party. They would've seen each other there for the first time, as far as I know, since Rome's UCLA graduation..."

"You were there. Did you see them talking to each other?"

"I didn't, but it was crowded, and I wasn't watching them. If they've reconnected, I'll bet it happened then." He blew out a deep breath. "I think I'm going to be sick."

"Don't take it on, honey. If it's true, and right now we know nothing for certain, it's got nothing to do with you kids this time around."

Julian so wished that were true. "Doesn't it, though? Everyone in town would be talking about them and us and relitigating the past. The thought of that is more than I can bear to consider."

"Do you want me to see what I can find out?"

"Don't do any digging but let me know if you hear anything."

"You'll be the first to know."

He made a huge effort to shake off the existential dread so he could focus on the details of the day ahead as Mattie reviewed his schedule with him.

"Nine a.m. mediation for *Hansen v. Hansen* in Century City. Twelve thirty lunch at the Beverly Hills Hotel."

"Is that the client who wishes to remain anonymous until we meet?"

"That's the one."

"No clue who it is?"

"Nope, but I expect it to be bombshell-level."

They used that term to describe a major celebrity laying the groundwork for a split that would dominate the headlines for weeks, if not months.

"I've prepared all the usual retainer paperwork and worksheets for you to take with you."

"Thank you. You're the best."

"I know, right?"

He chuckled at her saucy grin.

"At three thirty, you've got..."

As Mattie reviewed the rest of his day, Julian nodded at all the right moments, but he wasn't thinking about the day ahead or the bombshell-level client or the unsavory possibility of his parents getting back together. All he could think about was Isla and how sweet she'd been the night before as he'd gone on and on about the history of the house and the music. Even though she'd had no idea what he was talking about, she'd listened attentively and had seemed to enjoy their time together as much as he had.

Her gorgeous face kept popping into his mind, which had

him rattled in a way he rarely was when it came to women. He never allowed himself to get hooked on one, but for some reason, he found himself looking forward to seeing her again.

After Mattie left him alone to get to work, he texted Jackson, asking him to file for a restraining order against Stacey. He included her social media accounts as backup for the request. Julian chose not to look at them himself, because what did he care about whatever she was saying? It didn't matter to him, but he'd take the necessary steps to shut her down.

Oh shit, Jackson replied. *I'll get right on it.*

Thanks.

With a long day of work ahead of him, his parents' potential reconciliation weighing on him and annoyance at Stacey's nonsense, the last thing he should've been thinking about was Isla Santana, how their first night in the rental had gone and how long it might be until he could see her again.

ISLA HAD FALLEN asleep listening to one of the playlists Julian had sent her. She was in love with Mama Cass Elliot singing "Dream a Little Dream of Me," Joni Mitchell's "Both Sides Now" and Neil Young's "Heart of Gold," among many other beautiful songs that'd helped her understand more of the LA music history Julian had told her about. The era had a definitive sound that she'd immediately connected with. She could see why he loved it so much and couldn't wait for the chance to tell him that.

When she opened her eyes and saw it was after eight a.m., her first thought was for the kids, who were sleeping in for the first time ever. And then she realized her phone was vibrating on the table next to the bed with a call from Mrs. Ventura.

"Hi there."

"Isla, Gabriel is next door raising a ruckus, screaming your name and the kids' names. I don't know what to do."

She sat up and pushed her hair back from her face.

"Stay in your apartment and call the police."

"Are you sure? He needs help. There's got to be something else we can do."

"There isn't. He's refused all offers of help for years now.

"Okay. I'll make the call. Do you want me to keep you posted?"

She thought about that for a second. "No, thank you. It doesn't involve me anymore, but I'll always want to hear from you about other things."

"Okay, honey. Remember that I'm happy to sit with the kids any time you need me."

"I so appreciate that."

"They're such sweet kids. I'm happy to do it."

"I'll text you soon."

"I'll look forward to that."

"Please stay safe. Don't confront him or anything like that."

"I won't. Don't worry."

After they said their goodbyes, Isla ended the call and sat perfectly still for a long time, thinking about Gabriel and what would happen to him and then reminding herself that he was no longer her concern. He couldn't be. She had to focus on putting her own life—and her children's lives—back together, separate from him.

She sent a text to Julian. *My neighbor called to say Gabriel is at the apartment screaming for me and the kids. I encouraged her to call the police, since there's really nothing else that can be done unless he chooses to get help.*

He wrote back when she was in the bathroom brushing her hair. *Sorry to hear. I'm glad that you and the kids weren't there when he returned. Can I do anything for you?*

So many things, she thought with a small smile, even as she was filled with sadness for Gabriel, for the family she'd once hoped to build with him and for the fact that such a nice, sweet, sexy man like Julian had crossed her path at the worst-possible time.

I'm okay, she replied. *Will work on the documents today and get them back to you ASAP.*

Let me know when you're done, and I'll pick them up on the way home.

She replied with a thumbs-up, encouraged to know she'd get to see him again soon. That was good motivation to get the voluminous pile of documents completed soon.

Isla got breakfast for the kids, and when they were settled in to watch *Paw Patrol*, she began working on the packet that Julian had dropped off. Every time she thought of him, her skin tingled with awareness, as if he were still sitting across from her, looking at her with those gorgeous, compassionate brown eyes. Her soon-to-be ex-husband was probably getting arrested at the place they used to call home while she completed the initial paperwork to file for divorce, and what was she thinking about?

Her divorce attorney and how cute he'd been while telling her about the history of the house and sharing his knowledge of the Laurel Canyon rock 'n' roll scene that'd launched the LA music industry. She'd lived in and around LA her whole life and had never once given a thought to how the city's vibrant music scene had gotten its start.

Denny texted to check on them, and she updated him about the latest with Gabriel.

I was thinking I might have a chat with him. Any objections?

No, that's fine, as long as you aren't unkind to him. He's obviously ill or addicted or something, and he should be treated as such.

I'll talk to the cops about what we can do to get help for him.

That'd probably be more productive than talking to him. Thank you.

I'll let you know how it goes.

She sent a thumbs-up, appreciating that he'd take time he didn't have to help her—and Gabriel, whom he didn't even like. But he was doing it for her and the kids. The sooner they got Gabriel into treatment, the sooner he could work on reclaiming his life. And it was in the kids' best interests for him to one day have a relationship with them.

Mila brought her favorite pink blanket with her when she crawled into Isla's lap, pushing the papers aside as she went.

Amused by her daughter's ability to get what she wanted without saying a word, Isla wrapped her arms around Mila's sturdy little body and gave her a squeeze, incredibly thankful to be with her babies in a safe place, without the grinding fear of worrying about Gabriel coming home to ruin their peace.

Mila's soft blonde hair brushed against Isla's chin as she rested it on Mila's head.

Theo was transfixed by *Paw Patrol*, as always, running one of his character cars along the coffee table as he watched the action play out on the screen.

"Mommy," he said during a commercial. "When is Daddy coming over?"

Isla had been waiting for him to ask about his daddy, whom Theo loved despite the fact that he was sometimes afraid of him. "Come sit with me." She held out an arm to him and put it around him when he'd relocated to the sofa. "You know how I told you that Daddy is sick?"

He nodded while Mila sucked her thumb, listening but not really understanding.

"He's probably going to the hospital to get better, and that'll take a while."

"Like a week?"

"More likely a few months. Do you remember how long a month is?" They'd studied time in his preschool class that he could no longer attend out of fear of Gabriel trying to sign him out. Isla couldn't imagine letting either of them out of her sight, unless they were with Denny or Mrs. V.

"Thirty days, but some are more and one is less."

"That's right." Her little guy was so, so smart. He remembered everything he learned and was well ahead of his age group in development. "But it could be three or four months, which is like ninety or a hundred and twenty days."

"That's a lot of days."

"Yes, it is."

"Won't he miss us?"

"He'll miss us very much, especially you and Mila. But you can make some pictures for him that we can send to him. That'll make him feel much better."

"When we had to hide in the closet..."

Ugh. "Yes..."

"Was that because of Daddy's sickness?"

She wanted to lie to him, but everything she'd read about situations like theirs encouraged telling even the youngest kids as much of the truth as the parent felt they could handle. "Yes, honey."

"He broke our stuff."

"He did."

"Why did he do that?"

"It's because of the illness."

"Does he have a cold?"

"No, baby, it's something in here." She tapped on his head. "It's hard to explain to little guys like you and Mila, but the most important things to know are that Daddy loves you, and you're safe."

"But we can't go home?"

"No, honey, we're going to be looking for a new home. Doesn't that sound fun? We can find a place that has a playground nearby and maybe a pool."

"I love the pool."

"I know you do. But for now, we'll stay here and catch our breath and figure out what's next. Okay?"

"Okay." When the show came back on, he squiggled free

of her and went back to playing with the truck while the show had its usual mesmerizing effect on him. Thank goodness for the Paw Patrol, she thought, as she had many times before. Any time Theo was upset or out of sorts, a few minutes with his pals always made him feel better.

She glanced down at Mila, who was about to doze off for her late morning nap, so Isla gathered her up and stood to put her down in the portable crib she'd brought from home.

Mila rolled onto her side and was asleep in minutes.

Isla was thankful that her little girl was too young to understand any of what was happening. She fully expected many more probing questions from Theo, who was a deep thinker on a regular day. And this was most certainly not a regular day.

She sent a text to her friend Georgia, manager of the Whisky A Go Go. *Hi there. Hope you're doing well! I'm available to pick up a few shifts if you need any covered. Let me know when you can.*

With Mrs. V willing to babysit any time and an extra bedroom at the rental so she could sleep over, Isla was determined to get back to work a few nights a week. While it was nice to know there was money from her parents, she was under no illusions about being able to live off that forever. She would have to find a way to support her little family long term, without Gabriel's help. It was becoming clear that he'd be unable to work for quite some time, if not forever.

Taking care of their children would be her responsibility going forward, and working at the bar was the best way to make as much money as possible in the shortest amount of time. Thanks to the cushion she had from her parents, she could pay first, last and a damage deposit on a new apartment and buy the furniture and household items they'd need to get started. But after that, she'd continue to live as if she didn't have any extra money, so it'd be there in an emergency. After losing her parents so young, followed by years of marriage to an often unpredictable man, she'd learned to prepare for all contingencies. Thus, the hiding place in the apartment that'd quite possibly saved her and her children.

She was working her way through the worksheet of the assets—what few there were—and the long list of liabilities that Gabriel had run up on their credit cards when Georgia returned her text.

Nice to hear from you! Your timing is excellent. I had two girls quit this week. How soon can you start?

In a week or so? Not with the husband anymore (as of yesterday) and getting settled in the single-mom life.

Oh wow! That's a lot with little ones. Let me know if I can help.

Thank you!! That means a lot. Sorry to need a little time before I start back to work.

No prob. It's slower this time of year, but still better than most places. We've got new security, too, which is much better than when you were here last.

Great to hear. Sign me up for next weekend.

Fri, Sat & Sun?

Sure.

Done. See you soon, and good luck with everything.

Thank you so much!!!!!

What a relief to have work lined up. If she did three nights a week at the bar, she'd make enough to survive and be able to keep the kids out of daycare since she wouldn't be working during the day. That was a huge relief. Daycare was hideously expensive.

She texted Denny next. *Any news on Gabriel?*

I'm waiting to hear back from the police.

To Mrs. V, she said, *What's happening there?*

They took him away a couple of minutes ago. He was screaming the whole time that he hadn't done anything, it was his house, and he had a right to be there. He wanted to know what they'd done with his wife and kids.

Isla's reaction to hearing that was immediate and visceral. Thank God they hadn't been there when he returned. She'd hoped that being arrested, held overnight and hit with a restraining order would've kept him away from anywhere she and the kids might be, but clearly, it'd had no effect.

Chilled to her bones by that understanding, she could barely breathe or think or do anything other than be afraid for their lives. What if he found them? What would he do now that he felt cornered? What would happen when he was served with divorce papers that contained her request for full custody of their kids?

The questions—and the fear—had her calling Julian, who'd made her feel safe and reassured with his calm competence.

Her call went to his voicemail, so she left a message. "Um, this is Isla. Santana. I'm so sorry to bother you. I know how busy you are. It's just that my neighbor said Gabriel was screaming for his wife and kids when they took him away, and I just, well... Call me if you have a minute. Thank you."

Trying to stay busy so she wouldn't think about Gabriel being arrested again, she texted Mrs. V. *So it looks like I can do three nights next weekend at work. How do you feel about spending the weekend together? Haha. Kids would be asleep before I leave.*

She wrote back a few minutes later. *I'd love to. How's it going in the rental?*

I love it here.

I'm so glad! I lived in LC as a young woman. It's a wonderful neighborhood. Can't wait to see you and the kids.

We can't wait either.

The return of their old groove with each other made Isla realize how much she'd missed Mrs. V over the past couple of months. That was just another temporary loss she could chalk up to Gabriel and his rages. She thought of the lovely group of girlfriends she'd had once upon a time, each of whom had fallen off her radar as she'd focused on her kids and keeping them safe.

She composed a text to their group. *Hi, girls, it's me, your MIA friend who has no right to pop in out of the blue like this but is hoping you might still love her as she sticks her head out of the fog of dealing with a soon-to-be EX-husband. I've missed you all, and I'm sorry for going dark. It's been a rough couple of years. Anyway... If you haven't forgotten about me, I'd love to see you, talk to you, catch up and hear what's new with you. I'm sorry for being a shit friend. I love you guys.*

Isla read and reread the text that would go to the women who'd been her four closest friends once upon a time, before she married Gabriel and lost the rest of her life. Now that she was out of the center of the storm, she could look back with a bit of perspective and see how it'd happened swiftly after they were married. Suddenly, she was expected to spend all her time with him, to the exclusion of everyone else. He'd gone no-contact with his family and expected her to do the same with her people so they could build a future of their own without anyone else's influence.

Except... There was no way she would cut off Denny, and her insistence on keeping him close had infuriated Gabriel. He'd despised Denny from the start, probably because her brother had seen through Gabriel's bullshit, his big talk about always being on the verge of a career breakthrough and his lofty ambitions that'd never panned out.

Because he'd refused any sort of medical intervention to address his erratic behavior, she'd done her own research. All signs pointed to manic depression or addiction—possibly both, which was a potent combination—but she'd also learned that as long as he was unwilling to address it, she was powerless to make him. He had rights, and as such, the impetus to get help had to come from him. With his behavior increasingly more violent, she'd looked into psychiatric holds and other such options but had refrained from pulling those triggers out of fear of what would happen when he was released.

Her friend Lana replied to the group text. *Isla... I'm SOOOO glad to hear from you. We've been so worried. I'm relieved to hear you refer to him as your ex-husband, and I'm sorry things have been rough. We'd love to see you any time. We've missed you, too, and we've been so afraid for you.*

Isla read the text with tears in her eyes. *I just moved out yesterday, so things are in flux, but I wanted you guys to know... I'll be in touch. I promise.*

We've missed you, too, Jodi said. *So happy to hear from you.*

Isla put a heart on the comment and used her sleeve to wipe her eyes.

She went through the motions of making Theo's lunch and wrapping up a PB&J for Mila to have when she woke up. Theo ate his sandwich and carrot sticks with his usual cheerful disposition while continuing to play with his trucks. Thank goodness for him, she thought for the millionth time. He was the sweetest, easiest little guy, endlessly curious and funny. Isla was sad for what Gabriel was missing out on with their children and sad for herself that she needed to be afraid of the man she'd once loved with her whole heart and soul.

CHAPTER TWELVE

Julian's mediation had dragged on for most of the morning, with the husband questioning every item on the extensive list of assets and debts that were being divided evenly by the divorcing couple.

Julian's client, Victoria Hansen, had begun to wilt from the emotional and physical drain of dissecting the life she'd once treasured with a man who'd cheated on her with his younger assistant. She'd told Julian she felt like the ultimate cliché, the wife who never thought for a second her husband would betray her and the family they'd built together.

The entire proceeding had devastated her, and now that it was so close to being finished, Julian slipped her a note that said, BE STRONG. WE'RE ALMOST THERE.

She gave him a smile and a small nod as she sat up straighter. "Actually, I don't agree with that change," she said of an amendment that would've given her ex-husband their place in Lake Tahoe in exchange for her getting the house in Pasadena, where they'd raised their family. "I don't want the Pasadena house. I want Tahoe."

Her husband, Larry, was a distinguished-looking guy with salt-and-pepper hair and a goatee that Victoria had told Julian was the first sign that something had gone awry between her and the man who'd once disdained facial hair on other men. Apparently, the girlfriend liked him with a goatee.

Clearly, he hadn't expected her to toss the Tahoe bomb into the proceedings.

"You know how much I love Tahoe," he said.

"And you know how much I once loved you," she replied with a casual shrug that filled Julian with pride for her. When they first met, she'd been so devastated to learn her husband had been unfaithful that she hadn't been sure she wanted to continue living. Now, more than a year later, the shock had worn off, and thanks to a lot of therapy, she'd learned how to advocate for herself.

"Vic... Come on. Be reasonable. The Pasadena house is worth much more than Tahoe."

"I know. We can sell it, divide the proceeds and you can get yourself a new love nest in Tahoe for you and your child bride."

"You don't even like it there! Every time we went, you said it was a tourist trap."

"That's right."

"So why do you want it?"

"It'll be a very lucrative rental property."

He sat back, seeming shocked. "So you aren't even planning to use it?"

"Not that it's any of your business, but I plan to use it as an investment."

"You're getting half of everything else as well as spousal support. You won't need it."

"I want it."

Larry looked to the mediator, who was known for allowing couples to talk it out at his table. He intervened whenever things took a turn toward the ugly.

"If you can't agree on a disposition for the Tahoe property, we'll have to sell it and divide the proceeds."

"Which is also fine with me," Victoria said.

Larry seemed to understand all at once that she didn't care what happened to it as long as he didn't get to enjoy it with the woman he'd left her for.

Julian had sat back and allowed her to enjoy this moment she'd been looking forward to for weeks as they'd prepared for the mediation.

"This would be a good time to break for lunch," the mediator said. "Both sides should use the break to determine whether you've tendered final offers on these matters. We'll see you back here in an hour."

While Larry huddled with his attorney and directed dirty looks at Victoria, Julian escorted her from the conference room at the mediator's Century City office.

"Damn, that felt good," Victoria said with a big smile. "When he realized I don't care about selling Tahoe... That was my favorite moment since this started."

Normally, Julian encouraged his clients to avoid vindictive moves that only extended the process and cost them even more money than they were already spending on attorney fees. But in this case, he'd understood why Victoria had wanted to exact her pound of flesh.

While Larry had built a successful psychiatry practice, she'd raised their four children, kept a beautiful home, lavishly entertained his colleagues and friends and, as she'd said, played by all the rules. Finding out about his affair with a woman half her age had been shocking, demoralizing and, once she'd caught her breath, infuriating.

"You're resolved to stick with selling it if he's unwilling to let you have it?"

"Fine by me. I don't care about any of it anymore."

"I need to check in with the office. Do you want to grab something to eat?"

"I'd rather go out for a walk. I could use some air."

"Then I'll meet you back here in an hour?"

"See you then."

After she headed for the elevators, Julian ducked into an empty conference room to check his messages and listened to the one from Isla. Concerned by her fearful tone as much as his own reaction to the sound of her voice, he called her right back.

"Hi, Julian." She sounded better than she had in the message. "Thanks for getting back to me."

When his stomach dropped at the sound of her voice, he realized he had a very big problem on his hands. "Sorry for the delay. I was in a meeting."

"I can only imagine how busy you are."

"No worries at all. Is there anything new?"

"Denny was going to try to figure out where the police took Gabriel and suggest a mental health evaluation."

"Would you like me to find out where it stands?"

"Could you?'

"I can try."

"It's strange that even after everything that's happened, what he did to our home... I'm worried about him."

"That's totally understandable. I'll see what I can find out and get back to you."

"Thank you so much."

"I want to add... Right now, he's in custody, and I'm fairly certain they'll hold him after two incidents in two days. But just in case he's released, he shouldn't have any way to find you and the children. However, if you ever feel unsafe, call the police immediately."

"I will, and I hope they do hold him until he can get some help."

"I'll make a few calls. Hang in there."

"I'm trying."

He needed to say goodbye and start making those calls, but he didn't want to let her go yet. Alarm bells were ringing so loudly he couldn't hear anything else. "Are you all right, Isla?"

"I think so. I've gotten a few things done today despite this new issue with Gabriel."

"That's good. Stay focused on the future."

"That's the goal. Thanks for everything."

"I'll be in touch."

After he ended the call, he stood in the conference room, staring out the window without seeing anything other than red flags dancing before his eyes. As much as he might wish otherwise, he was attracted to her, and as such, he couldn't represent her.

"*Fuck.*"

Releasing a deep breath, he closed his eyes and took a minute to process a situation he hadn't seen coming when Denny had asked him to meet with his younger sister.

Damn it. Denny would be pissed, and who could blame him? He'd asked his friend to help his sister deal with a nightmare. The last thing Denny—or Isla—needed was Julian developing feelings for her.

And what, exactly, did he plan to do about those so-called feelings?

Not a goddamned thing.

He had no room in his life for a single mom with two little kids, even if she was the first woman who'd made him feel *anything* since Aimee.

The last thing he needed was an ethics breach, which was why he decided to assign Isla's case to Jackson. He stared at his phone for another long moment before he made the call.

"Hey," Jackson said. "How's it going with the mediation?"

"Not bad. Victoria made a play for the Tahoe house that Larry didn't see coming, and that was interesting."

"Good for her. How much longer will you be there?"

"We have one more hour scheduled this afternoon, and then I've got that meeting at the Beverly."

"I was going to call you to say the bombshell client canceled. He'll reschedule when he can."

"Ah, okay." It wasn't uncommon for clients to cancel several times before they actually met with a divorce attorney. "I'm calling because I need a favor."

"I work for you, Julian. You don't have to ask me for favors. I'm a sure thing."

Julian cracked a grin at his brother's cheekiness. "This is a bit delicate. My friend Denny from the band..."

"You're representing his sister, right?"

"Yeah, that's the case I want you to take over."

"I thought you wanted to handle that one personally."

"I did. Until I didn't."

"Um, okay. You're being weird."

"I'm aware, but I need you to take over, starting with some calls to our contacts at the LAPD about what's going on with her husband, Gabriel Santana. He was detained a second time after he showed up at the apartment where they lived together and raised a ruckus when she and the kids were nowhere to be found. I need you to find out what's going on with him and then report back to her. You ready for her number?"

"Yeah, go ahead."

Julian found her number and recited it.

"Got it."

"Thank you."

"Are you going to tell her about this change in counsel?"

"I'll take care of it. Put together the new retainer agreement with you as her counsel. I'll drop it off to her when I pick up the assets and liability worksheets from her."

"Okay..."

"Thank you."

"You're not going to tell me what's going on?"

Julian wanted to air it out with someone, and Jackson was good about keeping their professional business private, but this wasn't professional. This was as personal as it got, and he couldn't tell anyone why he was handing Isla off to his brother without it blowing up into a big deal.

"That's an awfully long pause, brother."

"With the Smithson trial starting next week, I need to stay focused. That's all it is."

"Okay, I'm on it. Let me know when you've informed her of the handoff."

"Will do."

Julian ended the call feeling a little sick over having to tell Isla—and Denny—that he was turning her case over to Jackson. They would think it was because he had more important clients who'd pay him top dollar. He wished that was the reason.

Why her?

Why, after all this time in which he'd gone without a single attachment to any woman, had she appeared to shake up his entire existence? Was it because he'd recently seen Aimee and been reminded of what it'd been like to truly love someone the way he'd loved her? He'd forgotten the breathless ecstasy of it all... And he'd been better off without the reminder. His reaction to Isla had to be tied up in seeing Aimee and all the shit that had resurrected, things he hadn't thought about—or felt—in ages.

He wanted to go back to before the Godfreys' anniversary party so he could come down with a cold or something that would keep him from seeing the only woman he'd ever loved. Going into it, he'd understood he would see her and expected it to be nostalgic and maybe a bit amusing.

Instead, it'd been devastating.

Coming face-to-face with the one woman who'd worked her way all the way into his soul, resurfacing emotions he hadn't experienced since the last time he'd been with her, had left him rattled and off his game for weeks now. It'd been a mistake of epic proportions to go to that party. If he'd had any sense of how upsetting it would be to see Aimee, to talk to her, to remember how insanely in love with her he'd been once upon a time... He would've stayed far, far away, despite both his parents telling their adult kids that they expected them all to attend their longtime friends' party.

And into that strange state of being had walked Isla Santana to remind him he wasn't immune to the kind of reaction that would thrill a normal person, who'd welcome a connection with a potential partner. He wanted nothing to do with that, which was one of two reasons he'd called in Jackson. The other was that he couldn't effectively represent her when being in the same room with her sent him into a weird tailspin that he had neither the time nor the patience to deal with.

He could almost talk himself into being angry with her for forcing him to have to manage something so ridiculous, but he couldn't let that happen. It certainly wasn't her fault she was beautiful, sweet, sexy and incredibly resourceful. That last thing had really done it for him, the way her planning for potential catastrophe had very likely saved their lives. That was incredibly impressive.

She was incredibly impressive.

And easy to talk to and funny and a wonderful mother.

"Fuck my life," he muttered as he checked the time and found he'd wasted half an hour thinking about a woman.

Enough of that.

She was great. No question about it, but she was no longer his concern. Jackson would take excellent care of her and would consult him if he had any questions. Julian would remain detached from the situation, protecting his heart and his ethics from any complications.

It was better that way.

CHAPTER THIRTEEN

The kids were out of sorts all afternoon and extra cranky at bedtime. They didn't like the bathtub in the rental because it wasn't as big as the one they'd had at home, and Isla had forgotten to pack their bath toys, which was another source of irritation for Theo. He wanted his boats, and she couldn't immediately provide them the way she could at home. That sparked a thirty-minute meltdown focused on the unfairness of not being able to have all his things when he wanted them.

Isla agreed with him. She'd forgotten her favorite pair of Nikes and the hair clip she used every day.

As comfortable and safe as she felt in the rental, it was unsettling for the kids to be out of their usual routine in the only home they'd ever known. She supposed she'd been delusional to think she could smoothly move them somewhere new with no bumps or bruises.

When Isla read them a story at bedtime, Theo started crying for Daddy, which got Mila upset, too. If he cried, she cried.

With them finally settled down for the night, she went

straight to the fridge for a glass of the chilled rosé she'd been looking forward to all day and checked her phone for the first time in two hours to find a message from Julian.

Will stop by around eight, if that's okay, to drop off some additional paperwork and pick up what you have so far.

It was now seven forty-five.

Shit. That didn't give her much time to change out of the shirt that'd gotten wet during bath time and run a brush through her hair.

Yes, that's fine, she replied, her heart racing with anticipation because she'd be seeing him in a few minutes.

Jeez, get yourself together, girl. He's dropping off papers and picking up others. That's all this is.

She knew that. Of course she knew, but it'd been so long since she'd experienced butterflies over the thought of seeing a man. It'd been like that with Gabriel at first. He'd been the most romantic, thoughtful boyfriend she'd ever had. Marrying him had made perfect sense, and at first, everything had been great. He'd been a hard worker who was always thinking of ways to make her happy. When Theo was born, he was absolutely in love with their little boy from the first second he ever saw him.

For a time, she'd felt like she was living a dream, but it'd all come crashing down in a flurry of increasingly disturbing incidents, none of which could be easily explained or addressed. She'd have been hard-pressed to describe the scenarios that had each unfolded differently.

Prior to the baseball bat, the worst thing, other than him missing Mila's birth and not meeting her until she was a month old, had been the time she'd been trying to pay for groceries with a debit card that had gotten declined. A kind woman in the line behind her had paid for Isla's groceries, and when she'd gotten to her car, she'd checked her bank app and seen nothing but zeros. All their money was gone. To this day, she still didn't know what he'd done with it, but it'd been terrifying to have no money at all for weeks until he'd gotten paid again.

The more she'd pushed him for answers, the more hostile he'd become.

Isla had buttoned up a denim shirt and brushed her hair when a soft knock sounded at the door. That Julian knew not to ring the bell with the kids sleeping earned him big points. As she ran to the door, all troubling thoughts of Gabriel and his erratic behavior were forgotten. With Julian Remington standing on her doorstep in a gorgeous navy pinstripe suit with a lighter blue tie, she didn't want to think about anything other than him.

"Come in." She headed for the kitchen, where she'd left the envelope containing the worksheets. "I've got the paperwork for you. I did as much as I could. There're more liabilities than assets, unfortunately. Oh, and I wanted to tell you... I listened to the music you sent, and I loved it. 'Both Sides Now' made me weep! I listened to it ten times."

When she turned back to him and saw his tormented expression, her smile faded. "What's wrong? Are you okay?"

"I'm glad you liked the music."

She noticed he hadn't answered her questions.

"I loved it! I get now why it's so cool that I'm living in Mama Cass's house. And 'California Dreamin'" ... It's everything you said it would be. I loved that, too." She reached for the wine bottle. "Drink?"

"No, thank you. I can't stay. I've got to be somewhere in twenty minutes."

"Oh, sorry, and here I am going on and on. But I did want you to know that I really love the music. I feel I've been missing out by not listening to it before now."

"That's the beauty of music. It's always there, waiting for you to discover it."

"I like that. It's a really nice thought."

He handed her a new document.

"What's this one?"

"It's a new retainer that names my brother Jackson as your counsel in the divorce case."

"Oh." Stunned and strangely hurt, she glanced up at him. "Why?"

"I... I have a huge trial starting next week, and I'm afraid of dropping balls. I want to make sure you get the attention you need. Jackson is a great attorney. He'll keep things moving forward and arrange service of the divorce papers to Gabriel as soon as he's released from custody."

Julian put the printed form on the counter.

Feeling unreasonably sad to learn he wouldn't be handling her case after all, she sat on one of the barstools to look at the form that he'd already signed to be rid of her. That he seemed exquisitely uncomfortable only made it worse. What happened to the easy groove they'd had the night before? How was it possible to miss something she'd never really had?

These were the questions running through her mind as she signed the form that released him from his obligation to her.

She pushed it across the island to him.

He reached for it, folded it and tucked it into the envelope with the other documents she'd completed. "Jackson made some calls to the LAPD. Gabriel's public defender has requested a medical evaluation for him. That could take a few days to complete, so he'll be held until then."

"I'm surprised he agreed to that."

"Since he violated the restraining order by going to the apartment, I'm sure his attorney suggested he allow it, to possibly avoid additional charges."

"This is all so surreal, but I'm not as surprised as I should be. It's been more than two years of total chaos, and every time I've suggested he seek medical care, he's told me to mind my own goddamned business."

"I'm sorry for all you've been through, but I'm glad you and the kids are safe."

"It's a relief to be free of him and the fear of what might happen next."

"I hope you can find some peace in your life."

She forced a smile as she understood he was saying goodbye to her. "That's the goal."

"I've got to get to band practice. Take care of yourself, Isla."

"You, too. Good luck with the trial."

"Thanks. I'll, ah... I'll let myself out."

For a long time after she heard the front door click shut behind him, she stared straight ahead, trying to make sense of what'd just happened. The night before, he'd been relaxed, engaged in their conversation about the house and its musical pedigree. He'd sent her playlists to listen to and had started to feel like a friend as well as her attorney.

Tonight, he couldn't get away from her fast enough.

Had she done something to annoy him?

"How could I have done anything annoying when I've been with him for less than two hours total?" She poured another glass of wine and took it to the living room to curl up on the sofa with a soft fleece blanket over her lap to ward off the chill that'd overtaken her as Julian had beaten a hasty retreat. "Anyway, who cares if I annoyed him in some way? That's his problem, not mine."

It'd been nice to feel something other than terrified, demoralized and outraged. For a brief shining moment, she'd felt excited again, hopeful and grateful to know she could still enjoy the company of a man after the tumultuous final years with Gabriel.

Before she'd met Julian, she would've said no way, no how to being interested in anyone else, possibly ever again. She'd wanted to hunker down with her kids and build a new life for the three of them separate from Gabriel. The last thing in the world she'd wanted was another man.

But then she'd crossed paths with her brother's sexy lawyer friend, and the spark of interest had reawakened a part of her that'd been sealed off for so long she'd forgotten it existed. While she was glad to know it was still there, she was flattened by the way he'd exited as quickly as he'd entered the picture.

Granted, he probably couldn't be "friends" with her while representing her in the divorce.

That thought stopped her short. Was that why he'd offloaded her to his brother? Because he wanted to be friends with her? But would someone who wanted to be "friends" beat feet out of her house like his pants were on fire?

What the hell was going on?

JULIAN FELT like absolute shit as he drove away from Isla's and headed for practice in the Valley. Witnessing her stunned expression when he'd told her Jackson would be handling her case had been like a hot arrow hitting his chest. He hated that he'd somehow managed to hurt her feelings by doing the right thing for both of them.

She was in a vulnerable spot, and though she wouldn't realize it right away, he'd done her a favor by bowing out of the entire situation. The last thing she needed was a commitment-resistant guy encouraging an attraction that became stronger every time he saw her and remained on simmer in between meetings.

It'd taken every ounce of fortitude he could summon to leave her just now, and that wouldn't do. He couldn't encourage something with a single mom of two kids that had nowhere to go, even now that he was no longer representing her. That didn't change the equation for him.

When things calmed down for her, she'd find a great guy

who wanted to be a husband to her and a father to her kids, a thought that made him feel slightly sick to his stomach.

Julian gripped the wheel tighter as he kept the car directed toward the practice, resisting every opportunity for a U-turn that would take him right back to her.

This, right here, this *turmoil*, was exactly why he avoided relationships. Who needed to feel this way about something he could no more control than he could the changing tides or that the sun would rise and set each day? Not him. He thrived on control and was determined to maintain it in every aspect of his life.

Maybe a night at Club Quantum to work out his frustrations would be in order to get things back on track. That'd worked for him in the past any time he'd felt things getting out of hand. Not that it happened very often, and it'd never been because he'd met someone he had trouble walking away from. That'd happened only once before, when he and Aimee had broken up, and it'd nearly killed him.

"Think about how hard that sucked," he said as he took Laurel Canyon Boulevard toward the Ventura Freeway. "Remember what you said at the time, that you'd never put yourself through anything like that again." For weeks after they'd split up for good, he'd felt like he was underwater, struggling to breathe, sleep, eat and function. That was the only semester he hadn't made the Dean's List at USC. He'd been a total wreck, and in the ensuing years, he'd done everything in his power to keep from ever again finding himself in that hellish mental state.

After three times in the presence of Isla Santana, he somehow understood that she posed the same kind of threat to his peace of mind that Aimee once had.

Spending more time with her wouldn't make anything easier, so if he knew that and understood the stakes with her being his close friend's precious younger sister, why then did he have to stay in the right lane to avoid the overwhelming desire to make that U-turn?

The band had a three-day engagement next weekend at the world-famous Whisky A Go Go on Sunset Boulevard, which was the most exciting thing to ever happen to any of them. The Whisky was a legendary club that dated back to the 1960s, having hosted luminaries such as The Byrds, The Doors, Mötley Crüe, Janis Joplin and Led Zeppelin. Booking a gig there was one of the pinnacles for anyone in the LA music scene, and thanks to Troy's relentless efforts, they'd finally gotten in.

That was another reason why Julian couldn't make that U-turn. The band was counting on him to be at their second-to-last practice before they hit the big time. For the others in the band, especially Vixen, Stix and Troy, the Whisky gig could be a gateway to bigger and better things. Julian worried about the band taking off and him having to bow out due to his day job. Denny had the same concerns, since he had a business to run and teenagers to finish raising and couldn't tour with the band.

Julian had made his choice years ago when he'd chosen the college-law school path over the music, and he'd never had regrets about that. And while he hoped for bigger and better things for the band, he and Denny were tied to LA in a way the others weren't.

They practiced in a warehouse in Glendale that Julian paid for since the others couldn't afford to contribute. When he pulled up next to Denny's truck, he realized he was the last to arrive.

With his stomach still in knots over the tense scene at Isla's, he grabbed the bag containing a change of clothes from the back seat and went inside to find Denny waiting for him.

"What the hell, man? You pawned my sister off on your brother? Isn't he fresh out of law school?"

"That's not what happened. He's four years out of law school and an excellent attorney."

"I asked you to handle this for me, not your brother."

"Jackson has more time to devote to her case. We're still doing it pro bono, so don't worry about that."

"I don't give a shit about the money. I care about Isla and her kids getting the best-possible attorney. That's why I wanted *you*. Supposedly, you're the best."

"I'm Jackson's boss and mentor. She's in very good hands. I promise."

"Why do I feel like there's something else going on here that you're not telling me?"

"There's nothing going on, and it's going to stay that way. Don't worry."

When Julian started to turn away, Denny grabbed him by the arm and spun him around.

"What the fuck does that mean? 'Nothing going on, and it's going to stay that way'?"

Julian pulled his arm free. "Just what I said."

"What was going on?"

"Nothing."

"Can we practice, boys?" Stix asked from the stage, where their equipment lived between gigs.

"Let's do it," Julian said as he walked away from Denny, certain their conversation was finished only for now since he'd been stupid enough to use those particular words.

Julian went into the cramped bathroom and changed out of his suit into faded jeans, a Foghat T-shirt and a flannel, because it was always freezing in there, especially in January. He pulled on fingerless knit gloves and shoved his feet into a pair of black Vans that were almost as old as the jeans. A Dodger's ball cap worn backward was the finishing touch to keep hair that needed to be cut out of his face.

Before he joined the others, he took a second to get his head together. It was ridiculous to feel so unsettled after seeing someone exactly three times. Not to mention he was fighting with Denny, one of his oldest friends. They'd hardly ever had a cross word between them until now.

When he thought of Isla and the hurt expression on her sweet face, he wanted to howl at knowing he'd done that to her when she was already hurting.

"Are you coming, Julian?" Troy said from outside the bathroom door. "We got shit to do."

"Yeah," he said, exhaling a deep breath that did nothing to calm the storm raging inside him. "I'm coming."

CHAPTER FOURTEEN

Practice was a mess. Julian missed half his cues and kept losing the beat, two things that rarely occurred for any of them, let alone multiple times during one practice or gig.

"What the actual fuck, Julian?" Stix said after they'd stopped for the fifth time because of him.

"I'm sorry. Let's go again."

"This is feeling kind of pointless tonight, man," Troy said. "Your mind is obviously elsewhere."

Since Julian couldn't deny that, he didn't try.

"You want to talk about it so we can get back on track?" Vixen asked.

"No, thanks. I'm okay. It was just a crazy day in the divorce wars."

"I don't know how you deal with that shit every day," Stix said. "Listening to people fight over the family china would make me insane."

"That's the least of what they fight over," Julian said with a small grin, relieved that they were homed in on work stress and hadn't picked up on the far bigger concern that was screwing up his concentration. How, *in the world*, could he have actual feelings for someone he'd met *three fucking times*?

"Jules..." Troy's exasperation was apparent. "You're not even listening. Let's call it. This practice is a bust. We gotta get our shit together before the Whisky, so let's practice one more time. Who can do Monday?"

While the others checked their calendars, Julian tried to recall what he was doing Monday night.

Vixen said she had to work Monday, so they moved on to Tuesday.

They were at Wednesday when he snapped out of his own thoughts and pulled his phone from his back pocket to check the calendar. "I can do Wednesday." He created a new event on the spot so he wouldn't forget.

"Wednesday it is," Troy said. Turning to Julian, he added, "And whatever's going on with you, man, *figure it out* before then. This gig at the Whisky is the biggest thing to ever happen to any of us. We can't blow it."

"I will. I'm sorry about tonight."

"Shit happens," Stix said. "But let's get it right for next weekend."

The others were gone by the time Denny and Julian walked out together fifteen minutes later.

"I've known you a long time, Jules. You've never screwed up a practice like that or reneged on a commitment to a friend. Something's up. It might be easier to tell me what it is, so I don't have to be pissed with you."

"It'll piss you off either way."

Denny stopped and turned to face Julian. "Tell me."

Julian hoped that what he was about to say wouldn't end a friendship he treasured. "I like her."

"Who?" Denny asked, brows knit in confusion.

"Isla."

Denny's brows shifted from confusion to surprise in the flash of an instant. "Wait. *What?*"

"You heard me. I like her. That's why I asked Jackson to take over her case. I'm ethically bound to step aside because

I'm... you know... attracted to her."

"You just met her!"

"Trust me," Julian said with an ironic grunt, "I know. It makes no sense to me either."

"You don't 'like' women. You sleep with them and cut them loose."

"That's not fair. I like them all. I just don't want forever with them."

"And you expect me to believe that my *sister* is somehow different from all the others?"

Julian removed the ball cap and ran his free hand through his hair as he tried to find the words he needed to explain something to Denny that made no sense to him. "I wish I knew, but it was immediate and undeniable."

Denny stared at him, incredulous. "I don't even know what to do with this."

"Neither do I, but I did the one thing I ethically had to do by stepping away from her case. Please tell me you understand that part."

"I guess so, but none of this makes sense."

"Remember when you first met Kath? You said you knew in five minutes that she was it for you."

"This is like *that*? For real?"

"The immediacy, yes, but I'm not going to do anything about it, so don't worry."

"Why not?"

"Because she's the kind of woman who'd expect and deserve forever, and I don't have that in me."

Denny placed his hands on his hips as he stared Julian down. "Because of your work?"

"Among other things. Remember the shit show with my parents? Kinda spoiled us for the whole happily-ever-after song and dance."

His friend tilted his head, studying him in a way that made

Julian wish he hadn't said anything about something that was never going to happen.

When the silence stretched on to the point of discomfort, Julian said, "What?"

"Hear me out on this."

"On what?"

"I think you'd be good for her."

Julian was shaking his head before Denny finished the thought. "I wouldn't be good for her or anyone else because I don't want the things they want—the white picket fence in the suburbs, with the kids and dogs and Christmas trees. That's not my life. It'll never be my life."

"Who says?"

"I do, Denny. It's not for me."

"Because your folks messed it up, you assume you will, too?"

"No. Because my folks messed it up, I never want to put myself in a situation where that could happen to me, too. I don't want it."

"So it's not that there's something wrong with my sister, then. There's something wrong with you."

"There's nothing *at all* wrong with her," Julian said with a sigh. "That's the problem. Trust me, with everything she's dealing with, the last thing in the world she needs is a guy like me sniffing around."

"Maybe you're exactly what she needs—someone solid and steady and reliable."

"What is wrong with you? I'm telling you I'm toxic to women, and you're pushing me toward your suddenly single sister who's one of the most precious people in the world to you?"

Denny looked away for a second before he shifted his gaze back to Julian. "She's not the only one who's been through a lot with Gabriel. He came between me and my sister. If I'd had any idea what was really going on with them, I would've gotten her the hell out of there ages ago. So when I tell you that having her with you would give me peace of mind, I mean it."

"Don't give me permission, man. That's the last freaking thing I need right now when I'm trying to forget this ever happened."

"How's that going for you?"

Julian's deep sigh was his only reply.

"Think about what I said."

He wondered how he'd think about anything else.

"She deserves a big love with a guy who deserves her. That's what she's always wanted. When she was little, she played bride and wedding and was Mommy to her dolls. After our parents died, she never played those games again. She was forced to grow up overnight, and the minute she was old enough, she found a guy to marry and committed to him with her whole heart, even though he never deserved her. She's the best mom ever and the absolute sweetest person I know. It's been so, so hard having to keep my distance out of fear of driving her away with my obvious, intense dislike of Gabriel."

Picturing little Isla playing dress-up as a bride gave him a warm feeling inside, until he remembered that going anywhere near a woman who'd fantasized about love and marriage was the last thing he ought to do.

"I hope she finds that. She deserves the best of everything."

"Yes, she does." After a long pause, Denny said, "I appreciate you being honest with me. I know it wasn't easy to tell me this."

"It wasn't, but I don't want trouble between us. Whatever this was has been nipped in the bud, and life will go on. Don't give it another thought, okay?"

"Yeah, okay."

"And don't say anything to her about it, please?"

Denny nodded.

"I'll see you Wednesday, then."

"See you then."

"We're all good?" Julian asked, needing to be sure.

"All good."

They headed to their vehicles.

"Hey, Julian?"

He turned back to his friend. "Yeah?"

"Has this ever happened before? Where you had to step away like this from a case?"

"Not for this reason."

"Huh. Interesting."

That wasn't the word Julian would've used to describe it, he thought as he hung his suit in the back of the G-Wagon and tossed his backpack onto the seat. Julian would've said it was shocking, unsettling and a bit... devastating. He felt the same way he had after he and Aimee broke up, which made no sense. They'd been together for three years. He'd seen Isla *three times*, for less than *two hours* total.

Make it make sense.

He drove home on autopilot, exhausted and annoyed and out of sorts like he'd been since he saw Aimee last month. That should've been a reminder of why he needed to steer clear of these sorts of things. Not that he'd gone looking for this.

Hardly.

He was almost relieved when his phone rang with a call from Griffin. "Hey."

"Jules... The kid is mine."

GRIFFIN REMINGTON HAD BEEN in complete shock since he'd received the call from McKenna's attorney letting him know the paternity test results revealed that he was her daughter's father. He had a child, and his entire world had spun out of control the second he got the news.

"Griffin."

"Yeah, I'm here," he said to Julian, who'd been his first call. His eldest brother always knew what to do.

"Where are you?"

"At home."

"I'll be right there."

"You don't have to—"

"I'm already on my way. I'll be there in twenty minutes."

Griffin put down his phone and dropped his head into his hands. *How in the hell* was it possible he had a kid and hadn't known she existed until a few days ago?

He hadn't moved when he heard his front door open and close. All his siblings had the code to his beachfront condo in Malibu, and he had codes or keys to their homes, too.

Julian landed next to him on the sofa and put his arm around Griffin's shoulders. "What can I do?"

"Tell me this is some sort of weird dream and that I don't actually have a kid?"

"Is that what you want me to say?"

He looked over at the brother who'd always been there for him and the others. Julian was usually their first call when shit went sideways, and his shit was most definitely sideways and upside down at the moment. "What am I going to *do*, Jules?"

"You're going to be a father to a child who didn't ask to be born but is here now and needs both her parents in her life."

"I'm not ready for this. I have no idea what to do with a kid."

"You'll figure it out the same way everyone else does."

He buried his head in his hands again, not wanting his brother to see the tears in his eyes. The thought of being responsible for a baby... a little girl... was terrifying. What if he screwed it up somehow?

His phone vibrated with a text.

"You're going to want to look at that," Julian said.

Griffin was almost afraid to take the phone from his brother. The message was from McKenna. *I'm sorry, Griffin. I know this isn't what you wanted. I have no idea how this could've happened. Trust me... It was as big a surprise to me as it is to you. We don't need anything from you. I just wanted you to know about her. She's the sweetest little thing. If you ever want to meet her, you know how to get in touch. Her name is Hadley Jane, and she was born on December 23 at 6:35 p.m. She was seven pounds, six ounces and nineteen inches at birth. Here are a few photos of her.*

He scrubbed at the stubble on his face, afraid to look at photos that would make her real. "Her name is Hadley Jane. McKenna sent pictures."

"Are you going to look at them?"

"Yeah." Griffin felt like he was having a heart attack, or something equally dramatic, as he called up the photos. Upon first glimpse at her tiny, precious face, the one thing that stood out to him was that she looked just like him. "Oh my God."

"She's you all over again."

The massive lump in his throat made it impossible for him to say anything. Hell, he could barely breathe as he stared at the photos. "I'm a father."

"Congratulations. I'm an uncle."

"I have a kid, Jules."

"Yes, you do. Mom is going to flip out."

Griffin grunted out a laugh. "Yeah, she is. She'll make Hadley call her Kate." Hadley. His child's name was Hadley.

Julian laughed. "No one will ever call her Granny."

When Griffin rubbed at his face again, he was surprised to find his skin wet with tears. What the hell was happening? He couldn't recall the last time he'd cried about anything. "We thought there wouldn't be any kids to call her Granny. That was the plan."

"Plans change. Shit happens." He picked up Griffin's phone and handed it to him again. "You should reply to McKenna."

"Right." He stared at the reply screen as he tried to think of what he should say.

"Tell her the baby is beautiful, which she is. Tell her you love her name. Tell her you want to meet her."

He'd never been more thankful for Julian than he was right then as he replied exactly the way his brother had suggested.

You can meet her any time. Just let me know when. She'd love to meet her daddy.

Her daddy.

He was her daddy.

Hadley's daddy.

Christ have mercy...

He was a disaster of tears and emotions he'd never experienced before. "What the hell is wrong with me?"

"You just had a baby," Julian said. "Your reaction is totally normal."

"She's really gorgeous, isn't she?"

"Despite looking like you, she is, in fact, gorgeous."

Griffin chuckled at the predictable comment. The normalness of that brought him comfort during the strangest moment of his life. "Just when you think you've got it all figured out... Not so fast."

"I know, right?"

Something about the way Julian said that had Griffin wondering what was up with him, but he didn't have the bandwidth to ask right then.

He stared at the phone screen, scrolling through the photos over and over again, his desire to see Hadley in person growing with every minute that passed. Replying to McKenna's last text, he wrote, *Would tomorrow be okay?*

She has a doctor's appointment with shots that'll make her cranky tomorrow, so Friday would be better. What time is good?

He started to say after work, but stopped himself, realizing he wouldn't be able to think about work or anything else until he'd met his daughter. *Would eleven be okay?*

Noon would be better. She'll be up from her morning nap by then.

Noon it is. Same address as before?

Yes.

See you then.

"Friday at noon."

"Do you want me to go with you?"

"Thank you for offering, but you don't have to. I can handle it."

"Are you sure?"

Griffin nodded. "I appreciate you coming when I called. It really helped to have you here when I saw pictures for the first time."

"I'm glad I was here, too. Congratulations, bro."

"Thank you," Griffin said with a laugh. "I think."

"It'll be okay. I promise."

Since Julian had never broken a promise to him, Griffin took his brother's words to heart as he counted down to noon on Friday when he would meet his daughter.

CHAPTER FIFTEEN

Following Julian's decision to hand her case off to his brother, Isla discovered that Jackson was an excellent attorney and was great about keeping her updated. From him, she learned that Gabriel had declined medical attention and had posted bail—again.

From him, she learned that Gabriel had been served with divorce papers and had tried to beat up the process server, leading to him being arrested—again.

And from Jackson, she learned that Gabriel had collapsed in jail and had been rushed to Cedars-Sinai's emergency department, where he was being evaluated.

She began to wish that Jackson was a little less good at his job as each update was tougher to hear than the one before.

Hanging over everything was the pervasive sadness she'd felt since Julian had exited her life, taking with him the one thing, other than her babies, that'd given her some joy in the midst of chaos. She missed him, which made no sense whatsoever. She barely knew him.

When she updated Denny on the latest news, he'd come over with pizza for her and the kids, giving her a shoulder to lean on.

"I don't understand anything anymore," Isla told her brother. "What is happening with Gabriel, how can I miss a man I met three times, how is all of this going to shake out, and what does it all mean?"

"The man you met three times..."

"Julian. He made an impact."

Denny took a sip of the beer he'd brought with the pizza and salad that Isla was picking at. "Did he?"

She nodded. "As if I'm in any position to be impacted by a guy when my husband is getting himself arrested three times in a week."

"He's about to be your ex-husband."

"Right. It's over. It has been for a long time. But I still shouldn't be thinking about someone else when all this is going on."

"He's thinking about you, too."

Denny's words hit her like a lightning bolt from above. "What?" she said softly.

"You heard me."

"He's thinking about me?"

"Yes."

"He quit me like a bad habit!"

"Not because he wanted to."

"What does that mean, Denny?"

"He quit your case because of ethical concerns."

"He said he has a big trial..."

"Maybe he does, but that's not why he left your case."

"Will you please tell me what you're talking about and not one sentence at a time?"

"He left the case because he's attracted to you, and because of that, he can't represent you without risking his career."

It would be strange to say at that juncture that nothing had ever shocked her more, because she'd had some pretty big shocks in her life, but this one was right up there at the top of the list.

"W-why didn't he just say so?"

"Several reasons. One, you're not exactly free and clear for a guy to state his intentions. Two, he's very determined to remain single and unencumbered, and you're rather encumbered." He glanced at the kids, who were playing with Theo's trucks in the living room while she and Denny sat at the kitchen counter. "Third, he had no idea what I'd think of it until I told him I thought he'd be great for you."

"You told him *what*?"

"Just what I said. Problem is, I don't think it's a good idea."

She didn't want to ask. She really didn't. But curiosity would make her crazy. "Why do you say that?"

"The guy doesn't do relationships. He's had one girlfriend in all the years I've known him. Everything else has been… transactional."

"Why is he like that?"

"Two reasons. One, he dismantles marriages for a living, and two, his parents went through one of the nastiest divorces in human history, dragging him and his eight siblings through hell for a decade while they fought over them. You don't remember it being on TV?"

"Not really. I wasn't paying much attention to anything but my own life back then."

Isla couldn't believe what Denny was telling her. Julian Remington had been so attracted to her that he'd bowed out of her case because he'd had to for ethical reasons. But he also had no intention of doing anything about that attraction because he didn't do relationships.

"Why are you telling me this?" she asked Denny. "What good does it do for me to know this when there's nothing I can do about it?"

"Who says there's nothing you can do about it?"

"You just said he wouldn't be good for me."

"Maybe you could be the one to crack the code with him."

"Because that'd be a great thing for me to get into after this mess with Gabriel."

Denny shrugged. "You never know what might be possible. From what I can see, you both had the same reaction to each other, which is a pretty good place to start."

"Why are you encouraging this?"

"I like him. I trust him. He's an incredibly successful, smart, stable, cool dude, and he's crazy talented. Plays the guitar and the bass and has an awesome voice. I've known him half my life, and I've never seen him be anything other than an upstanding kind of guy. If I had to trust my sister to anyone, I'd want it to be someone like him. That is... If he wasn't bound and determined to stay away from cozy domestic situations like you and your sweet little kids."

"We are not a *situation*," Isla said indignantly.

"To him, you are."

Isla thought about all that for a few minutes as she sipped her wine. Then she reached for her phone and opened a text to Julian.

I've been obsessively listening to the music you sent. I listened to "Our House" a hundred times. I could picture the cozy scene in a little house with a fireplace, the cats, the love... The other one I've been listening to on repeat is "When Will I Be Loved" by Linda Ronstadt. I can really relate to that one, especially lately. Thank you for introducing me to Laurel Canyon's musical history. I've really been missing out.

"What're you doing?" Denny asked.

"Texting him."

"About what?"

"Music."

Denny chuckled. "You've already got him figured out."

"Not yet, but I'd like to find out more."

"Just be careful. Remember what I said. He's not a forever kinda guy."

"Maybe not, but he could be a 'for now' kinda guy to get me back on my feet after a huge disappointment."

"That kind of situationship is his specialty."

"The fact that you trust and respect him means a lot."

"I hope I don't regret telling you this."

"I'm in the no-regrets part of the program. Don't worry. I can handle him."

Denny muttered something that sounded like, "I sure as hell hope so."

Before she could confirm what he'd said, her phone rang with a call from Jackson. "I have to take this. It's my new attorney." She pushed the green button. "Hi, Jackson."

"Isla... I heard from Gabriel's attorney that he's been diagnosed with a serious illness. He's asking for you."

The bottom fell out of her stomach. "What kind of serious illness?"

"The lawyer wasn't at liberty to tell me the details due to HIPAA regulations. Are you able to go to Cedars on Beverly Boulevard?"

"I, um, yes, I will. Thank you for calling."

"Of course. Let me know if you need anything."

"I will. Thank you again."

Her hands were trembling as she ended the call and updated Denny.

"I can stay with the kids while you go."

"Are you sure?"

"I am. Go ahead."

She kissed Denny's cheek and ran to the bedroom to change her clothes, brush her hair and teeth and find her keys.

Then she told the kids she had to go out for a little while, and Uncle Denny was going to stay with them. They were thrilled by that news because Denny was always willing to get on the floor and play with them.

"I'm scared," she whispered to her brother. "What now?"

"Go find out. It may explain some things."

"Yeah, maybe." She was filled with dread over what she might hear at the hospital and how it might change her life as well as Gabriel's. "I'll call you as soon as I know anything."

"I'll be waiting to hear." He gave her a hug. "Drive carefully."

On the way to Cedars, she focused only on driving and tried not to think about what this could be about. There was no sense in speculating and making herself crazier with theories. It could be anything at this point.

At the reception desk inside the main entrance, she asked for Gabriel and was directed to a room on the fourth floor. In the elevator, she stared straight ahead and tried to force breath past the weight in her chest. Outside his room, she took another deep breath and released it slowly, preparing herself to see him for the first time since he'd destroyed their home.

Isla was surprised to find an older couple, people she'd never met, standing next to Gabriel's bed, watching over him. Gabriel's curly, dark blond hair hadn't seen a comb in days. He had deep, dark circles under his eyes and a bruise on his cheek.

He extended his hand to her. "Isla."

She approached his bed but didn't take the hand he offered.

"These are my parents, Ramon and Maggie. Mom, Dad, this is my wife, Isla."

"Oh, um, it's nice to finally meet you," Isla said, feeling as if she were living in some sort of surreal universe.

"You, as well," Maggie said tearfully. "Gabriel has told us all about you and your children. They're absolutely beautiful."

What the hell was happening? Gabriel hadn't spoken to his parents or siblings in more than ten years after a falling-out he'd refused to talk to her about

"I... I called them because... Isla... I have a brain tumor. They say it's benign but inoperable at this point. I don't have a lot of time left, so I asked my parents to come."

"We've made arrangements to bring him home with us on hospice care," Ramon said.

Isla stared at the man she'd loved and married and had two children with, blindsided by this news.

"I signed the divorce papers so you can be free of me."

"A brain tumor," she said softly.

Tears filled his golden-brown eyes, Theo's eyes, as he nodded. "I'm sorry I didn't listen to you when you begged me to see a doctor. The tumor... It's the kind that affects personality and judgment, and it's the reason why... I'm sorry. For everything."

At long last, an explanation, albeit a devastating one.

"They think it started as long as fifteen years ago," Maggie said. "It's explained a lot to us, as well."

"They've got me on something that has me thinking clearer than I have in years, but they told us it won't last. That's why I asked you to come. I wanted to see you before..."

"I, uh... I don't know what to say."

"You don't have to say anything. I've put you through hell, and I want you to move on with your life. And the kids... I love them so much, but I don't want them to see me like this." His voice caught on a sob. "It wouldn't be fair to them. They're too little to understand."

He reached for her hand again, and this time, she let him.

"I'm so, so sorry for everything," he said. "I didn't know what was happening to me, and I was so scared. Rather than find out, I... I'll always be sorry that I did this to us."

Isla wiped away a tear. "You're sick. It's not your fault."

"Don't let me off the hook. If I'd listened to you, things might've been different."

His mother wept silently as she watched over him.

Isla couldn't imagine what she must be feeling and hoped to never find out.

"When it's over, I want the kids to see my parents, okay?"

"Yes, of course."

"Gabriel gave us your number," Maggie said. "We'll keep in touch."

"Okay." Isla had no idea what to do or say or feel. Nothing in her life could've prepared her for something like this.

"The signed papers are there, on the tray."

She looked to where he pointed.

"You were a perfect wife and mother. I never deserved you."

"That's not true."

"It is true." He kissed the back of her hand. "I want you to be happy. I want the kids to be happy. Do that for me, will you?"

"Gabriel." A sob erupted from her chest as she leaned over to hug him, trying to accept that this could be the last time she ever saw him.

"I love you, Isla. I always have, and I always will."

She didn't love him anymore and hadn't for a long time, but she considered the words her final gift to him. "I love you, too. The kids love you so much."

"I hope they remember the good things."

"I'll make sure they do."

"That's more than I deserve from you."

"No."

He ran his fingers through her hair the way he used to after they'd made love. The memories of that sweetness resurfaced from the deepest part of her consciousness. It'd been so long since she'd thought of him as sweet or kind. "You can go, Isla, and don't ever feel guilty about anything, okay? None of this was your fault."

"Thank you for my babies. I'll take good care of them."

"I know you will. They're lucky to have you. I was lucky, too."

She had no idea how long she stayed like that, leaning over him, his arm around her as he told her again and again how much he'd always loved her while his parents sobbed. How sad for them to get him back right when he'd be leaving forever.

How sad for all of them.

"Go on and live your life, Isla. It's okay. Everything is okay."

No, it wasn't, but his final gift to her was setting her free, and she'd always be thankful to him for that.

She raised her head off his chest and looked at him, studying the face she'd fallen in love with so many years ago, committing every detail to memory, including the scar that ran through his right eyebrow and the bump in his nose from it being broken while playing high school football. Someday, she'd tell her kids the story of how he'd gotten the eyebrow scar from a snowball with a rock in it that his cousin had thrown at him, thinking it'd be funny.

"Godspeed, Gabriel. I'll pray for you."

"Thank you for that. For everything."

She kissed him one last time, for all the good times, and stood upright, feeling like she'd been knocked off her feet.

"We'll be in touch," Maggie said as she wiped at tears.

Isla nodded, and with one last glance at Gabriel, she left the room. On the way to the elevator, it began to set in that she'd probably never see him again, and she began to cry again. Yesterday, that would've been the best news she could've gotten. Today, knowing what she did now, it was devastating.

In her car, she sat for a long time, staring straight ahead, blinded by tears that wouldn't stop.

Gabriel had a brain tumor and was going to die.

Probably soon.

She'd left the divorce papers on the tray table, because what did it matter now?

She wiped her face with her sleeve.

Her phone rang, and she took the call from Denny.

"What's going on? Are you okay?"

"Not at all okay." She filled him in on what she'd learned at the hospital. "He's going home with his parents on hospice."

"Oh my God. Isla..."

"I know. I can't believe it. They said he's probably had it for at least fifteen years."

"How is it possible he had something like that and didn't know it?"

"I have no idea, but it explains everything, including the estrangement from his parents."

"Maybe he did know and didn't want to deal with it."

"Possibly."

"How do you feel now that there's an explanation for everything?"

"I'm numb. I can't believe he's going to die, or that all of this might've been preventable if only..."

"That's so sad. Wow. What can I do for you?"

"I have no idea."

"Are you okay to drive home?"

"I think so."

"If you're not, get an Uber. We'll get your car tomorrow."

"I can drive."

"Okay. I'll be here waiting for you to get home."

"Thank you, Denny, for everything. Always."

"I love you, kid. You're stuck with me."

She was crying so hard, she couldn't speak.

"Islands... please take your time and be careful driving."

"Uh-huh, I will."

Isla waited until she was sure she could drive safely and stayed in the right lane all the way home, looking straight ahead and trying not to think about anything other than getting to her babies in one piece.

She was all they had now.

Even though that'd been true from the minute Gabriel destroyed their home, it felt more real now that she knew he was never coming back.

He was thirty-six years old and going to die.

By the time she pulled into the driveway at the rental, her entire body was trembling, and her teeth were chattering.

Denny came out of the house, opened the car door, helped her out and into his embrace. "I'm here. I've got you."

The second she was safe in his arms, Isla wailed. No other word could describe the way she let go of the myriad emotions she'd kept bottled up inside for years. She and her brother stood there in the dark for a long time, him consoling her while she cried harder than she had since they lost their parents so suddenly.

In many ways, this reminded her of that terrible time, when she and Denny had clung to each other in the aftermath of disaster.

At some point, he guided her into the house, closed the door and locked it before helping her out of her coat and onto the sofa. He put a blanket over her and then went into the kitchen, returning with a cup of tea made just the way she liked it, with a little bit of milk and some honey.

"Thank you."

"I wish there was more that I could do."

"This is what I need right now, my big brother making me tea and telling me it's going to be okay."

"As awful as it is right now, it will be okay, eventually. You and I know that all too well, don't we?"

She nodded and took a sip of tea. "I haven't cried like that since then."

"I hope you never have a reason to cry like that again. You've already had far more than your share of reasons to cry."

"This is just unbelievable. I mean... I suspected something was medically wrong with him, but he refused to seek treatment, so there was nothing I could do. To find out it was something that was slowly killing him and stealing all the things that made him who he was..."

"It is unbelievable, like something you'd read about in *People* magazine."

"I'm comforted to know that the violent stuff wasn't because he hated me or wanted to hurt me and the kids."

"Yeah, definitely. I couldn't reconcile the way he professed to love you guys with all his heart and then burned through your money and made you so afraid of him you built a shelter for you and the kids. I'll never get over you doing that."

"I had a feeling I'd need it." She looked over at Denny, who was nursing a beer. "Did I do the right thing letting his parents take him home for hospice? Shouldn't it be me seeing him through that?"

"No, it shouldn't be you. He called his parents because he didn't want to put you through that after everything else that's already happened. He wants you to take care of yourself and the kids and start building a new life. That's why he called them and not you when he got this news."

"He said he wanted that for me. And the kids. How will I ever explain this to Theo? He's been asking for Gabriel every day."

"You tell him the truth, that Daddy got very sick. Maybe you even wait until the time comes when you can say he went to heaven, so Theo won't ask to see him."

"Is it wrong not to let him see Gabriel?"

"I don't think so. He's so little. How would he ever understand it?"

She brushed away more tears. "All I ever wanted for my kids was a safe, happy, joyful childhood."

"And they'll have that with you, Islands. They will."

Isla dropped her head onto her brother's shoulder, the way she'd been doing for as long as it'd been the two of them against the world.

"I wish you'd told me sooner how bad it had gotten."

"I didn't want anyone to know, especially you, because you told me not to marry him."

"I never should've said that. It wasn't up to me to tell you who to marry."

"Who else would tell me the truth, if not you? I didn't want to hear it. I was in love."

"I know. I'm sorry it worked out this way. I never wanted that. I hope you know... I only ever wanted the best of everything for you."

"Of course I know that. Thank you for always protecting me—and my money."

Denny chuckled. "I've felt so guilty about that."

"You did the right thing. He would've blown through it for sure, but at least now we know why he'd have done that."

"Do you feel better knowing why things happened the way they did?"

"I guess so. I just wish he'd listened to me when I said he needed to go to the doctor to figure out what was going on. He refused to acknowledge that anything was wrong."

"Because he couldn't tell that from the inside," Denny said. "It probably seemed normal to him if the tumor was affecting his judgment."

"I suppose that's true."

"You must be exhausted."

"I am, but I'm not sure I could sleep."

"You should try. The kids will be up and at it early."

"Yes, they will."

"Go ahead. I'll crash on the sofa so I'm here if you need me."

"You don't have to do that. I'm okay. I swear. Go home and get some good sleep."

"Are you sure?"

"I am. Thank you for everything."

He helped her up and then hugged her. "Always."

Isla walked him to the door and waved him off before locking up and shutting off the outside lights. She checked on her sleeping babies, kissed them and tucked them in before heading to her room to change into her favorite flannel pajamas. Even though it was in the sixties outside, she was chilled to the bone.

Having experienced shock before, she recognized it for what it was—a full-body experience.

When she was in bed, she checked her phone for the first time in hours and found a text from Jackson Remington.

Checking in to see how it went at the hospital and if there's anything you need. I heard from Gabriel's attorney that he signed the papers, which is good news.

Thank you for checking on me. The news at the hospital was devastating. Gabriel has an advanced brain tumor and is entering hospice at his parents' home. Apparently, this is the reason for his erratic behavior and poor judgment. Needless to say, this news has hit me hard. He told me he signed the papers, but I left them there, since there's no point in continuing the divorce proceeding.

Jackson wrote back a few minutes later. *I'm so sorry, Isla. I can't imagine how hard it must've been to hear that news. If there's anything we can do to help, please don't hesitate to reach out.*

Thank you so much, Jackson. I appreciate your kind words.

Isla put her phone on the charger and shut off the light. For a long time, she lay awake thinking about Gabriel and her time with him. With the benefit of hindsight, there were signs from the start that something was "off." She'd chalked it up to eccentricity and had always thought he was more interesting than any other guy she'd ever met. Now that she knew the truth, she could see that nothing had added up like it should have.

Perhaps she'd been so desperate to create a family of her

own after losing her parents so tragically that she'd ignored things that should've been red flags.

But she could never regret her time with Gabriel, because it had brought her beautiful kids into her life, and they were the greatest gifts she'd ever been given.

If she kept her focus on them, she might just survive this latest catastrophe.

CHAPTER SIXTEEN

Julian stared at the text from Isla for so long, his eyes watered. Was she sending him some sort of subliminal message with her song choices? Why was it that he could picture that cozy little scene from "Our House" with her staring at the fire for hours and hours next to him on the sofa while he played love songs for her? Why did he ache at the simple sweetness of the scene with the two of them playing the central characters?

He was losing control of his emotions, which normally would terrify him. But with her, he couldn't bring himself to care as he wrote back to her.

I've got a whole lot of love songs I could play for you next to that cozy fireplace. Let me know when and where. I'll bring the firewood.

Before he pressed send, he read and reread the message. If he sent it, he'd be opening a door to something he'd spent his entire adult life trying to avoid. Who was he kidding? She'd thrown that door wide open just by walking into his office and saying hello. It also wasn't lost on him that if she was sending him not-so-subliminal messages, Denny must've told her why he moved her case to Jackson's care, which meant his friend approved.

Julian sent the message.

And then he waited.

And waited.

And waited.

But it never showed that she'd read it.

He thought about reaching out to Denny to check on her, but did one unanswered text warrant such a dramatic response?

He hoped she was okay and was disappointed that he hadn't heard back from her. Maybe her kids had needed her, or she'd crashed early for the night.

Anything was possible.

And he needed to stop acting like a sixth grader in the throes of first love, watching his phone like it was the most important thing ever invented.

He put the phone on the charger and went to bed but tossed and turned as he wondered why she hadn't read his text and replied.

It was probably because he'd taken her commentary about the music and turned it into something she didn't want.

"For fuck's sake," he said to the dark room. "Stop acting like an idiot and go the hell to sleep so you can function tomorrow."

The tossing and turning continued for most of the night, until his alarm provided a rude awakening. His first move was to check his phone. Nothing from Isla, but he had a text from Jackson.

Isla's husband is in the hospital. His lawyer said it's serious. He asked for Isla last night, and she went. He has a brain tumor that's caused all the behavioral issues. His parents are back in the picture and taking him home on hospice.

"Oh my God," he said as he reread Jackson's message.

Julian wanted to go to her, to offer comfort and anything

else she wanted or needed. The need to be there for her was so great, he had to actively talk himself out of going right to her house. The last thing she needed in light of this new catastrophe was him coming around looking like an opportunist in the midst of her tragedy.

But, oh, how he wanted to go to her.

He had another full day ahead of him, but none of that mattered as the biggest internal struggle he'd experienced in years raged inside him.

Go to her. Go to her. Go to her.
Do not go to her. Do not go to her. Do not go to her.
Go to her. Go to her. Go to her.

Julian had to force himself through the motions of getting ready for work—knot tie, don suit jacket, tie shoelaces, go downstairs, get keys, leave house, drive by Isla's street without looking her way, stop for coffee, go to office. If he stayed focused on each task as it stood before him, he could resist the maddening desire that pounded through him like an extra heartbeat. Since he was starting to run late, he'd text Denny to check on her as soon as he got the chance.

At the office, Julian said, "Good morning," to Hector and handed Mattie her latte like it was any other day, even as the storm continued to rage inside him. What Isla was going through had nothing at all to do with him, and he needed to stay the hell away from her.

Keep telling yourself that until you listen to your own advice.

Mattie brought her coffee with her when she came into his office to go over the schedule. "Everything all right?"

"Yes, let's get to it."

She gave him the rundown of client appointments, Smithson trial prep with Jackson, who'd be his second chair, and a late-day court appearance on behalf of Beverly Hills grandparents seeking visitation with their young grandson.

Just another day in family law paradise, dealing with people who'd once loved each other warring over money and possessions and children who were treated more like commodities than human beings.

Some days, like today, the entire business turned his stomach.

Mattie ran through his packed schedule for the day. "Julian, are you listening to me, honey?"

"Yes."

"No, you're not. You're a million miles from Wilshire Boulevard. What's the matter?"

"Nothing. I'm fine."

"You can lie to some people, but never to Ms. Mattie. I know my boy. Something is weighing heavy on your heart."

He made a face at her. "I wish I worked somewhere that no one knew me outside of work."

"Well, today is not that day, young man, so why don't you tell me what's wrong so we can find a way to fix it? And while you're at it, wipe that scowl off your handsome face. It'll give you wrinkles."

Julian laughed at that last part.

"What's wrong, sweetheart?"

"There's a woman."

Her brows lifted in surprise because he never talked to her about women. "Is there now? Tell Mattie everything and leave nothing out."

"We're at work, not a middle school cafeteria."

She waved away the comment. "Speak."

"It's ridiculous. Not worth our time."

"Julian Michael Remington, in all the years I've known you, I've never once seen you in a dither over a woman, so whatever's going on, it must be a big deal. Pretending otherwise will only make everything worse."

"What even is a dither?"

"Stop stalling and start talking."

"I've met her *three* times. It's nothing."

"Oh, my darling, is that what you're telling yourself? How's that working out?"

"Your sarcasm will be remembered on your next performance evaluation."

Her left brow lifted toward her hairline. "The one I write for you because you can't bear to evaluate the best assistant you'll ever have?"

"Yes, that one."

She laughed. "Talk to me, honey. Tell me what's going on. I want to help."

Because she'd never breathe a word of anything he told her, and he knew she wouldn't give up until he told her the truth, he said, "It's my friend Denny's sister, Isla, who was here the other day."

"*Oh.*" Mattie sat back in her chair as she smiled. "She's *lovely* and such a wonderful mother. Those kids were sweet as could be and so polite."

"I had the strangest reaction to her."

Her eyes went wide all of a sudden. "*That's* why you turned her case over to Jackson? Oh my heavens. This is serious!"

"No, it isn't. It's not serious, and it's never going to be. It was a momentary distraction. I'm dealing with it."

"Are you?"

"I am."

"How are you dealing with it?"

Julian glanced her way. "By pretending everything is fine when I've been told she's going through something major, and it has nothing to do with me, even if all I want to do is go to her and offer to help in any way I can. Since I can't do that, I'm here, and it'd be good to get to work so I can think about something other than what she's dealing with and how incredibly upset she must be."

"Oh, honey... What a dilemma."

"It is indeed, but I'm staying put. I'll let Denny know I'm here if they need anything, and I'll get on with my day."

"I'll leave you to it and remind you I'm right outside the door if you need me."

"I take great comfort in that every day, but especially on days like today."

She stood to leave. "Point of order, Counselor. There's *never* been a day like today."

After dropping that truth bomb, she left the room and closed the door behind her.

Julian took the time to text Denny to say he'd heard that Isla's husband was ill and that he hoped she was doing okay.

Then he forced himself to give work his full attention, beginning with a call to Carson about how he was making out with finding Cresley's ex.

"Hey, man, I was just going to call you. This guy Beckett is a piece of work."

"How so?"

"He's actively dealing something... Not sure if it's meth or coke or possibly heroin, but he's not even trying to be sly about it. He's just going about his business like it's totally legal and nothing to see here."

"Jeez."

"He's also keeping tabs on her and the kid."

"What do you mean?"

"He's watching the school and the house, following her when she leaves. You know, the usual stalker stuff. I'll send you a full report by the end of the day, but you need to get this guy into court ASAP and slap him with an RO."

"Your thoughts mirror mine. Thanks, Carson."

"You got it."

Julian ended that call and sent Jackson a message, asking him to schedule an emergency hearing in Cresley's case.

Then he called her and got her voicemail. "Hey, it's Julian Remington. I have some updates for you, one of which is that

Marlon is following you, so I have to urge you to be cautious. Don't let on that you see him, and if you feel unsafe in any way, contact the police right away. Give me a call when you can. Thanks."

He hated having to leave a message like that on her voicemail, but he wanted her to know as soon as possible what Marlon was doing.

His phone vibrated with a text from Denny. *Dude... he's got a brain tumor that's going to kill him. Soon. Isla is shocked, of course, and sad that he didn't listen to her and others who urged him to seek medical care. He called the parents he hadn't spoken to in years, and they're taking him home on hospice. Effed-up situation all around.*

Julian read the text twice, trying to process what Denny was telling him.

It was the reason for the behavior that'd ruined his marriage and cost him his job and his relationship with his parents.

What the hell kind of tumor caused all that chaos?

A few minutes on Google taught him about benign meningiomas that often formed on the frontal lobes, causing changes in personality, irregular social behavior and loss of inhibitions, among other things. If left untreated, they could become life-threatening.

He had no way to know if that's what Gabriel had, but it must be something like that if he'd had it so long and was now going to die from it.

He felt sick for Isla and her poor kids. What a heartbreaking situation for them.

Julian realized he was rubbing the area over his heart, which ached for her. While she finally had an explanation, it had come with a terminal diagnosis.

Mattie buzzed his desk phone to tell him his client had arrived for their nine o'clock meeting in conference room four.

"I'll be right there." He tried to shake off the emotional

turmoil, reminding himself that Isla's tragedy had nothing to do with him. They barely knew each other.

Perhaps this was the sign he'd needed to rein this thing in before it got further out of control. He was a big believer in signs from the universe and had rarely ignored one as blatant as this one. There was a reason he'd steered clear of romantic complications his whole life, and this situation had become as complicated as it could get.

He stood, stretched, grabbed his notes for the client meeting and took his coffee with him when he left the office, nodding to Mattie as he made his way to the conference room to get on with his day.

ISLA HAD BEEN AWAKE all night, reliving every minute with Gabriel from the day they met to the devastating hospital visit. Even though everything made sense now, it didn't change anything for her or the kids. Their lives had been nearly destroyed by a battle they hadn't even known they were fighting. If only he'd listened to her years ago and sought medical attention for the wild personality swings, everything could've been different for them.

Maybe he'd known it was something awful, and that's why he'd ignored the troubling symptoms.

The last few years ran through her mind like a horror movie with occasional glimpses of the true love that'd once made him essential to her. His disappearances, the unpredictable moods, the violent outbursts, the cutting words... Without the resources to change their circumstances, she'd been forced to adapt within the hellish bubble of their dysfunctional marriage.

In the days since she'd left the home they'd shared, she'd felt like she was coming off a years-long bender, sobering up for the first time to meet her new reality as a single mother of two young children who'd be looking to her to figure out a way forward for all of them. Coming down from the endless heightened state of alert, always gearing up for trouble she couldn't see coming until he was right in front of her, would take time and patience.

It would also take time to stop blaming herself for things that'd been so far outside her control. No, she couldn't have left sooner, because she hadn't had thousands of dollars sitting around to make it possible to leave—and she'd refused to let her brother bail her out of a situation he'd told her not to get into in the first place. No, she couldn't have called the police, because then she'd have had to fear he'd be released and come right back home, looking for vengeance. She'd been trapped in a nightmare, and no amount of Monday-morning quarterbacking or learning the true cause of his actions would change what'd been a terrifying reality for her.

She got up with the kids, went through the usual motions of snuggling and soothing and making breakfast for them when her heart had been shattered into a million pieces. As soon as she was sure Mrs. V would be awake, she called her.

"Oh, hi, honey. I was going to call you this morning to see how you're doing. I miss having you right next door."

"Something has happened." She filled her friend in on what she'd learned at the hospital.

"Good Lord. All this time, and he had no idea?"

"No, because he refused to see a doctor. My theory is that he was afraid of what they might say. It had to be terrifying for him."

"I never thought I'd feel sympathy for him after everything he's done, but here we are."

"I know. Same." She tried to contain the sob that snuck out anyway. "It's so terribly sad."

"I'm coming over. I'll stay with you and the kids for as long as you need me."

"You don't have to do that."

"Let me help, Isla. You need some space to breathe, and

you can't do that with two little ones clinging to you. I want to help."

"I'd love to have you here with us."

"I'm on my way."

"Thank you so much."

"I love you all, and we'll get through this together. I'll see you soon."

Isla was so thankful to her friend for realizing she was drowning. At some point over the last few years, Mrs. V had become like a mother to her and a grandmother to the kids, and she needed someone to lean on right now. Her parents had been gone so long, she barely remembered what it'd been like to have them around. Thanks to Mrs. V, the aching loss was a little less painful than it'd been before she'd come into Isla's life.

True to her word, Mrs. V arrived an hour and a half later, pulling a suitcase behind her and carrying grocery bags.

The kids shrieked with delight at seeing her and showered her with hugs and kisses that made the older woman laugh with delight. "Did you guys grow a foot since I last saw you?"

"We can't grow that fast!" Theo said, laughing.

Isla was so relieved to see her friend and to hear her little boy laugh. She wiped away new tears that refused to quit, even as she tried to hide them from the kids.

"Mommy is sad," Theo said.

"I know, sweetie," Mrs. V said. "Sometimes even mommies get sad, but she'll be okay because we love her so much, and we'll take very good care of her, right?"

"Right!"

After Theo ran off to play with his toys, Isla sat with Mrs. V on the sofa, holding her hand and resting her head on the other woman's shoulder.

"I still can't believe this news," Mrs. V said. "I've been reeling since you called."

"I know. It's hard to believe."

"How do you feel about him calling his parents and going home with them?"

"I think it was the right thing. I'd rather not have the kids witness his decline, and after everything that's happened, I'm not sure I'd have it in me to care for him like that. I mean, I'd do it if he'd wanted me to, but he made it clear he didn't. I'm kind of glad I don't have to. And just saying that out loud makes me feel horrible and guilty."

"Don't feel guilty. Even though we know why now, that man still put you through a hellish ordeal, and knowing the reason doesn't change the reality you endured. You owe him nothing."

"I met his parents for the first time last night."

"Doesn't that tell you everything you need to know about how you were always fighting a force bigger than you?"

"I guess so, but it's still so shocking and devastating that he's going to die. Like he's actually going to *die*."

"I'm so sorry for all of you. It's a terrible tragedy, but Isla, I want you to hear me on this. He let this happen to himself by ignoring everyone who pleaded with him to get help. Even I did once."

"You did? You never told me."

"Because it went in one ear and out the other, but I begged him to think of you and the kids and do whatever it took to get well for you guys."

"What did he say?"

"That he was fine and didn't know what I was talking about. Then he said it would be best if I minded my own business."

"Ugh," Isla said with a grunt of dismay. "I'm sorry he spoke to you that way. He knew what you mean to me and the kids."

"Did he, though? Who knows what he understood or didn't understand?"

"That's true." She released a deep sigh. "Thank you so much for coming. I feel much better now that you're here."

"I'll stay for as long as you need me."

"That's apt to be a minute."

"Luckily, all my minutes are mine to do with as I please, and right now, I want to be right here with you and our babies."

"Love you," Isla whispered.

"Love you more."

CHAPTER SEVENTEEN

Griffin shifted his schedule for Friday to his brother Ethan, who was his associate, to give himself an unexpected day off.

To meet his daughter.

He ran a trembling hand through hair that was already standing straight up and tried to calm himself as he stepped into the shower.

Ethan had been pissed with the last-minute disruption to Griffin's schedule that would make for a hell day for Ethan, but hopefully, he'd understand when he found out the real reason Griffin had taken the day off.

Not once in his entire life had he ever imagined what it might be like to have kids, because he'd never expected to have them. He had no freaking clue what to even do with a kid since he'd rarely been around them once his younger siblings had grown up.

What the hell was he going to do with a little girl?

The thought of being responsible for her made him weak in the knees as he combed wet hair before getting dressed in jeans and a Henley pullover. What did a guy wear to meet his kid for the first time, anyway?

His phone rang with a call from Julian.

"Hey."

"How're you holding up?"

"I'm spinning."

"Take a breath and calm down. It's going to be fine. It's a baby, not a bomb."

"Feels like a bomb going off in my life."

"It is, but everyone will be okay. I promise."

"Easy for you to say when you didn't just become a father without the usual nine months' notice."

"I'm not saying it'll be easy. Take it one minute at a time and send pictures."

"I will. Thanks for calling, Jules."

"Of course. You've got this, Griff. Remember, one minute at a time."

"Got it."

"And don't forget to take pictures."

"I won't."

He felt better after talking to Julian, which wasn't unusual. His eldest brother had always been there for him—for all of them. He wasn't the only one who went running to Julian any time something went sideways.

Did finding out you had a baby you didn't know about count as something going sideways? How about if her mother was the one woman who'd managed to crack your resolve to stay stubbornly single? Julian didn't know that part. No one did, or how he'd run away from her like his ass was on fire when he realized he'd developed feelings for her.

And now he had to see her—and the child they'd created together. Was it any wonder he was freaking the fuck out?

At eleven fifteen, he left his condo in Malibu to drive south to Santa Monica in his Chevy Silverado 1500 High Country, counting on the midday traffic to be lighter than it would be later in the day. Thinking about traffic was easier than trying to anticipate what was waiting for him at the other end of this short drive.

McKenna had been different from the start. Not only was she gorgeous and sexy as all hell, with curly light blonde hair and hazel eyes, but she was the funniest person he'd ever dated. She was a flight attendant who dabbled in acting and was away a lot, so the relationship, such as it was, had worked out well for him as he'd still had plenty of time to surf and see his friends and family. They'd done nothing but laugh—and screw—for months before he'd gotten scared of the emotional overload and headed for the hills.

He'd hurt her with his sudden withdrawal, and he hated that he'd done that to her, but one day, he'd woken up to the fact that she was becoming essential to him and decided he couldn't let that happen. It wouldn't be much consolation to her to hear that he'd suffered through genuine heartbreak for the first time in his life after walking away from her, or that his decision had screwed him up for months after.

It was no wonder she hadn't told him about the baby until she was born, or that she'd engaged a lawyer to reach out to him rather than texting him the news. She had no reason to have an ounce of faith in him after the way he'd behaved. Not to mention, knowing he was a family law attorney, she was probably afraid of what he might do next. Not that she had any reason to be afraid of him wanting custody of her child. He didn't.

So in addition to the considerable anxiety about meeting his daughter, he was also mortified about the chickenshit way he'd treated her mother.

Good times.

The vow they'd taken to stay single, so they'd never be part of a nasty split like their parents', had been easy enough to stick to until he'd met McKenna and had to reckon with the reality of letting go of someone he truly cared about. Steering clear of the kinds of nightmares they saw every day in their practice had turned out to be harder than expected when real feelings were involved.

But he'd done what he had to do, and now...

Today, he'd face the consequences in more ways than one. Considering the way he'd walked away from her, he was lucky she was allowing him to visit her home or meet their daughter.

Needing comfort wherever he could find it, he put down the window to let in the salt-air scent that always soothed him. The sound of gulls squawking as they went about their scavenging further calmed the rampaging emotions. He'd give anything to be spending this day surfing rather than having to face a woman he'd treated badly and the baby they'd made together.

Guilt, embarrassment, anticipation and curiosity were all present as he pushed the button on the panel outside her building to announce his arrival. "Hey, it's Griffin."

"Come on up."

How strange it was to hear her voice again after trying so hard to forget her. The woman who answered the door at apartment 4B bore little resemblance to the polished, put-together professional he'd met at a cocktail party in town. This version of McKenna wore no makeup, her hair was in a ponytail, and she had on a long-sleeved T-shirt with sweats, and somehow, she was even more beautiful than he recalled. There was a radiant, joyful aura to her that hadn't been there before, and he wondered if that had come from motherhood. If so, it looked good on her.

"Come in." She stepped back to admit him into the warm, cozy space he'd enjoyed so much when they were together. He'd enjoyed it too much, which had led to his retreat.

"You look great, Mac."

Grimacing, she said, "That's nice of you to say. Having a baby is tough stuff."

"You've never been more beautiful."

"It's okay. You don't have to say what you think I need to hear."

"It's the truth."

"Thank you. Hadley is just waking up. You can come in to see her room, if you'd like."

"I'm nervous about meeting her."

She glanced at him over her shoulder. "Why?"

"What if she takes one look at me and says, 'Nah'?"

"When was the last time a woman took one look at you and said, 'Nah'?"

"It happens."

"When has it happened?"

Was she teasing him or being serious? He had no idea until she smiled and immediately put him at ease. "She's going to like you, Griffin. All you have to do is show up, and she'll like you. She might even love you."

Griffin rubbed the spot on his chest that ached at the thought of his daughter loving him. What would that even be like? He couldn't begin to know.

He followed Mac into a room that'd been done in neutral, soothing colors with animals playing a central role in framed photographs and a mural on the wall next to the crib. Every detail had been seen to with loving care, including the rocker in the corner and the stuffed animals in a hammock. "This is such a nice room."

"Thanks. It kept me busy while I was waiting for her to get here." She bent over the crib to pick up the baby. "We have a special guest today, sweetheart." Mac turned so Griffin could see the baby's face, and holy shit...

She was the prettiest baby he'd ever seen, not that he'd seen many up close, but at first glance, he could tell this baby was special.

"She's gorgeous."

"She really is. I find myself staring at her for incredibly long stretches of time."

"I can see why."

He watched as she efficiently changed the baby's diaper, talking to her the whole time. The way the baby's legs were constantly moving and how Mac kept a hand on her at all times to hold her in place was fascinating to him.

Mac picked her up and turned to Griffin. "Do you want to hold her?"

"I'd love to, but I'm a bit scared I'll drop her or something."

"You won't drop her." She used her chin to point to the rocker. "Have a seat, and I'll bring her to you."

"Okay." He felt stupid, inept, out of his element and already on his way to being in love with the little being she lowered into his arms, bringing the familiar, fresh scent of Mac's hair and baby smells that were all-new to him.

Griffin was surprised by the solid weight of the infant as well as the heat she generated as she looked up at him with big blue eyes that seemed to see all the way through him. Could she tell he was a novice, a fraud and way less of a man than she deserved for a father?

He hoped not.

"Let her grasp your finger. You won't believe how strong she is."

Griffin gave her his index finger and was indeed surprised by her tight grip. "She's…" The huge lump in his throat caught him off guard.

"She's everything," Mac said. "And then some."

He nodded in agreement because that was all he could manage thanks to the huge swell of emotion that overtook him as he gazed at the face of his daughter.

He had a daughter.

"You want some photos with her?"

"That'd be great."

While he held the baby, Mac took photos that he'd use to

introduce his daughter to his family. He wondered how long he'd have to wait until he could see her again.

CARSON HAD BEEN WATCHING Marlon Beckett for hours as he staked out Cresley's home in the Hollywood Hills and their son's private school in Beverly Hills. So he happened to be perfectly positioned to see Cresley arrive to pick up her son and spot her ex in his vehicle across the street.

"Shit," Carson muttered as she got out of her SUV to walk toward Beckett's truck.

Cresley was quicker than him, though, and got to Beckett well ahead of Carson. She opened the truck's door and punched Beckett in the face while Carson ran toward the two, who were now locked in a physical struggle across the street from their son's school.

Noticing other parents pointing cell phones in their direction, Carson put himself between Cresley and the prying eyes.

"Stop." He wrapped an arm around her to pull her off Beckett. "People are recording you."

She froze.

"I'm Julian's brother Carson." When Beckett surged toward them, his lip bleeding and an abrasion on his cheek, Carson shoved him back and turned his focus on Cresley. "Let's get you out of here."

"I... um... I lost it when I saw him there."

"I know. Keep your face down so they can't get good pictures of you."

She pressed her face into his chest as he walked her back to her vehicle.

He'd no sooner gotten her settled in the driver's seat than a police officer approached them.

"Ma'am, I need you to step out of the vehicle."

"Why?"

"We have numerous witnesses claiming you assaulted the man across the street, who's bleeding from being hit by you."

"He's stalking me—and my kid!"

Carson handed the officer his card. "It's true, Officer. I've been watching him all day. He's been staking out her home and their son's school."

"So this is a custody matter?" the officer asked.

"No!" Cresley said. "I have full custody, and he's trying to extort me for money. My attorney can confirm this."

"I'll need you to come with me while we sort this out."

"I have to pick up my son! He'll be out any second."

"I'll take him," Carson said. "And I'll call Julian."

She looked at Carson and then at the school, where the children were now coming out to meet their parents and guardians.

Carson locked in on the gorgeous blue eyes that'd helped to make her a superstar. "I promise he'll be safe with me."

"I can't be seen leaving with police. It'll ruin me."

"Can we follow you to the station, Officer? We'll leave right from here. She's a victim of a crime. You wouldn't want to further victimize a woman who was defending her child from a stalker, would you?"

The young officer was clearly torn.

"Cresley, go get your son and get in the car."

She took off while Carson kept his gaze trained on the officer. "The one you should be arresting is him." Carson used his chin to gesture to Beckett, who was gleefully watching the scene with the cop unfold. Carson had no doubt that Beckett was the one who'd called the police in the first place. "He's been following her all day."

"That's not a crime."

"Isn't it a crime to shake her down for money and use the kid he doesn't give a shit about as leverage?"

"I'd need more information to determine that."

"Please make sure you're asking the right questions and not just assuming that she attacked him out of nowhere."

Cresley buckled her son into his booster seat in the back of her SUV and got into the passenger seat.

"We'll follow you to the station."

"No games."

"Understood."

Carson used his key fob to lock his own car and got into the driver's seat of Cresley's Lexus SUV, nearly crushing his knees on the dashboard before he adjusted the seat to his height. Then he navigated a U-turn into traffic to follow the officer to the Hollywood Community Police Station on North Wilcox Avenue.

"Ty, this is Mr. Remington. He's going to hang out with you for a bit while I take care of some business, okay?"

Carson glanced in the mirror at the child, who was the mirror image of his mother. Lucky kid. "You can call me Carson, buddy."

"Why are we following the policeman?"

"Mommy has to answer some questions for him, but it's nothing to worry about, okay?"

Carson looked up in time to see the little guy's chin quiver and his eyes fill with tears.

"I'm scared, Mommy."

"Nothing to be scared about, love. I promise."

When her voice broke on that last word, he reached over to cover her cold, trembling hand with his and noticed her right hand was bleeding. "You got a tissue or anything for that?"

She looked down and gasped at the sight of her bloody knuckles.

Carson withdrew his hand so she could root around in the glove box for a napkin, which she used to clean up the blood.

When they pulled into the parking lot at the station, Carson kept the car running as he handed her his business card. "I'll call Julian right away. Hit me up when you're done here, and I'll pick you up."

She looked at him. "Thank you."

"No problem."

"I won't be long, Ty. Be good for Mr. Carson."

"Want to get some ice cream?" Carson asked the boy.

"Sure," Ty said as he watched his mom get out of the car and go inside with the officer. "Is she okay?"

"She's fine. By the time we get some ice cream, she should be done with her meeting."

He texted Julian so Ty wouldn't overhear. *911—Cresley is in custody in West Hollywood for punching Beckett outside the son's school. Can you get over there right away?*

Julian replied a minute later. *On it. She actually punched him?*

Confirm. He'd been following her all day and should be the one charged. I've got her son, taking him for ice cream. Let me know when she's released.

You've got her son?!

That's what I said. Get her out of there!

Exasperated with his brother for making a thing of him taking care of Cresley's kid, Carson used his phone to find an ice cream shop close by and headed in that direction, hoping Cresley wouldn't be held for long. Julian was right to question him watching Ty. What the hell did he know about kids, anyway?

Not one thing, but he figured he was about to learn real fast.

TURNED OUT, Ty was a trip, with keen observations about everything they encountered during their outing, from the ridiculous number of steps involved to pay for parking to the guy busking for tips on the street to the ninety-two varieties of ice cream he wanted to sample before he chose his flavor.

Normally, Carson would've been annoyed to be spending an afternoon with a kid, but this kid was funny.

"How old of a man are you, anyway?" Carson asked as they sat across from each other and ate their ice cream.

"I'm seven, and I'm just a kid, not a man."

"Huh, I thought seven was a man these days."

"You don't know much about kids, do you?"

"Nope. What should I know?"

"That we're not men—or women—until we're eighteen to start with. Weren't you a kid before you grew up?"

"Yeah, but that was a long time ago. I don't remember."

"How old are you that you don't remember being a kid?"

"I'm thirty-six."

"That is pretty old."

"Hey! No, it isn't."

His belly laugh cracked Carson up.

"Only old people eat coffee ice cream," Ty said, wrinkling his cute little nose.

"That is not true."

"Is too."

"It's coffee *crunch*, I'll have you know, and at least I didn't sample ninety-two flavors before I got boring old strawberry."

Ty smirked. "Who got the most ice cream? Me or you?"

Carson sat back, eyeing the kid with new respect. "So that's a racket you've pulled before?"

"Maybe. Maybe not."

"You missed your calling as a con man."

"Still a kid over here. I've got time to become a con man."

Carson chuckled. The kid was awesome.

"Could I ask you something?" Ty said in a more serious tone.

"Sure."

"Is my mom in trouble because she hit my dad?"

"You saw that, huh?"

"Yeah. I've also seen him hanging out by the school the last couple of weeks, but I didn't say anything because she doesn't like talking about him."

"I think she'd want to know you've seen him around."

"Yeah, probably. I don't get why he sits outside the school watching me on the playground but never tries to hang out with me or anything."

"I don't know why he does that, but he's missing out. You're fun to hang out with."

"I know, right?"

Carson laughed.

"Are they going to put her in jail?"

"My brother is a really good lawyer, and he's taking care of it. Try not to worry. Even if she gets charged, it'd be a minor thing. And there's a case to be made for him following you guys around."

"So he's following her, too?"

Shit, I walked right into that... "Yeah, he has been."

"How do you know that?"

"That's a long story, but it's part of my job to know what's going on with clients of our law firm."

"Are you a lawyer?"

"Nope, but my five brothers and three sisters are."

His big blue eyes widened. "You have... *nine kids* in your family?"

"I do."

"And they're all lawyers?"

"The last one is still in law school and has to pass the bar exam, but the other seven are lawyers."

"Why aren't you?"

"Didn't want to go to school that long."

"How long is it?"

"Three years on top of college, plus months of preparing to take the state bar exam that makes you officially a lawyer. I had better things to do with my time."

"Like what?"

"Surfing, basketball and chasing girls, to start with."

"I'd *love* to learn how to surf. It looks like so much fun."

"It is. I'd be happy to give you some lessons if you'd like to try it." The words were out of his mouth before he could take even a second to consider what he was saying. If there was one thing he remembered from back in the day, it was that it wasn't cool to promise a kid something and not deliver. Plus, he needed to ask Ty's mom if it was okay with her.

"You would? Really?"

"Sure."

"I can't wait to tell my mom! Do you know how much longer she'll be there?"

"Let me text my brother."

Julian wrote back a few minutes later that Cresley was going to be released with a court date the following month on a misdemeanor assault charge. *I'm calling in a friend in criminal law to help make it go away, and I've got Jackson requesting an RO to keep Beckett away from her and Ty.*

Tell Jackson I've observed him following her and sitting outside Ty's school and can testify to that if needed. I've got photos. Ty told me he's seen him lurking at the school the last couple of weeks, but he didn't want to tell his mom that.

Good to know. I'll tell him.

I've got her car. When should I be there to get her?

Twenty minutes.

"She's getting out of there in a few minutes," he said to Ty. "Let's go pick her up."

Outside, he held the back door of the Lexus for Ty. "You need help?"

He gave Carson a withering look. "Please. I'm *seven*, not three."

"'Scuse me for asking."

"You're excused, but only cuz you're gonna give me surfing lessons. When can we do that?"

"That's up to your mom."

"She'll say it has to be on the weekend because of school."

"And because I actually work for a living during the week."

"That, too," Ty said with a cute little snort of laughter.

Carson never would've expected to enjoy spending an hour with a seven-year-old, but from what he could tell, this kid wasn't your average seven-year-old. He was sharp, witty, observant and freaking cute. Carson was actually looking forward to teaching him how to surf—that was, if Cresley was cool with it.

And seeing her again wouldn't be any hardship either.

He was still recovering from the impact of meeting her and finding out she was far more stunning in leggings and a T-shirt, her hair in a ponytail and not an ounce of makeup on her perfect face, than she was on the billboards around town that featured her in all her exquisite beauty.

If he'd had a type, Cresley Dane would be it. But he wasn't interested in the kinds of things the mother of a young child would want, even if she and her young child were awesome. He'd loved the way she'd marched across the street and smacked that son of a bitch right across his smug, sanctimonious face.

That'd been hot as fuck.

He was waiting outside when she emerged from the cop shop with Julian and headed straight for the waiting vehicle.

When she got into the passenger seat, she immediately turned to check on Ty. "Are you okay?" she asked.

"I'm fine. How are *you*?"

"All good."

Carson put down the window to speak to his brother. "Julian, this is Ty Dane, coolest seven-year-old you'll ever meet. Ty, this is my brother Julian."

"Good to meet you, Ty."

"You, too. Who's older?"

"Him." Carson used his thumb to point at Julian. "Can't you tell just by looking at him?"

Julian slugged Carson in the shoulder, which made Ty cackle with laughter.

"Let's get out of here before the press finds me," Cresley said.

"I'll be in touch," Julian said to her.

"Thanks for everything."

"Any time."

Following Cresley's directions, Carson drove them home to a house on Mulholland Drive that clung to the side of a steep hill.

Carson walked them in to make sure no uninvited guests were waiting inside.

The back side of the house was all glass, with a stunning view of the city below. "This is quite a spot."

"I never get tired of the view, especially at night."

"It's like a million twinkling stars," Ty added. "Do you want to see my room, Carson?"

Carson glanced at Cresley, who smiled.

"*Mr.* Carson."

"That makes me feel kinda old. Carson is fine with me if you're okay with it."

"He's gonna teach me how to surf, Mom. I can't call him Mr. Carson when we're surfing."

"He does have a point," Carson said, earning a big grin from Ty.

"How has ninety minutes of ice cream undone seven years of parenting?"

"We're guys, Mom. It's just how it is."

"Is that right?"

"Yep." Ty took Carson's hand and gave a strong tug. "Come see my room."

"Is it okay with you?" he asked Cresley.

"Of course. Go right ahead while I pour myself a big drink."

"Put some ice on those knuckles, too, killer."

She laughed. "Good idea."

Carson let Ty pull him down the hallway to his room on the left side. Right away, he saw that the boy was a huge fan of LA sports teams, with Dodgers, Lakers, Rams and Kings swag on the walls, along with a life-size poster of LeBron James. Mixed in with the sports were robots, Legos and superheroes.

"What do you think?" Ty asked.

Carson took a long, assessing look at every detail, from the Spider-Man comforter to the hat collection for each team to the signed jersey from Clippers star Kawhi Leonard. "I think you're a man of many interests."

Ty smiled, pleased with the review. "I do like a lot of things. Have you ever ridden on an electric scooter?"

Carson sat on the floor for a closer look at a remote-controlled truck with all the bells and whistles. He would've loved one of those as a kid. "Can't say I have."

"My friend Jonah has one, but my mom won't let me go on it because she says it's super dangerous. It goes pretty fast."

"You should listen to her. Moms know things."

"My mom knows all the things. None of the other moms can name the starting lineup of the Dodgers or know what it means to be offside in hockey. She's super cool."

"Sounds like it." Carson was impressed that she knew the Dodgers lineup. "Which sports do you play?"

"All of them. Little League baseball in the summer, flag football in the fall, rec league basketball and hockey in the winter."

"Wow, you're a busy guy."

"I am. Mom says that'll keep me off the streets and out of trouble."

Carson laughed. "Another thing she's right about."

"Do you want to come to one of my hockey games sometime?"

"I'd love to."

"I'll ask Mom to give you the schedule. When can we surf?"

"It's a little chilly this time of year, but if we got you a wet suit, we could probably make it work."

"That'd be *so* cool."

"I'll look into it. What size are you? Like a double extra-large?"

His belly laugh was delightful. "You know nothing about kids."

"I know less than nothing about kids."

"Clearly. I'd probably be a small in a kids' wet suit."

"Good to know."

"Time for homework, Ty."

He groaned. "We're having fun."

"I'm sure Mr. Carson has things to do."

When Carson looked up at her, he experienced the oddest sensation. Goddamn, but she was beautiful. And then she smiled at him, and all bets were off.

"You need to listen to your mom, buddy," he said to Ty. "She's going to make sure you don't grow up to be a dumbhead."

Ty's laughter would never get old to him. "That's true. What do you know about second-grade math?"

"Less than you."

"So you're a dumbhead, then?"

"In many ways, yes, and in some ways, no. It's a mixed bag."

Ty got up and offered Carson a hand up, tugging mightily. "Thanks for hanging out. This was fun."

"It was the most fun I've had in ages."

"You should hang out with kids more often."

Carson patted his blond head. "Probably so."

"Go get started on your homework," Cresley said. "I'll be right there."

After Ty ran off, Carson glanced at her. "He's an incredible kid."

"I know. I got really lucky."

"It's not all luck. He's also polite and articulate and funny as hell."

"I love that he's funny. That's my favorite thing."

"I can see why. So, about the surfing... I told him it's only if you say it's okay."

"It's okay. He'll probably love it."

"I'm sure he will. Most people do once they get the hang of it. If you give me your number, I'll get the stuff we need and hit you up about a date. For the surfing, that is."

She smiled. "That'd be very nice of you. Thank you."

"My pleasure. I truly enjoyed every minute with him."

"As do I, except for the second-grade math, that is."

Carson laughed as he followed her to the foyer, where she asked for his phone to put in her number.

When she handed it back to him, her hand brushed against his, making him feel like he'd been touched by electricity itself.

Over his shoulder, he said, "See you later, Ty."

"Bye, Carson! Thanks for the ice cream and stuff."

"My pleasure." To Cresley, he said, "I'll text you, so you have my number. If there's any more trouble with the ex, don't hesitate to call me."

"I won't." She reached her hand out to shake his. "Thanks for everything."

Later, he'd wonder what'd come over him as he took her hand and brought it to his lips, brushing a kiss over the back of it, realizing his error when the scent of roses and spice enveloped him in a cloud of fragrance he wanted to get much closer to.

"I'll be in touch," he said.

"We'll look forward to that."

He would, too. In fact, as he walked out to meet the Uber he'd take back to his car, Carson couldn't wait to be in touch with her and her adorable son.

CHAPTER EIGHTEEN

Julian's day had been a mess from start to finish. In addition to getting Cresley out of lockup, he'd dealt with a screaming fight between divorcing spouses at mediation, and Bryan McDavid tried again to sign his sons out of school, a clear violation of the restraining order, which had led to a warrant for his arrest. That was still pending when Julian took the elevator to the parking garage. He'd made sure Rachel and her sons were in a safe location before he left the office, promising to update her if he heard anything from the police, who were looking for Bryan.

Julian removed his suit jacket and tie and laid them out on the back seat. As he drove home, he realized he hadn't eaten since the bagel he'd had for breakfast and tried to think of what he had at home. Not much. He hung a left onto Laurel Canyon Boulevard and headed up the hill, stopping at the Laurel Canyon Country Store to pick up something for dinner.

He thought of Isla as he parked in the lot. When he'd told her about their historic neighborhood, he should've mentioned the prodigious history of the store, where Cass Elliot had once lived in the basement. The Doors had included a mention of the store in their song "Love Street." But he couldn't tell her that or anything else while she was dealing with something so tragic and heavy.

Hopefully, he'd get the chance to tell her all about it someday.

The store was cramped and crammed with grocery items, and he was careful not to knock anything off the shelves as he made his way to the freezer section in the back. He rounded a corner and nearly slammed into a woman, managing to save her from falling by grasping her arms.

He looked down to find Isla looking up at him.

"Oh," she said. "It's you."

"It's me." Julian drank in the sight of her sweet face, noting her eyes were rimmed with red and framed by dark circles. As she gazed up at him, her chin quivered, and her eyes filled.

Without thinking about implications or complications or anything other than whatever she needed, he put his arms around her and held her close while she sobbed. When she tried to pull back, he said, "Shhh, it's okay. I've got you."

She sagged into his embrace.

Her hair brushed his face, filling his senses with the essence of her, an herbal-tinged fragrance that he wanted to memorize for time immemorial as hers.

Isla's.

They had that back corner in the cluttered store all to themselves. For the moment, anyway.

He drew back to study her face, brushing her hair back and wiping away her tears. The need to care for her, to make things better, to fix the unfixable was as powerful as anything he'd ever felt. "What can I do?"

She shrugged as she shook her head. "There's nothing anyone can do."

"Where're the kids?"

"Home with my friend Mrs. Ventura. She came when she heard and said she'll stay as long as I need her."

"I'm glad you're being well supported. What'd you come in here for?"

She looked up at him, blinked and cracked a small grin. "I don't remember."

So freaking adorable, in every possible way.

"You want to come to my house for a burrito?"

Nodding, she said, "I think I'd like that very much."

"Pick your poison." He gestured to the freezer case behind them. "Literally."

Isla chuckled when she realized he was referring to the frozen burritos. "I'm partial to chicken."

"As am I, and I've had this one before, so I can attest that it's edible."

"That's a ringing endorsement."

He was encouraged by her witty reply and hoped he could help alleviate some of her terrible stress. "Do the kids need anything? Is that why you stopped here?"

"No, I remember now. I wanted a Mountain Dew and a few minutes to myself, so I told Mrs. V I was running to the store."

He grabbed four burritos from one case and two bottles of Mountain Dew from another and cradled them in his left arm. "Let's go." With his right hand on her back, he guided her toward the front of the store, where a young guy named Travis was working the register. He wore a tie-dyed Grateful Dead shirt and had shoulder-length blond dreadlocks.

"Hey, Julian, how goes the divorce wars?"

"Brutal as usual. How're you doing?"

"All good in the hood."

"My friend Isla is having some car trouble. Would it be okay if she left her car in the lot for a bit until we can get back for it?"

"Sure thing, no prob. What kind is it?"

"It's a red Hyundai SUV," she said.

"Got it. I'll let everyone know."

He rang up Julian's items, and when he tapped his card to pay, Isla said, "I wanted to pay."

"I've got it. All set."

Travis handed him the paper bag with their purchases. "When you guys playing out again?"

"The Whisky next weekend. We're pumped."

"Oh, that's cool. I'll be there."

"Bring your friends."

"Will do, man. Take it easy."

"You do the same," Julian said as he guided Isla out of the store and to the passenger seat of the G-Wagon, making sure she was settled before he shut the door, stashed the bag in the back seat and got into the driver's side. When he glanced over at her, she was staring straight ahead, so he reached over her for the seat belt and secured it for her.

"Thank you," she said with a small smile. "I'm such a mess."

"No, you're not. You're upset, and with good reason."

"I should just go home. The last thing you need to be dealing with is a weepy, heartbroken, unpredictable woman."

"I promised you a burrito, and I'd like to deliver on that, if you'll let me."

"Are you sure you don't have better things to do?"

"I'm very sure." Though he'd found himself with a rare free night, he would've canceled anything and everything to have this time with her. Even when she was weepy, heartbroken and unpredictable, she stirred him in a way only one other woman ever had. And while that should've terrified him, strangely enough, it didn't. Rather, it left him feeling exhilarated, even though he knew she was in no condition for anything like exhilaration from him. Tonight was about food and comfort and nothing else.

If he was thrilled to be with her, she didn't need to know that.

Not now, anyway.

ISLA TEXTED Mrs. V to tell her she'd connected with a friend and was going to have dinner with him if everything was under control at home.

We're doing just fine. Take all the time you need with your friend.

Thank you. Give the kids kisses for me and tell them I'll tuck them in when I get home.

Will do.

Isla sent heart emojis.

She couldn't believe she was in Julian Remington's fancy SUV on the way to his house. Could this day get any stranger? When she'd looked up in the store to realize he was the one she'd crashed into, the profound feeling of relief had made her legs feel wobbly.

She'd had one thought and one thought only: *He would make everything all right.*

How and why she'd known that, she couldn't say, but every instinct she had was telling her the evidence was irrefutable.

Julian was beautiful and brilliant and kind and talented. He was the real deal, and he was taking her home with him to feed and comfort her when he certainly had better things he could and should be doing.

After the past few weeks, months, *years* of turmoil, she would give herself this moment with him, carved out of the changing landscape of her life, and simply be with him for as long as he'd have her. She would draw comfort from his rock-solid presence and then go home better for having known him.

During this moment of respite, she'd not think about Gabriel or the past or what the immediate future might look like. For right now, for tonight, it was the two of them and a couple of burritos, and, strangely enough, that was all she needed.

They went up into the hills, so high her ears popped before he brought the SUV to a stop in front of a smoked-glass double garage. He pressed a button on the dash, and the door went up to reveal a small black sports car parked on the other side.

He pulled into the garage, cut the engine and shut the door, sealing them off from the outside world.

Isla released her seat belt and got out of the car, following him inside into a gorgeous kitchen. "Oh wow. This is so nice."

"Thanks. I did it mostly myself. Took almost two years."

"Why'd you do that?"

He waggled his brows. "So someday I could tell a beautiful woman that I did it myself and impress her."

"I hope that goes well for you when you get the chance to do it."

Over his shoulder, he flashed a grin. "I just did, and I feel like it went pretty well."

Isla couldn't stop the gurgle of laughter or the tearful response that followed.

Julian handed her a tissue.

"I feel guilty for thinking something's funny. I feel guilty for being happy to be here, with you, when Gabriel is dying. I feel guilty for being relieved that our marriage is over, because I never would've wanted it to end this way."

"He knows that, Isla. Everyone knows that."

"I tried so hard to make it work."

"You were fighting a battle you couldn't win—and so was he." Julian put a bottle of Chardonnay and another of rosé on the counter, raising a brow in inquiry.

"Do you have vodka, by any chance?"

"I do. How do you take it?"

"With ice would be good."

"You got it."

She tucked her hair behind her ear as she wondered what she must look like and decided it was probably better not to think about that. He'd said she was beautiful, which was a lovely thing to hear. "I read this thing online a while back... about how men can be super weird about seeking medical attention even when they know something is wrong. It's, like, a thing..."

"My dad is very proud of the fact that he hasn't been to a doctor in twenty-five years."

Her eyes went wide. "Seriously?"

Julian put an icy cocktail glass on the counter in front of her and opened a beer for himself. "Yep. We tell him he's a fool, but he points to his dad, going strong at almost ninety-four with minimal medical involvement, as proof that doctors are a waste of time he could be billing to clients."

"That's nuts."

"I know, right?"

"Your grandfather is ninety-four? That's amazing."

"His birthday is next month. He'd want me to say he's only ninety-three, but I'm rounding up. He's the coolest dude I know. He founded our firm sixty years ago, and it's been supporting our family ever since."

"That's an amazing legacy. Does he live independently?"

"In an assisted-living apartment, but he still cooks for himself, drives occasionally and plays at least one round of golf a week, if not more. The last time I played with him, he beat me by four strokes."

"Wow, that's impressive."

"It was annoying. He's still gloating about it."

She laughed. "I love that."

"He's great. He was a big part of our childhood."

"I heard you have eight siblings."

"Guilty as charged."

"What number are you?"

"Number one, baby. Leader of the pack."

"And they let you lead them?" she asked skeptically.

"When they're smart."

"Are you close to them?"

"They're my best friends and often my adversaries. My sisters work for my mom's rival firm, Kate Remington Family Law. Sometimes we're on opposite sides of the same case."

"That must be interesting."

"It can be, but we try very hard to leave work at the office. It's important to us to stay close."

"You're all lawyers?"

"All but one. Carson, who's number two behind me, is our lead investigator. He chose not to go to law school, but after years of telling us he could easily pass the bar exam, he's taking it in July to shut us up."

"Is that even doable without law school?"

"I mean… It can be done, but not easily. I think he's in for a rude awakening. That exam is a bitch. Number nine, Roman, is due to graduate from law school in May, so he's not technically a lawyer yet, but he's on his way."

She sipped from her glass. "It's cool that you guys are close. That's rare these days."

"We went through a lot together as kids. It bonded us for life."

"Oh." She *so* wanted to ask what happened from his point of view, but it was none of her business, so she didn't ask..

"Custody battle between the lawyer parents," he said, filling in the blanks for her. "Went on for almost a decade. It was a nightmare."

"Yikes. I'm sorry. That must've been rough."

"It was."

"And yet, you guys became divorce lawyers."

"I know. It's funny, right? But when your last name is Remington, you'd be a fool to practice any other kind of law in LA, thanks to the aforementioned sixty-year legacy."

"But is it hard for you? After what happened when you were a kid?"

"It can be. At times. Like when I see parents doing to their kids what was done to my siblings and me. I want to tell them that some wounds never heal..."

"I'm sorry that happened to you."

He put the burritos in a fancy toaster oven/air fryer combo thing that she was immediately obsessed with. The things she could cook in that! "We got through it."

"What're your siblings like?"

"Hmm, well, let's see. Carson is number two, and he's always been super inquisitive and resourceful, two skills that serve him well in his work as our chief investigator. He fought a ferocious heroin addiction for seven years until he finally got clean, and now he helps other addicts."

"I'm so glad he beat it."

"You and me both. It was a nightmare. Then there's Griffin, who wanted to surf professionally until he ended up underneath a monster wave in Portugal and almost lost his nerve for any kind of surfing."

"Oh my God. That must've been terrifying."

"He still can't talk about it without shaking. It took two years for him to get back in the water, but he eventually rediscovered his love for it even if his professional aspirations were over after that. Next is Jordan, a certified bad ass. She's into Krav Maga, and I honestly think she could kick my ass."

She laughed at the face he made as he said that. "Have you ever tested her?"

"I wouldn't dare. I'm scared of her. We all are."

"That's funny."

"Kaidan comes after her, and she's known for being really funny. Any time I need a laugh, I call her. She never disappoints me. Then comes Ethan, and he's the quietest of all of us. He always says he should've been an only child but ended up in the wrong line."

"I'd say so."

"Despite his jokes about wishing he was an only, he'd do anything for any of us. Jackson comes after him. He's my associate."

"Which means what?"

"He's my bitch at work, but don't ever tell him I said it that way."

Smiling, she said, "I see how it is."

"He's my right hand and a damned good lawyer or I never would've given him your case."

"That's good to know."

"He plays lead guitar in a band and sings, so we have that in common. Number eight is Gillian, the sweet, sensitive one. She feels everything so deeply. I worry about her sometimes. The things she encounters at work really affect her. More so than the rest of us."

"I don't know how any of you handle all the stuff you must deal with."

"You get used to it after a while, but some cases are harder than others."

"What about number nine?"

"That'd be Roman, the baby of the family and one of my favorite people ever. I'm thirteen years older than him, but he's always been very special to me. I'm looking forward to him being done with school in May, so we can get him back home with us. He plays the drums and is looking to find a band when he gets done with school and has the time."

"You obviously love them all very much."

"I really do. They're very important to me."

"What's it like working for your parents after all the custody craziness?"

"It's... often a delicate balancing act. At times, they're oblivious to what it was like for us, which infuriates us. But most of the time, it's not an issue. I go days without even seeing my father, and my sisters have a decent groove with my mom."

"How did you end up boys with boys and girls with girls?" Was she being too nosy? Asking too many questions? He didn't seem to mind, but would he say so if he did? She hoped not, because she was fascinated by everything he had to say.

"That's how they divided us as kids when they were fighting over us, and it just sort of happened that way with work, too."

"It's a very interesting story."

"Yes, so interesting that they made a reality TV show about it while I was in high school. That was a real blast."

"Ew, they did not!"

"Did too. We were on billboards all over Hollywood for months."

"I bet I saw them. I grew up in that neighborhood. I wasn't really aware of the show, though. I was in my smoking, drinking, chasing boys and driving my brother crazy era back then."

Smiling, he said, "Where'd you go to high school?"

"Hollywood High."

"Ah, the home of the Sheiks."

"That's right. I worked at the Roosevelt after school, bussing tables and cleaning up the pool area." The Hollywood Roosevelt was an iconic hotel in the heart of the tourist district.

"Is it true that place is haunted?"

"Well, I never had an encounter with Marilyn, but other people swear they have. I've served room service to the Marilyn Monroe Suite, which is as close as I've come to her. Where'd you go to school?"

"Beverly Hills High School."

"90210."

"Without the drama. It was actually kind of boring when I was there."

"Except for the reality TV show."

He chuckled. "My fifteen minutes of fame."

"It must've been dreadful. At that age, the last thing most people want is that kind of attention."

"It was pretty awful. My younger siblings ate it up. Those of us who were old enough to know better hated every minute of it. My dad said it would be great for business, and it was, but at what cost, you know?"

Isla grimaced.

"I'm not sure how you've managed to get me talking about things I never talk about with anyone."

"I'm sorry."

"Don't be. It's fine. You're easy to talk to."

"That's nice of you to say, but don't feel like you have to talk about painful stuff if you don't want to."

"It was a long time ago now. Doesn't hurt the way it used to." After a pause, he said, "You want to hear something really crazy?"

"Um, yeah?" Could he tell she was hanging on every word he said like an obsessed teenager? She hoped not.

"My mom's house in the Palisades burned in the fire."

"Oh no. That's terrible."

"It was a nightmare. We didn't know for sure she got out for almost a full day."

"I can't imagine."

"With the PCH being the only way out of there, it was a madhouse and terrifying for people trying to evacuate. Anyway, she's rebuilding out there and staying with my sister Kaidan in town during the week. Kaidan thinks she and my dad are back together."

Isla gasped. *"What?"*

"That's what we said, too."

"You guys must've been shocked to hear that."

"Shocked and a little outraged." He put the burritos on

navy blue plates and served them with salsa on the side. "Our gourmet dinner is served."

"It smells delicious. Thank you."

"Nothing but the best for you."

He made her feel lighthearted and giddy inside, which was tinged with guilt whenever she thought of Gabriel. So she tried not to think of him and instead enjoy the interlude away from reality for as long as she could.

They ate in companionable silence for several minutes. The burrito was surprisingly tasty and was the first thing she'd eaten all day that didn't get stuck on the huge lump that'd settled in her throat the night before.

She took a napkin from the pile he'd put on the counter and dabbed at her lips before taking another sip of vodka, which was making her feel warm and tingly inside. "I'm not sure what I'm doing here one day after I learned that my ex-husband—or actual husband or whatever he is—is going to die. Soon."

"You're living your life, which is the only thing you can do."

"I know that's what I have to do, but this, with you..."

He reached across the counter to put his hand on top of hers, electrifying her with his touch. "We're two people eating grocery store burritos and talking about life. No harm in that."

Maybe it was the vodka making her brave. "Is that all it is? Because it feels like more than that. You dumped me onto your brother because you were attracted to me."

"Damn Denny," he muttered before he added, "*Am* attracted. Present tense. And the last thing I wanted to do was turn you over to Jackson, but I had to. Lawyerly ethics can be a bitch about things like attraction to a client. I hope you understand."

"I'm trying to." She put her other hand on top of his, trapping him. "I have no business being equally attracted, or sitting in your cozy kitchen, holding the hand of a man who avoids commitment like the plague."

Julian winced. "Denny told you that, huh?"

"He mentioned that you're not a forever kind of guy. Because of your parents, right?"

He stared at her for a long moment, so long she wondered if she'd messed up by mentioning his parents. "That's a big part of it."

"Why do you look surprised that I asked that?"

"Because most people don't connect the two things—my desire to remain unattached and the mess my parents made of our childhood. They think it's only because of what I see every day at work. I let them believe that, but the wound runs deeper, you know?"

"I get it. Why would you want anything to do with happily ever after when you witnessed an ugly divorce and spend your days taking apart marriages?"

He nodded as he looked down at their hands, piled together on the counter. "Weird thing, though…"

"What is?"

"That I have no desire to warn you off me or tell you to look out for yourself around me the way I normally would."

"Is that unusual?"

"It's unprecedented." He put his free hand on top of the pile. "What do you make of that?"

"I don't know which end is up right now."

"I want you to know that if I hadn't run into you at the store, I would've left you alone for all the reasons."

"But you wanted to see me?"

"So, *so* much. You're all I've thought about since the minute we met, even when I'm getting paid to think about other stuff."

"I'm not sure what to make of this situation."

"Neither am I. I'm in completely uncharted territory with you."

"Can I tell you something?"

"Anything you want."

"Even though he told me I don't have to be, I think I should be involved in caring for Gabriel or at least visit him."

"Where will he be?"

"In Santa Barbara with his parents, who I just met for the first time at the hospital last night. Ours wasn't the only relationship to suffer from his illness." She ventured a glance at him. "Do you think I'm crazy, after everything he put me through, to want to be there for him?"

"Once upon a time, you loved him enough to marry him and have kids with him."

"Yes," she said with a sigh of relief that he understood. "That's it exactly, and I want to have a clear conscience going forward about honoring my vows. As I say that out loud, I realize it sounds incredibly quaint."

"As someone who works on the front lines of the broken-vow brigade, I think it sounds admirable. But..."

"There's always a but," she said, smiling. "Okay, let me have it."

"I'd be concerned about the toll it would take on you emotionally to be on the front lines of such a tragic situation after everything you've already been through."

"I've thought of that, and I'm not going to lie. It does give me pause. My number one priority is being able to care for my kids and to be there for whatever they need."

"Are you afraid that the emotional toll of seeing Gabriel decline and helping to care for him would make that too difficult?"

"I don't know. I've never been in a situation like this before. Well, except when I lost my parents, but that was a little different because it was an accident, not a slow decline."

"But the emotional toll was probably similar, right?"

Isla tried to never think too hard about that time in her life, but she let her mind wander to the immediate aftermath of calamity. She was shocked by how easily she conjured up feelings of utter despair.

Julian pulled his hands free and moved around the island to put his arms around her. "Breathe, Isla. Just breathe."

As she leaned her head on his chest, she did as he instructed, focusing on getting air to her lungs and then doing it again. "I'm okay."

"Take another minute." He ran his hand over her back, making her want to purr from the way he cared for her as if she were precious to him.

Stop, Isla. He's already told you that you'll never be precious to him because he doesn't want that with you or anyone. Self-preservation had her pulling back from him when that was the last thing she wanted to do.

What was it about this man that had her head spinning? It'd been so long since she'd felt anything resembling desire for Gabriel that the sharp sting of need nearly took her breath away. What would Julian say if she asked him to take her to bed and make everything better? The thought was so shocking, and the need so overwhelming, she had to bite her tongue so she wouldn't say something that could never be unsaid.

He kept a hand on her shoulder while he watched over her, seeing her in a way she could've only dreamed of being seen in her marriage. So often, she felt like she was invisible to Gabriel, which had led her to expect nothing from him so she wouldn't be constantly disappointed.

"What're you thinking?"

"I can't tell you."

"Why not?"

She glanced up to find him gazing down at her and noticed once again how stunningly handsome he was. "Because it's wildly inappropriate."

CHAPTER NINETEEN

Was it possible to die from an overload of desire? Julian never would've thought so before right now, when she looked up at him with those bottomless brown eyes and said her thoughts were wildly inappropriate.

He recognized he was in big trouble with this woman because he would've given everything he owned and every dime he had to hear those wildly inappropriate thoughts.

"Julian."

"Hmm?"

"Are you all right? You're, um, staring at me."

He blinked. "Sorry, it's just the words 'wildly inappropriate' have my imagination doing handsprings."

A giggle exploded out of her, and the joyful sound only made everything worse—and better at the same time. How was that even possible?

She covered her mouth to contain the laughter that soon led to more tears. "It feels so wrong to be laughing and joking when Gabriel is going to *die*. He's actually going to die. It's unbelievable."

Julian used a napkin to dry her eyes.

Her gaze connected with his like a punch to the chest.

"I, um..." He intended to back away. The last thing he'd ever do was take advantage of her when she was hurting.

But she reached for him, fisted his dress shirt in both hands and pulled him back to her with a force that couldn't be resisted. Not that he tried very hard to resist as his lips connected with hers, sending lightning streaking down his spine in a blast of desire that made anything he'd felt before seem trivial and insignificant.

Holy. *Shit*.

She curled her arms around his neck and rubbed her tongue against his, making him delirious with the need for more of her incredible sweetness.

He put his arms around her and lifted her right off the barstool to carry her into the living room to the sofa. As he came down on top of her without breaking the hottest kiss of his entire life, a brief moment of sanity had him thinking he should put a stop to this while he still could. But then she put her hand on his face and moaned as she arched into him, and all thoughts of stopping were lost in a frenzy of need.

The heat of her body against his was the sexiest thing he'd ever experienced, and they were only kissing, albeit like two people who feared kissing would be outlawed the next day.

He came up for air only out of absolute necessity and stared down at her, noting her closed eyes, flushed cheeks and damp, swollen lips. A surge of tenderness took him by surprise as it became clear he'd do anything for her, anything at all, even break his own rules to have her in his life.

Her eyes fluttered open. "Why'd you stop?"

"I needed to breathe."

She smiled, and he was lost to her, captivated, spellbound.

He brushed a soft, sweet kiss over her lips and rested his forehead on hers as she ran her fingers through the hair that curled at the ends against his neck, sending a shiver down his back.

"Julian..."

"Hmm?"

"It's okay if you want to keep kissing me."

"There's nothing I want more than that, but..."

"No buts. It's what I want."

He'd never felt so torn between what he wanted just as much as she did and what he knew to be right. "Can we talk about this for a minute?"

"Only a minute."

"I can't talk to you when you're pressed against me like this."

She curled her legs around his, trapping him, and he whimpered. "Don't go. Not yet."

"Isla..."

"Yes, Julian?"

He huffed out a laugh at the prim way she said that. "I'm trying to do the right thing here."

"And I'm begging you not to."

As his head dropped to her shoulder, he released a groan that came out sounding like a tortured moan. His lips found the warm skin of her neck, and he forgot all about why he'd thought it was a good idea to put a stop to this or slow things down or do anything other than what every cell in his body wanted to do.

He'd been taken over by some sort of invisible force that was leading him to something so much bigger than he could comprehend, with her sweet scent filling his senses and her hands under his shirt, searing his back with her heat. He was falling off a cliff, and a fall had never been so exciting.

"Take me to bed, Julian. Please."

Her words were like gas on an already out-of-control fire. He was on the verge of complying when her phone rang, and she froze.

"I have to get that."

They disentangled themselves, and she got up to return to the kitchen, while he sat back on the sofa and tried to catch his breath. He could hear her talking on the phone but couldn't make out what she was saying over the loud drumbeat of desire that had overtaken him.

When she came back into the room, the first thing he noticed was the bare shoulder peeking out from under her sweater, the kiss-swollen lips and the hair he'd messed up with his hands.

"My magic coach has just turned into a pumpkin. Mila is throwing up and screaming for Mommy. I have to go home."

"I'll take you."

"Sorry."

"It's okay."

He got up and went to her, stopping when she placed her hands on his chest.

"To be continued?"

Nodding, he kissed her quickly. "Let me get my keys."

In the kitchen, Julian took two seconds to breathe and get his head straight before he followed her to the garage and into the G-Wagon. They were quiet on the short ride down Laurel Canyon Boulevard to the store. He pulled up next to her car, which was the only one left in the lot.

"Let me know how Mila is feeling," he told her, desperate to ensure he'd hear from her again soon.

"I will." She released her seat belt and leaned over the center console to kiss his cheek. "Thank you for tonight. You were just what I needed."

She got out of the car before he could formulate a response.

He watched her until her car was started and her lights were on. Then he waved and drove back up the hill toward home, changed forever by the past two hours.

ISLA ENDED up with two kids who were sick all weekend. Thank God for Mrs. V, who was by her side through it all, until they fell into bed, completely exhausted at the end of each day. By Sunday, the delightful interlude with Julian might never have happened, even though he'd texted to check on her and the kids a couple of times and offered to bring them anything they needed, which she appreciated.

As she settled into bed and closed her eyes on Sunday night, she relived every dreamy, perfect moment with him, recalling his heated kisses and the way he obviously wanted her as badly as she wanted him.

It'd been so, so long since she'd felt wanted like that. She actually couldn't remember the last time. No, wait, it was once about two years ago, and from that, she'd gotten her precious Mila. But jeez... two years? No wonder she'd been so shameless with the incredibly sexy Julian Remington. Not that she regretted it, because she didn't. It had felt so good to be held and kissed and *desired*.

She fell asleep, smiling as she relived every minute of the two hours she'd spent with him, from their near collision in the store to making out on his sofa. He showed up in her dreams, handsome, smiling, listening to her as if everything she said was the most important thing he'd ever heard.

He was reaching for her, and she was melting into his warm embrace when her ringing phone woke her out of a sound sleep.

As she reached for it on her bedside table, she felt her heart beat hard with the kind of fear that came from crack-of-dawn phone calls. "Hello?"

"Isla... This is Maggie Santana, Gabriel's mother. I'm so sorry to call you at this hour, but I thought you'd want to know that he passed away at four o'clock this morning."

She sat up in bed. "What? Already?"

"Yes, it was very sudden. He was still in the hospital. The tumor... It possibly caused a hemorrhage. They said it happened fast, and he didn't suffer."

"I... I don't know what to say. I'm so sorry."

"I'm sorry for you, too. And the children."

God, she'd have to tell Theo...

"We'd very much like to meet them..."

"We'll make that happen soon. I promise."

"Gabriel told us you were a wonderful wife and mother and that he hoped you'd find a way to be happy. He also said again how sorry he was for what he put you through."

"Thank you for telling me that." She wiped away the tears that streamed down her face. "Is there anything I can do?"

"We'll need your help to settle his estate, but we don't need to worry about that today."

"Whatever I can do. I'm glad you were with him."

"We'll be thankful for these last days with him for the rest of our lives. We'd missed him terribly."

"It may sound strange to say, but I'd missed him, too. Who he used to be."

"I understand."

"I know you do."

"Let's stay in touch, okay?"

"Yes, please. I'd like that. It'll help the kids to hear your memories of him."

"We've got plenty to share."

They ended the call after promising to talk again soon.

Isla fell back against the pillows, sobbing for him, for her, for their kids, for his parents... for all the people who'd loved Gabriel once upon a time but lost him to an illness that might've been prevented if he'd done something about it when the symptoms first appeared.

It would be a challenge, she realized, to properly grieve the man she'd married without letting him off the hook for all the chaos and despair he'd caused. Her heart hurt for all of them and mostly for Theo, who was old enough to understand his daddy being gone forever but too young to hold on to his memories of him.

Would he only remember that long night hiding in the

closet, or would he also remember the daddy who'd held him over his head, making him shriek with delight? She hoped there were some of the good times left for him, not that there'd been many of them in the few years Theo and Gabriel had had together.

Mila would have no memories of her father, except for the ones Isla and Gabriel's parents were able to give her.

Isla was on her second cup of coffee when Mrs. V came out of the third bedroom at around eight, looking as tired as Isla felt. She was so cute in a purple zip-up bathrobe. "Are they sleeping in?"

"Yes, thank goodness."

"Why aren't you?"

"Get some coffee, and I'll tell you."

"Uh-oh." She sat next to Isla a few minutes later. "What's going on?"

"Gabriel died early this morning."

She gasped. "Oh, Isla..."

"His mother called. She said it was sudden, and he didn't suffer. It was probably a hemorrhage."

"That's so sad. I'm so sorry for your loss, honey."

"Can I tell you something?"

"Whatever's on your mind."

"It doesn't feel like my loss. I hadn't felt like his wife or partner in a very long time."

"I get it. The marriage was over long before it officially ended."

"Yes, that's it exactly. I have no idea how I'm supposed to feel about him dying. I mean, of course I'm sad that his life was cut short, but I'm sad for him and the kids, not for me. I'm sad for the version of me who loved him and married him and had children with him, but I haven't seen that guy in a long, long time. Well, except for at the hospital. He was more like himself because he was finally on medication."

"The one thing I don't want you to feel is guilty. Do you hear me?"

"Yes, ma'am," Isla said with a small smile. "I'm going to work really hard to not feel guilty."

"Do that. You stood by him much longer than most people would've."

"Only because I couldn't afford to leave, and I was too ashamed of what my life had become to tell my brother I needed help. I wish now I'd involved him sooner."

"No guilt. No regrets. None of this was your fault, honey."

"It wasn't his either."

"To be fair, not seeking medical attention for an obvious issue was entirely his fault, as were the consequences of that failure."

Isla leaned on Mrs. V's shoulder and reached for her hand. "Thank you for being here with us."

"You're the daughter and grandchildren I never had. I'm here for the long haul."

"That makes me feel so much better."

CHAPTER TWENTY

Julian's first meeting of the day was with Liam Rossi, a top Hollywood producer. Since this was an initial consultation, Julian met with him in his office rather than the conference room, sitting in upholstered chairs with coffee in hand. He preferred the more informal approach to these get-to-know-you sessions, during which he tried to determine if he and the potential client were a good fit.

Liam had graying dark hair, brown eyes and a tense demeanor. He wore a charcoal-colored suit with a burgundy tie that he fiddled with as they got settled.

"I'd ask what brings you in today, but the answer is almost always the same," Julian said, using a line that usually got a chuckle from the client of the moment and served to break the ice in an often-emotional situation.

"I need a divorce," Liam said without an ounce of humor to lighten the mood. "I've spent twenty-three years trying to fill the shoes of a dead man, and I just can't do it any longer."

He was on the verge of tears, which wasn't unusual in these first meetings as people came to terms with the fact that their marriage was over and they needed a divorce lawyer.

"Is your wife aware of your intentions?"

"Not yet. I want to have my ducks in a row before I tell her."

"Will it come as a surprise to her?"

"I'm sure it will, and I'm sorry about that. But our entire marriage has been stalked by the ghost of a man I've never met and will never know. I can't live in that shadow anymore. I just can't."

"Who's the man you're referring to?"

"Her fiancé was killed in a rock-climbing accident three weeks before their wedding, which was four years before I met her. In my opinion, she's mourned him and the wedding she had to cancel ever since."

"That's an incredibly traumatic event. I hope she had good support afterward."

"She did—and does. Her family is amazing, and she's had a great therapist helping her, and then us, to cope with the fallout. I love her. I truly do. But I've never felt that she loved me as much as she loved him. He lives on a pedestal in her heart in a way I could only dream of achieving."

"Do you have children?"

"Two teenage sons."

"I assume you intend to seek joint custody?"

"Yes, I do, although they'll probably be so furious with me for leaving their mother that they won't want anything to do with me."

"You're willing to risk that to proceed with a divorce?"

He leaned forward, elbows on his knees, expression earnest. "You have to understand that I simply can't bear to live this way any longer. We've been in therapy throughout our entire relationship. She's spoken more of him than she ever has of me." After a pause, he added, "Of course, I knew about her heartbreaking loss going in, but nothing can prepare you to live your whole life in the shadow of a man who died tragically. It's become unbearable."

"I can start the process as soon as you give me the green

light. I urge you to notify your wife and sons of your intentions so they aren't blindsided when she's served with divorce papers, which would make a difficult situation a thousand times worse."

"I'll talk to them."

"I have to ask this because it may turn out to be relevant... Is there someone else?"

He hesitated, only for a second, but long enough to answer Julian's question. "Nothing has happened."

If he had a dollar for every time he'd heard those exact words...

"I swear. Nothing has happened. But I want to be with her. I want to experience what it might be like to be truly loved and not merely tolerated as an unsatisfactory replacement for a man who died."

"I understand." Julian went over the fee structure that included various costs for mediation versus a trial, which was much more expensive for everyone involved. "We charge on a fee-for-service basis, rather than hourly, but there're additional costs based on your needs, such as accounting, investigation and other add-ons should the case go to trial."

"I'm hoping it'll be fairly straightforward," Liam said.

That was another thing almost every client said and thought. It was almost never *fairly straightforward*.

"We'll do what we can to facilitate that for you."

He guided Liam through the signing of the retention agreement and directed him to Mattie, who'd collect the initial retainer.

They stood and shook hands.

"Thank you for your help."

"Of course. I'll wait to hear from you on next steps."

The second the door closed behind Liam, Julian went to his desk to check his phone, hoping for a text from Isla. He was disappointed that she hadn't reached out and furious with himself for caring so much. What the hell was wrong with him since he'd met her? Why was he so interested in her sick children and whether Isla had gotten any sleep?

Mattie knocked and came into the office, catching him staring off into space, contemplating his next move with her.

"Everything all right?"

"Yep. What's up?"

"I wanted to remind you that today's the deadline to RSVP to the premiere of *Valiant*." She laid the embossed invitation from Quantum Productions on his desk. In light of his history with Flynn Godfrey's sister, he'd been surprised to be invited to the film about Flynn's wife, Natalie, and her brave journey to bring a rapist governor to justice. But the entire Remington family had been invited in deference to the longtime friendship between his parents and the Godfrey parents.

As he gazed at the invite, an idea came to him. "I'm allowed a plus-one, right?"

"Yes."

"Go ahead and accept for two."

"They'll want the name of your date for security purposes."

"Isla Santana."

She gave him a curious look but wrote down Isla's name. "I'll take care of it."

"Thanks." The thought of taking Isla to a movie premiere filled him with the kind of excitement he rarely experienced. He endeavored daily to keep his emotions even, omitting things like excitement, joy and anger. It was easier to function when he wasn't all over the place.

But regulation had become a huge challenge since Isla had strolled into his office and turned things upside down. After their encounter at his house, all he wanted was more of her and the fully alive, electrified way she made him feel.

He was aware enough to recognize he was standing on a slippery slope where she was concerned. He'd never once wavered on the vow to remain single or even been tempted to waver.

Until now.

He'd seen her a handful of times and already knew he'd do whatever it took to keep her in his life. Why her? Why now? Had seeing Aimee made him vulnerable, creating an opening to his heart that Isla had walked straight through? If so, how did he get her out? He didn't want to be vulnerable to anyone. The whole reason they'd made the vow in the first place was to protect themselves from the very situation he was now in with Isla.

Even as he tried to figure out how to undo what'd already been done, he wondered how she was, how the kids were feeling and if she was thinking of him as much as he was of her.

And ugh... He was a grown-ass man with a shit ton of work to do and was wasting time wondering if a woman was thinking about him.

Ridiculous.

A knock sounded on his door.

"Enter."

Jackson came in, shutting the door behind him.

Without looking up from the file he'd only just flipped open, he said, "What's up?"

"Jules..."

Julian looked up and noticed the stricken expression on Jackson's face. "What's wrong?"

"Isla's husband died early this morning. His attorney called to notify me. I thought you'd want to know."

For a second, Julian was certain he'd heard him wrong. "He *died*?"

Jackson nodded.

Julian was on his feet and reaching for his suit coat before he'd made the decision to stand.

"What're you doing?"

"I'm going to her."

"Um, is that a good idea?"

"Yeah, it is."

"Jules... Her husband just *died*. You might want to give her a minute before you go flying over there."

Jackson was right. Of course he was. But every instinct Julian had was propelling him toward her, and his instincts rarely did him wrong.

"I need you to cover my day."

"*What?* I'm not prepared for that."

"Yes, you are. You're up to speed on all my cases. I need this, Jack. Please."

"What's your plan when you get there?"

"That'll depend on what she needs."

"And you're fully aware that you're marching into something with this woman that could change your life forever when you said you'd never let that happen?"

Jackson's words stopped him cold.

Was he prepared for his life to change forever? Only if it was changing to make room for her. Yeah, he was okay with that. "I know what I'm doing."

"Do you?"

Julian put a hand on Jackson's shoulder. "Thank you for caring, but I've got this. I need you to cover for me today. All right?" Julian, Carson and Griffin, all of whom were full partners, tried very hard never to pull rank on the younger brothers who worked for them, but Julian wouldn't hesitate to play that card if it meant getting to Isla that much sooner.

"Yeah, boss, whatever you need."

"Thank you. I appreciate it."

"I hope you're being careful here, Jules. I've never seen you act this way about a woman."

Because there'd never been one like Isla. "I'm okay. I promise. I'll check in later." Without waiting for his brother to reply, he rushed out the door, stopping for a second to speak to Mattie. "I have something I have to do. Jackson is covering my day."

Maddie raised her left brow, which was the only indication she gave that he was behaving wildly out of character. "Is everything all right?"

"Yes. I'll see you tomorrow."

"Okay."

He felt her watching him as he moved toward the elevator, hoping no one would stop him before he could make his escape. All he could think about was Isla and what she must be dealing with. He wanted to help if he could and hoped he'd be welcome.

What if he wasn't?

He'd never been in a situation remotely close to this, so he had no idea what to expect. All he knew was that he couldn't *not* go.

The elevator arrived and got him out of there before anyone else tried to stop him. He had no illusions about Jackson keeping this news to himself and fully expected to hear from each of his siblings imminently. He'd deal with them later. First, he'd see what Isla needed. She was all that mattered right now.

Driving as fast as he dared through traffic, he thought only of her and of their time together the other night and the things she'd shared with him about her complex emotions in regard to Gabriel. His mind raced with thoughts and implications as his phone rang with calls from each of his brothers, right on schedule.

Julian declined each call and then declined them again when they called a second time.

The dash screen lit up with texts.

At a red light, he saw one from Carson: *What the hell are you doing? Come back to the office. Let's talk about this before you go off a cliff.*

He didn't want to talk about it. Even knowing he was

heading for a cliff couldn't stop him from hanging that left turn onto Laurel Canyon Boulevard and racing up the hill to her, taking the curves faster than he ever had before.

Julian had no clue what he'd be walking into and didn't care.

Thanks to some lucky breaks with traffic, sixteen minutes after leaving the parking garage, he pulled into the driveway at her rental, relieved to see her car was there. That was sixteen minutes too long, he thought, as he pressed the doorbell.

An older woman answered.

"You must be Mrs. Ventura."

"That's right."

"I'm here to see Isla."

"And you are?"

"Julian Remington."

"It's okay, Mrs. V," he heard Isla say from inside as relief washed over him. "Let him in."

Mrs. V stepped aside to admit him, and he went right to Isla, who was standing in the foyer.

He stopped short of immediately embracing her the way he wanted to. She looked so small and lost that he wanted to wrap his arms around her and do anything he could to make this better for her, even if that was an impossible task. "I came as soon as I heard."

"Thank you." Her chin quivered as she looked up at him with swollen eyes that were shiny with new tears. "I still can't believe it."

"I know." He couldn't stop himself from reaching for her.

She came to him like she'd been doing it all her life, slipping her arms inside his suit coat and around his waist as he drew her in close to him while she sobbed.

He noticed that she fit perfectly in his arms as he rested his chin on the top of her head while breathing in the unmistakable scent he was already addicted to. "I'm so sorry, Isla."

"You shouldn't be here."

Oh shit. "I know, but I wanted to be here for you."

"No, I mean because the kids have had a stomach bug. I don't want you to get it."

"I don't care about that. What can I do for you?"

"This," she said, snuggling into him and sighing, "is just what I need."

"How are the kids?"

"They're napping after a rough weekend."

"What do you need?"

"More of this," she said, holding on tighter to keep him from getting away.

That was absolutely fine with him.

HE'S HERE.

That was all Isla could think as she luxuriated in the scents of starch and citrusy cologne and sexy man. And as soon as she had that thought, she immediately felt terrible. Gabriel was dead, and she was thrilled to see Julian, to know he cared enough to come running to her after hearing about Gabriel's passing.

What kind of person did that make her?

She was relieved to have his support and company, especially since Denny was working in San Diego for a few days, finishing a job that was already running late. When she'd called him with the news about Gabriel, he'd felt bad that he couldn't come home. Isla had told him not to worry about it, that Mrs. V was with her, and she was okay, but she was more so now that Julian was there. It made no sense, but it was true. His presence was a comfort to her.

"I know you must be so busy. I'm all right if you need to go back to work."

"I cleared my day."

Swoon. He'd cleared his day. For her.

Mrs. V was probably thinking she'd lost her mind as she

clung to the handsome man in the suit who'd cleared his day for her, but Isla couldn't bring herself to worry about that when it felt so good to have his arms around her and his heart beating fast beneath her ear.

With his phone ringing incessantly, he pulled back from her to shut it off and then put his arm around her to lead her to the sofa, where he sat next to her and reached for her hand. His was so warm compared to hers. She'd been freezing since she got the news.

"How did you hear?"

"His mother called me at five a.m."

"Oh wow. That must've been so shocking."

"It was. I really didn't expect it to happen so fast, but I keep thinking it's a blessing for him that he won't suffer a slow, painful decline."

"That's a good way to look at it."

She leaned her head against his shoulder because he was there and he cared and that meant so much to her. "You know what else?"

"What, honey?"

Her heart did a funny stutter when he called her that. "I'm filled with this strange energy today, knowing that I no longer have to be on full alert like I've been for years now, anticipating the next disaster."

"It's an adrenaline response. I've seen it happen before when someone who's been in danger finds out the risk has been alleviated."

"So it's normal to feel almost amped up about that?"

"Totally normal."

"My first thought should be grief for him and the kids, but instead, I'm oddly relieved to know that I don't have to be afraid of him anymore. And then I immediately feel guilty, because he couldn't help the things he did."

"Regardless of the reason, you were terrorized by the things he did, Isla. You have every right to feel relieved that the threat has been permanently removed from your life, even if you feel sad for him and your kids."

"It's a lot of emotion all at once."

"I can't even imagine."

"In the middle of it all is this lovely sparkle of joy, thanks to you."

CHAPTER TWENTY-ONE

"Oh. Well..." He was adorable when he was flustered, which she suspected didn't happen very often.

"I can't believe you left work to come here."

"You can't? Really?"

"No one has ever done anything like that for me, except for Denny and Mrs. V, of course."

"Well, that's a damned shame. You should be treated like the queen you are."

She fanned her face.

"Cut it out," he said with a grunt of laughter.

"I will not cut it out. I was so happy after the other night."

"I was, too."

"I'm tired of being sad and devastated. I want to feel like I did with you. I felt so alive and young and..." She hiccupped on a sob.

"Shhh, it's okay. Everything is going to be okay. You're strong and resilient, and you're going to get through this and find your way to being happy all the time rather than just some of the time."

"My kids make me so happy, but that night, with you... That was different."

"It was for me, too."

"I haven't felt good like that in so long. Thank you for giving me that."

"Please don't thank me. It was a great night for me, too. I'm just so sorry you're hurting."

"I'm in shock more than anything. The past several days have been a lot."

"Yes, they have, which is why I should probably go and give you some space to cope."

She turned so she could look up at him. "Do you want to go?"

"Not even kinda."

"Then please don't. I feel better when you're here."

"Can I tell you the statistics for relationships following a divorce or the loss of a spouse?"

"Do you have to?"

"I feel obligated to tell you that we're possibly setting ourselves up for disaster here."

"Because you don't do relationships, right?"

He winced. "That's not what I mean in this case."

"What do you mean?"

"There's an attachment forming here, and it wouldn't be fair for me not to tell you that this is the worst-possible time for you to become attached to me or anyone else."

"And it's always a bad time for you, right?"

"Usually, but not with you. It's different with you."

"Why?"

He laughed. "The hell if I know, but it just is, and all my usual rules of engagement don't seem to apply to you."

"What're those rules?"

"Be honest from the beginning, keep it casual, no emotions, no commitments, no promises, nothing that would give the other person hope that there's a future with me."

"That sounds like a pretty grim way to live, even if you're doing it to protect yourself."

"It's worked for me."

"I know." She snuggled in closer to him and put her arm around his waist. "If you feel like this is too much for you, I'll totally understand, because we're a lot, and this situation is a lot, and I wouldn't blame you at all if you ran for your life back to the office, where things make sense to you."

"Things make sense to me here, too."

"Really?"

"Uh-huh."

"Does that scare you?"

"Not nearly as much as it probably should."

Theo came into the room, dragging his light blue blanket behind him. He stopped short when he saw her cuddled up to Julian.

She sat up and held out her hands to him. "Are you feeling better, sweetie?"

"A little." He eyed Julian. "Did you bring the fishies?"

Julian's lips quivered with amusement. "No, they have to stay at the office with my dad."

"I love the fishies."

"They're so pretty," Isla said.

"Lots of colors."

Isla ran her lips over his forehead and was relieved that his fever had broken. "Are you hungry?"

Theo shrugged. "A little bit."

"You want some animal crackers?"

He nodded.

"Do you want to stay here with Mr. Julian while I go get them?"

"Okay."

Isla kissed the top of his blond head and settled him with his blanket against a sofa pillow.

"I see the puppies."

She glanced at Julian. "Code for 'please turn on *Paw Patrol*, Mom.'"

"I love *Paw Patrol*," Julian said, earning a skeptical look from her.

"For real?"

"What's not to love? Maybe Theo can remind me of their names."

"He'd love to." Isla turned on the TV and handed the remote to Theo, who was better at finding things than she was.

"That's Rubble!"

"Who's that guy?" Julian asked.

"Zuma!"

Smiling, Isla left them to get the animal crackers.

Mrs. V was in the kitchen with a cup of tea and one of the many catalogs she enjoyed receiving so she could "window-shop" without leaving her home—or Isla's. She glanced at Isla with a million questions in her expression.

"Theo wants some animal crackers."

"How's he feeling?"

"Much better. The fever has broken."

"That's a relief."

"I hope we don't get it next."

"Who's that handsome drink of water you were hugging in the foyer?"

"My ex-divorce attorney."

"I figured when he said he was a Remington, and he looks like a lawyer."

Isla filled a small bowl with animal crackers and a sippy cup with apple juice that she diluted with some water. "What do lawyers look like?"

"They look successful like him. What's up with him?"

"I have no idea, but I like having him around."

"Is he the one you ran into at the store the other night?"

"Uh-huh."

"Be careful, Isla. You're already dealing with a lot."

"I know, and he's done nothing but try to help. Having him around makes me feel better. I can't explain it. It just is."

"Do you want me to go home?"

"No, not at all."

"I don't want to be underfoot."

"You're not. We love having you here. Please don't go."

"If you change your mind, you need only say so."

She went to Mrs. V and hugged her from behind. "I'm not going to change my mind. I need all my people right now, especially you."

Mrs. V patted her hand. "I'll stay for as long as you need me."

"Thank you."

"Be careful with that sinfully handsome man. He's got 'dangerous' written all over him."

"Is he sinfully handsome? I hadn't noticed."

Mrs. V snorted with laughter. "Liar."

Isla smiled at her friend and then took the crackers and juice to Theo, who was talking Julian's ear off about the *Paw Patrol* characters and their various roles in the story.

"Mawshall is the fire dog. He keeps everyone safe."

"That's an important job."

"He's a Dal... a... Mommy, what is he again?"

"A Dalmatian."

"I can never remember that," he said with a grin for Julian.

"They made a movie about Dalmatians," Julian said.

Isla shook her head. "Too scary."

"That movie wasn't good at all," Julian said.

"I wanna see it!"

"Sorry," Julian said with a grimace.

Isla laughed. "Hopefully, he'll forget about it."

"No, I won't." Theo pointed to Julian's burgundy silk tie. "Why do you have to wear that?"

"That's a very good question, sir."

"Does it squeeze your neck?"

"Every day."

"Why don't you take it off?"

"I think I will."

Isla and Theo watched, fascinated for different reasons, as Julian slid the tie free and released the first two buttons of his gray dress shirt.

Then he hooked the tie around Theo's neck. "Want me to show you how to make the knot?"

Theo nodded eagerly.

"Come sit on my lap." When Theo was seated facing away from Julian, he reached around him to show him the moves to make the knot.

"That looks hard."

"You get so you can do it in your sleep."

"You can't do anything in your sleep but sleep!"

Julian laughed.

"Three-year-olds are very literal," Isla said.

"So I'm discovering."

Mrs. V came into the room, carrying Mila. "Miss Priss is up and asking for Mommy."

Isla held out her arms to the little girl. "Here I am, sweet pea."

Mila gave Julian the side-eye.

He wiggled his fingers at her, and she dove into Isla's shoulder to hide from him.

"She's grumpy when she first wakes up," Theo told Julian as he continued to try to replicate his moves with the tie.

Julian guided him patiently until they had the knot tied.

"I did it, Mom! Look, I did it!"

"You sure did. Great job, honey."

"I want to do it again."

Julian untied the knot and walked him through the steps a second time.

Isla thought about the much more important things Julian probably should've been doing but couldn't bring herself to tell him to go back to work, that she'd be fine. She didn't want him to go, and he didn't seem in any particular rush to depart.

He glanced over at her while Theo worked on his tie.

She met his gaze, still holding Mila. "This is my life."

"I know."

"You should be *running for your life*."

"I know that, too."

Mila squirmed to get free from her mother, so Isla put her down to play on the floor with Theo, who had Julian's tie looped around his neck. "So why aren't you?"

"I don't want to. Unless…"

"What?"

Julian took her hand and linked their fingers. "Would you rather put this on hold for now? I don't want to intrude during such a difficult time for you."

"You're not intruding. I'm glad you're here, and as hard and shocking as the past several days have been… I'm trying to focus on the future rather than the past and figure out what's best for myself and the kids and… I don't want to put anything on hold, even though the timing is less than ideal."

"That's good news, because I don't want that either, but I do want you to promise me something."

"What's that?"

"If it starts to feel like too much on top of a lot, you have to tell me. You won't hurt my feelings, and I'll still be here when you're feeling ready."

"I can do that."

"Promise?"

"Promise."

With their heads resting on the back of the sofa, gazes locked, hands joined, a thrill of anticipation zinged through her. It'd been so, so long since she'd looked forward to anything or been excited about something that wasn't related to the kids that she'd almost forgotten what it felt like.

"What're you thinking?" he asked.

"That it feels good to feel good."

"I'm glad you're feeling good."

"I'm still sad and stunned, but I'm glad you're here, too. I guess all those things can be true at the same time." After a pause, she said, "Will you promise me something?"

"Anything."

"You should hear what it is before you say anything."

"Not changing my answer. What do you want me to promise?"

"That if this..." With her free hand, she included the kids. "If it turns out to be more than you bargained for, or if you decide you want to stick with the stubbornly single life, will you tell me? I'd rather you come right out and say it than disappear or ghost me or whatever people do these days."

"I'd never ghost you, and I promise I'll tell you if things change for me. But... I need you to tell me if I screw up, because I haven't done anything like this in almost twenty years, and I'm afraid I've forgotten how."

"You're doing great so far."

"It's early days. Don't let me screw this up, okay?"

"I won't." She looked down at their joined hands, marveling at how natural and normal it felt to be holding hands with him when she'd met him less than a week ago. "Do you need to go back to work?"

"I'm covered for today."

She still couldn't believe he'd covered his day, no doubt a complicated proposition, to be with her. He'd done that for her.

"Do you want to get out of here for a while? Take a ride maybe?"

"That'd be nice. We've been cooped up all weekend. Where do you want to go?"

"I need to take a run up to Ojai. We've got a ranch up there with horses and other animals that my grandfather wants one of us to check on. The kids might enjoy that."

"They'd love it. Are you sure you want to do that?"

"Yeah, I'm sure."

CHAPTER TWENTY-TWO

They took Isla's car because the car seats were already installed, and after a quick stop at Julian's so he could change clothes, they headed north to Ojai on a beautiful, mild, blue-sky Southern California day.

When he'd been changing into jeans and a pullover, he'd taken a quick look at his phone and found thirty missed calls—twelve of them from his siblings, several of whom had called multiple times—and forty-six texts. He powered down the phone but stuck it in his back pocket in case he needed it later.

He hadn't taken a day completely off the grid in years, even when he was on "vacation," so he refused to feel guilty for one day away from it all. Tomorrow would arrive all too soon, and he'd pay the piper then. For now, for this one day, he was going to enjoy the time with Isla and her kids, who were thrilled to be going on a "mystery ride," as he'd referred to it.

When they were on their way north to Ojai, Theo started asking questions about where they were going.

"Is it the beach?"

"Is it a pool?"

"Is it a toy store?"

"Is it Disneyland?"

Julian looked over at Isla, who seemed to have relaxed a bit since he'd suggested the outing. "He knows about that, huh?"

"Sometimes I think he knows about everything."

"Mickey," Mila said. "Minnie."

"And he's teaching his sister."

Isla had a mirror affixed to the visor that allowed him to see the kids in the back seat. They were beautiful, well-behaved children, and he was enjoying spending time with them. Would he enjoy being with them every day, or was it because he was so new to kids that they intrigued him almost as much as their lovely mother did? He had no way to know, so he intended to proceed with caution where they were concerned.

There'd be hell to pay tomorrow with his family. They'd demand an explanation for his seemingly irrational behavior and would want to know why he'd run off to be with a woman he barely knew after she'd found out that the husband she'd been divorcing had died suddenly.

He had no doubt their sibling group chat was probably on fire with speculation that Julian had lost his mind all of a sudden and what were they going to do about it? They'd be formulating a plan for how they might rein him in and get him back on track with the program they'd all committed to years ago.

A week ago, if any of them had behaved the way he had today, he'd be having that same conversation with the others.

Now, everything was different, and the only thing that'd changed was the arrival of the woman in the passenger seat, who held his hand as if it was something they'd been doing for years. Everything about being with her felt natural and almost effortless, as if he'd been meant to find her and vice versa.

While it was easy to get lost in this moment of domestic tranquility, he had to remember that she'd recently survived the emotional equivalent of a massive earthquake, and in many ways, her life was still in shattered pieces. The wounds she carried wouldn't heal overnight, and he was under no illusion that the path forward would be easy.

Him wanting to be by her side while she traversed that path made this situation an earthquake in *his* life.

He'd never been so happy to be caught up in someone else's disaster, with his well-ordered life spinning out of control with every minute he spent with Isla and her kids. Would he wake up from this odd new state of being in a week or two to discover he'd made a huge mistake and then go back to normal? That was certainly possible, but he didn't expect it to happen. Nothing about being with Isla felt like a mistake. If anything, it seemed a bit like... well... *destiny*, a word that would've given him hives a few days ago.

How else to explain the series of events that had him at the wheel of an SUV owned by a woman with two young kids, driving them up to the ranch in Ojai on a Monday afternoon after blowing off a workday for the first time ever?

He'd promised his grandfather he'd check on things at the ranch, not that the ranch needed checking with their outstanding ranch manager, Miguel, in charge of things. But Spence wanted the family to put eyes on the place every few weeks, so that's why he'd asked one of them to go up.

With horses, goats and chickens running around, the kids would love it, and perhaps the spectacular scenery in the mountains would give Isla some peace, too.

"So your family has an actual ranch in Ojai."

Julian winced. "That sounds pretty fancy, huh?"

"Just a tad. How long has it been in the family?"

"My grandfather bought it in 1980 because he wanted a place the family could go to get away from the city."

"Is your dad his only child?"

"Yep, which means we're his only grandchildren, so we're all close to him. Growing up, we spent a lot of weekends up there. We couldn't wait to get there... until we were in high school, that is, and wanted nothing to do with him, the family or the ranch."

Isla laughed. "So you were rotten, huh?"

"For a while. I snapped out of it after college. How about you? Were you an awful teenager?"

"Denny would say I was the worst."

"I knew him back then, and I can't imagine he was in charge of a teenage girl."

"I was a monster to him. It's a wonder he still speaks to me."

"He adores you."

"And I adore him, even if he drives me crazy sometimes with the protectiveness. Although, if I'd listened to him years ago, things might've been different. Not that I'd change anything, because being with Gabriel led to my babies, the best things to ever happen to me."

"My grandma Freida was a big believer in the universe bringing exactly what's intended for you."

"Do you believe that?"

He gave her hand a squeeze. "I'm starting to."

She sighed. "Julian…"

"Yes, Isla?"

"I don't know what to think of this."

"You and me both."

"Does it scare you?" she asked.

"It scares the s-h-i-t out of me."

"Are you scared of me?"

"Terrified," he said, smiling at her. "But you should be more afraid of me."

"How come?"

"Denny told you I'm a risky bet, right?"

"He did. He said you go out of your way to avoid things like suddenly widowed single mothers with two very young children."

He winced at the way she described herself. "I always have, and PS, you're the first suddenly widowed single mom with two very young kids I've met, and if I had ever met a woman like you before you, I probably would've run screaming in the opposite direction."

"So why are you taking my kids and me to Ojai?"

He shook his head as he grunted out a laugh. "That's a very good question." After a pause, he said, "All I know is that when I heard about what'd happened overnight, I needed to be with you. It was like a force bigger than me propelling me toward you." He glanced at her again. "And trust me, that sounds as ridiculous to me as it does to you."

"It sounds incredibly romantic to me."

Julian scoffed. "I'm not romantic at all."

"I think maybe you could be if you had the right inspiration."

"Is that right?"

"Uh-huh." After another pause, she said, "Will you do me another favor?"

"Anything."

"Will you talk to me about how you're feeling, even if it's not what I want to hear?"

Julian had never had such an emotionally charged conversation with a woman, even Aimee. "Yeah," he said gruffly. "I will."

He was about to tell her there was nothing he wouldn't do for her, but he decided he ought to save something for tomorrow.

ISLA HADN'T EXPECTED to feel so calm after receiving the news about Gabriel earlier. But knowing he was finally at peace had diffused the constant state of turmoil she'd lived in for years. And having Julian come running to her, wanting to be there for her... That was heady stuff from a man who'd avoided such things his entire adult life.

She wouldn't be the one to make him want forever with one woman, but there was no reason she couldn't enjoy a little swoon-worthy romance with a kind, sexy, interesting man for as long as it lasted. If anyone deserved that, she did, and after the years of pure hell she'd endured with Gabriel, she was going to enjoy it without feeling guilty.

Isla took in the mountainous scenery leading into the quaint town of Ojai, which she'd never visited before. "Oh, this is so pretty."

"I love it here. It's been a home away from home my whole life. We'd come up here with my dad on the weekends, and my brothers would want to surf, so he'd drive us out to Ventura. My sister Gillian always got car sick because the road is hilly and winding, so she got to sit in the front seat. She used to gloat about getting to sit in the front."

"How did he move around with nine kids?"

"In a very large Suburban. Both my parents had them when we were all at home."

"Your family required its own school bus."

He laughed. "Pretty close. You want to get some lunch before we go up to the ranch?"

"Sure."

"What do the kids like?"

Isla spotted a pizza place on the town's main street. "That'd work."

Julian parked in a public lot and went to help Theo out of his seat.

Theo giggled when Julian couldn't figure out how to release the safety clasp.

"Are you laughing at me, mister?"

"Yes!" Theo let loose with his trademarked belly laugh. Anyone who heard that and didn't laugh along with him wasn't truly alive.

Julian proved he was truly alive by cracking up with Theo as he continued to try to figure out the clasp. "I went to law school, for crying out loud. Why can't I undo this thing?"

"It's a secret," Theo told him.

"Tell me how."

Theo shook his head as he continued to laugh.

"Isla, come help. Theo's being mean to me."

"I'm coming." With Mila in her arms, she walked around to the other side of the car and reached in with one hand to release the clasp.

"What? Come on. How'd you do that?"

"Should we tell him?" she asked Theo as Julian lifted him out of the seat.

"No! It's a secret!"

They crossed the street and entered Ojai Pizza Company.

"My dad used to bring us here for dinner on Saturday nights. We loved it. I haven't thought about that in years."

"I'm trying to picture your dad wrangling nine kids by himself."

"He was better at it than my mother was. We drove her insane. He just rolled with it." Julian helped her to settle Theo in a booster seat while Isla kept Mila on her lap. "It's possible he was medicated."

Isla laughed. "I'd be surprised if he wasn't. What's the age difference?"

"Thirteen years between me and Roman."

"What are the others' names again?"

"Carson, Griffin, Jordan, Kaidan, Ethan, Jackson, Gillian and Roman."

"All your names end with n."

"Our parents' names do, too. Corbin and Katherine both have an n sound. So they made it a thing."

"I like it. I still can't believe there're nine of you. That's wild. I've never known a family that big."

"Growing up, I knew of one family with twelve kids and

another with eleven. I negotiated a divorce for a mother of eight last year."

"That's a lot of kids. I can barely handle two. How in the world does anyone wrangle eight or nine?"

"Well, in our case, we weren't all little at the same time. And for another, they had a lot of help from a long string of nannies, who are probably still in therapy after dealing with us. The older kids helped with the younger ones. We made it work."

"It sounds like a fun way to grow up."

"It was. For a time. What looks good to you?"

"Mama, chicken!"

"How about pizza?" Isla asked her son.

"No, Mama. Chicken."

"They have boneless chicken bites," Julian said.

"Chick," Mila said, parroting her brother, like always.

"The people have spoken," Julian said with a smile. "What do you feel like?"

"I'd love a salad and a bite of whatever you're getting."

"Want to split a large, tossed salad and a small pizza?"

"That sounds good to me. No onions on the salad?"

"You got it. What do you like on the pizza?"

"Will you laugh when I say onions?"

His laughter was a lovely sound and made him even sexier than he already was. "You're a woman of contradictions."

"Only with onions. Cooked good. Uncooked bad."

"Got it." He pretended to make a note. "Anything else with the onions?"

"You pick."

"Pepperoni?"

"That works."

"Want me to order for us?"

She appreciated that he'd asked and didn't just assume she'd be fine with it. "Sure, go ahead."

When the waitress came to get their drink order, Julian

asked if they had Mountain Dew. It was such a small thing, but it meant so much to her that he remembered what she liked.

"I'm sorry that we don't. Second choice?"

"Sprite is fine," Isla said.

"I'll have unsweetened iced tea, please," Julian said. "What about the kids?"

"I have drinks for them."

"Do you want to order food, too?" the waitress asked.

Julian gave her their order and asked for two orders of the boneless chicken bites.

"One order is more than enough," Isla said. "They won't eat that much."

"Are you sure?"

"Very sure. One is good."

"Mom's the boss," Theo said.

"I see that," Julian replied. "Thanks for letting me know."

Theo giggled at the face Julian made.

"You're good with him," Isla said.

"Am I? You should know..." He leaned in and added, "I have no clue what I'm doing."

"You're a natural."

"No way."

"Yes way. You make him laugh. That's honestly all it takes to win over a three-year-old."

"What does it take to win over a one-year-old?"

"Patience. She's in her shy, I-want-Mommy stage."

"I get that. Mommy is pretty great."

HER SMILE HIT him in all the feels, filling him with a sense of absolute rightness that would've been unthinkable before she'd walked into his life and changed everything. "I ought to be pissed at you," he said in a teasing tone.

"Pissed," Theo said with a grin.

Julian winced. "Whoops."

"He's a parrot. Are you going to tell me why you should be PO'd with me?"

"I was just thinking how you came strolling into my office and turned my well-ordered life upside down in the course of an hour, and I'd like to know how exactly you did that."

"First of all, I do not *stroll*."

"Trust me. There was strolling."

Her lips quivered with amusement. "You're being ridiculous."

"My siblings tell me that every day. Anyway, there I was, minding my own business and dealing with other people's nonsense. I was perfectly fine until you showed up with two of the cutest kids I've ever met. Tell me the truth... Are you some sort of witch with magical powers who cast a spell on me or something? Because that's the only possible explanation for why I'm at a pizza place in Ojai on a Monday afternoon with one kid in a booster, another on her mother's lap and a very pretty mommy trying not to laugh at my soliloquy."

"You found me out. I cast a spell on you."

"I knew it."

"I can undo it if you want me to."

"Can I get back to you on that?"

"It's a limited-time offer."

"Is that right?" Had he ever had more fun simply talking to a woman? Not since Aimee...

The waitress brought placemats and crayons for the kids that immediately captured their attention.

"Can I tell you something?" she asked quietly so the children wouldn't overhear her.

"I wish you would."

"I feel so guilty for having fun when..."

He covered her hand with his. "I know, but what would he want for you?"

"He said he wanted me to have fun, to be happy with the kids and new friends who make me laugh."

"There's absolutely nothing else you can do for him besides your best to raise your kids to be great people and try to make yourself happy along the way. The choices he made for himself took a terrible toll on you. There's nothing wrong with making this next phase the Age of Isla—and her kids. And wow, that sounds incredibly self-serving, doesn't it?"

Smiling, she said, "No, I get what you mean, and you're right. This is my chance to forge a new path."

"That's right. It'll always be incredibly sad that his story ended the way it did, but it doesn't have to define you or your story. I tell my clients all the time that they're the authors of their own destinies and only they can decide the outcome. Granted, we're all hit with things that force us to make course corrections, but at the end of the day, we're in charge of our own paths in life."

"I like the sound of that, but so far, I've had very little control over my destiny other than deciding to get married. I feel like outside forces, from my parents' accident to Gabriel's struggles, have charted much of my course for me."

"Well, you're the captain of this ship now. The future is yours to shape to your liking."

"That feels kind of daunting, if I'm being honest." She glanced toward the kids, who'd pushed their placemats together to make one big, scribbled picture. "Being solely responsible for two little beings is so overwhelming."

"Haven't you been mostly responsible for them all along?"

"I mean… I guess so? But I wasn't technically a single parent."

"Weren't you?"

"Are you cross-examining me, Counselor?"

He laughed. "Sorry, no. I'm just saying that in some ways, nothing will change for you, even though the title has become official."

"That's true."

"I've had single-parent clients tell me that the benefit of sole-custody single parenthood is that there's no one to question your decisions. You're in charge of everything, which is a lot, no doubt about that, but it's also freeing in the sense that you don't have to consider anyone else's opinion about what's best for your kids."

"I'm afraid I won't always know what's best for them."

The kids were now driving Theo's trucks over the "road" they'd drawn on the placemats. They were so good at entertaining themselves, which was a huge gift to her as she stared down full-time single parenthood.

"Yes, you will. You have all the skills and sensibilities you need to do a brilliant job. I have full faith in you."

"How's that possible? You barely know me."

"How's any of this possible? I just know. It's that simple—and that complicated."

She flashed him a saucy grin. "Are we still talking about my sensibilities?"

"You're so freaking beautiful," he said gruffly.

Before she could catch her breath from hearing those words from him, the waitress arrived with their food, and she was occupied with cutting up chicken while she reeled from what he'd said and how he'd looked at her as he'd said it.

AFTER HE INSISTED on paying for lunch, they buckled the kids back into the SUV and headed up into the hills on winding roads that delighted Theo with their twists and turns.

"Is this the road that made your sister sick?" Isla asked.

"One of them."

"What goes on at this ranch of yours?"

"Well, we grow lemons that we sell to fruit distributors all over California."

"That must be a lot of lemons."

"We farm about two hundred acres of lemons, olive trees and grapevines."

"So it's a huge operation."

"You could say that. My grandfather's goal was to make the ranch self-sustaining, and it's more than succeeded in that regard. This is the start of our property now." He gestured to the groves of lemon trees on either side of the road.

Isla took in the rugged beauty of the landscape. "I love the cacti."

"It comes in every shape and size around here."

"It's so different from the city but has a lot of the same Spanish influences."

"I've always loved how different it is from home. It's only like ninety minutes north of LA but seems like a world away."

"I can see why you love it here."

"I'd live here full time if it wasn't for the pesky day job in the city—and the band."

"I'm excited to see you play."

"We're at the Whisky next weekend if you want to come by."

"Um, well, I'll be there. I picked up three shifts cocktailing. My friend is the manager."

He looked over at her, seeming startled. "Oh. I, um... I thought Denny was going to make your money available to you."

"He did, but after I secure us a new place to live, I'm going to put away most of that to pay for the kids to go to college someday."

"Are you sure you want to work in the bar? I mean... it can get crazy."

"I know. I've done it before. It's the best way I can make a lot of money quickly at a time when the kids are asleep. Mrs. V will stay with them. It's all worked out."

She could tell he wanted to say more, but thankfully, he kept his thoughts to himself. On this new path of hers, she was calling the shots, and no one would ever again tell her what to do or how to live. That was a hard line in the sand for her.

They drove for miles past an olive grove and long rows of grapevines that were dormant in the winter before pulling up to a large Spanish-style home with a terracotta roof and tile accents that was situated across from a modern white barn with black trim.

"Can we get out, Mama?" Theo asked, bouncing in his seat.

"You sure can."

She'd shown Julian the secret to the car seat latch, and he had Theo out of his seat in record time.

"See?" he said to Theo. "I can be trained."

Laughing, Theo ran off toward the horses inside a paddock with Julian in hot pursuit. "Horsies! I wanna see the horsies!"

Mila perked up to see what had Theo excited. Her pretty green eyes went wide at the sight of the horses.

"Can you say horse?" Isla asked her daughter.

"Horse."

"That's right."

"Puppy."

"No, puppies are different from horses."

She'd no sooner said that than three golden retrievers came into the yard, barking when they saw Julian and Theo, who was now standing on one of the rails with Julian holding him so he could see the horses.

When Theo saw the dogs, he wanted to get down to greet them and so did Mila.

While Julian lowered Theo to the ground, Isla put Mila down to toddle along on her own to see the dogs. Her little girl resembled a drunken sailor on liberty call on her new legs, so Isla stayed close to catch her if she fell.

The dogs surrounded the kids, who were delighted by them.

"They'll talk about this for weeks," Isla told Julian. "They love animals of all kinds."

"Let's go see the chickens and goats."

"Gochas," Mila said.

"That's her word for goats," Theo told Julian.

"We have a book we read at bedtime with all the animals," Isla added.

"Gochas it is," Julian said as he put Theo on his shoulders and Isla picked up Mila to walk toward the barn, with the dogs leading the way.

"Doggy," Mila said.

"Three doggies."

"Twee?"

"That's right. One, two, three."

"One, two, twee."

"It's three, Mila," Theo said. "I am three. Say three."

"Twee."

Theo laughed. *"Three."*

"Twee."

They all laughed at Theo's dramatic moan.

Julian took them past the barn to visit a wire coop, where they sprinkled feed for the colorful chickens, and then on to play with the goats in the yard. Dogs and goats ran in circles around the kids, who laughed so hard they almost hyperventilated.

When one of the goats knocked Mila over, Isla rushed to pick her up and brush her off. "You're okay, pumpkin. The gocha was just playing."

"Play."

"That's right."

Mila pulled loose to resume the game.

"Thank you so much for this," Isla said to Julian. "It was just what we needed today."

"I'm so glad."

"I thought that was you, Julian," a man said from outside the fence. "To what do we owe the honor?"

"Hey, Miguel. This is Isla and her kids, Theo and Mila. They wanted to see the gochas."

"The *what*?"

"That's one-year-old-speak for goat," Isla said. "Nice to meet you."

Miguel's smile stretched across his sun-weathered face. "You, as well. Your kids are cute."

"Thank you."

With a curious expression on his face, Miguel watched Julian chasing the kids and animals.

While Julian wrangled the kids, Isla wandered closer to the fence, hoping Miguel might share his thoughts.

"Never seen him with kids that little before. Surprised he knows what to do with them."

"He's great with them."

"Interesting."

"Is it?" Isla asked.

"Yes, ma'am. Julian Remington isn't the type of guy to play with kids, goats and dogs in the middle of a workday. That's just not who he is."

Isla was overtaken by a sinking sensation as Miguel's observations landed. Was Julian doing all this to get her into bed, after which he'd suddenly lose interest in her and her kids?

He wouldn't do that. He's Denny's good friend. That has to count for something.

Julian grabbed Mila before one of the goats could crash into her and resituated her before he grinned at Isla over his shoulder.

That man wouldn't play me, she thought. How she knew that, she couldn't say, but her absolute certainty couldn't be denied. He wasn't like other guys. He didn't have time to play games or take a Monday off to spend it with a single mom and her kids just so he could get laid. He could get laid without putting forth that kind of effort.

No, there was a reason he'd chosen to spend this day of all days with them, and if she had to guess, sex was the least of the reasons.

If she turned out to be wrong about him, she'd never trust her gut again.

CHAPTER TWENTY-THREE

Julian drove Isla and two dirty, tired kids back to the city late in the afternoon after showing them the house and walking out into the lemon grove to pick a few to take home.

"This was such a wonderful day," Isla said. "Thank you so much for taking us."

"We'll do it again. Any time you want."

She glanced back to make sure the kids were still napping. They'd conked out shortly after they'd left the ranch. "Don't say that in front of them, or they'll drive us crazy asking to go back."

"I really enjoyed it, too. I haven't been around young kids in a long time. I'd forgotten how inquisitive they are."

"Theo never runs out of questions. Ever. One time, we were coming home late, and I wanted to get them into bed as fast as possible. I had one of them under each arm, and we saw a huge spider in the hallway. Before I could get to it, it'd scurried away and disappeared under the carpet. Well, Theo wanted to know where it had gone. Before I fully thought through the ramifications, I said the spider had gone to the guts of the house. Let me tell you how many thousands of questions I've answered about what goes on in the guts of the house. 'Is his mommy there?' 'Does he have toys there?' 'Is there *Paw Patrol* in the guts of the house?' 'Mom, in the guts of the house, does he have his own house?'"

Julian was rocking with silent laughter. "He doesn't mess around."

"Nope. That was six months ago. He asked about the guts of the house last week."

"It's so funny. I used to be obsessed with spiders and where they came from and how they got into the house. If my mom or dad had mentioned the guts of the house, I would've been similarly obsessed with what went on down there."

"I realized I'd made a huge mistake about ten minutes later when he was sitting up in bed, firing questions at me."

"He might grow up to be a lawyer with that skill."

"I've had that thought more than once. He's an interrogator when he gets ahold of something."

"Allegedly, that's how I was as a little kid, too. I was told I questioned everything and basically drove the adults in my life crazy with my curiosity about all things."

"And look at where that's gotten you."

"I was also told I was lucky I had any siblings, let alone eight of them."

"How'd they end up with nine kids if their marriage was shaky?"

"I don't think it was shaky until it was. We've never heard what caused the rupture, but it was sudden. At least that's how it seemed to us."

"Have you heard any more about them allegedly being back together?"

"Not yet, and we may not be able to prove it. They know how to cover their tracks."

He pulled into the driveway at Isla's rental, shut off the engine and handed the keys to her.

"Thank you for driving."

"No problem. Let me help you get the kids inside."

Julian carried Theo while she had Mila and the backpack she'd brought with changes of clothes, diapers for Mila, drinks and snacks. He'd been impressed by how she was prepared with anything the kids needed. Not once in his entire life had he considered what was involved with taking children somewhere. Now he knew they required a lot of contingency items for whatever might happen.

Isla led the way to the bedroom the kids were sharing, where she removed shoes, changed Mila's diaper, wiped their hands and faces and put them down to finish their naps.

"You're good at that," he said when he followed her to the kitchen after the children were settled.

"At what?"

"Giving them whatever they need when they need it."

"That's motherhood for you."

He tucked a strand of silky hair behind her ear. "You make it look easy."

"I don't know about that."

"I do. It's true. You're a wonderful mother."

"That's nice of you to say. And thank you again for a beautiful day. I'm not sure what this day would've been like if you hadn't shown up to give me something else to think about."

"I'm glad I could be with you."

"I am, too."

"Do you want me to go?"

She shook her head. "Not unless you've had enough of us."

He took a step closer and put his arms around her. "This is a really tough time for you. Please tell me if you want me to leave you alone for a while. I'll come back when you're ready."

She rested her hands on his chest as she gazed up at him. "I don't want you to go anywhere."

"I feel like I should give you some space..."

She shook her head, and with her hands on his face, she

drew him into the sweetest, sexiest kiss of his life, the kind of kiss that stopped traffic and changed lives, even lives that hadn't been looking to be changed.

"I know we're a lot," she whispered against his lips. "I know this isn't what you wanted. But I have to tell you..."

"What? What do you have to tell me?" He felt like his entire life and any chance he had to be happy would come down to whatever she said next.

"I really, really want you to stay."

"For how long?"

She smiled, and his heart expanded, making his chest tighten. "As long as you'd like to stay."

He groaned and dropped his head to her shoulder while acknowledging that she was changing everything one sweet word and one sexy kiss at a time.

And he was allowing it.

If anyone had told him a week ago that he'd be clinging to a woman, about to beg her to give him everything, he'd have thought they were insane.

Julian Remington didn't do forever or happily ever after.

So what in the world was he doing with his arms around a suddenly widowed single mom, kissing her like the world was expected to end at any second?

He had no idea, but being with her felt better than anything ever had, and all he wanted was more.

The hottest kiss in history was interrupted by the sound of the front door opening and closing.

Isla jumped back from him so suddenly, he nearly stumbled.

Mrs. V. Shit.

He sat on one of the barstools so the older woman wouldn't see the prominent evidence of what she'd interrupted.

"Hi, honey. How was Ojai?" She glanced at Julian. "Hello."

"Hi there."

"Ojai was amazing. The kids had the best time. They saw horses, goats, chickens and three of the cutest dogs."

Isla's lips were red and swollen, her cheeks flushed.

Her friend knew exactly what they'd been doing before she'd come in.

"I'm going to lie down for a bit. I'll see you for dinner?"

"Sounds good."

She nodded to Julian as she left the room.

Ugh. Mortifying.

He smiled at the face Isla made. "We weren't fooling her."

"Not at all."

He reached out to her.

She took his hand and let him draw her back into his arms where it seemed like she belonged.

"This is happening really fast."

"I know." She stepped between his legs, put her hands on his shoulders and leaned her forehead against his. "But it feels so good. Better than anything has in longer than I can remember."

"For me, too. Things are complicated for you. I don't want to make anything worse."

"You're making everything better just by being here."

He held her close and rubbed soothing circles on her back.

"I know it must seem unreal that I can be clinging to you right after my husband died, but please know... as sad as I am for him and the kids, and I'm really, *really* sad, but that relationship has been over for me for a long time. Years, really."

He nuzzled her neck. "I like when you cling to me. You should feel free to do that as often as you'd like."

Her soft laughter sent shivers down his spine. "That might be very often."

"Okay."

A sense of peace came over him, as if he'd been on a long

journey and had finally found his way home. "I'm going to go for a bit while you have some time with the kids. If Mrs. V will be here with them, maybe I could come pick you up later."

"Where do you want to go?"

"My place so we can be alone?"

She nodded. "I'd like that."

Neither of them seemed to want to let go, even for a couple of hours.

"You'll come back, right?"

Wild gochas couldn't keep him away. "Yeah," he said. "I'll come back."

AS JULIAN DROVE the short distance from her house to his, he felt dazed, as if he was under the influence of something much bigger than him, bigger than anything he'd ever experienced. He couldn't wait to be with her again.

When he got home, he landed on the sofa, reliving every extraordinary minute he'd spent with her since Jackson told him the news about Gabriel. He was almost afraid to check his phone.

He'd no sooner had that thought than Carson and Griffin came into his house, looking like a pair of angry bears.

Carson put his hands on his hips. "What—and I say this with love—*the actual fuck*, Julian?"

Griffin used his thumb to point to Carson. "What he said."

"Sorry to disappear. I had something I needed to do."

"You had to go to Ojai with Isla Santana and her children on a workday?"

Goddamned Miguel. He was like a gossipy old woman sometimes.

"Yes, I did."

"While you were gone," Griffin said, "Rachel McDavid shot and killed her ex-husband when he tried to break into the house where she and the boys were staying. She's been arrested and booked on manslaughter charges."

"Oh my God." Julian sat up straight. "There's no way she should be charged for defending herself. We need to get her a criminal defense attorney."

"Already done," Griffin replied. "Jackson has had one hell of a day. You might want to check in with him."

"I will. I'm sorry, guys. I needed a minute."

"For what?" Carson asked. "What in the world could you be thinking, swooping in on a recently widowed woman with two kids?"

"I'm not swooping in on anyone. She's had a rough week, yes, but she'd tell you herself that the marriage had been over for years, and the only reason she stayed with him as long as she did was because she couldn't afford to leave."

"What do we tell all our clients about relationships after divorce, Jules?" Griffin asked.

They cautioned their clients to tread carefully when getting into entanglements after ending a marriage that'd made them unhappy. Those entanglements often ended in disaster for people who were already raw from the ordeal they'd been through with their spouse. Several of Julian's clients had ended up back in court with romantic partners who'd tried to take advantage of newly divorced people with fat settlements.

He'd been feeling so good before the buzzkillers showed up to ruin the best day he'd had in years.

"By anyone's standards, Isla has had a week from hell," Carson said. "She's the last woman on earth you should be spending time with right now. Tell me you know that."

"It's what she wants."

"Are you *hearing* yourself?" Carson asked. "What the hell, Julian? What the fuck are you *doing*?"

"I don't know, but it feels pretty damned good."

"It feels great in the moment, but how will it feel when it

blows up in your face because she's no more ready for something like this than you are?"

"I might be ready for it."

"Fuck you," Griffin said. "You're not ready for anything with a widowed mom of two very little kids. This is the exact scenario *we've spent our entire adult lives trying to avoid, for fuck's sake.*"

"I'm aware."

"Are you?" Carson asked. "Because it seems to us like you've lost your damned mind or something. You've known her a couple of days, and you're blowing off work to take her and her *little kids* to Ojai? She has *little kids*, Julian."

"Yes, I've noticed, and they're actually very cute, well-behaved little kids. You should've seen them with the goats today. It was so adorable."

"What is happening?" Griffin asked Carson.

"Hell if I know, but it stops right here, you hear me?"

"Um, no, I can't hear you, especially when you're yelling at me."

"Someone needs to yell at you before you screw up your entire life—and hers. Are you thinking about her, Julian?"

"She seems to be all I can think about."

"Did you *hear what you just said about a freaking woman with little kids*? That's the last thing in the world you want anything to do with!"

Julian shrugged helplessly. He could no more explain this situation to his brothers than he could to himself. All he knew was that nothing was going to keep him from her now that he'd found her.

Had he been looking for this? God no, but now that he knew her, he couldn't—and wouldn't—walk away from her. "Look, you guys, I want you to know... I hear what you're saying, and if the roles were reversed, I'd be in your faces, too. All I can say is... Well, she's different."

His brothers stared at him as if they'd never met him, let alone been his closest friends for his entire life.

"She's *different*," Carson said to Griffin, his tone incredulous. "This one is *different*."

"Have you forgotten the many, many, *many* reasons we made that vow to each other in the first place?" Griffin asked. "Do we need to remind you what it was like to be dragged through a vicious custody battle *for ten goddamned years* or all the absolute *insanity* we see in our practices between people who thought they'd *found the one who was different*?"

"No," Julian said, "you don't need to remind me. I'm fully aware."

"Are you?" Carson asked. "Because it seems to us like you've lost all awareness of the things you've always said were important to you, including not allowing yourself to get into situations in which you give someone the power to *wreck your goddamned life*."

"She's not going to wreck my life. It's quite possible she could *make* my life."

Carson's jaw went slack. *"What?"* he whispered. "What're you saying?"

"You heard me."

Carson stared at Julian for a long moment before he said, "Eff this shit." He turned and walked away.

Griffin shook his head. "I hope you know what you're doing, man, because you're off the freaking rails, and when it blows up in your face, I'm gonna say, 'I told you so.'"

With that, he left, too, slamming the door on his way out.

For a few minutes, Julian sat perfectly still, stunned and dismayed by the unusual argument with his brothers. They loved to drive one another crazy, but they never fought for real like that. Griffin and Carson had landed a few well-placed hits to his certainty where Isla was concerned.

And the news about Rachel McDavid had rocked him. He

needed to check in with Jackson about that, but right now, he was sure his other siblings were hearing all about how Jules was off the rails over a woman he'd only just met, who'd been a new client, then not a client, then widowed, all in the span of a few days.

He understood their concern. If any of them had done what he had this week, he'd have been all over them, too.

Remingtons didn't skip out of work to take a single mom and her kids to visit the goats in Ojai. They didn't lose their minds over one woman when there were plenty of women to spend time with and not get into something they couldn't easily get out of if need be. With every moment he spent with Isla, he became more enmeshed in a situation that was rapidly spinning out of his control. The fact that he had zero desire to extricate himself before it was too late should've been terrifying.

Rather, it was the most exhilarating thing he'd ever experienced, and as soon as she told him her kids were asleep for the night, he'd be going back for more.

CHAPTER TWENTY-FOUR

After Julian left, Isla went into the bathroom attached to her bedroom to splash cold water on her heated cheeks. When she caught a glimpse of her reflection in the mirror, the rosy cheeks and kiss-swollen lips were almost startling. How long had it been since she'd had kiss-swollen lips?

Years…

The last time she'd had sex with Gabriel, she'd conceived Mila, and that'd been a moment of weakness after months of upheaval. He'd come home full of tearful apologies and promises that he'd get help and that everything would be different. Only because she'd been so lonely and scared had she given in, knowing his promises would most likely turn out to be empty.

In a matter of days, he'd been gone again. She hadn't seen him for six weeks that time, and by then, she knew she was pregnant. At first, she'd been furious with herself for allowing that to happen, but as Mila grew inside her, she'd fallen deeply in love with the little being who would turn out to be her baby girl. Thankfully, wherever he'd gone, Gabriel hadn't cut off the money she needed to survive.

Isla had no regrets when it came to Theo and Mila. They

were the best things to ever happen to her, even if everything else in their lives was a mess. She'd done her best to keep them insulated from Gabriel's demons.

As she ran a brush through hair that'd been mussed by Julian's fingers while he kissed her, she couldn't wait to see him again.

Julian...

Quite simply the kindest, sweetest, handsomest, sexiest, smartest man she'd ever met in her life, and she was completely smitten with him, even if she had no business being smitten by anyone when her entire existence was in an uproar.

Somehow, some way, he'd become the calm in the storm for her, even if she felt anything but calm when he was around. She'd never had the kind of physical reaction to a man that she'd had to him, almost from the second they first met in his office when he'd been so kind to her and the kids. Right away, she'd felt safe with him in a way that she never had with Gabriel. It was as if she could finally exhale and allow someone else to pick up part of the load she'd been carrying on her own for so long.

Not that she needed a man to come swooping in and fix everything for her and the kids. Only she could do that. But there was no reason she couldn't enjoy something special that was all hers—and his—while she figured out the rest. At some point, when he was a little older, Isla would explain to Theo what'd happened to his daddy. How in the world would she ever make sense of it for him when she was still processing it herself?

Mrs. V cleared her throat.

Isla spun around to find her friend standing in the doorway. "Oh, hey. I thought you were lying down."

"I lied. You know I don't nap."

She said naps were for babies and old people—and that seventy-two didn't count as old.

"Sorry my arrival was poorly timed just now."

"It wasn't."

"Now you're the one who's lying." Mrs. V smiled as she leaned against the doorframe. "That man sure is handsome."

"Is he? I haven't noticed."

Mrs. V snorted with laughter. "Sure you haven't. I hope you're being careful with your heart with that handsome man."

"I'm not being careful at all. I lose all perspective and sensibility when he's around."

"I wanted to know more about him, so I poked around a bit online."

"Wh-what did you find out?"

"By all accounts, he's a brilliant attorney who cares tremendously about his clients and helping them get the best-possible settlements. He's also a strong advocate for mediation over costly litigation that mostly benefits the lawyers, which makes him better than most in that regard."

"That's nice to hear."

"It's his personal life that concerns me."

"How so?"

"He doesn't seem to have one. There were photos of him at various fancy events, always with a gorgeous woman on his arm, but there's never a second photo with the same woman."

"There's a reason for that." Isla immediately felt the need to defend him. "His parents dragged him and his siblings through an ugly custody battle for ten years, not to mention what he deals with every day at work. He's reluctant to get himself into things he can't get out of."

"Interesting."

"How so?"

"Well, on paper, he seems like a great guy. But is someone who avoids commitment like the plague the right guy for you, especially in light of recent events?"

Isla didn't want to squirm under the heat of Mrs. V's gaze or face the reality of her keen observations. She'd much rather exist in the heightened state of euphoria that came with Julian.

Julian.

She loved his classy, elegant name. It suited him.

"Isla."

When she glanced at Mrs. V, she realized she'd zoned out on thoughts of the very man her friend was trying to warn her about. "I hear you, and I appreciate you."

"I can't bear to see you get hurt again after everything you've been through. You're finally free to make a new life for yourself and the children. Please be careful not to get serious about a man who doesn't do serious."

"I'll be careful. I promise. Thank you for caring about me."

"Oh, honey, I love you so much. And I also love that dazzled look in your eyes. You so deserve a man who can love you the way you deserve, but I'm not sure he's the guy for that job."

"Maybe not. It's quite possible he'll be a lovely interlude on the way to something else down the road."

"Which is totally fine as long as you don't fall for a man who doesn't do love or forever or happily ever after."

"Don't worry. This isn't about any of that stuff."

Mrs. V gave her a skeptical look. "If you ask me, you're already halfway in love with him."

"No, I'm not. I'm enjoying his company. I feel calmer when he's around, and I can forget—just for a time, anyway—that Gabriel destroyed our home and then died. He actually *died*. From the thing that caused all this in the first place. Julian gives me a place where I can step away from the nightmare for a few minutes and just breathe. I'm not going to fall in love with him. I promise."

"Don't make promises you might not be able to keep, sweetheart."

"I never do. Do you mind babysitting after the kids are asleep?"

"Not at all, as long as my big kid is protecting her fragile heart."

Isla hugged her friend. "She is. He's a very nice guy. You don't have to worry."

"Didn't Goldilocks say that about the Big Bad Wolf?"

Isla laughed. "No, she never said that about him. You're mixing up your stories."

"Huh," Mrs. V said as she turned to leave. "I could've sworn she did."

BY THE TIME Isla texted him at eight forty-five, Julian was on pins and needles, waiting to hear from her and hoping she wouldn't change her mind about wanting to see him tonight.

All clear over here.

I'll be right there.

Julian pulled into her driveway seven minutes later, intending to go to the door.

She came out before he could release his seat belt and was in the car two seconds later. Then she leaned in to meet him halfway for a devouring kiss that set him on fire in the span of an instant.

He lost all sense of space and time as her tongue tangled with his in the single-hottest kiss of his entire life.

Before her, he would've said nothing about women or sex could surprise him anymore. He would've been very, very wrong about that as she taught him something brand-new and more exhilarating than anything he'd known before.

By the time they resurfaced, in desperate need of air, the G-Wagon windows were steamed up, and he was certain the dazzled look on his face matched the one looking back at him.

Then she giggled, and he fell deeper into this thing that was taking him over like nothing else ever had.

He cracked a window to let in some cool, fresh air—and so he could see to back out of her driveway.

When they were on the way up the hill to his place, he reached for her hand and held on tight.

She put her free hand on top of their joined hands, trapping him in her silken web.

He'd never been so happy to be trapped.

Everything about her did it for him, from the scent that made him want to bury his face in her neck to get closer to it, to her soft lips, her sweetness, the beautiful way she mothered her kids, her resilience and the fortitude that was guiding her through one of the hardest times in her life.

He wanted to make everything easier for her going forward but already understood that she didn't need a man to do that for her. She'd be fine on her own, which only made him want to do everything he could to help her.

It was a strange state of being for a man who'd never wanted any of the things that came with her, but the thought of letting her get away now that he knew she existed was unthinkable.

When they walked into his kitchen, she dropped her coat and purse on the floor and turned to him just as he reached for her.

This kiss made the one in the car look like child's play.

Holy. *Shit*.

His better judgment had him briefly thinking they should maybe slow this down a bit, but then her hands wandered under his sweater, and the heat of her skin against his pushed every thought out of his head except one.

He wanted her. Right now.

Without breaking the kiss, he wrapped an arm around her waist, lifted her and headed for the stairs.

She wrapped her arms and legs around him and held on tight for the ride upstairs.

They came down on Julian's king-sized bed, wrapped up in each other and not losing a beat in the kiss to end all kisses.

He'd spent a lifetime trying to avoid the very trap he was now walking into, fully aware that she was changing his life with every stroke of her tongue and caress of his face. Her touch sent shivers down his spine and filled him with a craving for more of her sweet sexiness.

"Isla," he whispered against her neck.

He wanted to drown in the scent of her hair and skin.

She tilted her head to the right to give him better access to her neck. "Hmm?"

"Are you okay?"

"Uh-huh. Are you?"

"I think so." He rested his forehead on hers as he tried to catch his breath. "Do you want me to stop?"

"God no. That's the last thing I want." She tugged on his sweater to make her point. "Take this off."

He pulled back from her only long enough to pull the sweater over his head.

She ran her hands over his arms and shoulders, giving him goose bumps that made her smile. "You're hiding some serious muscles under those sexy suits, Counselor."

It was strange to realize in that moment of extremely charged awareness that he'd never wanted anyone the way he wanted her and that he ought to be scared shitless about feeling that way about someone. He'd never wanted that, but now that it was happening, he couldn't imagine not wanting it —or her.

He slid a hand under the hem of her gauzy top and gave a gentle tug to help her out of it, moving aside to get a better look at what he'd revealed. A sheer bra put full breasts on tempting display as he buried his face in the plumpness spilling out of the cups.

Her fingers gliding through his hair had him trembling

from the effort it would take to go slow, to make this good for her.

Julian released the front clasp of her bra and pushed the cups aside to reveal the lush beauty of her breasts. He sat back to take in the gorgeous sight of her full-body blush, the flawless skin and dark pink nipples that stood up tall, as if they were waiting for him to give them some attention.

He cupped her right breast and took her nipple into the heat of his mouth, running his tongue back and forth over the tip while she squirmed beneath him. The sweet flavor of her skin was immediately addicting as he went back for more, sucking on her nipple until it popped free of his mouth. Then he moved to the other side, keeping it up until she was moaning and pressing her heat against his hard cock.

"Julian..."

"What, honey?"

"You're making me crazy."

"You're making *me* crazy."

"I haven't even done anything yet," she said.

That single word—*yet*—was like gas on a fire.

"You're here, and you're breathing, and you smell so good, and you're so warm and soft and sweet... How can you say you haven't done anything?"

"I want to touch you, too."

"Feel free to touch me any time you want, all the time if you want."

Her smile lit up her pretty face and made him so thankful to be in this moment with her in his arms. "Don't mind if I do."

"I promise I won't mind at all, but..." He pressed a kiss into the valley between her breasts. "This one time, I want to be all about you. Close your eyes, quiet your busy mind, relax and let me love you."

He peppered her torso with kisses as she squirmed beneath him.

"I, um..."

"Shhhh," he whispered against her quivering abdomen. "Relax. Let it all go."

She exhaled and seemed to try to settle as he tugged at the button of her jeans, unzipping them slowly before pulling back to ease them down her legs, leaving her covered only by a tiny pair of panties. His mouth watered at the sight of her spread out before him.

He'd had a lot of sex in his life, probably too much if he was being honest, but never before had it felt as important as this did. After everything she'd endured with her husband, he wanted to give her more pleasure than she'd ever had.

Starting at her left ankle, he left soft kisses up the inside of her leg, smiling at the goose bumps that erupted on her sensitive skin.

"Julian..."

"You're relaxing, remember?"

"Um, yeah, sure..."

His soft chuckle against her inner thigh brought even more goose bumps and a wild shiver that shook her entire body. "Easy, sweetheart. Keep breathing."

"I can't breathe with you doing that."

"What am I doing?"

She made a sound that was full of exasperation. "You know what you're doing."

"Do I?"

"Are you doing this on purpose?"

Goddamn, she was cute. "Yeah, I am, and it's so much fun."

"For whom?"

"It's hot when you use words like 'whom.'"

"Proper English makes you hot?"

"You make me hot, and you have from the second you *strolled* into my office."

"We already had this debate. I don't stroll."

"You most definitely do stroll, and it was the sexiest thing I've ever seen. I was immediately hard for you."

"Stop it. You were not."

He pressed his mouth to the silky fabric that covered her. "Was too. I was afraid to move out of fear that you and Denny would notice."

"Don't talk about my brother when you're doing *that*."

Julian laughed again but kept his mouth tight against her, nuzzling her as she raised her hips to push against him. The movement seemed almost involuntary, as if her body had taken over and was now in charge. That'd be good. He wanted her brain out of the mix so she wouldn't somehow be convinced that she didn't deserve to feel good or to be cared for this way or to take as much pleasure as she could handle.

With her hips raised off the bed, he reached under her to remove the panties, sliding them slowly down her legs as she watched him. Then he removed his jeans and boxer briefs, reveling in her wide-eyed expression as she took a good look at him, fully aroused for her. Returning to his former post, he used his shoulders to part her legs and settled between them.

"W-wait... What're you doing? Julian..."

He ran his tongue from top to bottom and then back up to focus on the tight knot of her clitoris, sucking on her as he drove two fingers into her tight channel.

She made a sound that seemed to come from the deepest part of her as he doubled down, stroking her with deep thrusts of his fingers.

Her grip on his hair reached the point of pain, but he didn't let up on her for a second until she came with a sharp cry of completion, clamping down so hard on his fingers, he lost his breath when he thought about how it would feel to be inside her when that happened.

Julian moved quickly to roll on a condom and replace his fingers with his cock, pushing gently but insistently into her as she contracted with aftershocks that had him on the verge of release in a matter of seconds.

He forced himself to slow down, to find some of the legendary control that had made him a preferred partner at Club Quantum, to make this memorable for both of them. But control was hard to come by with her soft sweetness wrapped around him, pulling him deeper into this web from which he never wanted to be freed.

Buried deep inside her, he held still for as long as he could before he had to move.

Her fingertips dug into his back as he took them on a fast, wild ride that had them clinging to each other as they chased the big finish.

He came down on top of her, breathing hard as his head spun from the surge of emotions that came with the absolute feeling of rightness in this surreal moment.

She held him tightly, as if afraid he might try to get away.

He wasn't going anywhere as long as she wanted to hold him close.

After shifting ever so slightly, he felt dampness on his face and realized she was silently weeping. He raised his head to check on her and found her eyes tightly closed as tears slid down her cheeks.

For a second, he was paralyzed with fear that he'd hurt her, or she had regrets, or… "What's wrong, honey?"

"Nothing at all."

"Then why are you crying?" He kissed away her tears, gutted by every one of them. "Does something hurt?"

"Only my heart for settling for less for so, so long."

"Oh, baby, you'll never have to settle for less than you deserve ever again."

"Thank you for showing me how it's supposed to be."

"I've only begun to show you how it should be."

"You're not supposed to be making promises you can't keep."

"I never do, and I never will."

"Julian..."

"Yes, Isla?"

"I have two very little kids."

"You do? What the hell? When were you going to tell me that?"

She laughed, as he'd hoped she would. "Be serious."

"I've never been more serious about anything than I am about you and us and your kids and all of it." He was already hard again and began to move slowly, drawing a groan from her. "Especially after this. You've got me completely addicted to all things Isla."

"I've got you addicted? What about that wizardry you perpetuated on me?"

"Was there wizardry?"

"There were two orgasms. That's wizardry to me."

"So you hadn't..."

"Hardly ever, and he didn't care if I did or not."

"That's a goddamned crime."

"Thus the tears."

"Sweet, sweet Isla..." He kissed her as he replaced the condom and made love to her again, already addicted to everything about her. "You deserve all the good things, everything..."

If the first time was fast and frantic, this time was about slow, sweet, eyes-connected intensity that seared him all the way to his soul.

He was in deep trouble with this woman, and he'd never been happier to be in trouble.

CHAPTER TWENTY-FIVE

With Julian wrapped around her after a second round of thrilling lovemaking, Isla stared up at the ceiling, processing what'd transpired in his bed. To call it life-changing would be dramatic but true. Her entire body hummed with sensation after three orgasms.

Three!

She hadn't thought that was even possible for her until he'd shown her otherwise.

While she ought to feel guilty about being naked in a bed with another man less than twenty-four hours after her husband passed away, guilt was the last thing on her mind. She'd done everything humanly possible to make the best of a horrible situation, and she'd be damned if she'd feel bad, sad or guilty about feeling *good* for the first time in forever.

She ran her hand over his hairy forearm to a muscular bicep and shoulder.

He was a finely built man with muscles in all the right places. She'd never seen actual washboard abs until he'd removed his shirt, revealing a sculpted chest and abdomen. How did he manage that when he worked an ungodly number of hours and played in a band after work?

She couldn't wait to ask him that and the million other questions it would take to fully know him the way she wanted to.

In the back of her mind was the nagging concern that came from Denny's warning to not lose her head over a man who wanted nothing to do with the sorts of commitments that made up her daily life, including children. What made her different from all the other women he'd run away from when things got too intense? Would he do that to her, too? He'd said he wouldn't. He'd told her this was different. Did he always say that to women, or did he mean it? How would she know?

Every minute she spent with him, especially the last two hours' worth of minutes, had her more invested in whatever this was, and if it suddenly went away, if he suddenly went away, she'd be devastated. He'd brought light and joy and hope into her life in the short time she'd known him, and she'd become immediately addicted to the high that came with him.

"Stop fretting," he whispered gruffly. "Everything's okay."

"How do you know I'm fretting?"

"There's smoke coming out of your ears."

"That is not true!"

He grumbled out a laugh. "It's very true. I'm choking on smoke over here."

She elbowed his ribs, drawing a grunt from him.

"Ow."

"Stop talking nonsense."

"Are you or are you not fretting?"

"What does that even mean?"

"Are you thinking about all the ways this could blow up in your face and cause total devastation when it ends?"

"Shut up."

He laughed hard, and she found another thing about him to like—the sound of his unrestrained laughter.

"No, really, shut right up."

That made him laugh even harder.

"You're very cute when you're annoyed."

"If that's true, I must be extremely cute right now."

"You are." He leaned in for a kiss, and she turned away from him, even though that was the last thing she wanted to do.

"Hey."

"What?"

"Look at me."

"I'm mad at you."

"No, you're not."

"Yes, I am!"

"Isla..."

"Yes, Julian?"

"Please look at me."

Because she already missed looking at him, she turned her head. "What?"

"I don't want you to fret or worry or be afraid or any of the things your mind is telling you to be concerned about. I'm as lost in this as I've ever been in anything, and every minute I spend with you only makes it worse in the best-possible way."

"That makes no sense."

"Trust me. I know. But it's true. I can't get enough of you, and after tonight... All I'm going to want is more of you." He twirled a length of her hair around his finger. "Please don't be afraid of anything having to do with me."

"It's not just about me. You know that, right? I come with attachments."

"Who are as adorable and sweet as their mother."

"They're very young, Julian. I'm looking at twenty more years of intensive parenting before they're launched and on their own. Raising them to be decent, productive humans will be the most important thing I'll ever do, and I'll be doing it on my own."

He tightened the arm he had around her. "I know."

"In fact, I should be getting home soon."

"Not yet. It's not even midnight."

"Don't you have to work tomorrow?"

"I do, but I'll be fine. Stay for a little longer. Please?"

"I need to get some sleep so I'm not a zombie tomorrow. Dealing with little kids while in zombie status is no fun."

"Ten more minutes." After raising himself up on an elbow, he moved in for a kiss that quickly turned ten minutes into sixty.

"I really have to go," she said when she'd caught the breath he'd stolen from her lungs—again.

"I know. I've got to sleep, too, before I get myself fired."

"You can get fired from a family firm?"

"Well, technically, as a partner, I'm also an owner, but the last thing I want is my dad, the senior partner, up in my grill asking me what the hell is wrong with me lately when nothing is wrong. Everything is just right."

"You really think so?"

"I really know so. As long as you're in the picture, everything is perfect."

"I hope you still think so when you see my kids freaking out or sick or—"

He kissed her as sweetly as anyone ever had. "It'll be fine. I'm sure of it."

Isla wanted to take his reassurances to the bank and make a deposit on a future that looked awfully sweet all of a sudden, but she'd learned to be cynical. Even the best sex of her life couldn't erase the self-preservation instinct that was telling her to proceed with utmost caution.

She got up, found her discarded clothing and got dressed while he did the same on the other side of the bed. After a quick trip to the bathroom, she followed him downstairs, where she'd left her coat on the floor.

He picked it up, held it for her and then put his arms around her and kissed her neck. "Thanks for tonight. I had the best time."

"Me, too."

"Don't worry about anything, okay?"

"I'll try not to."

They drove to her house in silence, hands clasped as usual, but she couldn't deny that everything had changed between them during the unforgettable hours they'd spent in his bed. This was no longer just a heated flirtation that'd taken them both by surprise with its intensity. Now it was something else altogether, something serious and full of potential and possible pitfalls.

If she hadn't been so close to it, she might've laughed at the sheer absurdity of finally deciding to leave her husband, only to fall for her divorce attorney days before her husband died.

Like... *what*?

It wasn't like she didn't already know how arbitrary and strange life could be, but by anyone's standards, this last week had been exceptional.

Julian pulled into her driveway and let the engine idle while he turned to her. "Are you okay?"

She nodded.

"It's a lot. I know it is. But it feels so good to feel this way..."

"Yes, it does."

"Let's stay focused on that, okay? The rest will sort itself out how it's meant to."

"Do you really believe that?" she asked.

"I never used to, but I'm starting to see how there's some truth in that."

"I've had no reason to believe that anything ever works out, so you may find me to be a tough convert on that philosophy."

"I wish I didn't have to leave you when you're having doubts."

"They're not doubts so much as realities."

He tipped her chin up to receive his kiss. "My reality suddenly and totally revolves around you, so keep the faith, okay?"

"I'll try."

"Get some rest and text me when you wake up."

"Okay."

He kissed her once more, with all the passion and heat he'd shown her from the second they'd arrived at his home earlier and seemed to be tearing himself away from her when he let her go.

"I'll walk you to the door."

"No, I'm fine. Go on home and get some sleep."

"I'll wait until you're inside, then."

"If you must."

"I must."

"Thank you for tonight. It was amazing."

"Yes, it was. Thank *you*."

Isla leaned across the center console for one more kiss before she got out of the SUV and headed for the breezeway door, where she punched in a code to get into the house. She waved and turned off the outside light.

After checking on her sleeping babies, Isla got into bed and exhaled a deep breath as she tried to calm her racing heart. Her body was still tingling from the aftereffects of epic orgasms with a man who clearly knew his way around the female body. While she might've been jealous to think of him with countless other women, if all that experience had shown him how to bring her the most pleasure she'd ever known, then she supposed she could forgive him for his past.

It would take days, if not weeks or months, to process what'd transpired in his bed.

That her body could respond that way, that a man would tell her to relax and let it all go and think of nothing but her own pleasure... What world was she living in all of a sudden? Every pleasure point pulsated in response to the memories that played on repeat, the most sensuous, delicious movie she'd ever seen.

She turned onto her side, hugging the pillow and wishing it was him. If only she could bottle the way it felt to be wrapped up in his arms so she could have a dose of it any time she needed it.

Mrs. V had made her promise not to fall in love with a man who'd avoided relationships for his entire adult life, but here she was, falling deeper by the minute into the sort of thing that couldn't be undone or unlearned once it had seeped into her heart and soul. The euphoric feeling that came with him was heady, addicting stuff that had her already yearning to see him again.

Her last thought before she drifted into sleepy dreams of him was that she hoped it would happen soon.

She woke in the morning to a text from Gabriel's mother, letting her know there'd be a wake for him in Santa Barbara on Thursday afternoon. *No pressure to attend,* Maggie had written along with the address for the funeral home where the service would take place. *He didn't want anything religious, so we're just doing the wake and a private burial for the family. We know how busy you are with the children. Hopefully, we can find a time to get together in the next few weeks so we can meet our grandchildren. We'd so love to know them—and you, of course. Gabriel spoke so highly of you in the short time we had together.*

Isla thought about what she wanted to say before she replied. *Thank you for letting me know. I'll try my best to be there, and of course you can meet the children. They'd love that, too. Thank you also for letting me know he was remembering me fondly at the end of his life. That's nice to hear. Our time together was challenging and very difficult, especially toward the end, but I'm trying to remember that much of what happened was because of his illness.*

As she reread the message before she sent it, she decided to strike that last sentence. There was no sense in revisiting things that couldn't be changed. What difference did any of it make now? Gabriel had done what he'd done, he'd refused to seek the medical care that might've saved his life and their marriage, and now he was gone forever.

She had to live in the present rather than the past, and the present was looking rather lovely with a text from Julian that popped up after she'd replied to Maggie.

Morning, beautiful. Hope you slept well. I had dreams of you and was sad when I woke up and you weren't here. I wish you were here.

Isla smiled as she typed her reply. *I dreamed about you, too, and wished you were here. Hope your busy day isn't too awful. What's first on your agenda today?*

Attending the arraignment for my client who shot and killed her ex-husband when he broke into the home where she and her kids were staying. I need to figure out what's up with her kids and who has them.

Isn't her case self-defense?

It should be a slam dunk for that.

Then why's she being arraigned?

That's routine procedure. Once the judge hears the ex was under a domestic violence restraining order and had a hunting knife with him when he broke in, she should be released on bond. Her criminal attorney will hopefully make it go away before it gets to trial.

I'll be rooting for her—and you.

Thank you. When can I see you again?

What are you doing after work?

No plans—and if I did have plans, I'd cancel them for the chance to see you.

Awww, you're so sweet. Gabriel's mom texted to tell me there's a wake for him on Thursday afternoon in Santa Barbara.

Are you thinking you might want to go?

Probably.

I can drive you up there if you don't want to go alone.

That's very kind of you, but you have to work so you don't get fired.

I won't get fired. I'll take the afternoon off in case you need me.

Is this real? Are you real? Or am I dreaming?

If it's a dream, I don't want to wake up.

The phone rang with a call from him.

"Yes?" she asked with a chuckle.

"Why are we texting when we could be talking?"

"That's a very good question. Where are you?"

"In the car on the way to the courthouse."

"Where is it?"

"Downtown."

"Is the traffic bad?"

"Is that a rhetorical question?"

She laughed. "I guess so."

"I've got my pal Ernie driving me, so I don't have to worry about parking. Thank God for him."

"That's a nice perk."

"Sure is. I couldn't do this job without him."

"No, you couldn't," a man said in the background.

"And he's entertaining to have around."

"I see that. Has he been with you for long?"

"Years. While I was talking to you, I cleared my schedule for Thursday afternoon. No pressure, but if you want a ride, I'm happy to take you."

"That's very nice of you to do that. I know how busy you are."

"It's fine. I rarely take time off."

"How come?"

"Because I haven't found anything I like to do more than work."

"That's very sad, Julian."

"I'm beginning to realize that. Can I ask you something unrelated to this depressing topic?"

"Sure."

"How do you feel about going to a movie premiere?"

"Like an actual premiere?"

"Yep."

"What movie?"

"*Valiant*. It's the new Quantum—"

She let out a shriek. "*Are you kidding me?* I'm dying to see that movie. I'm a huge Natalie Godfrey fan. She's such a badass, and her husband is dreamy, *and oh my God! Are you kidding me?*"

Julian was cracking up from the first "are you kidding me" all the way through to the second one. "Not kidding. The Godfreys are family friends, so we're all invited and allowed a plus-one. You wanna be mine?"

"I'm dead."

"Don't do that!"

"It's a saying, Julian. Get with it. 'I'm dead' means I can't believe this is happening, and yes, I want to go. When is it?"

"A week from Saturday."

"What would I wear?"

"I'll hook you up with a stylist."

"Do you have stylists on speed-dial for all your dates?"

"Put your claws away, killer. I've never once called a stylist in for any date, but I've needed one a few times myself, so I have a few names."

"Oh. I see."

"In case I haven't mentioned it before, I don't do stuff like this, so you don't have to worry that you're just another in a long line. It's not like that with you."

"You're making me all fluttery."

"Is that a good thing?"

"It's the loveliest thing to happen to me in, well, ever."

He sighed, desperately wishing he could tell Ernie to turn

the car around and take him right to her. "Same, sweetheart. I'll call you later, okay?"

"I'll be here."

"Can't wait."

"Me either."

Julian ended the call with the same dazzled feeling he'd had last night when he'd had her warm and naked in his arms.

"Um, excuse me, boss," Ernie said, glancing at him in the mirror, "but... what the hell is going on with you?"

CHAPTER TWENTY-SIX

"I'm not sure exactly."

"What was all that just now?"

"There's this girl, you see... And she's unlike any other girl I've ever met, and... It's the worst-possible time for her, but she's not pushing me away, and well... It's amazing, actually."

"Didn't you recently tell me I didn't know you at all when I said you ought to make a play for the supermodel?"

"She's not my type."

"Since when do you have a type?"

"It's a recent development."

"People were talking about you going missing yesterday."

"I heard."

"Where'd you take off to?"

"I took my friend and her kids to Ojai for the afternoon."

"You took her... and her kids... to Ojai."

"That's what I said," Julian replied, amused by the gobsmacked expression on Ernie's face in the mirror.

"You bailed out of work to be with a woman who has kids."

"Yep. Little kids. They're three and one, and they loved the gochas and the horsies and doggies."

"What the hell is a gocha?"

"It's a goat. Duh."

"Are you feeling all right, man?"

"I'm feeling better than I ever have before."

"What. Is. *Happening?*"

Julian bit back a laugh. "No idea, but whatever it is, I want as much of it as I can get."

"Are you the same guy who was about to call the exterminator to get rid of smokeshow Stacey a week ago?"

"Yeah, that was me."

"And now..."

"And now everything is different. Can't really explain it. Just is."

They pulled up to the Stanley Mosk Courthouse ten minutes before Rachel McDavid's arraignment.

"I'll text you when I'm done."

"Julian..."

"Everything's fine, Ernie. Don't worry."

"Right. What do I have to worry about when my friend is going off the deep end over a woman for the first time ever?"

"Nothing to see here."

"Whatever you say, Counselor."

Julian got out of the car, looked both ways and dashed across the street and up the stairs to the courthouse that was his home away from home. He greeted the security officers by name and thanked them for ushering him through the metal detector with their usual respect for the time of busy people.

He entered the courtroom in time to see Rachel, wearing an orange jumpsuit and handcuffs, being led into the room. The cuffs were removed before she sat at the defense table.

Julian sat behind her. "Rachel."

The woman who turned toward him bore almost no resemblance to the woman he'd last seen a week ago. "Julian, you have to find my kids! They took them... They should be with my sister. She can't get anyone to tell her where they are."

"I'll find them and do everything I can to reunite them with your sister. What else can I do for you?"

"I... I don't know. I did what I had to. He... he was going to kill us. He had a hunting knife."

"That'll matter to the judge."

The courtroom was called to order for the arraignment of Rachel McDavid in the matter of the fatal shooting of her ex-husband.

"How does your client plead?" the judge asked the defense attorney.

"Your Honor, my client pleads not guilty due to self-defense. She was under the protection of a domestic violence restraining order when her ex-husband broke into the home where she and her children were staying. Police found a hunting knife on his person. We believe he intended to kill her and the children after losing custody of them in a recent family court matter. Mrs. McDavid defended herself and her children and likely saved their lives. We ask that she be released on bond while this matter is adjudicated."

The judge turned to the district attorney at the other table. "We have no objection as long as she remains local."

Julian stood. "Your Honor, Julian Remington, Mrs. McDavid's divorce attorney. May I please address the Court?" After the judge gestured to give him permission, Julian said, "Her minor children were taken into emergency custody, and we'd request that they be returned to her as quickly as possible."

"Are there other firearms in the home?" the judge asked.

Rachel shook her head.

"No, Your Honor," the defense attorney said.

To the DA, he said, "Please see to the return of the children by the end of the day. I'll set a hearing in this case for one month from today. What's next?"

As the judge and his clerk turned to the next case, Julian

leaned in to speak to Rachel. "I'll wait for you to be released and drive you home."

"Thank you," she said tearfully as she was led away by the sheriff's deputy.

While he waited for Rachel, Julian texted Mattie to let her know he'd be at the office as soon as he got Rachel settled at home.

Glad to hear they're letting her out.
Me, too. Were you able to push my morning meetings?
All set for this afternoon.
Great, thanks.

He and Jackson had blocked out three hours later in the afternoon to do Smithson trial prep, and he had two other client meetings, as well as a partner meeting at lunch. After all that, maybe he'd get to see Isla again.

Ernie was probably still trying to figure out when Julian had been abducted by aliens, which was amusing to him. Julian from a week ago wouldn't recognize the version of him that was counting the hours until he could see a woman.

But she wasn't just any woman. She'd touched him in ways that no one else ever had, even Aimee, and she'd done it in a matter of minutes. That was the part that was still unbelievable to him, too. After spending a lifetime avoiding the very thing she represented, he'd been sucked into her silken web so quickly he'd already been trapped before he'd even realized he'd been captured.

He scrolled through his texts while he waited for Rachel and read one from Griffin to their sibling group chat.

Kids, I have shocking news. I recently heard from an ex that I am the father of her daughter. I took a paternity test that came back positive, and, well... meet Hadley Jane. I'm already in love. Her mom, McKenna, is a great person, and if this had to happen with anyone, I'd pick her. So... other than that... LOL

He'd included gorgeous photos of the baby and one of him holding her, looking stunned but elated, too.

The *holy shit, bro* responses from their siblings were amusing and heartfelt.

I'm an auntie, Jordan said. *She's gorgeous! When can we meet her?*

Have you told Mom that she's a grandmother? Ethan asked. *If not, can we be there when you do?*

What he said, Roman replied with an emoji arrow pointing to Ethan's text as the others chimed in with congrats and questions and compliments on the beautiful baby girl who'd made them aunts and uncles for the first time.

Haven't told the folks yet, Griffin said. *Will get to that. Eventually. Will arrange a sibling meeting soon.*

She's wicked cute, despite having your DNA, Jackson said. *Congrats, bro.*

So happy for you, Griff, Julian wrote. *She's a stunner.*

Oh, look who it is, Carson said. *Our fearless leader is back on the grid after a quick trip to somewhere he said he never wanted to go... Are you back to stay, Jules, or will you be entering temporary insanity once again?*

Julian didn't want to be pissed at Carson's snarky text, but it stung nonetheless, coming from the brother he'd always been the closest to. He chose not to dignify Carson's comment with a response and stuffed the phone in his suit coat pocket so he wouldn't have to see what the rest of them had to say about his recent departure from normal.

He got it. If one of them had acted the way he had in recent days, he'd be worried, too. He'd probably be planning an intervention, which was no doubt happening in a separate group text that didn't include him.

He thought of Isla and how she'd looked after the third time they'd made love the night before and had to quickly think of something else to avoid an embarrassing and obvious reaction to some of the sweetest memories he'd ever made with anyone.

Was he out on a limb in this situation? Absolutely. They'd

made their vow to one another for damned good reasons, and he'd fully intended to honor that commitment—until he'd met someone who made him want more.

Would he marry her? No. He'd never marry anyone, but that didn't mean he couldn't have a meaningful life with her and her kids if that's what she wanted, too, and he wouldn't justify himself to anyone, even the siblings who'd sustained him during their darkest times. He loved them more than anything, but they weren't going to tell him how to live his life.

His phone rang with a call from Rachel. "Hey."

She told him where she was, and he walked to meet her while holding the phone to his ear. "I'm coming."

He texted Ernie to make sure he was ready to pick them up at the curb.

On the way.

Rachel emerged through a door, wearing her own clothes and carrying a plastic bag. She looked ragged and terrified. "Have you heard anything about the kids?"

"Not yet, but I'll check on that when we're in the car. Let's get you out of here."

They emerged into bright sunshine and a crush of bottom-feeding "reporters" who tended to show up for only the most salacious cases shouting questions at Rachel about why she'd shot and killed her ex-husband and how she'd managed to get released when she'd murdered someone.

Julian put an arm around her and led her through the scrum, keeping his gaze locked on Ernie, who stood outside the SUV with the back door open for them. "Keep your head down and just keep moving," he said to Rachel, who shook with silent sobs.

"Did your kids see you shoot their father?"

"Had he threatened you before?"

"How long did you have the gun?"

Ernie met him about twenty feet from the car and helped

to form a barrier around Rachel. They had her in the car and speeding away from the courthouse in a matter of minutes while she silently wept.

"S-so it's blown up into a b-big story while I was locked up," she said.

"They're always tuned in to the salacious stuff, but they'll lose interest as soon as the facts become clear," Julian said.

"By then, my name and my kids' names will be forever tied to this."

"Names can be changed. We'll do everything we can to protect you and your kids."

She wiped tears from her face. "No offense, because I know your intentions are good, but everything you could do wasn't enough to keep him from finding us and breaking in with the intent to kill us rather than let us be happy without him."

"You're right. It wasn't enough. I'm sorry that there wasn't more I could do to keep you and your sons safe."

"I'm not blaming you. I'm blaming a system that can't stop stuff like this from happening."

"It's a valid complaint. Restraining orders are often not worth the paper they're printed on. The restrained people know the cops can't be everywhere, so they risk it. It's a screwed-up system, but it's the only one we've got."

"It needs to be reformed before more people end up dead." She looked over at him. "I didn't want to kill him." Her chin quivered. "That's the last thing I wanted to do, but if it was a choice between him and my babies…"

"You did what you had to do to keep them safe."

"I'll never regret that."

"I'm texting my contacts for an update."

"I guess we can actually go home now," she said, seeming to realize that for the first time. "How long will it take until my hands stop shaking?"

"Your nervous system has had a shock. It'll take a minute to catch your breath."

"Do you think I'll go to prison?"

"I highly doubt it. He showed up with a knife and broke in. He had a restraining order, so it's on the record that he was legally considered a threat to you. But your defense attorney is a better resource on those questions."

"I won't get Bryan's life insurance now."

"If it doesn't go to you, it'll probably go to the kids as his heirs."

"Oh. I hadn't considered that possibility."

"I know it all seems horrible right now, and it is. It's sad and tragic and infuriating and all the things, but you and your boys will get through this. I know you will."

"I hope you're right."

EIGHT HOURS after Julian delivered Rachel to her home, he received word that her sons were back in her custody. Rachel's sister texted him to let him know they were upset and tired but seemed to be doing as well as could be expected under the circumstances.

His day had been one shit show after another, with things blowing up for multiple clients at the same time.

Liam Rossi's wife had "lost her shit" when he'd told her he wanted a divorce, and now he was rethinking leaving the marriage. *I'm not sure I can do this to her,* Liam had written in a text to Julian.

What about what you want for yourself?

How can I be happy knowing I've devastated her?

How can you be happy in a marriage where you're competing with her late first love?

I don't know what to do.

Sit with it for a bit and see how you feel in a week or two. I'm here if I can do anything to help.

The Smithson trial prep had been stalled by a possible breakthrough between the warring parties. Julian's client, the husband, had agreed to a ten percent increase in alimony that would add an additional fifteen thousand dollars to the wife's monthly payment. She'd been convinced throughout the process that he was hiding assets. He swore he wasn't. Since she'd been unable to prove the accusation, she'd been willing to go to trial in the hope of forcing him to reveal hidden resources.

They were waiting to hear if Mrs. Smithson was going to accept what Mr. Smithson had called a final offer.

In the meantime, Julian and Jackson were ready for trial.

"I'm going to be out on Thursday afternoon," Julian told Jackson. "I need you to cover a couple of meetings for me."

"Your clients want you, not me."

"I've told them you're just as capable as I am, which you are."

"That's not the point. They're paying for a partner, not an associate. If you want to stay off of Dad's radar, you need to stop taking unscheduled time off."

"I haven't taken time off in years, Jack. *Years*. If I want to take a little time here and there, I can do that without feeling guilty. I'm still involved with the cases they're paying me to handle and will continue to be."

"Whatever you say, boss man."

"If you've got a beef with me, why don't you just say so?"

"I thought I just did."

"You're my associate, Jackson. That means you do what I ask you to do. I'm asking you to take two client meetings for me on Thursday afternoon, the way you would if I was sick or injured or otherwise unable to work."

"You're not sick or injured. You're something else that makes no sense to any of us."

"What I'm doing is a favor for a friend who just lost a

loved one. I assume that falls under acceptable reasons to take time off."

"Do what you've got to do, Jules. You don't want to hear what we have to say about it."

"What do you have to say?"

"The same things Carson and Griffin tried to say to you. The same things you didn't want to hear."

Julian went to grab his suit coat off the back of his chair and put it on, eager to get out of there after his day had run super late due to the situation with Rachel. He hoped Isla was still awake. "I'm glad you got a full report from them that'll save us from having the same argument I already had with them."

"What're you doing with this woman, Jules?"

"I'm having a nice time with her. Is that illegal?"

"Why're you being so defensive about it? I thought we had a deal… We're supposed to avoid things like single mothers with little kids who just lost their husbands."

"Her relationship with him was over a long time ago."

"But he *just* died. If I was losing my mind over a woman in this situation, you'd be having a fit over it."

"I appreciate the concern, Jack. I really do. But I'm okay."

"Don't stand there and act like you haven't taken leave of your senses since you met her. Don't disrespect me by lying to my face about being okay, because none of this is okay."

"I'm not going to marry her. Don't worry."

"You say that now."

"I say that forever. I'll never get married. Nothing that matters has changed. Okay?"

"If you say so."

"Go on home. I'll see you in the morning."

Jackson grabbed his suit coat off the sofa and walked out.

Julian decided to give him a minute to exit the building before he headed out. He reached for his phone to text Isla. *Hey… Finally done at work. What are you up to?*

*Long day for you. I'm having a glass of wine and reading.
Can I stop by on the way home?
I wish you would.
Be there soon.*
She tagged his text with a heart.

Just that quickly, the day's tension slipped away, and the ecstatic feeling that came with knowing he'd see her again soon was back. It propelled him out of the office to the elevator and out of the parking garage five minutes later. Traffic was lighter at this hour, allowing him to zip through Beverly Hills and take the left onto Laurel Canyon Boulevard in record time. As he pointed the G-Wagon up the hill, he pressed the accelerator, eager to get to her.

CHAPTER TWENTY-SEVEN

Julian was tired, hadn't eaten since lunch and hadn't had time to work out that morning. His well-ordered routine had been obliterated by Isla's presence in his life, but every second with her was worth the chaos when he was away from her. He wasn't so far gone that he couldn't see what his brothers were upset about. His behavior was so far out of character as to be inconceivable to them. It would've been inconceivable to him before he'd met Isla and instantly felt everything inside him shift to make room for her.

He pulled into her driveway, cut the engine and was out of the vehicle so quickly he nearly stumbled in his haste.

She was waiting for him at the door, smiling as she held out her arms to him.

He picked her up, making her squeak with surprise as he carried her inside, kicking the door closed behind him. As he let her slide down the instantly aroused front of him, her lips connected with his in a kiss full of pent-up desire. *Finally*, he thought as it occurred to him that his entire day had been about doing whatever it took to get back to her.

"Mrs. V," he whispered against her soft, sweet lips.

"She went home for the night."

Hearing they were alone—and knowing the kids were sleeping—Julian was lightheaded with desire. He kept his arm around her as he kissed her and walked her backward toward the hallway where the bedrooms were. "Which way to your room?"

With her arms curled around his neck and her body pressed against his, she directed him to the last door on the left.

Julian stopped next to the bed for another tongue-twisting kiss as he ran his hands over her soft curves. She was wearing a white tank and pajama pants. He untied the bow at her waist to push the pants out of his way as she pulled his suit coat over his shoulders.

He took a step back to remove his tie, unbuckle his belt and take off his shirt by pulling it up and over his head. All the while, he held her gaze as they undressed and fell onto the bed in a wild burst of need that took his breath away.

"I couldn't wait to get back to you," he said as he slid his lips over hers.

"I thought I wasn't going to hear from you."

"Today was a mess, from start to finish. Until right now, that is."

"I'm sorry you had a tough day."

He kissed her neck and breathed in the scent that so bewitched him. "How was your day?"

"Pretty good. The kids and I went to the park and had lunch at In-N-Out. They loved that."

"I love In-N-Out."

"We're still talking about the restaurant, right?"

He laughed as his hands slid down to cup her bottom. "I love all the various ins and outs."

"I'm not sure I can do that tonight. I'm a little sore from last night's trifecta."

Julian immediately pulled back from her, and just as

quickly, she drew him back into her embrace. "Oh no. Why didn't you tell me?"

"I just did."

"I mean earlier."

"You were busy at work, and I'm fine."

"I'm sorry I caused you discomfort."

"Trust me, it was totally worth it. I've been in this state of dazed disbelief all day."

"Is that right?"

"Uh-huh. It's never been like that for me."

"Tell me more."

Her giggle was the new sound of joy for him.

"Come snuggle me."

"Nothing I'd rather do."

She rested her head on his chest and sighed. "This is lovely."

"Sure is. You were going to tell me more about how it's never been like that for you..."

"I've only been with Gabriel, so I didn't know anything else. When we were first together, it was really great between us. He made me feel wanted and sexy and you know..."

"I know." A wild feeling of possessiveness caught him off guard as he tried not to picture her with another man.

"But there were things he didn't like to do."

"What things?"

"You want, like, details?"

"I'm here for anything you want to tell me."

"It's kind of embarrassing."

"Don't be embarrassed with me. You have no idea how obsessed I am with you—in the best-possible way, of course."

"Of course."

He felt her lips curve into a smile against his chest as he ran his fingers through her silky hair. "Don't be shy, Isla. I want to hear all your thoughts, even the naughty ones."

"He didn't like oral."

"Giving or receiving?"

"Giving. Receiving was never a problem."

"Why did I know you were going to say that?"

"It was fine with me. The few times he did do that, it didn't do much for me."

"Because he didn't want to be doing it, so he intentionally sucked at it. No pun intended."

She laughed. "I could tell you like doing it."

"I *loved* doing it to you." He was so hard he ached. Talking about sex with her was better than doing it with anyone else had ever been. "In fact, a little more of that might help to soothe the soreness. It's commonly known to be the best cure."

"You're a bit shameless, aren't you?"

"Only with you."

She ran her hand over his chest and down to cup his erection through his boxer briefs. "Maybe I could do that for you."

He got even harder when she said that, and she laughed again. "He approves."

"He's all in with you."

"Is it weird that I already feel like we've been together this way forever, rather than just a few days?"

"Same. I can't remember what life was like before you strolled into my office."

"I do not stroll!"

"Oh yes you do, and it was hot as fuck."

"I had a kid on each hip. How is that hot?"

"It just was."

"Whatever you say."

"Mmmm, does that apply to all things, or is it selective?"

Julian nuzzled her neck as they moved against each other, simulating intercourse, which was almost as hot as the real thing.

"Is that your way of saying you like being in charge?"

He cupped her breast and ran a thumb over her tight nipple. "Only when it comes to your pleasure. You can be in charge of everything else."

"Is that, like, something you're into?"

"I have been in the past, but it's not required."

"Tell me more."

The thought of her being interested in dominance and submission nearly sent him right over the edge.

"I, um... Well..."

She laughed. "Articulate, Counselor."

"You've got me all flustered."

"What did I do?"

"You're you, and you smell so good, and you feel even better. And then you want to up the ante to talk about my dominant side, and it's all I can do not to implode."

"Is it always like this for you?"

"Like what?"

"Hot, frantic, desperate."

Hearing her describe their insane attraction with those words almost did him in. "Never. Not like this."

"What makes this different?"

"Damned if I know," he said with a laugh, "but it's been unlike anything else from the minute you strolled—"

She pinched his lips.

Laughing, he twisted free of her grip to add, "Onto the scene."

"That strolling thing is going to get you in trouble."

"Oh goody. What does trouble involve?"

"You really are shameless."

"Not usually. You bring out my shameless side."

"I'm trying to understand how this is even possible."

"Some things just *are*, or so I've heard. I've never experienced anything like this either."

"Denny asked me today if I'd heard from you."

"What did you say?"

"I believe my exact words were, 'You could say I've heard from him.'"

"Which of course left him with more questions than answers."

"He doesn't need to know everything."

"No, he certainly does not."

"He... He told me again that you're not a wife-and-kids kind of guy."

Julian winced at the vulnerable tone of her voice as she said that. "I'm not."

"But here you are with a single mom..."

"You noticed that, huh?"

"Haha, yes, I noticed. And I noticed that you're great with my kids. All they've talked about since we went to Ojai is when we can go back to see the gochas and when they might see their new friend Mr. Julian again."

"They asked about me?"

"A hundred times today alone."

His heart suddenly felt too big for his chest. "That's so cute."

"You made a big impression."

"Wow."

"Can I say something that has no place in a brand-new situationship, or whatever you want to call this?"

"You can say anything you want to me any time you want."

"I'm not sure I can be seriously involved with a man who has a no-wife-and-kids policy."

He winced. "Why did I know you were going to say that?"

"Please understand... I'm not a big fan of marriage myself after the last few years with Gabriel, but my kids deserve a real family and maybe a dad to be there for them since Gabriel can't be. I don't know what the future holds, but I don't want to rule out any possibilities."

The same heart that had expanded when she'd said her

kids had asked about him wanted to shrivel up and die at the thought of having to let her go to find some other guy to help her raise her kids. "That's fair."

"I want you to know I get why you feel the way you do. I... I watched a few episodes of that reality show about your family, and I ached for you, imagining what it must've been like to have that story on blast."

He hated that she'd watched that but didn't blame her for being curious about who she was sleeping with. "It was brutal. I hated that the whole world knew our business and that my parents ate it up because it was so good for their divorce practices. The phone rang off the hook with new business."

"It's just gross."

"That's a very good word for it."

"But you were very cute back then. Not as cute as you are now, though."

"I was never *cute*."

"Hate to break it to you—you were and *are* very cute." She kissed him. "And sexy and sweet and hot."

"That last part is all fine, but the cute shit is *not*."

Smiling, she said, "I give you and your siblings so much credit for not only maintaining relationships with your parents but also working with them. That can't be easy."

"It's easier than it would've been back in the day when it was all so raw. That was a long time ago now. A lifetime ago, really."

"But the scars are forever."

"Yeah, they are."

"I get that. I'll never get over some of the things that happened in my marriage, such as him going missing for weeks at a time and then swearing to me that everything would be different if we had kids, and for a while, it was better. We had Theo, and he was great with him. Being a father seemed to change everything for him. But, of course, it didn't last. When I was pregnant with Mila, he started disappearing again, and then when she was born, he was nowhere to be found. He didn't meet her until she was a month old."

"God, Isla. I'm so sorry you had to bring her into the world on your own."

"It was rough. I had some postpartum depression after she was born that really rocked me, and having to take care of two little ones in the midst of wondering where the hell my husband was and what he was doing and where all the money had gone…"

He held her as tightly as he dared, wishing he could take away all the hurt she'd experienced.

"That was when the marriage truly ended for me. After that, I was all about trying to save enough money to leave, but I could never seem to get ahead of the day-to-day needs of two kids, rent, car payments, insurance and all the things. People like to say, 'Why don't women just leave?' Well, that's why we don't leave. Because we can't. And I was too ashamed to go to Denny, especially since he'd told me not to marry him in the first place. He had a bad feeling about him from the beginning. I think maybe he saw the future with Gabriel from the start."

"Not much gets by him."

"He didn't know the truth of what was going on with us. When he came to meet Mila, I told him Gabriel had been called into work on an emergency job. I'm not sure if he believed me, but he didn't ask any questions."

"He probably knew something was off but didn't want to add to your stress at an already tough time."

"I have no doubt he sensed trouble, but I was stubborn and proud and stupid, as it turns out. I wish I'd gone to him when it got really bad."

"You're far from stupid. That hiding place in the apartment is one of the baddest-ass things I've ever heard of in more than thirteen years of family law practice. Seriously impressive."

"Desperate times and all that."

"Incredible ingenuity. From the second I heard about that, I was eager to meet the person who'd figured out a plan like that. And then you strolled—"

She kissed him hard. "I never want to hear that word again."

"Aw, don't say that. It's part of our story."

"We have a story?"

"I'm starting to think you might be the story of my life."

"But you'd never marry me, no matter what, right?"

"No, I wouldn't, but if we decide to be together, I'd have your back in every other way."

"I'm not sure how I feel about that. This is already seeming kinda..."

"Serious?"

She nodded. "I should probably get out while I still can."

He hugged her closer. "I'm not letting you go."

"When I got married, I really believed it would be forever. He was the one I wanted to spend my life with. I was devastated by the way it turned out, but that wouldn't stop me from taking that chance again with the right person."

"Do you still trust your judgment after what happened with Gabriel?"

"That's a good question, and I can understand why you might ask that since I was so wrong about him and jumped right into this with you when my life was in turmoil."

"I haven't had either of those thoughts about you, if that matters. Gabriel's illness changed him profoundly, and when you met me, things with him had been over for quite some time, or so you said."

"Both those things are true, and I don't know if it counts as trusting my judgment, but everything in me wanted to trust you from the second I first met you. I felt like I could exhale because you were there, and everything was going to be all right as long as I trusted you. I've never experienced such certainty toward a stranger before."

"I haven't either, and it's got me questioning a lot of things I thought I knew to be true about myself."

"Like what?"

"Well, to start with, hearing you say you should get out while you still can has me wanting to promise you whatever it takes to keep you here with me, because I'm honestly not sure I'd survive if you walked away and never looked back."

"I didn't say I'd never look back."

He caressed her cheek. "Everything has changed in the span of one week. Before this, before you, I would've said that would never happen to me."

"And now that it has?"

"You've got me reconsidering my lines in the sand."

She leaned over to kiss his chest. "I should probably make sure you know what you'd be getting if you cross all these lines of yours."

"Um, getting?"

"You know, the full package." She looked up at him, smiling as she moved so she was on top of him, positioning his cock between her breasts. "No pun intended."

Julian gasped. "What is happening?"

"It's your turn to close your eyes, quiet your busy mind, relax and let me love you."

"Wait, but..."

She slid down to take his cock into her mouth, and the words died on his lips as she applied tongue and suction at the same time.

"Isla..."

"Hmmm?" She made sure her lips vibrated against the head as she said that.

He moaned. "Sweetheart, wait..."

"I don't want to wait."

Over the next ten minutes, she made him swear, sweat, beg

and plead. Every time she brought him close to release, she backed off and started over. His legs were trembling, and his hands were wrapped up in her hair as she started the whole thing again, this time taking him all the way to the finish line.

He bit back the urge to shout from the power of his release.

She stayed with him until he sagged into the bed, his muscles going slack.

The only sound in the room was his labored breathing.

Isla kissed the rippling muscles on his abdomen, then moved up to his chest and lips.

His eyes opened, and the heated look he gave her seared her soul. "How soon do you want to get married?"

She laughed as he wrapped his arms around her. "Does that mean you enjoyed the full package?"

"My full package enjoyed it very much."

His chest was like a bellows until he finally caught his breath and relaxed somewhat.

"Do something for me," she said tentatively.

"Anything."

"Don't make jokes about getting married if it's never going to be in the cards for us."

"I won't. I'm sorry."

"I mean, don't get me wrong... Getting married is the last thing on my mind after these last few years. But..."

He couldn't seem to stop playing with her hair when he was with her. It was so soft and slid through his fingers like spun silk. "What, honey?"

"It's just that since I lost my parents so suddenly, I think I've been kind of chasing the sense of family and belonging to something that was lost with them. Denny did his best, but it wasn't the same, and then Gabriel came along, and I thought maybe he'd be the one to fill that gaping hole inside me. For a while, I thought I was healed, you know?"

"Yeah, I get what you're saying."

"But it didn't last, and now here I am having to rebuild again from scratch, and here you are when the last thing I was looking for was something like this. I certainly don't think that marriage is the be-all and end-all, but I do think it's something I want again someday, when the time is right and the person is right." She sighed. "I feel like I'm making no sense."

"You're making perfect sense, and you deserve to have everything you want in life."

"My kids are everything to me, and they fill a big part of that hole my parents left, but it's not the same as having a partner who belongs only to me, who commits to me for a lifetime and is there for all the ups and downs that come our way. I'm in no way actively looking for that right now, but I don't think I can get into a situation where it's never going to be a possibility."

Julian's heart sank deeper with every word she said. He totally understood where she was coming from, but the thought of never seeing her again was physically painful, as was the thought of legally binding himself to another person after swearing he never would. Picturing himself taking those vows and signing that marriage license made him feel physically ill, but the idea of losing her forever made him ache like nothing else ever had.

"I want to reassure you, to tell you I might be able to give you all the things you want in this life, but I can't do that and be truthful with you, too. It's important to me that I always tell you the truth, because I'd never want to hurt you or your kids."

"I appreciate that, even if I wish things were different."

Julian had never wished more that he'd been raised differently, that he'd seen less of the many, many ways that people could hurt the ones they'd once loved so much they'd pledged to love and honor them for the rest of their lives.

If there was one thing he knew for certain, it was that nothing lasted forever.

Though it was the last thing in the world he wanted to do, he sat up, got out of bed, found his clothes and got dressed.

Isla was the most amazing woman he'd ever met, and there was no way he would add to the hell and heartache she'd been through in her life by stringing her along on a path to nowhere.

When he was ready to go, he sat on the edge of the bed, feeling as heartbroken as he ever had. Leaning in, he kissed her bare shoulder and then her lips.

The tears that slid down her cheeks broke something in him that could never be put back together the way it'd been before he'd known her.

"I want to take you to Santa Barbara on Thursday, and I want you to come to the premiere, okay?"

She nodded as she caressed his face. "No matter what happens next, you restored my faith in people and showed me what I need to aim for next time."

Julian's heart ached like it never had before, even after he'd lost Aimee. "I can't bear to picture you with someone else."

"Same."

She reached for him, and he held her close, possibly for the last time ever, breathing in the distinctive scent that was now etched upon his heart and soul. He never wanted to forget a single detail of her or their time together.

"I'll text you about Thursday."

"Okay. Thank you for going with me."

"Of course."

"Do you think, maybe, we could stay friends?"

"I'm not sure I can be just friends with you. I'll want to hold you and kiss you, among other things, and friends think you're weird when you do things like that."

She smiled and reached up to place her hand on his face. "I hope you'll find a way to be happy in your life. You deserve all the good things."

"So do you."

"I don't want to let you go."

"I don't want to be anywhere but with you."

They held each other tightly for a long time before he forced himself to let her go, to stand up and to leave the best thing to ever happen to him. And yes, he was certain of that despite the short time he'd known her.

He was also certain he'd miss her for all the days that remained in his life.

CHAPTER TWENTY-EIGHT

The next day was a blur for Julian, with nonstop fires at work to put out, band practice where he had to force himself to concentrate so he wouldn't screw up an amazing opportunity for his friends and a sleepless night during which he'd stared up at the ceiling for hours, contemplating which would be worse—to break his vow to his siblings or to live without Isla for the rest of his life.

With every minute that passed without her, the vow became less important. All he wanted was her. He longed for her. He had to force himself to drive by her street on the way home when everything in him was pulling him in her direction.

"Julian," Mattie said Thursday morning as he stared into space while she went over the schedule for his half day in the office. The wake wasn't until four, so he'd leave around two to pick up Isla.

He tuned in to Mattie, realizing he'd checked out on her. "Sorry. What did you say?"

"What's wrong, sweetheart? You've been wildly distracted lately."

Everything was wrong. Every freaking thing had been

wrong since the minute he'd left her weeping in her bed because he couldn't be the man she needed. "Nothing's wrong. What time is Cresley coming in?"

"You can lie to some people, my love, but Mattie isn't one of them. What's weighing on you? Is it that sweet young woman that has your head turned all around?"

Of course she knew. He could never get anything past her and usually didn't care that she knew him as well as anyone did. Today, he wasn't up to baring his soul to anyone, even someone who loved him like she did. "It's complicated."

"Always is when it matters."

Goddamn, but she could cut to the chase like nobody's business.

"Are you in love with her, bebe?"

"Hell if I know."

"Yes, you do. That's the problem, right?"

He shrugged, feeling as helpless as he had back when his parents had been fighting over him and his siblings. He hated that feeling more than anything. Trying to prevent that was why he'd gone to law school, so nothing could ever make him feel that way again. And now here he was... Locked in a situation he hadn't seen coming, a situation that had taken over his heart and soul and his entire life, if he was being honest.

Was he in love with her?

Probably, yet there was nothing he could do about it.

"I hate seeing you like this, Julian. It's so unlike you as to be frightening."

"I'm sorry to worry you. I'll be okay."

"What's the worst thing that could happen if you allowed yourself to love this woman?"

His huff of laughter burst out of him. "Do I really need to list the worst things that could happen? We see the litany of things that can go wrong every damned day around here."

"Oh please. Ninety-nine percent of that stuff would never apply to you. You'd never cheat on your wife or beat her up or try to steal her money or be abusive to her kids or get hooked on drugs or—"

"You've made your point."

"Have I? My point is that if you're looking at what goes on around here, or even what went on between your parents back in the day, and thinking you need to deny yourself the experience of truly loving this woman and her children, then you're not as smart as I've always thought you were."

"There're a lot of things far short of cheating or abuse that can doom a marriage."

"Absolutely, but will you let your fear of those things stop you from fully living? From fully experiencing love and contentment and all the things?"

"I hate to point out that you've been perfectly content without being married."

"I would've loved to have gotten married and had children. I never met anyone I loved enough to have those things with. If I had, I would've jumped on him. Literally."

Julian laughed. "I'm sorry it didn't happen for you."

"My life is full of so many things, but I've never been truly in love. I'm not sure I would've been strong enough to turn away from that if it had happened."

"I'm not sure I am either."

"Then don't." She put her hands on his desk and leaned in. "Don't spend the rest of your life yearning for what you let get away. I'd think that'd be worse than gambling on her and having it not work out. Regrets are a bitch, my love. Ask yourself how you'll feel when your friend Denny tells you his beautiful sister is getting married again—to someone who isn't you."

Julian ran an absent hand over his abdomen, which felt as if it'd taken a direct hit from a closed fist. "Years ago, my siblings and I promised each other we'd never put ourselves in a situation like this. We promised we'd never get married, never turn over everything to another person who could ruin us in all the ways."

"That's a very stupid promise to make when you're too young to know better."

"We were old enough to know... We saw it firsthand."

"My mother said once that no one knows what goes on inside a marriage except the two people in it. Whatever went down between your parents was something only they knew about, because to my knowledge, neither of them has ever said what led to their split. What they put you kids through was all about wanting to win and not about what was in the best interests of their children. Those of us who watched that happen have never forgiven them for that."

Her expression was as earnest as he'd ever seen it.

"If you let what those two fools did keep you from the woman you love, then you're a fool, too. And the one thing you've never been is a fool, Julian Remington. Don't start now when the stakes are as high as they might ever be."

"My siblings would never forgive me."

"Don't be ridiculous. Of course they will. You're their hero. You led them through hell and have never wavered in your devotion to them."

"I'm nobody's hero."

"Oh, Julian. Yes, you are. That you don't even see it only proves my point. They'd never stand in the way of your happiness."

"You missed your calling as an attorney."

"I've been attorney-adjacent my entire adult life. I've learned a few things along the way, and the number one thing is that true love is rare and precious. Don't have regrets, my love. They're a bitch."

With that parting shot, she turned and left him to think about everything she'd said and how desperately he wanted to follow her advice.

His parents might've been fools back in the day, but their

actions had left deep scars in Julian and the siblings who were old enough to remember the details of those seemingly unending years they'd spent at war with each other, with their nine children trapped in the middle.

They'd understood at an early age that the only way to keep from reliving that experience was to remain unmarried. And here he was, thinking he might be able to overrule a lifetime commitment to staying single if it meant giving Isla what she wanted.

He would've laughed at how intensely tempted he was to cave if the stakes hadn't been so high.

Twenty minutes later, when Mattie buzzed to tell him his first client of the day had arrived, he'd done nothing but stare off into space, thinking about Isla. Every moment with her had been pure bliss. He'd never experienced a connection with another human being that could rival the one he'd found with her—even with Aimee.

If there was any one indicator that this was different, it was that. Aimee had been his only love until now. No one else had ever come close to making him feel the way she had.

Until Isla.

And now...

Julian gathered the case file, his notebook and pen and headed for the conference room where his client waited for him, taking thoughts of Isla and the things Mattie had said with him.

He wondered how he would think about anything else.

ISLA HAD PUT the kids down for naps, showered and done her hair when Mrs. V came in, bringing salads for both of them. She'd come over to stay with the kids while Isla went to the wake in Santa Barbara and would spend the weekend with them while she worked at the Whisky.

They sat at the kitchen table to eat. "Thanks for bringing lunch."

"No problem. How're you feeling?"

"My stomach is in knots for multiple reasons."

"You want to talk about it?"

Isla picked at the salad with grilled chicken, goat cheese and walnuts, usually one of her favorite meals. Today, she couldn't seem to work up enthusiasm for food or anything else, for that matter.

"I'm anxious about the wake."

"Which is only natural. It's a very sad thing."

"Yes, it is. I'm doing the right thing by not taking the kids, right?"

"Absolutely. They're far too young to understand, especially if it's an open casket."

"Ugh, I hope it isn't."

"It's apt to be. His appearance didn't change much, despite his illness."

"I can't bear to see him like that."

"As his wife, you could request that the casket be closed."

"His parents should have whatever they want."

"You have a say in it, too. If it's too upsetting for you, you can request that it be closed."

"I'll think about that."

"What else?"

Isla looked up at her, knowing she shouldn't be surprised that Mrs. V saw right through her. "Julian and I have decided to just be friends."

"How come?"

"We want different things."

"What different things?"

"I'd like to eventually get married again someday, and he's determined to never get married."

"So live in sin. It's all the rage. It's not even a sin anymore."

"I know, but I don't want to rule it out forever, and he's

not into it at all because of his parents and the things he sees in his work. We decided it's easier to stop it before it really gets started, rather than set ourselves up for heartache in the future."

"Huh."

"Huh what?"

"Nothing... Even though I've had my concerns about the situation, it was nice to see you smiling again. It's been a while since I saw you like that for reasons that don't involve the kids."

"It was nice while it lasted."

"Is he still taking you to Santa Barbara?"

"Yes, he said he wanted to do that. We're still friends. We're just keeping it real."

"Is that right?"

"What is it you're really asking?"

"I might've been widowed for a long time, but what I walked in on the other night didn't look like 'just friends' to me."

"We had a really exciting and immediate connection."

"Had? Past tense?"

"I mean... it's still there, but we've decided to take a step back before it goes too far."

"Are you sure that's what you want?"

"Not really, but I can't handle any more heartache."

"Heartache has a way of finding you even when you're trying to avoid it."

Her friend's words were devastating in their simple truth. Being with Julian could be heartbreaking. Being without him would be more so. That much she already knew for certain. However, she couldn't and wouldn't pressure him to change the rules he lived by for her. Nothing good could come of that either. The rules he'd set for himself had served him well thus far, and he'd stayed true to them for thirty-eight years. She had to respect that and find a way to move on.

If only she didn't ache from head to toe when she thought about never being close to him again.

Today, she needed to focus on saying a final goodbye to Gabriel while trying to stay strong when it came to Julian. She appreciated that he wanted to help her through a difficult day and was determined not to make it worse than it already was by yearning for things that could never be.

Julian arrived right on time at two thirty, wearing a blue sport coat over a checked blue dress shirt and khaki pants. He looked so handsome that she had to curb her first impulse to hug and kiss him.

"You look beautiful," he said with a hint of sadness in his voice that hadn't been there before.

"Funny, I was thinking the same about you."

Isla had worn a black wrap dress with matching heels. She'd spent extra time on her hair and makeup, hoping she looked dignified for her last moments with Gabriel. "This is surreal. I'm going to my dead husband's wake with my former divorce attorney. Have you ever experienced that scenario in your practice?"

He replied with a small smile. "This entire situation is unprecedented in every possible way."

Mrs. V came out of the kitchen. "Oh, hello, Julian."

"Hi there, Mrs. Ventura."

She handed a black sweater to Isla. "Don't forget this. It's apt to be chilly later."

Isla hugged her friend. "Thank you for everything."

"I'll be thinking of you today. Let me know how it goes."

"I will."

"You should go before the babies wake up and want Mommy."

"We're going," Isla said as she reached for her purse, which was hanging on a hook by the door.

"Julian," Mrs. V said.

"Yes, ma'am?"

"Take good care of my girl today."

"I will. I promise."

"Don't worry about rushing home. We'll be just fine."

Isla hugged her again. "Love you."

"Love you more, sweet girl. You'll be in my thoughts and prayers today."

"Thank you."

Julian put his hand on her lower back to usher her out the door into warm, bright Southern California sunshine that was almost offensive on a day of mourning. She would've expected dark clouds and a stormy sky on such a day. The heat of Julian's hand was comforting but also disconcerting because all she wanted to do was ask him to take her back to his place, where she could forget all the sad stuff.

But that wasn't an option today.

He held the door for her, waited until she was settled and then closed it.

After he got into the driver's side, he asked her for the address of the funeral home and punched it into the vehicle's GPS. The map showed a ninety-minute ride through Calabasas, Thousand Oaks and Ventura before hooking north on the Pacific Coast Highway.

Unlike their previous rides together, he didn't reach for her hand the minute they were underway, and the sense of loss was profound. Their easy rapport was gone, too, as if neither of them knew what to say to the other after what they'd decided. She wanted to ask him if he ached the way she did, but she couldn't bring herself to pose the question.

He kept his gaze straight ahead, but a muscle twitching in his cheek was new and might be a sign of internal struggle.

"Are you okay?" she finally asked when she couldn't stand the tension any longer.

"I've been better."

"Did you have a crazy workday?"

"No more than usual."

"Oh." Did she have any right to ask other questions? "I hate this."

He glanced at her. "What?"

"That it's weird between us now."

"I hate it, too."

She waited for him to say more, but what could he say? What could either of them say that would change their reality?

They drove in silence for a long time before he said, "I miss you desperately, and you're right next to me."

Isla reached across the center console for his hand and held on tight as tears stung her eyes. She fought them back so she wouldn't be red and puffy when they arrived at the funeral home. But she wanted to wail from the pain of it all, mixed in as it was with the sudden loss of Gabriel.

Julian had been such a bright light in the midst of incredible darkness. He'd come along at a time when she'd never felt so lost and shown her what might be possible. To lose him on top of everything else was nearly unbearable.

He brought their joined hands to his lips and kissed the back of hers.

With the breath stuck in her throat, it was all she could do to think or function when all she wanted was to crawl into his lap, let him wrap her up in his warm, loving embrace and stay there for as long as he'd have her.

A silent hour later, she could no longer remember why it had once been important to her to remarry someday, to give her children a stepfather to help raise and guide them. If it meant living without Julian Remington, none of that stuff seemed as important as it might've been if she'd never met him.

He took a call from Carson without releasing her hand. "Hey, what's up?"

"Where you at, bro?"

"Almost to Santa Barbara."

"What's there?"

"I'm taking a friend to a wake."

"Oh."

Carson's single word held the weight of everything that'd come between them. In it, she heard disapproval, concern and perhaps a hint of anger. All that from a single-syllable word.

"What do you need?" Julian asked him.

"Just wanted you to know that we had Beckett served with the RO and the C&D. He'd gone underground since the altercation with C, but we found the slippery little fucker and let him know we'll be watching to make sure he stays the hell away from her and her son."

"Great job, bro. Thanks."

"It'd be my pleasure to update the client, if you'd like me to."

"Sure, go ahead."

"I'll take care of it."

"Anything else going on?"

"Did you hear why Dad is out of the office today?"

"I didn't know he was out today, so no, I don't know why."

"Hmm. When was the last time he took a day off?"

"I can't remember. Not in years."

"I hate to say that Kaidan's theory may have merit."

"I can't even think about that right now."

"Me either. I'll check in later."

"Sounds good."

Julian ended the call and then changed lanes to take the exit to downtown Santa Barbara.

Isla hadn't been there since elementary school, when she'd spent a day there with her parents while they were shooting a commercial at Stearns Wharf. Signs for the wharf took her right back to a day she hadn't thought about in years.

"Have you been here before?" Julian asked.

"Once, with my parents, when I was very young. They

were shooting up here for the day and brought me with them."

"Who did they work for?"

"Themselves. They were freelance camera operators and worked on everything from movies to TV to commercials and sporting events."

"That sounds cool."

"They loved the variety of it and declined many offers to be in-house at the studios. They met when they were in film school at USC."

"I did undergrad there. Loved it."

"They did, too. They were diehard Trojans."

"As am I."

"They would've liked you. They liked anyone who went to USC. That was all it took."

He chuckled. "I'm glad to know they would've liked me. I'm so sorry you lost them the way you did."

"Me, too. I wonder all the time how my life would've been different if they'd lived. I probably wouldn't have been in such a rush to get married."

"Everything would've been different, I'm sure."

"I wouldn't change anything, though. I have the babies I was meant to have. I truly believe that."

"They're beautiful, sweet and lovely, like their mother."

"Stop saying nice things to me if I'm not allowed to fall for you."

"My apologies."

"Don't be too sorry. You're good for my ego."

"Isla..."

She shook her head and pulled her hand free, even though that was the last thing she wanted to do. "Let's not."

His deep sigh echoed through the space between them, which might as well have been a mile instead of a foot.

Ten minutes later, he turned into the funeral home parking lot. Before she could tell him she could get herself out, he was there to help her down with his hands on her hips. A long, charged moment passed between them before he released her.

"Do you want me to go in with you?"

"That's okay. I'll be fine."

"Are you sure?"

"No, but I'm going to try my best to be fine because my kids need me, and falling apart isn't an option."

"I'll probably take a ride out to the beach or something. Stay as long as you need to. I'm in no rush."

"I could've done this on my own, but it's so much better with you here."

He leaned in to kiss her cheek. "Call if you need me."

"Don't say that, or your phone will be ringing nonstop."

"I'll always take your calls. *Always.*"

She smiled softly and eyed the funeral home's Spanish-style building. "Well, here goes."

When she got to the main door, she looked back to find him waiting until she was inside before he waved and got back into the SUV.

Isla could feel his reluctance to leave her there to face the tragedy inside, but she appreciated that he understood she had to do this herself. No matter what the future held for her, she had to close the door to the past so she could move forward. For better or mostly worse, Gabriel had been a big part of her life for much of a decade, and it pained her to think of never seeing him again and their kids never really knowing the man he'd been before his illness took over.

She'd make sure they knew that version of him and that Theo didn't remember their night in the closet first when he thought of his father. Hopefully, that memory would fade in time, and others would come to the forefront when he saw photos of the joy his father obviously took in him.

When she walked through the main doors, a man directed her to the left for the Santana wake. She signed the guest book and took a couple of the prayer cards that had a photo of a smiling, much-younger Gabriel on the front and a prayer on the back. She'd put away one for each of the kids to have when they were older.

Maggie left her spot in the receiving line, which included Gabriel's father, Ramon, and several other people who must've been siblings and their partners, to come to the back of the room to hug Isla. "Thank you so much for coming."

"Of course. Thank you for planning everything."

"We prayed for reconciliation for all the years we were apart, and when he finally called to tell us he was so ill... We were just so thankful to hear from him. It was a gift to have those final days with him."

Maggie used a tissue she had balled up in her hand to dab at tears. "All he talked about was you and the kids and what a mess he'd made of everything. He had terrible regrets about not seeking care when you first asked him to."

"It helps me to know that. Thank you for telling me. I wanted so badly for things to work out with him, for our sake as well as the kids'."

She put her hand on Isla's arm. "You were fighting a losing battle. The doctors said the tumor was probably affecting every aspect of his personality since he was a teenager, and his infernal stubbornness ended up doing him in. It explains so much but doesn't make any of this any easier."

"No, it doesn't."

"Would you like to see him?"

Isla didn't want to see Gabriel in a casket, but she also didn't want to shy away from a final goodbye with someone who'd once meant so much to her. "Yes, please," she said, sounding much stronger than she felt.

Maggie hooked her arm through Isla's and led her to the front of the room.

When the other people realized who she must be, they fell silent to watch her approach the casket, which was surrounded by floral arrangements. The same photo of Gabriel on the prayer card had been enlarged and displayed on an easel. They'd also framed a photo of him with the kids that he must've given them.

Isla's hands were sweaty as she gazed down at Gabriel, whose hands were clasped around rosary beads. She was almost afraid to look at his face, but when she did, she was relieved to realize he was truly at peace now.

"That was his Abuela's rosary," Maggie said. "He was always close to her as a child. I figured he might want to take something of hers with him."

Isla reached into her purse for the photos she'd brought of Gabriel and her with the kids and Gabriel with each of the kids. She handed the pictures to Maggie, who looked through them. "I thought he might want to take these, too."

"You made a beautiful family together."

"Yes, we did."

"I hope we can find a way…"

Isla rested her hand on Maggie's arm. "We will." In another life, she would've known Maggie and Ramon well. She'd also know their other children and their families. In this next era, she'd make sure Theo and Mila knew them all. "I promise."

"Our son was lucky to be loved by someone like you, Isla. We'll always be sorry for the way he disappointed you."

"I'm looking forward rather than backward these days. My heart is at peace where he's concerned." As she said those words, she realized it was true. "My only goal now is to raise our children to be good people."

"Let me introduce you to the rest of the family."

"I'd like that very much."

CHAPTER TWENTY-NINE

With rare time to kill on a weekday, Julian headed for Hendry's Beach to get some air and enjoy the warmer-than-average day. He chose that beach since it was only ten minutes from downtown, so he could stay close for when Isla was ready to leave.

He left his sport coat in the car and rolled up his shirtsleeves when he walked toward the shore, taking a seat on one of the benches to watch the surfers. Julian hadn't spent much time in Santa Barbara, but he'd always thought it was one of the more beautiful towns in the greater LA area.

His mother adored all things Santa Barbara. She'd had a house there for more than twenty years. He'd been in college when she'd bought it and hadn't been there very often, except for an occasional holiday or birthday celebration.

Julian could see why she loved it there, but it was too far out of the city for him to make it more than once in a while. That he'd been there and in Ojai in the same week was highly unprecedented, but then, everything about the past two weeks was unprecedented.

What was he doing sitting on a bench at a beach in Santa

Barbara on a Thursday afternoon, watching the surfers enjoy larger-than-average waves?

Meeting Isla had changed everything, and as much as he'd tried to avoid it, he couldn't deny that he was, in fact, in love with her. Admitting that to himself was a huge relief, even if it didn't change the reality of their situation. What he still couldn't wrap his head around was how quickly and easily he'd fallen for her when he would've said, before he'd met her, that it couldn't happen like that. No way, he would've said.

Haha, the universe replied. *Hold my beer.*

If it weren't such an impossible situation, he would've been elated to feel the way he did for her. She was everything he could ever want and so much more than he'd allowed himself to dream possible. The way she'd survived the nightmare her husband had put her through, keeping herself and her kids safe in a volatile, unpredictable situation she didn't understand was truly admirable. There was so much to admire about her, which was what set her so far apart from most of the women he'd met who were far more concerned about things that didn't matter than they were with anything of real substance.

Isla had lived a life of substance. She'd known crushing loss far too early in her life and then experienced bewildering extremes with the man she'd married. She was a wonderful, loving, tender mother to her babies, and her warm, soft sweetness had filled an empty place inside Julian to overflowing. He hadn't even known that empty place was there until she'd arrived to show him everything he'd been missing.

Driving up here without her hand in his had taken all the self-control he could muster with every fiber of his being longing to touch her, to hold her, to kiss her, to make love to her, to make everything that was wrong in her life—and his— right.

He was beginning to understand that he'd never have a chance of being happy again if she wasn't in his life. In order to keep her with him, where he was now convinced she belonged, he'd have to open his heart and mind to the idea of one day getting married. That was what she wanted for herself and her kids, and if the choice was that or a life bereft of her presence...

He huffed out a laugh as his thoughts led him to the only possible conclusion to this dilemma. His brothers would kill him. They might even disown him. He wouldn't blame them if they did. When they'd taken that solemn vow to one another, they'd meant it.

But now... If he had to choose between making them happy and making her happy... Again, the choice was clear.

"How in the hell did this even happen?" he asked the same universe that had brought Isla into his life in the first place.

He laughed at the insanity of it all as he checked his watch to see how much time had passed while he arrived at the biggest decision of his life. Now that he knew she existed, there was no life without her and her kids and whatever came next. It was that simple and that complicated.

Julian turned his face toward the sun, soaking up the warmth as a feeling of peace settled over him. Fighting his love for her would be like trying to keep the tides from changing or the wind from blowing or any number of other impossible things.

A barking dog on the beach caught his attention, and he tuned in to watch the antics of the little white fluff ball that reminded him of his mother's dog, Snowball. Like Snowball, this dog was full of beans, running in circles, barking happily and totally oblivious to anything other than his or her own little world.

His gaze shifted to the right of the dog to see a man and woman holding hands, laughing as they followed the dog to the parking lot. He watched them for a full minute before he realized *he was looking at his parents*. They were hand in hand on a Thursday afternoon, laughing like newlyweds as they tried to keep up with Snowball.

They were completely oblivious to everything other than each other, not seeing their eldest child seated twenty feet from them as they walked past him on the way to the parking lot, laughing, talking, calling the dog as if nothing else in the entire world mattered.

Before Isla, he would've wondered how they could be so caught up in each other. Now he knew, but that didn't make him any less furious to see proof of their reconciliation with his own eyes.

For a second, he thought he might be sick. When he recalled what they'd put their children through as they dismantled their happily ever after publicly and with as much vitriol as they could muster, each wanting to win no matter the cost or the collateral damage to the nine children they claimed to love more than life itself...

Julian wanted to chase after them, to ask them what the hell they were doing, to ruin what looked to be a perfectly lovely day for them by reminding them of why none of their adult children had ever married and had sworn to one another they never would.

Just that quickly, the decision he'd made about Isla and what he was willing to do for her was back in play as memories he'd kept buried deep inside came surging to the surface to remind him of why he and his siblings had made that vow to one another.

Goddamn his parents.

How dare they?

He wanted to call Carson to tell him what he'd seen, but then he'd have to hear Carson remind him once again that he was off the deep end in Santa Barbara on a Thursday afternoon. He didn't feel like dealing with that on top of the gut punch of seeing his parents holding hands and laughing like young lovers newly in love.

In all the years of chaos and upheaval they'd caused, he'd never hated them more than he did right then. He seethed with outrage, hurt, bewilderment and determination to protect himself from the kind of pain they'd caused for most of his life.

What was their plan when it came to their kids? he wondered. Did they intend to soft-launch their reconciliation at some point, hoping to get their offspring to buy into their new happily ever after? Had it all been a big mistake back in the day? Had it been a huge misunderstanding that'd now been rectified, opening a path to a reunion? Whatever the story was, he didn't care.

Julian wanted to go back in time ten minutes, to before he'd seen them together and could no longer deny that Kaidan's theory was true. He didn't want to have to tell the others he'd seen them together and that there was no doubt they were back together.

He checked the phone he'd put on silent so he wouldn't be hounded by the world while he was off for the afternoon and found a text from Isla that she'd sent seven minutes earlier. *Ready to go whenever you are.*

Be right there.

Julian got up and walked toward the parking lot, wondering how he'd missed seeing one of his parents' vehicles in the lot when he'd arrived. Only because the lot was fuller than usual on a January weekday, he hadn't seen whatever car they were in. His state of disbelief continued as he drove to the funeral home and texted Isla to let her know he was out front.

She came out a few minutes later, and the second he saw her coming toward him, he forgot all about the bombshell experience at the beach. He got out of the G-Wagon and met her at the end of the sidewalk, waiting to take his cues from her.

She stepped toward him and leaned her head on his chest.

Julian wrapped his arms around her and breathed in the scent of love, for that's what she was.

Love.

His love.

"What can I do?" he asked.

"This helps a lot."

He had no idea how long they stood there holding each other while he fell deeper into something from which he'd never recover. She pulled back quite some time later to look up at him with those bottomless eyes that saw all the way through him. "I'm okay. We can go."

Relieved to hear her say she was okay, he put an arm around her, escorted her to the SUV and helped her up into the passenger seat.

He reached for her hand the second the vehicle was moving. "Do you want to talk about it?"

"I don't think so, other than to say it was nice to meet the rest of his family and to have the chance to say goodbye. It's just so very sad."

"Yes, it sure is."

"What did you do?"

"Went out to the beach."

"Would you take me there?"

He didn't want to because of seeing his parents there, but he'd do it for her. He'd do anything for her. "Of course."

A short time later, seated on the very bench he'd occupied before, holding her hand as they soaked up the warm sunshine, he wanted so badly to tell her what he'd seen there earlier. But he couldn't throw his shit on top of her already intense day.

"This is a beautiful beach. Have you been here before?"

"A couple of times, a long time ago. My mother bought her house up here when I was in college. I haven't spent a lot of time here."

"It's such a pretty town. I love the Spanish architecture and the rugged coastline."

Julian nodded in agreement as the turmoil within threatened to boil over. He couldn't do that to her. Not today.

"What's wrong, Julian? You're so tense."

"Am I?"

"Yes, did something happen? Other than, well..."

He knew she meant the decision they'd made together to stop this thing while they still could. How funny that seemed now that he understood there was no stopping destiny. "A couple of things happened, actually." So much for not dumping on her today of all days.

"Do you want to talk about it?"

"Desperately, but today is your day. You've got enough to deal with."

"Please give me something else to think about." She released his hand and put hers on his leg, branding him with her heat as she moved closer to him. "Talk to me."

Part of his job was knowing when all was lost in a situation, when he had to advise his client to take the best deal they were going to get and walk away with their dignity intact. In many ways, this reminded him of that as he threw up the white flag in surrender to the inevitable.

"I was sitting here before, watching the surfers, enjoying the day, and it occurred to me that I love you."

She gasped. "What?"

He glanced at her, enjoying her astounded expression, flushed cheeks, wide eyes and kissable lips. "I love you, Isla. I'm in love with you."

"You... I... I thought..."

"Yeah, so did I. We agreed this couldn't happen because we want different things out of life, but as it turns out, the only thing I seem to want out of life is you. And your kids, God help them. You've just been to your husband's wake, everything is in an uproar right now, it's the worst possible time for something like this, and yet... there's absolutely no denying that I love you."

"Julian..."

"It's okay. You don't have to say anything. I just wanted you to know."

After a long moment of silence during which he was increasingly focused on the feel of her hand on his leg, she said, "I'm pretty sure I love you, too. No, wait... I'm absolutely sure I do, because when we decided to call this off, the ache was unlike anything I'd ever felt, even when I lost my parents. I wouldn't have thought anything could've been worse than that, but losing you was."

"You haven't lost me. That is, if you're willing to take on a major fixer-upper who's probably emotionally stunted and the biggest skeptic in the history of the world that something this amazing can possibly last."

"It can last if we both want it more than anything."

"I want you more than I've ever wanted anything."

She looked over at him, smiling. "That's a pretty good place to start."

"I also want you to know that despite all my vows to avoid the trappings of marriage, I'd do it for you if it's what you really want."

She leaned her head on his shoulder and gave his leg a squeeze that made him instantly hard for her. "You said several things happened while you were gone. What else?"

"I saw my parents."

Her head came up as she spun around on the bench to face him. "*What?* Where?"

Julian pointed to the sandy path that led to the parking lot. "Right there. Holding hands, laughing, chasing after my mother's little dog, Snowball, without a care in the world. They never looked my way."

"Oh, Julian. My God. That must've been shocking."

"Not as shocking as it would've been without Kaidan tipping us off that she thought they might be back together."

"But still... To see it with your own eyes."

"Yeah."

"Have you told the others?"

He shook his head. "I was still processing it when I came to pick you up and using it to try to talk myself out of the thing I just told you." His face lifted into a small grin. "As you can tell, I failed miserably at trying to talk myself out of telling you how I feel."

"I'm glad you failed," she said, smiling, "but I want you to know, even though you love me and I love you, you don't owe me anything. I understand why you feel the way you do about marriage and divorce. I don't blame you for wanting to avoid the whole potential mess. I was also thinking after we talked the other night that I've learned, from my own experience, that there's something to be said for being able to leave, if need be, without having to legally dissolve a family."

He hated to think about dissolving anything with her. "As someone who dissolves families for a living, there's a lot to be said for the freedom to leave if it comes to that. I think it's actually a bigger deal to be together simply because you want to be and not because the law says you have to be after you put on a puffy white dress and make public vows."

"I hate being the center of attention. If I ever get married again, it won't be in a puffy white dress in front of people."

"I love learning new things about you, such as you hate being the center of attention. Would it be okay if you were the center of my attention?"

She gave him a saucy grin that lit up her lovely eyes. "I think I could live with that."

"That's good, because I don't think I could live without you now that I know you exist in the world."

"Same." She leaned forward to meet him halfway in a soft,

sexy kiss full of hope and anticipation. "So, what does all this mean?"

"I guess we're choosing to be together for as long as it works for both of us."

"That sounds perfect," she said with a sigh. "And you won't have to deal with your brothers if we're not getting married."

"I don't care what they think, and if it's all right with you, I'd like to reserve the right to possibly change my mind in the future about marriage."

"You can reserve all the rights you need to be comfortable in this arrangement."

"I want to make you comfortable to do anything you want, whether it's full-time motherhood or going to school or pursuing a career. Whatever makes you happy. But I do have one request."

"What's that?"

"I'd rather you not work at the Whisky. I've spent far too much time in bars and clubs, and it gives me hives to think about you being harassed by men while you're working. I wouldn't have a minute's peace knowing you were fending off morons—or actual creeps."

"I need to be financially independent."

"You *are* financially independent. The money your parents left is yours. I could set you up with the woman who manages my accounts to help you if you want some advice. I'll cover the day-to-day stuff, so you don't have to worry about any of that."

She bit her lip as she considered what he'd said. "I'm worried I might someday find myself back in the same situation I was in before—financially, that is—if this doesn't work out."

"Thanks to your brother and your parents, you'll never again, for the rest of your life, be in that situation. But no matter what happens between us, I'll always be there for you and the kids. That's my solemn vow to you—and one I'll keep no matter what."

"Even if I do something terrible?"

He gave her a side-eyed look. "What do you have in mind?"

"Nothing at the moment." She laughed at the face he made. "But life has taught me to prepare for all scenarios."

Julian turned to face her, tucking a strand of her lovely hair behind her ear. "I don't want you to worry about anything ever again. Whatever happens, we're in it together. I'll never leave you stranded or scared or uncertain. I think you've proven, beyond a reasonable doubt, that you can more than take care of yourself and your kids. How about you let me take care of you going forward? Let me make your life easier while you make mine worth living. What do you think?"

"I think that meeting with a divorce lawyer is going to turn out to be the best thing I ever did."

Smiling, he kissed her and then held her as close as he could get her on the bench. "I think you'll turn out to be the best ex-client I'll ever have."

CHAPTER THIRTY

Hours later, Julian made sweet love to her in his bed, and for the first time since she lost her parents so suddenly, she felt like she'd truly come home again. Denny had done what he could as a grief-stricken twenty-year-old to finish raising her, and Gabriel had given her a temporary respite that hadn't lasted.

And then there was Julian.

When the last thing she'd been looking for was what she now had with him, there he'd been, so handsome, calm, competent and gentle with her and her kids at the tender moment in which she'd concluded she had to leave Gabriel once and for all.

"I had no idea what I've been missing my whole life," Julian whispered as he pushed deep into her and held still, driving her wild as only he could.

"Without the condom?" After she mentioned that she was on long-term birth control, he'd told her he'd never once had sex without a condom, and that this might be quick. Fifteen minutes later, there'd been nothing quick about it other than the two orgasms she'd already had.

"That's incredible, but so are you. You're what I've been missing."

She curled her arms around his neck, lost in a kiss full of all the things she hadn't known she was missing until he came along to show her.

"I love you, Isla. I've only said that one other time, but even that... That was nothing like this."

"I've only said it to one other person, too, but this..."

"This is *everything*."

On a day when she might've been dwelling in the pain of the past, he'd shown her a future bright with love and commitment and the promise of a happily ever after that they'd write for themselves, with their own rules.

"Come with me, love."

"I don't know if I can again."

"That sounds like a challenge."

Within minutes, he proved her wrong with deep thrusts and fingers that knew just where to touch her and kisses that made her head spin.

After, they held on tight to each other, breathing hard and coming down from the highest of highs.

Eventually, he moved to his side, bringing her with him, wrapping her up in his love and warmth. "Are you okay?"

"You really have to ask?"

"Today's been a lot. Soaring highs, crushing lows—and I'm sorry both those things ended up happening today."

"Don't apologize for one of the sweetest moments of my entire life. I'll never forget our first trip to the beach."

"Okay, I won't apologize," he said, smiling. "How're you feeling?"

"I feel good, all things considered. I'll always be sad for Gabriel and the kids, but I'm thankful for you and for this and for a second chance at love. Not everyone gets that."

"No, they don't."

"How're you feeling?"

"Lucky, blessed, cautiously optimistic, a little nervous about suddenly having two little kids in my life who've just lost their dad."

"You're great with them."

"I'm okay with them for an afternoon, but how will I be on a daily basis?"

"I guess we'll see how that goes, right? We can ease you in."

"I don't want to be eased in. I want to go all in. Right now."

"Julian…"

"I want to show you something."

"Now?"

"Right now."

He got out of bed and extended a hand to help her up, steadying her when her legs wobbled under her.

"You've turned my muscles to jelly."

His smug, satisfied grin made her laugh. "That wasn't a compliment."

"Wasn't it?"

"I can't believe you expect me to walk around your house naked."

"Why not? There's no one else here." Taking her hand, he led her out of his room, down the hallway, past another bathroom, to show her three more bedrooms. "One for Theo, one for Mila and a third for guests or an office for you or whatever you want to do with it. I have an office downstairs that I rarely use that could be turned into a playroom for the kids. Do you want to see it?"

Deeply touched by the message he was sending, she said, "I'll look the next time I'm down there."

"There's plenty of room for you guys, or we could get another place that you help to choose if that's what you want."

"I love this house and that you have a little yard and the street isn't as busy as some of the others around here."

"There's an awesome elementary school in this neighborhood, too."

"I know. Denny's Realtor friend told me when we rented the house."

"How long is that rental?"

"Until the end of the month, with an option to renew beyond that if I want to."

He drew her naked body against his, kissed her neck and then nibbled her ear, making her shiver. "Move in here when the rental ends. Sleep with me every night. Let me take care of you and your kids and give you a soft place to land after what you've been through. I swear on my life and the lives of everyone I love that you'll always be safe with me."

"Jules! Are you up there?"

Isla gasped as Julian hustled her back into his room.

"Who's that?" she whispered.

"My brother Griffin."

"What's he doing here?"

Julian pulled on a pair of joggers. "I don't know, but I'll get rid of him."

Isla got back in bed and pulled the covers up to her chin, embarrassed to have nearly been caught naked by one of his many brothers while still processing Julian's offer for her to move into his house with the kids.

God, she wanted to. She wanted to spend every possible minute with him and to help him form a bond with the kids, but she was worried that she couldn't trust her own judgment anymore, that what felt so good today might not feel as good in a month or two or six or a year. What if she went all in with him, and it didn't work out? She'd be right back to picking up the pieces again, not to mention she would've allowed her kids to fall in love with a man who didn't do forever.

At least he never had before.

She believed him when he said everything was different

with her, but she was still hesitant to move in with him only a few weeks after they first met.

From downstairs, she could hear him talking to his brother but couldn't make out what they were saying. Her phone vibrated with a text that she checked since Mrs. V was with the kids and had reported they were both asleep when Isla had asked her friend if she minded her being gone for a while longer.

Take your time, Mrs. V had replied. *We're fine. I'm going to bed myself soon.*

The new text was from Tenley Black, a Hollywood stylist Isla had actually heard of. *Hi, Isla, this is Tenley Black. Julian asked me to reach out to help get you ready for the premiere next Saturday night. We're running tight for time, but if you're available tomorrow, I could come by and show you some options. I can also recommend hair and makeup if you're interested. Julian said to give you the works!*

Isla had responded to the surreal message, telling Tenley she was available tomorrow, when Julian came back into the room. "I just got a text from *Tenley Black*, the stylist to the *biggest stars in the world*, who wants to help get me ready for next Saturday night. *How do you even know her?*"

Julian, who'd looked a bit annoyed when he returned, smiled at her question. "Well, a funny thing happened a couple of years ago when *Los Angeles Magazine* did a feature on the city's most eligible professionals and named me LA's most eligible attorney in this silly article that went a little viral." He stretched out on the bed next to her. "It had me fending off marriage proposals while I dealt with my brothers, who thought the whole thing was hilarious."

Her lips quivered from the effort not to laugh at his pained expression.

"Don't you dare laugh. It's not funny."

"It's a little funny. I had no idea I was sleeping with LA's most eligible attorney."

He rolled his eyes. "Anyway, the article raised my profile in every possible way and led to invitations to things I was ill-prepared to handle on my own. So Flynn set me up with Tenley, and now I've set you up with her."

"Flynn, as in *Flynn Godfrey*?"

"Yes," he said, laughing. "I told you I've known him all my life. We went to high school together, and our parents are friends. That's why we're invited to the premiere in the first place." He linked his fingers with hers. "I should probably mention that the only other woman I've ever dated seriously was his sister Aimee, from the time I was eighteen until about twenty-one."

"Did you love her?"

"I thought I did at the time, and I was crushed that it didn't work out. Since I met you, I'm not as sure that I was in love with her the way you need to be with someone you want to go the distance with."

"What happened?"

"She wanted marriage and kids and the whole nine yards, and I was in no way prepared for anything like that, so we broke up, and it was devastating. I've never had an actual girlfriend again until now."

"But you dated a lot, I'm sure."

"Some. Ever since I joined the firm, I've been too busy for anything other than casual hookups every now and then."

"None of them got serious?"

"Not for me."

"But for them?"

"A few thought they'd be the one to change my mind about happily ever after and forever, but it turns out that you're the only one who's been able to do that."

"Why me?"

"Oh, Isla... How much time do you have? Every single thing about you does it for me. From the way you smile to how soft your hair is, to your sweetness and the way you are with your kids, to your fortitude in dealing with such a difficult end to your marriage. All of it. You touch my soul in a way that no one else ever has. And there's just this magical aura to you... There's no other way to explain it."

She shifted so she could snuggle up to him. "That's a lovely thing for you to say."

"I mean it. Every word."

"I know you do." She believed that this man, who'd never felt this way about anyone else, loved her like he said he did. If she was wrong about him... Well, she didn't want to entertain that possibility. "Is everything okay with your brother?"

"It will be. He recently learned he has a daughter, and he's trying to adjust to his new reality."

Julian put his arm around her and made her comfortable with her head on his chest.

"Is he upset about the baby?"

"Quite the opposite. He's already crazy about her, and he can't figure out how that's possible when he expected to never have kids."

"Life happens."

"That it does. We should know, right?"

She gave a little nod. "While you were downstairs, I was thinking about what you said about wanting us to move in."

"I'd love nothing more than to have you guys here with me."

"You say that now, but you have no idea what you'd be signing on for with two very young kids."

"I was the oldest of nine and was thirteen when the youngest was born. I'm not new to kids."

"It's different when they're leaving sticky fingerprints on your pristine walls or spilling something on your ten-thousand-dollar leather sofa."

"That sofa didn't cost ten grand."

"Okay, seven grand, then. You get my point."

"I understand what you're concerned about, but those

things don't matter to me. Fingerprints can be wiped off of walls, and leather is bulletproof. My mother always had leather sofas for that very reason. She's the one who said they were bulletproof and last forever."

"What I'd like to do is renew my rental for a couple of months so you can spend more time with the kids and make sure this is what you really want."

"It is what I really want. I don't need more time."

"I think I might." She rested her hand on his face. "You're the sweetest to want to take care of me and us, and I truly love you for that and many other reasons. But I need to be sure I'm making the right decisions for me and the kids. I'm not ready to make that one yet."

"We'll play this however you want. I'm not going anywhere, and the offer stands. Whenever you're ready, my home is your home."

"One other thing..."

"What's that?"

"I'm going to work my three shifts at the Whisky this weekend because my friend is counting on me. I'll see how that goes before I decide whether I'm going to continue or not. It's a great way for me to work while my kids are sleeping and make a lot of money."

She could tell he didn't like that, but thankfully, he only nodded and said, "Whatever you want to do is fine with me. The good news is the band is playing there this weekend, so I'll be around if anyone gives you a hard time."

"You'll let me handle it myself, or we're going to have a problem. You got me?"

"I've got you, sweetheart, and as long as you want me around, I'm never letting you go."

"That guitar in the corner over there. I assume you play that?"

"I do."

"Will you play for me?"

"I'd love to."

He got up and turned on the gas fireplace since it had gotten chilly after sunset. After fetching the guitar, he returned to the bed and sat against a pile of pillows to tune the guitar.

Bathed in the glow of the firelight, he was the most beautiful man she'd ever seen. And then he began to play and sing "Our House" to her, and it was all she could do not to weep from the sweet message he was sending with the song. With him, she could be perfectly content staring into the fire for hours and hours while he sang love songs to her. Listening to him, watching his fingers move over the strings, a feeling of absolute rightness came over her.

They would live here in this lovely home with him, eventually, and they'd be happy together. He was someone she could count on to be there for the long haul, to have her back, to help her raise her children and to love her through all of life's ups and downs.

Someday, when they were much older, she'd tell the kids the story of how she'd gone to meet with a divorce attorney and found true love in the last place she ever would've expected to find it.

She'd tell them how one of the best men she'd ever known had shown up when she was at her lowest point and changed everything for the better.

EPILOGUE

The weekend at the Whisky had been incredible for the band and torturous for Julian. He'd had to force himself to concentrate on the music when all he wanted to do was leave the stage to fight every man who dared to look at Isla in her short black skirt, Whisky T-shirt and sexy little apron.

In addition to that nightmare, she'd had her hair in a high ponytail and had worn a lot more makeup than he'd seen on her before. He'd been out of his mind over her from the first second he saw her decked out for work while he was doing a sound check with the band. His mouth had fallen open as she'd sent him a saucy smile and a little wave while he tried to keep his tongue where it belonged.

"That's not you looking at my baby sister like you want to eat her up, is it?" Denny had asked.

Isla had told her brother that she and Julian had decided to make a go of it together, and he'd told them both how happy he was for them. But that didn't mean he liked watching Julian ogle her.

"She's hot as fuck."

"Watch your filthy mouth."

"Sorry," Julian said with a sheepish grin for his friend. "I only speak the truth."

Denny glowered at him before they continued with the sound check. He kept an eye on Julian while Julian kept an eye on Isla during all three nights at the bar. Knowing he'd get to go home with her was the only thing that kept Julian from going insane.

On Sunday, they finished playing earlier than they had on Friday and Saturday and sat to have a drink together to celebrate a successful gig at one of the city's most celebrated venues.

Stix raised his beer in a toast. "Here's to sharing the stage with Janis, The Doors, Led Zep, The Kinks, The Byrds, Mötley Crüe and so many others."

"Hear, hear," Denny said when he leaned in to touch his glass to the others.

"You guys were all on fire this weekend," Troy said. "People noticed. Caleb heard from a promoter about sending us out on tour."

Caleb was a friend who managed them in exchange for references to other bands, when they needed managing, that was.

"What?" Vixen said breathlessly. "Are you for real?"

"I'd never lie about something like that," Troy said.

Julian and Denny exchanged glances as their friends' dream came true, but it was a dream they didn't share. For them, it was about the release of making music, not chasing the gold ring.

"Tell us exactly what he said," Vixen demanded.

As Troy relayed the conversation to the others, Julian noticed a dude standing a little too close to Isla. Her body language was defensive as she ran his credit card through a handheld reader and turned it to him to tip and sign. When he handed it back to her, he leaned in and said something that had her visibly recoiling from him.

Julian was up and out of his seat, walking toward her before he'd even decided to go. "Everything okay, Isla?"

That she looked relieved to see him told Julian that whatever the guy had said to her was upsetting.

"Back off," Julian said to the man, "before I make you sorry you were born."

"Who the fuck are you?"

"I'm her lawyer and your worst nightmare." Julian held the drunken man's gaze until he put up his hands and took a step back, which saved Julian from shoving him and starting something he in no way wanted to deal with. "Get lost."

Thankfully, the guy did as he was told.

"Are you okay?" Julian asked Isla.

She nodded.

"Almost done?"

"Another half hour."

"Take your time."

He'd driven her home the last two nights and spent most of each night in her bed, leaving before the kids and Mrs. V woke up. There'd been very little sleep either night, which had left him exhausted as he stared down a new workweek.

But he wouldn't trade a minute with her for more sleep. He'd catch up eventually.

They left together shortly before two a.m. and drove home in Julian's Porsche.

She was quieter than usual, which put him on edge. "What's wrong?"

"Nothing."

"Don't start lying to me now."

"I was handling that guy. You didn't have to get involved."

"I saw that he upset you. I couldn't sit there and do nothing."

"They all upset me. They're entitled and handsy and obnoxious, but we've got security for situations that get out of hand."

"I'm sorry I interfered."

"I want to be mad about it, but I was so freaking happy to see you."

"I know you can take care of yourself, love, but I can't help that I want to take care of you, too."

"Why did you tell him you were my lawyer rather than my boyfriend or partner or whatever word we're using?"

"Because I figured 'lawyer' would scare him off faster."

"Oh, I see."

He brought their joined hands to his lips for a kiss on the back of hers. "I should've told him you're the love of my life and if he knows what's good for him, he'd beat feet away from you."

"Aw, nice recovery, Counselor."

"It's the truth. If you knew how much time I spend thinking about you when I'm not with you…"

"Same," she said with a sigh. "It's a crush of epic proportions."

Julian was relieved that they'd quickly gotten back on track after a little bump in the road.

"Can I tell you something else that'll make you happy?" she asked.

"I'm always here for that."

"You were right about working in the bar. I'm too old for that shit these days, and even though the money is great, I can't do it."

"I'm really glad to hear you say that. I felt like every time I looked for you in the crowd this weekend, some dude was hassling you."

"It's exhausting. They're so much more entitled than they used to be. When did that happen?"

"I'm not sure, but their bad behavior has been good for my business."

"That's a sad statement."

"Sure is. I've heard and seen it all. Not that the women

aren't just as bad at times, but many of the men who come through my practice, whether they're my clients or the opposition, are pieces of work, to say the least."

"So what you're saying is that I got super lucky to find one of the good ones."

"That's exactly what I'm saying."

She laughed, which he'd hoped she would. "I definitely see that. Just so you know."

"I got one of the good ones, too. No manufactured drama just to see how I'll react. No unreasonable expectations or wanting me to buy you expensive things because I can."

"Ew. That's really happened?"

"More often than I care to recall."

"That's so gross. What's wrong with people?"

"Is that a rhetorical question? Because if you really want to know, I can entertain you for hours with stories about the many things that are wrong with people."

"No wonder you wanted nothing to do with this mess for yourself. You see the worst of the worst—and you've lived it."

"I didn't want the mess until you showed up and quickly made me see that my life would be ruined if you weren't by my side."

She turned her head to look at him. "You know I'm a sure thing, right?"

Laughter burst from his chest. That happened a lot with her. "That doesn't mean you shouldn't hear how much I love and value you every single day."

"I can live with that."

"Good, because I can't live without you."

A few minutes later, they tiptoed into Isla's house, where Mrs. V and the kids were sound asleep. While she checked on the kids, Julian went into her room to strip off his clothes and head for the shower to wash off the sweat from playing for hours.

He was standing under the warm water, eyes closed, when

Isla wrapped her arms around him from behind and pressed her naked self to his back. Just that quickly, he wanted her. "You might want to give me some warning next time you do that, unless you want me to have a heart attack in your shower."

Her soft chuckle vibrated against his back, where she pressed soft kisses to muscles gone tight from the rigors of performing for three straight nights.

"How do you feel about shower sex?" he asked.

"For other people or for myself?"

"I was thinking specifically of yourself."

"I feel pretty good about it, but you're exhausted."

"Never too exhausted for shower sex with you."

"Let me get clean first."

"I'd be glad to help with that."

He soaped up his hands and turned to face her, gliding them over every soft, sexy curve until she was squeaky clean and clinging to him, pressing herself against him as she initiated one of those hot kisses he craved when he was away from her. Moving carefully because he was so tired, he lifted her against the shower wall and brought her down slowly onto his hard cock.

"Mmm," he whispered in her ear. "I've been thinking about this all night."

"You were busy all night."

"I was busy counting the hours until I could be alone with you again. It seems to be all I think about these days."

"That's not true. You're very devoted to your clients."

"I'm very devoted to *you*."

Because they were both exhausted and her kids would be up early, he took them on a fast ride that had them clinging to each other at the finish line. Afterward, she held on tight to him, her face buried in his neck and her internal muscles squeezing him so perfectly that he started to get hard again.

"*No,*" she said, laughing. "Must sleep while we can."

"If you're going to be that way about it..."

"I am."

He set her down and washed them both again before reaching for towels and wrapping her up in one of them.

If this was what it was like to be in love, to spend every night with the same woman, to look forward to the morning because it meant more time with her... He was happier than he'd ever been, and it was all because of her.

After they crawled into bed and met in the middle, arms and legs entwined, she exhaled a deep breath.

"I don't think I've ever been this tired, even when I had newborns."

"We're getting too old to be up until three a.m. three nights in a row."

"Speak for yourself, old man."

"Hey, that's mean."

Her giggle was becoming his favorite thing. "What time should I set the alarm for so I can be out of here before Theo wakes up?"

"Don't set it."

"Umm..."

"He'll see you with me eventually."

"Are you sure he's ready for that?"

"He'll have questions, and I'll answer them. It'll be fine."

"If you say so..."

"Are you scared of my three-year-old?"

"I'm only scared of not doing the right things for him."

"Look at you, already starting to think like a parent."

"Am I?"

"Uh-huh. It's too soon for all of it. I know it is, but I so want to get on with the rest of my life, and since you're going to be at the center of that life, I want the kids to be there with us. If that's okay with you."

"It's more than okay."

"You say that because you have no clue what you're signing up for."

"I know."

"We'll see..."

That was the last thing he heard until he was awakened suddenly by something landing on him and nearly knocking the wind out of him.

Theo...

"Wake up, Mommy."

"Don't want to."

"Yes, Mommy. Why is Mr. Julian in your bed?"

"Because I like him."

Julian held his breath, waiting to hear what Theo would say.

"I like him, too. Can I watch *Paw Patrol*?"

"Sure."

"Mrs. V said I had to let you sleep, but I told her you'd want to see me."

"You were right." She hugged and kissed him until he squiggled free and left as quickly as he'd arrived.

They heard him tell Mrs. V that Mommy had a sleepover with Mr. Julian.

"Did she now?"

"Uh-huh. She *likes* him."

"Mortifying," Isla said, laughing.

The rest of their conversation was muffled after Mrs. V came to shut their door.

"My house has a basement with a bedroom, living room and bathroom that'd be perfect for Mrs. V," Julian said. "We need to keep her."

"Really?"

"Oh hell yes. She just bought us another hour in bed." He rolled on top of her. "However should we spend our time?"

"Sleeping."

He shook his head.

"Yes."

Kissing her, he said, "No."

"Wake me up when you're done."

THE FOLLOWING SATURDAY NIGHT, Julian left his home in a rented Bentley driven by Ernie, who was petrified about somehow damaging the priceless vehicle.

"Why can't we just take the G-Wagon?"

"Because. I want this night to be magical for my date, and there's nothing magical about the G-Wagon."

"You're kinda gone over this gal, aren't you?"

"That's putting it mildly."

"You ought to know that everyone at the office is talking about it."

"Why am I not surprised?"

"I mean, when one of the world's most confirmed bachelors falls flat on his face in love, it's gonna make headlines."

Julian had spent most of the past week dodging questions and comments from his brothers. His dad had cornered him in the break room to ask what was going on with him lately. Julian had bitten his tongue so he wouldn't ask the same question of his father. He still hadn't told anyone what he'd seen in Santa Barbara, mostly because he didn't want to deal with that when things were going so well in his own life. He was under no illusions. Eventually, his parents' rekindled relationship would come to light, and he'd handle it when he had to and not one minute before.

He'd simply told his father that he'd been extra busy, but all was well. All was better than well, in fact. It was exceptional, extraordinary, life-changing and life-affirming at the same time. Being determined to stay single and childless seemed like a long time ago now, when it'd been only a few weeks.

Julian could no longer imagine life without Isla, Theo and

Mila—and even Mrs. V—in the middle of it. He rushed through his workdays with newfound concentration so he could get everything done and get home to them as early as possible. He'd had dinner with them three nights that week and had even helped with bedtime.

Theo had asked Julian to read to him, and he'd loved snuggling in bed with the little guy while he read him three books, which was one more than Isla usually allowed.

"He's working you," she'd said.

"It's fine. I like being with him."

They were getting attached to each other, and nothing had ever felt more natural to him, which of course had his brothers —and sisters—on fire with concern, commentary and questions that he mostly ignored.

The band had booked two more big gigs at Sunset Boulevard venues, and Caleb was fielding more interest than they'd ever received.

And tonight, he got to take Isla to her first-ever Hollywood premiere, to see a film about a woman she admired and a man who'd been in Julian's life so long that he didn't remember a time when he hadn't known Flynn Godfrey.

That he'd grown up to be a global superstar still amused Julian, who'd played baseball and basketball with him and Hayden Roth back in the day. Now they were connected to several Academy Award-winning films, and they owned the hottest production company in town.

Hollywood was abuzz over *Valiant*, with billboards throughout the city and a huge marketing campaign already underway to promote Quantum's most personal project yet— the story of Flynn's amazing wife, Natalie, and how she'd fought back against the governor of Nebraska, a close friend of her father's, who'd attacked and sexually assaulted her as a teenager.

She'd sacrificed everything to get justice, including her relationships with her parents and two younger sisters, both of whom were now back in her life. Her youngest sister, Olivia, played Natalie in the film and was already generating Oscar buzz for her star-making performance.

Ernie turned into the driveway at Isla's home and put the Bentley in Park, exhaling a sigh of relief.

"Relax, will you? It's insured."

"It's a *Bentley*."

"It's an *insured* Bentley."

"Whatever you say, boss man."

"Be right back."

Julian was unprepared for the sight of Isla in a stunning red dress that put miles of creamy skin on display, with her hair in an elaborate updo and chandelier-style diamond earrings.

He could only stare at her while she stared right back at him.

"Mommy looks so pretty," Theo said.

"She sure does," Julian said in a gruff tone. "She's gorgeous."

She smoothed her hands over the long skirt. "In this old thing?"

"I've never seen anything or anyone more beautiful."

"That's surely not true."

He hooked an arm around her waist and kissed her cheek. "It's absolutely true."

"Oh my," Mrs. V said when she came into the foyer, holding Mila. "Look at you two. You're gorgeous."

"Will you take a photo for us?" Julian asked her. "I want to remember this forever."

"Of course."

Mrs. V put Mila down and took Julian's phone from him to take the picture of them and then another with each of them holding one of the kids. "I hope you two have a wonderful time. We'll see you in the morning."

He'd booked a room for them at the Beverly Hills Hotel to make a full night of their first, official, Hollywood date night.

Isla hugged and kissed her kids and then hugged Mrs. V. "Love you all."

"Love you, too, Mommy, and you, too, Mr. Julian," Theo said.

Julian leaned down to hug the little boy. "Aw, love you, buddy. Sleep tight."

"Tomorrow, we go to the park," Theo said.

"That sounds like fun," Julian replied. "Will you show me around the park? I haven't been in a long time."

"You're so silly, Mr. Julian."

He ran off to play with Mila.

"Get while the getting is good," Mrs. V said.

Julian picked up Isla's overnight bag and put his hand on her lower back. "We're going."

Outside, she gasped when she saw the Bentley and Ernie in a black suit, standing by the back door and waiting to open it for them.

"Isla, this is my friend Ernie. Ernie, meet Isla."

"Ma'am. You look lovely."

"Thank you, Ernie. It's nice to meet you. I've heard a lot about you."

"Uh-oh."

"It's all good, except how you hate driving in Laurel Canyon."

"I hate driving a Bentley in Laurel Canyon the most."

"Then let's get out of here," Julian said, amused by him as always.

ISLA WAS ENCHANTED by every aspect of the premiere, from the red carpet that stretched through multiple blocks in the heart of Hollywood, not that far from where she'd lived as a child, to the celebrities she'd admired from afar, especially

Natalie and Flynn Godfrey, who greeted Julian with a bro hug. When Julian introduced him to Isla as Denny Clarkson's younger sister, Flynn said it was nice to meet her and that Denny was an old friend.

She was so tongue-tied at meeting him and Natalie that she could barely squeak out a reply. "I so admire you," she said to Natalie, who was resplendent in a slinky silver sequined gown.

"That's so kind of you to say. My sister has done an incredible job of bringing my story to life on the screen. And my husband and his colleagues at Quantum did, too."

"I can't wait to see it."

She met director Hayden Roth and his wife, Addison, producer Kristian Bowen and his wife, Aileen, superstar Marlowe Sloane and her husband, Sebastian, and Flynn's sister, Ellie, who worked for Quantum, and her husband, cinematographer Jasper Autry.

"You're the divorce lawyer, right?" a feisty young woman with reddish hair asked Julian.

"That's right."

"You have no need for a divorce attorney," the man with her said. "I'm Emmett Burke, Quantum general counsel, and this is my wife, Leah, who does not need a divorce attorney."

"Not yet, anyway," Leah said, poking the bear. "A girl can never be too prepared."

Isla laughed at the couple's banter and decided she'd love to be friends with Leah. "Call me." Isla made a phone gesture with her hand. "I'll hook you up."

"Sounds good," Leah said, grinning.

"That does not sound good," Emmett said as his wife laughed at his outrage.

"I get that a lot," Julian said. "Guys telling me to stay away from their wives and how they have no need of what I'm offering."

"I bet there's a lot of double meaning in that."

"It's because I'm a divorce attorney."

"It's because you're hot and LA's most eligible attorney."

"Hush with that."

Isla laughed as she took his arm to walk up the stairs to the Dolby Theatre, where the movie would be screened for a select audience a week before the general release.

They were nearing the theater doors when Julian paused, seeming uncertain.

"What's wrong?"

"That's Aimee, Flynn's sister and my ex-girlfriend. And her husband."

"Oh. Do you want to say hi?"

"I guess it would be rude not to."

Aimee caught his eye and gave a tentative smile as they approached. She was wearing a midnight blue gown and diamond jewelry. Her sister Annie was married to a jeweler who'd probably outfitted the whole family for this big occasion.

"Hello, Julian."

"Hi, Aimee. This is Isla Santana. Isla, Aimee Godfrey."

"It's Morgan now." She shook Isla's hand. "Nice to meet you. This is my husband, Trent."

"Good to meet you," Trent said as he shook Julian's hand and then Isla's.

That Aimee never said Julian's name told her that Trent knew exactly who he was and what he'd once been to his wife.

"We'd better get to our seats," Julian said. "It was nice to see you. Enjoy the film."

"You, too," Aimee said.

He led Isla to their assigned seats and sat next to her. "Sorry if that was awkward."

"It was fine. Was it weird to see her?"

"Not like it was the last time I saw her."

"What's changed since then?" she asked with a sexy smile.

He glanced at her, returning her smile as he took hold of her hand. "Everything."

Flynn and Natalie took the stage a few minutes later to thundering applause.

"Thank you so much for being here," Flynn said to the full house. "As you know, this film was a passion project from beginning to end. Every shot, every detail, every aspect has been a labor of love for my amazing wife and her inspirational story. Natalie, it's an honor and a privilege to walk through this life with you by my side, and to raise our four babies together. Thank you for allowing me the honor of sharing your triumphant story with the world."

The audience clapped for his embarrassed wife.

She took the microphone from him. "Thank you, Flynn, for spearheading this special project from the start and for the love and care that was put into every frame you'll see tonight. To Hayden, Kristian, Aileen, Jasper, Ellie, Emmett, Leah, Marlowe and the entire team at Quantum, I'm deeply grateful for your hard work on this film. From the start, you've made me part of your Quantum family, and I love you all so very much. To my sister Olivia, who brought my story to light in the most breathtakingly beautiful performance I ever could've imagined, I'm so proud of you and our other sister, Candace, and everyone on screen and behind the scenes of this film. Thank you all for being here tonight."

"We're proud to present *Valiant*," Flynn said to applause.

"In case I forget to tell you later," Isla whispered to Julian, "this is the most exciting thing I've ever done. Thank you for inviting me."

"My pleasure, honey. I'm so happy you're here with me."

From the first minutes of the movie to the last, Isla was transported by Natalie's story. Olivia's performance was indeed breathtaking and captivating, and the Hollywood ending of Natalie's Las Vegas wedding to Flynn, mere weeks after they first met, had Isla wiping away tears of joy and deep admiration for the courage it'd taken for Natalie to start over after utter devastation.

As the closing credits rolled, everyone in the theater was on their feet, cheering as Flynn, Natalie, Olivia and everyone involved with the film took the stage to soak up the audience's enthusiastic response.

Isla glanced at Julian and saw him staring hard at someone across the aisle. "What's wrong?"

"Nothing. Just saw someone I know."

"Is everything okay?"

He put his arm around her and gave her a squeeze. "Yes, everything is fine."

Despite what he'd said, she could tell everything was not at all fine.

WHAT IS *Carson doing here with Cresley?* Julian wondered, his mind racing with thoughts and implications. As the firm's chief investigator, Carson avoided the spotlight like the plague so he could do his job without people recognizing him. So then, what in the world was he thinking coming to a Hollywood premiere with one of the most famous women in the world?

It took forever to leave the theater and walk the short distance to where the reception would be held. As they followed the crowd, Julian ignored his phone, which vibrated nonstop in his suit coat pocket.

"Is that your phone?" Isla asked.

"Yeah."

"Should you get it?"

Julian wanted to keep his full attention on her tonight. "Whatever it is can wait."

He spotted Jackson and Roman standing off to the side, looking at their phones with grim expressions.

"Hey," he said to them. "What's wrong?"

"You might want to check your phone," Jack said. "TMZ posted that Mom and Dad are back together, and the whole world is going nuts thanks to the freaking reality show that made them the poster children for ugly divorces."

Jack's words had barely registered when Julian became aware of people looking at them the way they'd observe survivors of catastrophe, with sympathy and anticipation of all the salacious details.

"Julian."

He'd almost forgotten Isla was there, which he wouldn't have thought possible a few minutes ago. He glanced at her.

"Let's go," she said.

"No, it's fine. We can stay."

"You guys shouldn't be exposed to the public and the paparazzi with this news hitting. They'd love to get a photo of you looking shocked. Let's get out of here."

Julian didn't want her to miss a minute of the most exciting night she'd ever had, but she was right. He couldn't bear to be caught in the public crossfire of his parents' nonsense again. Once had been more than enough.

"Come on, you guys," he said to his brothers. "Let's go."

On the way out, they ran into Carson and Cresley.

"Where're you guys going?" Carson asked.

"We're leaving," Julian said, "and you'll want to come with us."

"Why?"

"Trust me," Julian said to his brother. "You need to come."

"TMZ is reporting Mom and Dad are back together," Roman said, "and it's blowing up online."

Carson glanced at Cresley. "I, um, I need to..."

She wrapped her hands around his arm possessively. "Let's go."

As the group walked out together, Julian fell back to talk

to Carson in a low tone that couldn't be overheard by either of their dates. "What the hell are you doing?"

Carson shifted his gaze from Julian to Isla. "I could ask you the same thing, brother."

AHHH, there it is! Book one of the Remington Family Law Series is on the docket, with book two, CONTENTIOUS, coming later this year. That one will feature Carson Remington and is available now for preorder at *marieforce.com/contentious*! Since you guys LOVE my baby cliffhangers in the First Family Series, I figured I'd continue the tradition here by giving you several things to look forward to in the next book.

First and foremost, what is Carson doing with Cresley at the premiere, and how did that come about? Second, what will be the fallout of Corbin and Kate's reconciliation, and how will that play among their children? Third, what will the rest of the Remington siblings have to say about Julian bringing Isla to the premiere, and will she and the kids move in with him? Oh, and how's it going with Griffin and his daughter's mother as he adjusts to fatherhood? Will Roman come into the family business when he finishes law school, or does he have another path in mind?

There's so much fun to be had with this new family as the next few books transpire! Thank you for coming along on yet another series featuring a big family that works together, plays together and tries to stay single together. So far, that's not working out so well for them, the author says, rubbing her hands together with diabolical glee. LOL!

I truly loved writing Julian and Isla's story and leaving a few threads open to explore in future books. You know how I love to keep my couples present throughout a series, and this one will be no different. Julian and Isla's story will continue to unfold even as other characters are featured in upcoming books.

Join the Acrimonious Reader Group at *www.facebook.com/groups/acrimonious/* to discuss this first book in the Remington Family Law Series. Also, join the Remington Family Law Series Group at *facebook.com/groups/remingtonseries* and LIKE the series page at *facebook.com/RemingtonFamilyLawSeries* to stay up to date with all the news of upcoming books.

Preparing to write this series was intense! You may have seen my posts about taking a twelve-hour continuing education class on the basics of family law in California, which was extremely helpful in making sure I understood the profession I wanted to write about. One of the things that motivates me to take on what I hope will be a long series is the characters having interesting work that provides tons of secondary plot lines to go along with the romance stories. Family law is one of the most emotionally fraught areas of the law and is rife with stories that'll be featured in upcoming books.

A special thank you to California family lawyer Marnie Smith (and to my author friend Lauren Rowe for connecting me with Marnie), for her help in identifying resources that might be helpful to my research. Marla Polin volunteered to help as soon as she heard about my new series and was an amazing resource. Any legal mistakes made in this book are entirely mine. Some things may have been tweaked to serve my story, so it's important to remember that, while I'm attempting to keep the legal details as accurate as possible, I may occasionally take creative license where needed.

Since I took the family law course, I've been joking that I went to "law school," and let me give you some advice... That's intended completely in jest, and nothing you "learn" from these books should be considered actual legal advice. Like many other aspects of the law, family laws differ from state to state, and should you find yourself in need of this kind of legal advice, please consult with a lawyer in your state (or country).

I read some interesting books about divorce, including *It Doesn't Have to Be That Way* by Laura A. Wasser, *I Just Want This Done* by Raiford Dalton Palmer, J.D., AAML, and *Divorce in California: The Legal Process, Your Rights, and What to Expect* by Debra R. Schoenberg, Esq., and Jennifer L. Knops, Esq.

I came out of all this research thinking that we ought to require anyone who wants to get a marriage license to read the divorce laws in their state to ensure they know what it would take to undo their marriage, should the need arise. My friends and family noted the irony of my cynical viewpoint on marriage in light of the fact that I've been married almost thirty-four years, and I write romance novels for a living—LOL! But remember, romance novels come with a guarantee of happily ever after (or at least happy for now), so it'll all work out for my characters, regardless of what I put them through.

I also spent a week in Los Angeles in November 2025, mapping out things like where the law office would be located, how Julian would get to work and where he lived. I've been interested in the 1960s and 1970s music scene in Laurel Canyon for years and getting to delve into that was so much fun. I'm a superfan of Crosby, Stills, Nash and Young, as well as The Eagles, Fleetwood Mac, Joni Mitchell, the Mamas & the Papas, The Byrds and other amazing acts that came from the era in which Laurel Canyon was the heart and soul of LA music. I read a great book about that time and place called *Laurel Canyon: The Inside Story of Rock and Roll's Legendary Neighborhood* by Michael Walker. I liked that book so much and talked about it so often that Dan read it after me, and he loved it, too. If classic rock—and folk—is your jam, check it out.

As always, a huge thanks to the team that supports me

behind the scenes, including my editors, Joyce Lamb and Linda Ingmanson, my beta readers, Kara Conrad and Tracey Suppo, and the Remington Series Beta Readers: Gwen, Jennifer A., Patti, Karen, Jenn, Kathy, Gina, Jennifer J., Patti, Lauren, Johanna, Irene and Jennifer T.

To my team, Julie Cupp, Lisa Cafferty, Jean Mello, Nikki Haley, Ashley Lopez and Emily Force, thank you for all you do to keep things running smoothly behind the scenes. In November, we celebrated Lisa's twelfth anniversary as our chief financial officer, and in January, we marked Julie's thirteenth anniversary as the chief operating officer. I'm so thankful to both of them for giving up perfectly good jobs to come on this ride with me, and also to the other team members who provide such amazing support. I'm indeed blessed to be surrounded by friends and family on this journey.

Most of all, thank you to my readers, who make all things possible, including this new series about divorce lawyers that I hope will keep us entertained for years to come.

Much love and gratitude,

Marie

ALSO BY MARIE FORCE

Contemporary Romances Available from Marie Force

Remington Family Law Series
Book 1: Acrimonious
Book 2: Contentious *(Sept. 2026)*

The Wild Widows Series—a Fatal Series Spin-Off
Book 1: Someone Like You *(Roni & Derek)*
Book 2: Someone to Hold *(Iris & Gage)*
Book 3: Someone to Love *(Winter & Adrian)*
Book 4: Someone to Watch Over Me *(Lexi & Tom)*
Book 5: Someone to Remember *(Full Cast)*
Book 6: Someone to Save *(Nov. 2026)*

The Gansett Island Series*
Book 1: Maid for Love *(Mac & Maddie)*
Book 2: Fool for Love *(Joe & Janey)*
Book 3: Ready for Love *(Luke & Sydney)*
Book 4: Falling for Love *(Grant & Stephanie)*
Book 5: Hoping for Love *(Evan & Grace)*
Book 6: Season for Love *(Owen & Laura)*
Book 7: Longing for Love *(Blaine & Tiffany)*
Book 8: Waiting for Love *(Adam & Abby)*
Book 9: Time for Love *(David & Daisy)*
Book 10: Meant for Love *(Jenny & Alex)*

Book 10.5: Chance for Love, *A Gansett Island Novella (Jared & Lizzie)*

Book 11: Gansett After Dark *(Owen & Laura)*

Book 12: Kisses After Dark *(Shane & Katie)*

Book 13: Love After Dark *(Paul & Hope)*

Book 14: Celebration After Dark *(Big Mac & Linda)*

Book 15: Desire After Dark *(Slim & Erin)*

Book 16: Light After Dark *(Mallory & Quinn)*

Book 17: Victoria & Shannon (Episode 1)

Book 18: Kevin & Chelsea (Episode 2)

A Gansett Island Christmas Novella *(Appears in Mine After Dark)*

Book 19: Mine After Dark *(Riley & Nikki)*

Book 20: Yours After Dark *(Finn & Chloe)*

Book 21: Trouble After Dark *(Deacon & Julia)*

Book 22: Rescue After Dark *(Mason & Jordan)*

Book 23: Blackout After Dark *(Full Cast)*

Book 24: Temptation After Dark *(Gigi & Cooper)*

Book 25: Resilience After Dark *(Jace & Cindy)*

Book 26: Hurricane After Dark *(Full Cast)*

Book 27: Renewal After Dark *(Duke & McKenzie)*

Book 28: Delivery After Dark *(Full Cast)*

Downeast

Dan & Kara: A Downeast Prequel

Homecoming: A Downeast Novel

The Quantum Series

Book 1: Virtuous *(Flynn & Natalie)*

Book 2: Valorous *(Flynn & Natalie)*

Book 3: Victorious *(Flynn & Natalie)*

Book 4: Rapturous *(Addie & Hayden)*
Book 5: Ravenous *(Jasper & Ellie)*
Book 6: Delirious *(Kristian & Aileen)*
Book 7: Outrageous *(Emmett & Leah)*
Book 8: Famous *(Marlowe & Sebastian)*
Book 9: Illustrious *(Max & Stella)*
Book 10: Momentous *(Olivia's story, coming 2026)*

*The Green Mountain Series**
Book 1: All You Need Is Love *(Will & Cameron)*
Book 2: I Want to Hold Your Hand *(Nolan & Hannah)*
Book 3: I Saw Her Standing There *(Colton & Lucy)*
Book 4: And I Love Her *(Hunter & Megan)*
Novella: You'll Be Mine *(Will & Cam's Wedding)*
Book 5: It's Only Love *(Gavin & Ella)*
Book 6: Ain't She Sweet *(Tyler & Charlotte)*

*The Butler, Vermont Series**
(Continuation of Green Mountain)
Book 1: Every Little Thing *(Grayson & Emma)*
Book 2: Can't Buy Me Love *(Mary & Patrick)*
Book 3: Here Comes the Sun *(Wade & Mia)*
Book 4: Till There Was You *(Lucas & Dani)*
Book 5: All My Loving *(Landon & Amanda)*
Book 6: Let It Be *(Lincoln & Molly)*
Book 7: Come Together *(Noah & Brianna)*
Book 8: Here, There & Everywhere *(Izzy & Cabot)*
Book 9: The Long and Winding Road *(Max & Lexi)*

The Treading Water Series**

Book 1: Treading Water *(Jack & Andy)*
Book 2: Marking Time *(Clare & Aidan)*
Book 3: Starting Over *(Brandon & Daphne)*
Book 4: Coming Home *(Reid & Kate)*
Book 5: Finding Forever *(Maggie & Brayden)*

The Miami Nights Series**

Book 1: How Much I Feel *(Carmen & Jason)*
Book 2: How Much I Care *(Maria & Austin)*
Book 3: How Much I Love *(Dee's story)*
Nochebuena, A Miami Nights Novella
Book 4: How Much I Want *(Nico & Sofia)*
Book 5: How Much I Need *(Milo & Gianna)*

Single Titles

In the Air Tonight
Five Years Gone
One Year Home
Sex Machine
Sex God
Georgia on My Mind
True North
The Fall
The Wreck
Love at First Flight
Everyone Loves a Hero
Line of Scrimmage

Romantic Suspense Novels Available from Marie Force

The First Family Series

Book 1: State of Affairs

Book 2: State of Grace

Book 3: State of the Union

Book 4: State of Shock

Book 5: State of Denial

Book 6: State of Bliss

Book 7: State of Suspense

Book 8: State of Alert

Book 9: State of Retribution

Book 10: State of Preservation

Book 11: State of Unrest *(July 2026)*

Read Sam and Nick's earlier stories in the Fatal Series!

The Fatal Series*

One Night With You, *A Fatal Series Prequel Novella*

Book 1: Fatal Affair

Book 2: Fatal Justice

Book 3: Fatal Consequences

Book 3.5: Fatal Destiny, *the Wedding Novella*

Book 4: Fatal Flaw

Book 5: Fatal Deception

Book 6: Fatal Mistake

Book 7: Fatal Jeopardy

Book 8: Fatal Scandal

Book 9: Fatal Frenzy

Book 10: Fatal Identity

Book 11: Fatal Threat
Book 12: Fatal Chaos
Book 13: Fatal Invasion
Book 14: Fatal Reckoning
Book 15: Fatal Accusation
Book 16: Fatal Fraud

Historical Romance Available from Marie Force

*The Gilded Series**

Book 1: Duchess by Deception
Book 2: Deceived by Desire

* Completed Series

ABOUT THE AUTHOR

Marie Force is the *New York Times* bestselling author of more than 110 contemporary romance, romantic suspense and erotic romance novels. Her series include Remington Family Law, Fatal, First Family, Gansett Island, Butler Vermont, Quantum, Treading Water,  Miami Nights and Wild Widows. She has also written 12 single titles.

Her books have sold more than 15 million copies worldwide, have been translated into more than a dozen languages and have appeared on the *New York Times* bestseller list more than 30 times. She is also a *USA Today* and #1 *Wall Street Journal* bestseller, as well as a Spiegel bestseller in Germany.

Her goals in life are simple—to spend as much time as possible with her adult children, to keep writing books for as long as she possibly can and to never be on a flight that makes the news.

Join Marie's mailing list on her website at *marieforce.com* for news about new books and upcoming appearances in your area. Follow her on Facebook, at *www.Facebook.com/Marie ForceAuthor* and Instagram *@marieforceauthor*. Contact Marie at *marie@marieforce.com*.

www.ingramcontent.com/pod-product-compliance
Lightning Source LLC
LaVergne TN
LVHW040036080526
838202LV00045B/3362